the Villain

USA TODAY BESTSELLING AUTHOR
L.J. SHEN

Copyright © 2020 by L.J. Shen

All rights reserved. No part of this publication may be reproduced, distributed, or transmitted in any form or by any means, including photocopying, recording, or other electronic or mechanical methods, without prior consent of the publisher, except in the case of brief quotation embodied in critical reviews and certain other noncommercial use permitted by copyright law.

Resemblance to actual persons and things living or dead, locales, or events is entirely coincidental.

Cruel. Cold-blooded. Hades in a Brioni suit.

Cillian Fitzpatrick has been dubbed every wicked thing on planet Earth.

To the media, he is The Villain.

To me, he is the man who (reluctantly) saved my life.

Now I need him to do me another small solid.

Bail me out of the mess my husband got me into.

What's a hundred grand to one of the wealthiest men in America, anyway?

Only Cillian doesn't hand out favors for free.

The price for the money, it turns out, is my freedom.

Now I'm the eldest Fitzpatrick brother's little toy.

To play, to mold, to *break*.

Too bad Cillian forgot one tiny detail.

Persephone wasn't only the goddess of spring, she was also the queen of death.

He thinks I'll buckle under the weight of his mind games.

He is about to find out the most lethal poison is also the sweetest.

Playlist

Sub Urban: "Cradles"

Bishop Briggs: "River"

White Stripes: "Hardest Button to Button"

Gogol Bordello: "Sally"

Milk and Bone: "Peaches"

Nick Cave and the Bad Seeds: "Red Right Hand"

To Cori and Lana.

> Lost in Hell, Persephone,
> Take her head upon your knee;
> Say to her, "My dear, my dear,
> It is not so dreadful here."
> —Edna St. Vincent Millay, *Collected Poems*

The bleeding heart is a pink and white flower that bears a striking resemblance to the conventional heart shape. It is also referred to as the heart flower or as lady-in-bath.

The flower is known to be poisonous to the touch and deadly to consume.

And, like the mythological goddess Persephone, it only blossoms in spring.

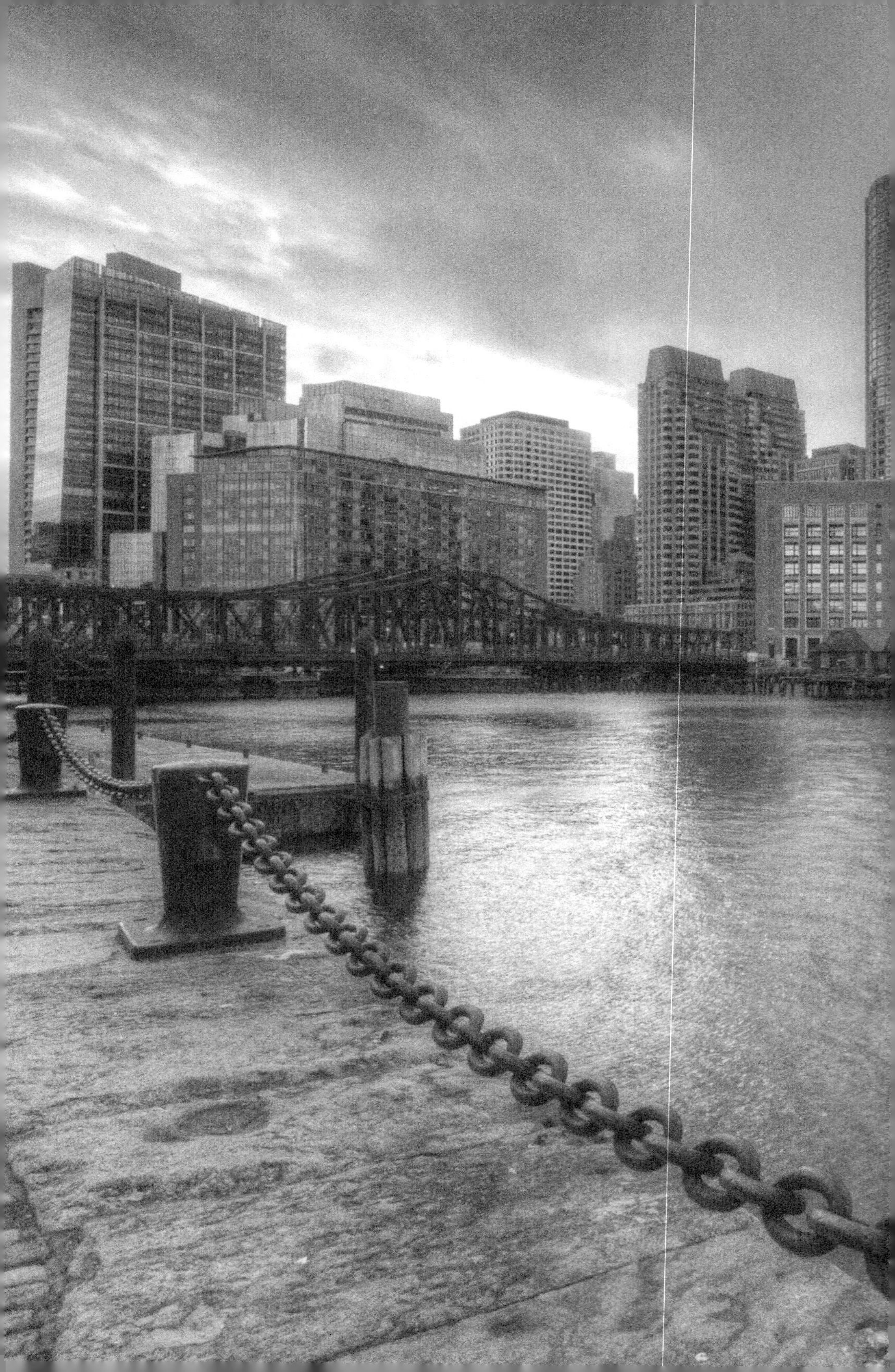

Prologue

Persephone

My love story started with a death.

With the sound of my soul shattering on the hospice floor like delicate china.

And Auntie Tilda, wilting inside her hospital bed, her breath rattling in her empty lungs like a penny.

I soaked her hospital gown with tears, clutching the fabric in my little fists, ignoring Momma's soft pleas to get off her ill sister.

"Please don't leave, Auntie. Please," I croaked.

The cancer had spread to her lungs, liver, and kidneys, making it excruciating for my aunt to breathe. For the past few weeks, she's slept sitting upright, falling in and out of consciousness.

At twelve, death was an abstract concept to me. Real, but also foreign and faraway. Something that happened in other families, to other people.

I understood what it meant now.

Auntie Tilda was never going to scoop me in her arms, pretending to strum her fingers on me like I was an air guitar again.

She'd never pick Belle and me up from school with Ziploc bags full of apple slices and strawberries whenever our parents worked long hours.

She'd never braid my hair again, whispering magical tales about Greek gods and three-headed monsters.

My aunt tucked wisps of blond curls behind my ear. Her eyes shimmered with sickness so tangible I could taste it on my tongue.

"*Leave?*" She belched. "Oh, my, that's a big word. I'd never do that, Persy. Dead, alive, and in-between, I will always be there for you."

"But how?" I tugged at her gown, clinging to her promise. "How will I know you're really here after your body is gone?"

"Just turn your face up, you silly goose. The sky will always be ours. That's where we'll meet, between the sunrays and the clouds."

On hot, sticky summers, Auntie Tilda and I would lie on the grass by Charles River, cloud-spotting. The clouds came and went like passengers at a train station. First, we'd count them. Then we'd choose the funny-shaped, extra fluffy ones. *Then* we'd give them names.

Mr. and Mrs. Claudia and Claud Clowdton.

Misty and Smoky Frost.

Auntie Tilda believed in magic, in miracles, and I? Well, I believed in *her*.

While my older sister, Emmabelle, chased after squirrels, played soccer with the boys, and climbed trees, Auntie Tilda and I admired the sky.

"Will you give me a sign?" I pressed. "That you're there in the sky? A lightning? Rain? Oh, I know! Maybe a pigeon can poop on me."

Momma put her hand on my shoulder. In the words of my sister Belle—I needed to take a chill pill, and fast.

"Let's make a deal," my aunt suggested, laughing breathlessly. "As you know, clouds are more reliable than shooting stars. Common, but still magical. When the time comes and you grow up, ask for something you want—something you *really* want—when you see a lone cloud in the sky, and I will grant it to you. That's how you'll know I'm there watching. You only get one miracle, Persephone, so be careful what you wish for. But I promise, whatever your wish may be—I will grant it to you."

THE *Villain*

I'd kept my Cloud Wish for eleven years, harboring it like a precious heirloom.

I didn't use it when my grades slipped.

When Elliott Frasier came up with the nickname Pussyfanny Peenrise sophomore year, and it stuck until graduation.

Not even when Dad got laid off and McDonald's and hot water became rare luxuries.

In the end, I wasted the Cloud Wish in one, reckless moment.

On a doomed desire, a stupid crush, an unrequited lover.

On the man every media outlet in America referred to as The Villain.

On Cillian Fitzpatrick.

Three Years Ago.

I was drunk before noon the day my best friend, Sailor, got married.

Typically, I was fun-drunk. *Responsible* drunk. The kind of drunk who talked a little louder, snort-laughed, and danced like no one was watching, but also called an Uber, saved her friends from bad hookups, and never let *anyone* in my vicinity get a tattoo they were going to regret the next morning.

Not this time.

This time, I was crank-up-the-Enola-Gay plastered. The kind of hammered to end up in the hospital with an IV drip, an oopsie baby, and a criminal record.

There were a variety of reasons I was so drunk, and I would point all of them out if I were able to hold a steady finger in the air.

The problem was, now was the worst possible time to be indisposed. I was on bridesmaid duty. The twenty-three-year-old—*drumroll, please*—flower girl!

Was it weird to be a full-grown flower girl? Why, not at all. It was an honor.

Okay, fine. It was a *little* embarrassing.

And by a little embarrassing, I mean soul-crushingly humiliating.

Yet saying no was out of the question.

I was Persephone.

The easygoing, even-tempered, roll-with-the-punches designated friend.

The one who kept the peace and dropped everything when someone needed help.

Aisling, who was about to become Sailor's sister-in-law, was in charge of holding the eight-foot train, **à la** Pippa Middleton, and my sister, Emmabelle, was responsible for the rings.

Thorncrown Chapel was a luxurious wedding venue on the Massachusetts coastline. The medieval castle looming over a cliff boasted fifty acres of old-world architecture, French-imported limestone, private gardens, and a view of the ocean. The bridal suite was an oatmeal-hued apartment that offered a claw-foot tub, a front porch, and four fully equipped vanities.

All expenses for the lavish wedding were paid by the groom, Hunter Fitzpatrick's family. Sailor was marrying up, climbing high up the social ladder.

The Fitzpatricks stood shoulder-to-shoulder with the Rockefellers, the Kennedys, and the Murdochs.

Rich, powerful, influential, and—at least, according to the rumors—with enough skeletons in their closet to open a cemetery.

It was crazy to think the girl I'd played hopscotch with as a kid and who let me cut her bangs was going to become an American princess in less than an hour.

It was even crazier that she was the one who introduced me to the man who now occupied ninety percent of my brain's capacity and virtually all my dreams.

THE *Villain*

The villain who broke my heart without even noticing my immortal existence.

Trying to sober up, I paced back and forth in the room, stopping at the window. I leaned over the sill, tilting my face up to the summer sky. A lone cloud glided lazily behind the sun, holding a promise for a gorgeous day.

"Auntie Tilda, fancy seeing you here! How've you been?"

It wasn't the first time I'd spoken to a cloud like it was my dead aunt, so I couldn't blame my level of intoxication on this particular quirk. "Weather's looking fine. Sailor is going to appreciate it. How do I look?"

I twirled in my pine-green gown in front of the window, giving my hair a playful toss. "Think he'll finally notice me?"

The cloud didn't need to respond for me to know the answer—no.

He wasn't going to notice me.

He never did.

I highly doubted *he* even knew I existed.

Five years I'd known him, and he had yet to speak a word to me.

Heaving a sigh, I grabbed the flowers I'd picked earlier outside the suite and pressed them to my nose with a greedy breath. They smelled warm and fresh, spring-like.

The flowers were pink and shaped like a Valentine's heart. I wove some of them in my hair, which was partly coiffed at the top.

One of their thorns pricked my finger, and I lifted it, sucking on the drop of blood it produced. The stickiness of the sap filled my mouth, and I groaned.

"I know, I know, I should just get over him. Move on."

I quickly licked all my fingers to get rid of the nectar. "There's a fine line between being a romantic and a moron. I think I've straddled it about four years too long."

I'd been harboring my obsession to the eldest Fitzpatrick brother for the past five years. Half a freaking decade. I'd compared every guy I dated to the unattainable tycoon, sent him starry-eyed looks, and compulsively read every piece of information about him in the media. Simply deciding to forget about him wasn't going to cut it. I'd tried that before.

I needed to go big or go home.

In this case, I needed to use Auntie Tilda's wish and ask to move on.

I opened my mouth to make the wish, but just as I began to utter the words, my throat clogged up.

I dropped the flowers in my hand, stumbling to the mirror. A rash fanned across my neck like a possessive male palm. The rubicund stain spread south, dipping into the valley between my breasts. Every inch of my flesh was turning scarlet.

How in the hell did I have an allergic reaction? I was too anxious to eat anything all morning.

Maybe it was jealousy.

A green, pointy-toothed monster clawing its way out of my heart. Reminding me that being a bride was *my* dream, not Sailor's, darn it.

Sure, it wasn't feminist, or inspiring, or progressive, but it didn't make it any less the truth. *My* truth.

I wanted marriage, a white picket fence, giggly babies in diapers roaming around freely in my backyard, and smelly Labradors chasing them.

Whenever I allowed myself to think about it (which wasn't very often), the unfairness of it rubbed me off my breath. Sailor was the most asexual thing in the world after a surgical face mask before she'd met Hunter.

Yet she was the one who ended up marrying before all of us.

A knock on the door snapped me out of my trance.

"Pers?" my older sister, Emmabelle—Belle for short—crooned from the other side. "The ceremony starts in twenty minutes. What's taking you so long?"

Well, Belle, I look shockingly similar to a Cheetos, both in color and complexion.

THE *Villain*

"You better get your ass in gear. Our girl has already puked in the limo's trash can twice, cursed the groom like a pirate for not eloping in Vegas, and one of her acrylic nails is playing Amelia Earhart."

"How do you mean?" I shouted back through the suite's door.

"It's disappeared. Hopefully not in her hairdo." I heard the grin in my sister's voice. "Oh, by the way. Can you bring Hunter's ring if his brother doesn't show up to take it? Technically, it's Cillian's job, but he's probably in the gardens, skinning a female employee and making fashionable coats out of her flesh."

Cillian.

My stomach clenched at the mention of his name.

"Roger that. I'll be there in five minutes."

I heard my sister's heels clicking as she left, heading back to the waiting limo.

I glanced around the room.

How can I make this stupid rash go away?

Mentally snapping my fingers, I looked around for Aisling "Ash" Fitzpatrick's purse, finding it on the bed. I rummaged through it, flicking away Band-Aids, a Swiss knife, and a thumb-size makeup kit. She must have Benadryl and antihistamines. She was a Girl Scout, ready for any occasion, be it a rash, a broken nail, a World War, or a sudden pandemic.

"*Bingo.*" I tugged a skin-soothing ointment tube from the diamond-studded Hermès. I scrubbed the lotion on my skin, pleased with my drunken self, when the door behind me flung open.

"Five minutes, Belle." My eyes were still glued to my blemished arms. "And yeah, I remember, Hunter's ring…"

I looked up. My jaw slacked as the rest of my words shriveled back into my throat. The ointment slipped between my fingers.

Cillian "Kill" Fitzpatrick stood at the door.

Hunter Fitzpatrick's older brother.

The most eligible bachelor in America.

A stonehearted heir with a face sculpted from marble.

Attainable as the moon, and just as cold and wavering.

Most important of all: the man I'd loved in secret since the first day I'd laid eyes on him.

His auburn hair was slicked back, his eyes a pair of smoky ambers. Honey-rimmed yet lacking any warmth. He wore an Edwardian tux, a chunky Rolex, and the slight frown of a man who regarded anyone he couldn't screw or make money out of as an inconvenience.

He was always calm, quiet, and reserved, never drawing attention to himself yet owning every room he entered.

Unlike his siblings, Cillian wasn't beautiful.

Not in the conventional sense, anyway. His face was too sharp, his features too bold, his sneer too mocking. His strong jaw and hooded eyes didn't harmonize together in a symphony of flawless strokes. But there was something decadent about him that I found more alluring than the straightforwardness in Hunter's Apollo-like perfection or the Aisling's Snow White beauty.

Cillian was a dirty lullaby, inviting me to sink into his claws and nestle in his darkness.

And I, aptly named after the goddess of spring, longed for the ground to crack open and suck me in. To fall into his underworld and never emerge.

Whoa. That last mimosa really killed whatever was left of my brain cells.

"Cillian," I choked out. "Hello. Hey. Hi."

So eloquent, Pers.

I peppered my greeting by scratching my neck. It was just my luck to be alone with him in a room for the first time ever while looking and feeling like a ball of lava.

Cillian ambled toward the safe with the indolent elegance of a big cat, oozing raw danger that made my toes curl. His indifference often made me wonder if I was even in the room with him.

"Three minutes until the limo leaves, Penrose."

So I *did* exist.

THE *Villain*

"Thank you."

My breathing became labored, slow, and I was starting to realize I might need to call an ambulance.

"Are you excited?" I managed.

No response.

The metal door of the safe clicked mechanically, unlocking. He took out the black velvet box of Hunter's ring, pausing to look at me, his eyes sliding from my red face and arms to the pink and white flowers crowning my head. Something passed across his features—a moment of hesitation—before he shook his head, then made his way back to the door.

"*Wait!*" I cried.

He stopped but didn't turn to face me.

"I need…I need…" *A better vocabulary, obviously.* "I need you to call an ambulance. I think I'm having an allergic reaction."

He swiveled on his heel, assessing me. Every second under his scrutiny dropped my temperature by ten degrees. Sharing a space with Cillian Fitzpatrick was an experience. Like sitting in an obscure, vacant cathedral.

At that moment, I wished I were my sister, Emmabelle.

She would tell him to stick his attitude where the sun don't shine. Then drag him into one of the private gardens after the ceremony and ride his face.

But I wasn't Belle. I was Persephone.

Timid, nice, Goody Two-shoes Persy.

Missionary-sex-with-the-lights-off Pers.

The awkward romantic.

The people-pleaser.

The *boring* one.

There was a beat of silence before he took a step back into the room, closing the door after him.

"Not much going on inside that pretty head, huh?"

He sighed, discarding his blazer on the bed, then unbuttoning his cuff links. Hiking his dress shirt up his muscled forearms, he stared me down with dissatisfaction.

My body had decided this was a great time as any to collapse on the floor, so it did just that. I crashed on the carpet, heaving as I tried to draw my next breath.

So that's how Auntie Tilda felt.

Unaffected by my fall, Cillian flicked the faucet of the claw-foot bath in the middle of the room, turning the tap to the blue side, so the water would be ice-cold.

Satisfied with the water temperature, he stepped toward me, rolled me over on my stomach with the tip of his loafers—like I was a sandbag—and leaned down, pressing his palm to the base of my spine.

"What are you—" I gasped.

"Don't worry." He tore the corseted dress from my body with one long movement. The violent sound of fabric ripping and buttons popping sliced through the air. "My tastes don't run to little girls."

There was an age different between us. Twelve years weren't something you could easily disregard. It never bothered me, though.

What *did* bother me was my new state of nakedness. I shivered like a leaf beneath him.

"What the hell did you do?" I shrieked.

"You're poisoned," he announced matter-of-factly.

That made me sober up.

"I'm *what*?"

He kicked the pink flowers next to me in answer. They careened to the other side of the room.

My breath became shallower, more labored. The vitality seeped out of my body. The echo of gurgling water pouring into the tub was monotone and soothing, and suddenly, I was exhausted. I wanted to sleep.

"I found them in the garden outside the suite," I murmured, my lips heavy. My eyes widened as I realized something.

"I tasted them, too."

THE Villain

"Of course you would." His voice dripped sarcasm. He hoisted me over his shoulder and carried me to the restroom. Dumping my limp body by the toilet, he lifted my head by fisting my hair. My knees screamed in pain. He wasn't gentle.

"I'm going to make you throw up," he announced, and without any further intro, he stuck two of his large fingers down my throat. Deep. I gagged, vomiting immediately while he held my head.

In the words of Joe Exotic, I am never going to recover from this. Cillian holding my hair while he is making me puke.

I emptied my stomach until Cillian was sure everything was gone. Only then did he wipe my face with his bare hand, undeterred by the puke residue.

"What're they, anywhmm?" I slurred, resting my head on the toilet seat. "The flowers."

He scooped me in his arms with frightening ease, walking across the room, and dumping me onto the bed. I was stark naked, save for a skin-colored thong.

I heard him rummaging through the cabinets. My eyes fluttered open. Grabbing a first-aid kit, he produced a small bottle of medicine and a syringe, frowning at the tiny instructions on the vial as he spoke.

"Bleeding Hearts. Known for being beautiful, rare, and toxic."

"Just like you," I murmured. Was I seriously cracking jokes on my deathbed?

He ignored my riveting observation.

"You were about to poison an entire chapel, Emmalynne."

"I'm Persephone." My eyebrows pinched.

Funny how I could barely breathe, but I still managed to take offense at being confused with my sister. "And my sister's name is Emmabelle, not Emmalynne."

"Are you sure?" he asked without looking up, sticking the syringe into the bottle and drawing the liquid into it. "I don't remember the younger one being so mouthy."

I was filed under The Younger One in his memory. *Great.*

"Am I sure I am who I am, or what my sister's name is?" I resumed my scratching, about as demure as a wild ogre. "Either way, the answer is yes. I'm positive."

My older sister was the memorable one.

She was louder, taller, more voluptuous; her hair was the dazzling shade of champagne. Normally, I didn't mind being overshadowed. But I *hated* that Kill remembered Emmabelle and not me, even if he got her name wrong.

It was the first time in my life I resented my sister.

Kill lowered himself to the edge of the bed, slapping his knee.

"On my lap, Flower Girl."

"No."

"The word shouldn't even be in your vocabulary with me."

"Turns out I'm full of surprises." My mouth moved over the linen. I knew I was drooling. Now that I was breathing better, I noticed the stench of puke from my breath.

I turned my head in the other direction on the bed. Maybe dying wasn't such a bad idea. The man I'd been obsessed with for years was a massive prick and didn't even know my name.

"I don't care if I die," I croaked.

"Ditto, sweetheart. Unfortunately, you'll have to do it on someone else's watch."

His arms came around my body, and he draped me over his legs. My breasts spilled over his muscular thigh, my nipples brushing against his pants. My butt was aligned with his face, allowing him a perfect view. Luckily, I was too weak to feel embarrassed.

"Stay still."

He eased the needle into my right buttock, slowly releasing the liquid into my bloodstream. The steroids hit my system immediately, and I sucked in a lungful of oxygen, my mouth opening against his thigh. I moaned in relief, my back arching. I felt a bulge nestling against my body. It was thick and long, splaying across most of my belly. That thing belonged in a rifle case, not a vagina.

THE *Villain*

And the plot thickens.

It wasn't the only thing that did just that.

We stayed like this for ten seconds, with me regaining my breath, gulping precious air, and him picking the flowers from my hair with surprising tenderness. He disposed of the flowers inside a napkin, then folded it a few times. He put one hand on my butt cheek and pulled the syringe out slowly, causing ripples of desire to run along my body.

My head dropped to the bed.

I was shamefully close to an orgasm.

"Thank you," I said quietly, pushing my palms up on the bed to rise. He plastered a hand over my back, lowering me down to lie across his lap.

"Don't move. Your bath should be ready any minute."

He had the eerie, irritating ability to treat me like dirt while saving me at the same time. Stuck in a state of drunkenness, gratefulness, and mortification, I followed his instructions.

"So. *Persephone*." He tasted my name on his tongue, rolling my panties down my legs with his strong, long fingers. "Did your parents know you were going to be insufferable and punished you in advance with a stripper's name, or were they on a Greek mythology kick?"

"My Auntie Tilda named me. She battled breast cancer, on and off. The week I was born, she got the all clear after her first round of chemo. My mother let her name me as a present."

In hindsight, they were too quick to celebrate. The cancer came back in full force a few years later, claiming my aunt's life. At least I had a few good years with her.

"They couldn't say no." Cillian tossed my panties on the floor.

"I love my name."

"It's tacky."

"It means something."

"Nothing means anything."

I whipped my head to flash him an angry look, my cheeks hot with anger. "Whatever you say, Dr. Seuss."

Cillian took off my heels, leaving me completely naked. He discarded me on the bed to stand up and turn off the faucet, then he took a seat on the edge of the bathtub.

"Lady-in-bath." He swirled his finger in the water, checking the temperature.

I cocked my head from my position on the bed.

"That's another name for the bleeding heart," he explained aloofly. "Get in."

He turned his back to me, allowing me some privacy. I stepped into the bath, sucking in a breath. The water was ice-cold.

Cillian texted on his phone while the arctic water soothed my skin. I was already feeling much better after the shot. Despite throwing up most of what I'd eaten and drank that morning, I was still lush. Silence stretched between us, punctuated by staff and event coordinators barking instructions beyond the suite's walls. I knew that despite the awkward situation, I only had one chance to tell him how I felt. The odds were against me. Other than his erection at having me buck naked on his lap, he seemed turned off by my very existence.

But it was now or never, and never was too long a time to live without the man I loved.

"I want you." I propped my head against the cool surface of the bath. The words soaked the walls and ceiling, and the truth filled the air, charging it with electricity. Using the L-word was too intimate. Too scary. I knew what I felt for him was love—despite his rude behavior—but I also knew he would never believe me.

His hands busied over his phone. Maybe he didn't hear me.

"I've always wanted you," I said, louder.

No response.

A glutton for punishment, I continued, my pride and confidence collapsing brick by brick.

"Sometimes I want you so much it hurts to breathe. Sometimes the pain from breathing is a nice distraction from wanting you."

THE *Villain*

A knock on the door made him dart up. Aisling was on the threshold, holding a replica of the bridesmaids dress we all wore.

"You said you needed my extra gown? Why on earth…" She trailed off, taking me in behind her brother's shoulder. Her eyes flared.

"Holy Mother Mary. Did you two…?"

"Not in a million years," Cillian snapped, plucking the dress from his sister's hand. "Stall the limo. She'll be down in five minutes."

With that, he slammed the door in her face, then locked it for good measure.

Not in a million years.

White-hot panic mixed with good ole embarrassment coursed through my veins.

Reality sank in.

I'd poisoned myself.

Rambled to Cillian drunkenly.

Let him undress me, make me puke, give me a shot, hurl me into the bathtub.

Then confessed my undying love for him with vomit pieces still decorating my mouth.

Kill threw a bathrobe into my hands, all business.

"Dry up."

I sprang up on my feet, doing as I was told.

He rounded on me with Aisling's spare dress, helping me into it.

"I don't want your help," I bit out, feeling my cheeks flush.

Stupid, stupid, stupid.

"I don't care what you want."

Pursing my lips, I watched his dark figure in the mirror as he fastened my corset, working quicker and more efficiently than any seamstress I'd ever seen in action. It was jarring. His fingers moved like magic around the ribbon, looping it into the hoops expertly to tie me like a bowed present.

It dawned on me he knew I was poisoned from the moment he

stepped into the room and saw the flowers in my hair, but hadn't offered to help me until I asked him to call an ambulance.

I could have died.

He wasn't kidding when he said he only saved me because he didn't want me to die on his watch—he honestly didn't care.

Cillian tugged at the satin strings of my dress, tightening it around me.

"You're hurting me," I hissed, narrowing my eyes at the mirror in front of us.

"That's what you get for having a bleeding heart."

"The flower, or organ?"

"Both. One is a fast poison. The other slow, but just as destructive."

My eyes clung to him in our reflection. Graceful and self-assured. He stood tall and proud, never used profanity, and was the most meticulous person I knew.

It was what I admired about him the most. The thin film of properness engulfing the chaos teeming inside him. I knew that underneath the flawless exterior laid something untamed and dangerous.

It felt like our secret. The perfect Cillian Fitzpatrick was, in fact, not so perfect. And all I wanted was to find out how.

"You weren't going to help me. You were going to leave me to die." My tone was frighteningly mild. I became more sober with each passing second. "Why did you?"

"A poisoned bridesmaid makes bad press."

"And they say chivalry is dead," I said sarcastically.

"Chivalry might be dead, but you're not, so shut up and be grateful." He gave the satin cords another yank. I winced.

He *did* have a point. Cillian not only saved me this morning but he also didn't try any funny business and was probably running just as late as I was now because my dumb ass had decided to pick poisonous flowers.

Begrudgingly, I muttered, "Thanks."

He arched an eyebrow, as if to ask—*for what?*

"For being a gentleman," I clarified.

Our eyes clashed in the mirror.

"I'm no gentleman, Flower Girl."

He finished with a final pull, then stepped away and picked up his blazer from the mattress. I had to think on my feet, fast. My gaze drifted to the window. The lone cloud was still there.

Watching me.

Taunting me.

Waiting to be used.

You only get one miracle.

This one was worth it.

I took a deep breath and said the words aloud, not wanting to half-ass it in case there was a fine print and I needed to do the whole Hocus Pocus thing.

"I wish you'd fall in love with me."

The words surged out of my mouth like a blizzard, making him freeze midstride on his way to the door. He turned around, his face a perfect mask of harsh brutality.

Drawing a breath, I continued.

"I wish you'd fall in love with me so hard you won't be able to think about anything else. To eat. To breathe. When my Aunt Tilda died, she granted me one miracle. This is the wish I choose. Your love. There's a world beyond your ice walls, Cillian Fitzpatrick, and it is full of laughter and joy and warmth." I took a step in his direction, my knees wobbling. "I'm going to pay back your favor. I'm going to save your life in my own way."

A curse.

A spell.

A hope.

A *dream*.

For the first time since he entered the room, I saw something resembling curiosity on his face. Even my naked body splayed on his lap didn't make him as much as blink twice. But this? This pierced his exterior, even if it only made the tiniest of cracks. His brows pinched, and he advanced toward me, erasing the space between us in three confident strides. Outside, Belle and Aisling banged their fists on the door, yelling that we were late.

My entire life spun out of focus at that moment. My carefully crafted fantasy unraveling into a nightmare.

Cillian tipped my chin up with his finger, his eyes hard on mine.

"Listen to me carefully, Persephone, because I will only say it once. You are going to walk out of this room and forget you know me, just as I've failed to notice your existence thus far. You will meet a nice, sane, *boring* guy. A perfect fit for your nice, sane, *boring* self. You'll get married to him, have his babies, and thank your lucky stars I wasn't horny enough to take you up on your less than subtle offer. I'm giving you the gift of turning you down. Take it and run for the hills."

He smiled for the first time, and it was so unpleasant, so twisted that it knocked the breath out of my chest. His smile told me he wasn't happy. Hadn't been for years. Decades, even.

"Why do you hate me?" I whispered.

Tears blurred my vision, but I refused to let them fall.

"Hate you?" He wiped the tears with the back of his hand. "I have no feelings, Persephone. Not for you. Not at all. I am incapable of hating you. But I will also never, *ever* love you."

One

Persephone

Present.

The cobblestone sidewalk dug into my feet through my cheap shoes as I secured my bicycle to the bike rack.

Darkness washed the street in North End. Pub workers hurled fat, soggy trash bags into the jaws of industrial containers, chatting and laughing, ignoring the sheets of rain falling from the sky.

I said a silent prayer they'd stay on the street until I made it safely to my building. I hated coming home late but couldn't say no to the babysitting gig I'd been offered after school hours. Collecting the hem of my wet dress, I hurried to my door. I pushed it open, pressing my back to it with a relieved sigh.

A hand shot to me in the dark, yanking my wrist and flinging me across the room. My back slammed against the stairway, and pain exploded from my tailbone to my neck.

"Mrs. Veitch. Fancy seeing you here."

Even in the pitch black, I recognized Colin Byrne's voice. It was smooth and low, a hint of mockery lilting his Southie accent.

"It's *Miss Penrose*." I rushed up to my feet, swatting strands of wet hair off my face and dusting my knees. I flipped the switch on. Yellow light pooled inside the hallway. Tom Kaminski—simply Kaminski to anyone who knew him—Byrne's errand boy and muscle man, stood behind the lean, wrinkled loan shark with his burly arms crossed at his chest.

Byrne covered the distance between us, the strong scent of his cologne prickling my gag reflex.

"Penrose? Nah, that's not the name on your driver's license, Persy baby."

"I asked for a divorce." I took a step back from him, schooling my face.

"Well, I asked for a threesome with Demi Lovato and Taylor Swift. Looks like we both ain't getting our wish, doll. The fact of the matter is, you're married to Paxton Veitch, and Paxton Veitch owes me money. A shit-ton of it."

"Exactly. *Paxton* owes you," I said hotly, knowing I was entering a lost war. Byrne wouldn't listen. He never did. "He was the one placing those bets. He was the one losing money at your joints. It's his mess to fix, not mine."

Colin lifted my left hand, rubbing at my naked wedding finger. The imprinted tan line where the ring used to be glared back at both of us, reminding me that my relationship with Pax wasn't ancient history.

Not only was I still married to him but I also still honored my vows. I hadn't dated anyone since Pax ran away. Hell, I still visited his grandma in the nursing home every week, bearing shortbread cookies and her favorite culinary magazines.

She was lonely, and it wasn't her fault her grandson turned out to be a dick.

"Pax's long gone now, and his pretty wife refuses to let me know where I can find him." Byrne's velvet voice pierced my thoughts while he played with my fingers.

"His wife doesn't *know* where he is." I tried to yank my hand away to no avail. "But she does know how to use pepper spray. Personal space here."

THE *Villain*

I didn't want Belle, who was upstairs, to hear the commotion in the hallway and come out of the apartment to investigate. She knew nothing about my situation, and I was pretty sure my savage sister would not hesitate to take out the Glock she owned and put a hole in each of these bastard's heads if she walked into this scene.

I didn't want to burden Belle with my problems. Not this particular problem, anyway. Not after everything she'd already done for me.

"Use your fine investigative skills to find out," Byrne beamed. "After all, you managed to catch the lousiest husband in New England. You found him before, and you can do it again. Have a little faith."

"We both know I haven't the greenest clue where to start looking. His phone is dead, my emails are bouncing back, and his friends won't talk to me. It's not like I haven't tried." I used the hand Colin held to push his face away roughly.

He didn't budge. Just wrapped his fingers tighter around mine.

"Then I'm afraid his debt is now yours. Whatever happened to in sickness and in health? For richer or poorer? How does the oath go?" Byrne snapped his fingers at Kaminski behind him.

Kaminski snorted, flashing a row of rotten teeth.

"Beats me, Boss. Never got hitched. Ain't planning to, either."

"Smart man."

Byrne brought my hand to his mouth, pressing a cold kiss to the back of it, darting his tongue between my index and middle fingers, showing me what he wanted to do to the rest of my body. I swallowed a ball of puke and breathed through my nose. He was doing a great job of scaring the bejesus out of me, and he knew it. Byrne was a loan shark who was notorious for collecting his checks rain or shine, and my husband owed him over a hundred thousand dollars.

He rested my damp palm on his cheek, nuzzling against it.

"Sorry, Persephone. It's nothing personal. I have a debt to collect, and if I don't collect it soon, people are going to assume it's okay to take money from me without paying me back. If you're interested in reimbursing me through a different currency, I can stitch together a plan.

I'm not an unreasonable man. But no matter how you look at it—you *will* pay your husband's debt, and you better hurry, because the interest is stacking up nicely as the weeks tick by."

"What are you insinuating?" My heart jackhammered its way through my rib cage, about to abandon ship and run out of the building without me.

This idea had never come up before in the months Byrne and Kaminski had been paying me weekly visits. I was a preschool teacher, for crying out loud. Where would I be able to find one hundred thousand dollars? Even my *kidneys* weren't worth that much.

And yes, I was desperate enough to Google it.

"I'm saying if you can't pay the outstanding balance, you'll have to *work* for it."

"Just spit it out, Byrne," I hissed, every nerve in my body ready to reach for my purse, grab the pepper spray, and empty that bitch into both their eyes. As sleazy as he was, I doubted he would give up a hundred grand just to roll me between his sheets.

"Serving men who are less than hygienic and not much to look at." Colin smiled apologetically. "You're a good-looking gal, Veitch, even in those rags." He tugged at the muddy, cheap dress I wore. "Six months working in my strip club doing double shifts every day, and we can call it even."

"I'll die before I dance on a pole," I seethed, pushing my fingers into his eye sockets with the hand he held. He dodged the attack by rearing his head back, but I managed to put a few scratches on his cheek.

Kaminski stepped forward, about to interfere, but Byrne waved him off, laughing.

"You won't be dancing," he said, his eyes glinting with amusement. "You'll be on your back in the VIP room. Although I can't promise you won't be on your hands and knees, too, if they're willing to pay extra."

The ball of puke in my throat tripled its size, blocking my windpipe. A cold film of sweat covered every inch of my body.

THE *Villain*

Byrne wanted to pimp me out if I didn't come up with the money Paxton owed him. In the eight months Paxton had been gone, I'd stupidly hoped he would do the right thing and show up at the eleventh hour to deal with the shitstorm he'd created, leaving me in the eye of it.

That he'd grant me the divorce I'd begged him for in the days before his disappearance.

I'd held onto my anger, refusing to let it turn into resignation because that meant accepting this was my problem.

Now, I was finally coming to terms with the hard facts Byrne had already known:

Paxton was never coming back.

His problems were mine to deal with.

And I had to come up with a solution, *fast*.

"What if I don't pay?" My jaw clenched. I wasn't going to cry in front of them, no matter what. I may not have been as feisty and fierce as my older sister, but I was still a Southie original.

A sweet romantic—but a savage, nonetheless.

Byrne's heavy boots clicked softly as he ambled toward the building's entrance. "Then I'll have to make an example out of you. Which, I assure you, Mrs. Veitch, would hurt me more than it would you. It is always a sad state of affairs when the wife has to take on the burden of her husband's mistakes." He stopped by the door and shook his head, wearing a faraway look on his face. "But if I let this slide, I'll lose my street cred. You *will* pay. Either in money, with the thing between your legs, or with your blood. Catch you later, Persy."

The door clicked shut behind the two men. Thunder rumbled, licking their shapes through the glass door in electric blue. They ran to a black Hummer parked across the street, slipping inside and gunning it back to the hellhole they came from.

I stumbled up the stairs to my sister's apartment. I'd been staying with her since Paxton took off eight months ago. Shakily turning the key inside its hole, I pushed the door open.

I didn't pay rent. Belle thought Pax stole all the money he and I had saved to buy a house when he ran away. That part wasn't a lie. He *did* take our money. What she didn't know was it wasn't only that he spent my entire life's savings in an underground casino—I was actually in debt because of him.

"Pers? Jeez, dude. There's a thunderstorm outside." Belle rubbed at her eyes, stretching on the couch. She wore a *Fries Before Guys* oversized shirt. A Korean drama danced across the flat TV screen, and a bag of peanut butter pretzels balanced on her flat stomach. A stab of jealousy pricked my chest as I watched her lying there. Trouble-free and relaxed.

She didn't have to wonder if she would make it to next week alive without selling her body in a dingy Southie strip club.

She didn't have her hand kissed, licked, and twisted by Colin Byrne, the scent of his cheap cologne lingering in her nostrils for days after each of his visits, making her stomach churn.

She didn't toss and turn at night, wondering how to save herself from a gory death.

I hung my tattered windbreaker by the door. Emmabelle's apartment was tiny but fashionable. A studio with hardwood flooring, trendy palm-tree wallpaper, deep green ceiling, and funky mismatched furniture. Everything she owned and wore dripped of her bold, sophisticated personality. We shared her twin bed.

"Sorry about that. Shannon's parents went to a drive-in and must've gotten carried away. I didn't even know drive-ins still existed. Did you?" I stepped out of my holed shoes at the entrance, concealing my despair with a smile.

Maybe I should admit defeat and do what Paxton did. Catch the next flight out of the States and disappear.

Only unlike Paxton, I was attached to the place where I grew up. I couldn't imagine my life without my sister, my parents, my *friends*.

Paxton had been lonely. Orphaned at age three, he was raised by his grandmother Greta and various relatives. Tossed between houses

THE *Villain*

whenever he got too difficult. That was what he told me when we first got together, and my heart went out to him.

"Drive-ins? Sure. Some of my favorite sexcapades happened at the Solano drive-in. But it's been raining so hard, I doubt they could watch anything there. You really should've called me. I'd have picked you up. You know tonight is my night off." She wiggled her toes under her throw.

Exactly. It was her night off. Who was I to take away the only free night she had for herself? She deserved to do exactly what she was doing. Binge on a TV show, junk food, and wear a discounted face mask from Ross.

"You already do too much for me."

"That's because that bastard, Pax, screwed you over. Remind me why you married him again?"

"Love?" Plopping down next to her on the mustard corduroy couch, I propped my chin on her shoulder with a sigh. "I thought I was respecting our pact."

Once upon a time, when we were in college, Sailor, Emmabelle, Aisling, and I made a pact to only marry for love. Sailor was the first to keep her word. But she happened to fall for a man who worshipped the ground she walked upon, looked like a Hemsworth brother, and had enough money to start a new country.

I was the second in the gang to say I do. A few hasty kisses behind carefully trimmed bushes were all it took for me to make the biggest mistake of my life. Paxton Veitch was Colin's previous Kaminski. A simple soldier who moonlighted as a security guy in the private sector. Paxton always maintained he was a bouncer at one of Colin's bars. Said he was going to quit as soon as he found a more stable job.

Spoiler alert: he never looked for one. Not only did he love being a thug, but he also enjoyed losing the money Byrne paid him in his joints when he was off duty.

It wasn't until I was too far gone that I found out Paxton wasn't a bouncer. He broke hands, noses, and spines for a living, and had a police record thicker than *Lord of the Rings*. I'd never told Belle, Aisling, and Sailor that Pax was a low-grade mobster. They'd loved him almost as much as they loved Hunter, and I didn't want to burst their bubble.

And anyway, Paxton wasn't all bad. He was handsome, funny, and incredibly good-hearted at the beginning of our relationship. He left me love letters everywhere, packed my lunch box for me each night, sent me flowers for no reason at all, and arranged spontaneous Disney World vacations where we'd drive down to Florida in our beat-up car, eating crappy gas station junk, and singing to my Paula Abdul and Wham! playlist from the top of our lungs.

A stand-up guy who'd offered to paint my parents' entire house for free before they sold it, bought me an engagement ring using every single cent he had to his name, and was always there when I needed him.

Until he wasn't.

I thought I could help him get on the right path. That love would conquer all.

Turned out, it couldn't conquer his gambling addiction.

"You still believe in that bitch?" Belle tilted the bag of pretzels in my direction in offering, pulling me out of my musings.

"In what?" I took a pretzel, munching on it without tasting it. I'd become scarily thin in the past few months. The side effect of inheriting Paxton's weighty problems.

"Love." Belle shot one eyebrow up. "Do you still believe in love after Pax took a dump all over the concept, then set it on fire?"

"Yeah." I felt my ears pinking, masking my embarrassment with a chuckle. "Pathetic, right?"

My sister patted my thigh.

"Wanna talk about it?"

I shook my head.

"Wanna *drink* about it?"

I nodded. She laughed.

"I'll heat some pizza, too."

The thought of eating made me want to vomit. But I also knew Belle was becoming suspicious, what with my weight loss and inability to sleep.

"Pizza sounds great. Thanks."

She stood and sashayed over to the kitchenette. I watched as she threw the fridge door open, shaking her butt to her off-key whistle.

"Belle?" I cleared my throat.

"Hmm?" She shoved a slice of pizza into the microwave, setting the timer for thirty seconds.

"What do you think is going to happen with Pax?" I grabbed a pillow and hugged it to my chest, pulling at a thread in it. "I can't stay married to him forever, right? I'll be relieved from this marriage at some point if he doesn't show up?"

Belle plucked a can of Pepsi from the fridge, tapping her lips as she contemplated my question.

"Well, marriage is not a public restroom. I'm not sure you can be *relieved* from it, but you for sure can get out of this if you put your mind to it. The man hasn't been around in almost a year. You need to save up, get a good lawyer, and finish with this mess."

Me. Paying for legal representation. *Right*.

"You'll have to do it at some point, you know," my sister said, more quietly now. "Seek legal help. Take the bastard down."

"With what money?" I sighed. "And please, don't offer me another loan. I'm just going to refuse it."

Belle was working as a club promoter for one of Boston's most outrageous joints, Madame Mayhem. She was a genius in her field and brought in clientele that made the owners foam at the mouth, but she was nowhere near financially established. Plus, I knew she was saving up to chip in on Madame Mayhem's looming remodel so she could become a partner.

"Let's say you're too proud to take money from me—your own *sister*, mind you—and still want legal representation. I would just go to Sailor and ask for a loan." Her voice grew heated, desperate. "The Fitzpatricks have enough fuck-you money to build a dick-shaped statue the size of Lady Liberty. Sailor won't be hard-pressed to get it back, you'll have zero interest, and she knows you're good for it. You'll pay it eventually."

"I can't." I shook my head.

"Why?" She took the pizza out of the microwave, put it on a paper plate, and sauntered over to the couch, dumping it on the pillow I was hugging. "Eat the whole thing, Pers. You're skin and bones. Mom thinks you have an eating disorder."

"I don't have an eating disorder." I frowned.

Belle rolled her eyes. "Bitch, I know. Your ass inhaled three Cheesecake Factory meals just eight months ago and washed it all down with margaritas, Tums, and regret. You're going through something, and I want you to snap out of it. Ask Sailor for the money!"

"Are you insane?" I waved the soggy pizza in the air. "She doesn't have time for my drama. She just told us she was pregnant."

Three days ago, on our traditional weekly takeout night, Sailor dropped the bomb. There were a lot of squeaks and tears. Most of them Ash's and mine while Sailor and Emmabelle stared at us blankly, waiting for us to get over our hysterics.

"*And?*" Belle cocked her head. "She can be preggo and give you money, you know. Women are known for multitasking."

"She'll get worried. Plus, I don't want to be that loser friend."

"It's just a few thousand dollars."

It's a hundred thousand of them.

But my sister didn't know that.

Which was the *real* reason I hadn't asked Sailor.

"At least think about it. Even if it feels weird for you to turn to Sailor and Hunter, that sociopath Cillian would give you the money. Sure, he'd make you sweat for it—I swear, that asshole is as annoying as his face is sitable—but you'll walk out of there with the money."

Cillian.

After the suite incident, my friends and sister demanded to know what happened between us. I'd told them the truth. Most of it, anyway. About the bleeding heart and the steroid shot, omitting the part where I told him I was in love with him and put a curse on him.

Why get into the small details, right?

I'd managed to forget Cillian over time. *Barely*. Even the memory of him saving me faded and was washed away along with the Wish Upon a Cloud performance I was determined to suppress from my memory.

I hadn't spoken to my Auntie Tilda since that day. That day, I stopped spotting lonely clouds in the sky and tried to move on with my life.

I fell in love.

Got married.

Almost got divorced.

Cillian, however, remained the same man who left that suite.

Ageless, timeless, and taciturn.

He was still single and as far as I knew, hadn't dated anyone, seriously or otherwise, in the time since he'd rejected me on Sailor and Hunter's wedding day.

Eight months ago—on the week Paxton had disappeared—Kill took the reins of Royal Pipelines, his father's petroleum company, and officially became CEO.

How did I not think of him before?

Cillian "Kill" Fitzpatrick was my best shot at getting the money.

He had no loyalties to anyone but himself, was good at keeping secrets, and seeing people squirm was his favorite pastime.

He'd helped me before, and he'd do it again.

One hundred thousand bucks was pocket change to him. He would hand me the money if only to watch me turn into a hundred different shades of red as I slid pitiful monthly checks that meant nothing to him down his mailbox. I'd even agree to take back the curse where I'd told him he'd fall in love with me.

For the first time in a long time, I felt my mouth watering.

Not because of the pizza, but because of the solution I could practically feel grazing the tip of my fingers.

I had a plan.

An escape route.

The older Fitzpatrick brother was going to save me, *again*.

Unlike my husband, all I needed to do was play my cards right.

Two

Persephone

"Sorry, sweetie, I don't think seeing Mr. Fitzpatrick is in your cards today." The malnourished PA made a show of tossing her platinum ponytail, a venomous grin on her scarlet lips. She wore a bubblegum-pink vinyl dress that made her look like BDSM Barbie, enough perfume to drown an otter, and the expression of someone who would die before letting another woman stake a claim on her boss.

I showed up unannounced at the Royal Pipelines' offices as soon as I finished work, asking to meet with Mr. Fitzpatrick. Sailor had mentioned that Hunter, who also worked for the family's company, was accompanying her to her first OB-GYN appointment, and dipped early. I didn't want Hunter to see me and pass the information to my friends.

When I showed up, Cillian's personal assistant pouted the entire time she spoke with him on the phone.

"Hiiiiiii, Mr. Fitzpatrick. This is Casey Brandt."

Pause.

"Your assistant for the past two years, sir."

Pause.

"Yeah! With the pink." She giggled. "Totes sorry to bother you, but I have Miss Persephone Penrose here without an appointment."

Pause.

"She said she needs to talk to you urgently, but, like, refused to give me any further information?"

I wasn't sure why the question mark was necessary. Then again, I wasn't certain why his PA looked like she belonged in a pink Corvette, driving around with her plastic boyfriend, Ken, and puppy, Taffy.

"Yes, I know it is my job to get the information out of her. Unfortunately, she's been most uncooperative, sir."

Pause.

"Yes, sir. I'll let her know."

She looked up at me like I was gum stuck on the bottom of her eleven-inch heels.

"Mr. Fitzpatrick cannot seem to fit you in his schedule."

"Tell him I'm not leaving until he sees me." My voice shook around the words, but I couldn't get out of here without seeing him. Without trying.

She hesitated, biting down on her glossed lip.

I jerked my chin toward the phone. "Go on, give him my answer."

She did, then proceeded to slam the switchboard phone.

"He said he's in a meeting that will likely last hours."

"That's okay. I have time."

That was two hours ago.

The grand lobby of the Royal Pipelines' management floor gleamed in gold accents. TV monitors following the company's stocks all over the world markets glowed in green and red.

Casey was growing restless, drumming the tips of her pointy fingernails on her chrome desk.

"I need to go to the ladies' room," she huffed, tugging a makeup kit from her bag under the table.

I looked up from the oil and gas journal I pretended to read.

"Oh?" I asked sweetly. "Are you not fully potty-trained? You know, I'm a pre-K teacher. Accidents don't faze me in the least. Need help in the big girl toilet?"

She shot me a murderous glare.

"Don't go anywhere, unless it's back to the trailer park you came from." She stood, running her eyes over my cheap clothes. "Or hell."

Her red-soled high heels stabbed the floor on her way to the restroom, leaving dents.

As soon as Casey was out of view, I jumped to my feet, sprinting ahead. Cillian's office was the largest and plushest on the floor. It was easy to spot the one fitted for the king of the castle.

I could only see his visitor's back through the glass door as I raced in his direction. The man who hid him from my vision was broad-shouldered with tawny blond hair, a sharp suit, and an impeccable posture. They seemed to be deep in conversation, but I didn't care. I threw the door open without knocking, barging in before I lost my nerve.

Unfortunately, my grand entrance wasn't enough to tear Cillian's gaze from the man in front of him. They were hunched over a mass of papers scattered all over his silver desk.

"…stocks going up, but I still noticed a trend in negative press. Saying the media doesn't like you would be an understatement. It'd be like saying the ocean is damp. That the sun is lukewarm. That Megan Fox is *merely* shagable…"

"I get the gist of it," Cillian clipped. "How do we rectify the situation?"

"I suppose a personality transplant would be out of the question?" the man drawled.

"The only thing that's about to be transplanted is my foot in your ass if you don't give me a solution."

Tough crowd. I'm about to face a very tough crowd.

"Bloody hell, Cillian," the posh man huffed, "you started your CEO journey by sacking nine percent of the company's management and drilling holes in the Arctic. You haven't exactly won any fans."

"I trimmed the fat."

"People rather like fat. The fast food industry rolls 256 billion dollars in revenue each year. Did you know that? The people you fired talked to journalists, adding fuel to the fire and making you truly one of the country's worst villains. Royal Pipelines is already considered the most hated company in the US. The refinery explosion in Maine, the Green Living climate rally where an eighteen-year-old broke both legs—"

"I wasn't the one who broke her legs," Cillian interjected, holding his palm up. "*Unfortunately.*"

"No matter how you spin it, you must clean up your act. Play their game. Promote a wholesome, jolly image. The company's reputation needs to be restored."

The man had a smooth, English accent. Princely, drenched with entitlement, and dripping authority. He was playfully detached. An enigma. I couldn't tell if he was a good or bad guy.

"Fine. I'll kiss a few babies. Sponsor some students. Donate funds to open a new hospital wing." Cillian leaned back in his seat, his eyes dropping back to the paperwork in front of him.

"I'm afraid we're quite past the kissing babies stage. It's time, Kill."

Cillian looked up, scowling.

"I will not sacrifice my personal life to pacify a few self-righteous, Tesla-driving pricks—"

"Cillian? I mean, Mr. Fitzpatrick?" I cleared my throat, jumping into the conversation before more information that wasn't meant for my ears was given.

Both men turned to look at me in surprise. With blue eyes charred with gold, a granite jaw, and an elegant nose, the British man was the kind of handsome that should be outlawed.

Cillian…well, he stayed gorgeous in his own go-screw-yourself way.

Kill raised an eyebrow. My appearance in his office didn't surprise him in the least.

"I didn't mean to interrupt—"

"Yet you did," he cut into my words.

"Sorry about that. May I have a word with you?"

"No," he answered flatly.

"It's important."

"Not to me." He dropped the documents to his desk, already looking disinterested. "Which Penrose sister are you? The older and loud one, or the young and annoying one?"

After all these years, he still couldn't tell Emmabelle and me apart. We didn't even look like one another. Not to mention, he'd seen me naked as the day I was born (also: just as red).

Yet again, I found myself torn between the need to seduce and stab him.

"I'm Persephone." I balled my hands into fists beside my body, recalling how badly it hurt when he broke my heart. How sublimely idiotic I'd felt after I tried to put that silly spell on him.

"That doesn't answer my question."

"Fine," I bit out. "I'm the *annoying* one."

He turned his focus back to the files at his desk, skimming through them. "What do you want?"

"To speak with you in private, please."

"Barging into my office unannounced is otiose. Expecting me not to kick you out implies you got your degree at the local Sam's Club. Spill it. Mr. Whitehall is my lawyer."

"Lawyers are people, too," I pointed out. My humiliation didn't need an audience.

"Debatable." The gorgeous blond man smirked viciously. "And actually ..." He pushed up from his seat, glancing back and forth between us with amusement dancing in his marble eyes. "I have better things to do than watch you two engaging in verbal foreplay. Cheers, Kill."

He gathered his documents, tapped the desk twice, and dashed out. Cillian's office temperature resembled that of an industrial freezer. Everything was neat, minimal, organized, and silver-chrome. Clinical and deliberately unnerving.

"May I come in?" I wrung my flowery dress. I hadn't even noticed my dress of choice when I left home this morning, but now, the irony wasn't lost on me.

He swiveled in his chair to face me, propping one ankle over the other on his desk. His five-piece dark gray suit looked like it had been sewn directly onto his body. Even though my obsession with Cillian Fitzpatrick morphed into resentment over the years, I couldn't deny he was the type of smoldering that made Michele Morrone look like Steve Buscemi.

"You have exactly ten, no, make it five minutes before I call security." He flipped an hourglass on his desk. "Give me the elevator pitch, Flower Girl. Make it good."

Flower Girl.

He remembered.

"You're going to call security on me?"

"My to-do list is long, and my patience is short. Four and a half minutes." He cracked his knuckles.

I rushed through the details so fast, my head spun. I told him about Paxton taking me to the cleaners. About Colin Byrne and Tom Kaminski. About the massive debt. I even told him about Byrne's promise he would pimp me out or kill me if I didn't come up with the money. When I was done, all Cillian did was nod.

"You managed to cram all of this in under three minutes. Maybe you're not completely useless."

A bang behind us made us twist our heads in unison. Casey was plastered to the glass door, wide-eyed. She pushed it open, baring her fake teeth.

"Gosh, I'm *so* sorry, Mr. Fitzpatrick. She promised she wouldn't..."

"Miss Brandt, leave," Cillian clipped.

"But I—"

"Save it for someone who cares."

"I—"

"That someone isn't me."

"Sir, I just wanted you to know that—"

"The only thing I know is you failed at your job and will be assessed accordingly. You're leaving in the next three seconds, either through the door or the window. Friendly advice: choose the door."

She bolted like the Looney Tunes Road Runner, nearly leaving a cloud of sand in her wake. Cillian turned back to me, ignoring the look of horror smeared on my face.

"You just threatened to throw Barbie out the window." I jerked my thumb behind me.

"Not threatened, heavily *implied*," he corrected. "You have less than two minutes, and I have about five hundred questions."

My palms dampened despite the temperature in the room.

"That's fair."

"One—why me? Why not Hunter, Sailor, or anyone who actually gives half a damn about you, pardon my forwardness?"

I couldn't tell him about Sailor's pregnancy. She still hadn't shared the news with her extended family. Or about my need not to be the loser one out of our group of friends. The one in need of saving.

I settled for half the truth.

"Sailor and Hunter don't know what Paxton did, and they're the only people I'm close with who actually have this kind of money. They know Pax left me and took the money we'd saved, but they don't know about the debt. I don't want to taint my friendship with my best friend by putting her in this position. I figured you and I share no history, no ties. With us, it will be a business transaction and nothing more."

"Why not Sam Brennan?"

Sam was Sailor's older brother and, as far as I was aware, a good friend of Cillian's. The reigning king of Boston's underground. A dashing psychopath with a peculiar taste for violence and pockets as deep as his soulless gray eyes.

"Mixing up with Brennan to try to pay back a street loan shark is like cutting off your arm because you broke your nail," I said quietly.

"You think I'm less dangerous than Brennan?" A ghost of a smile passed his lips.

"No." I tilted my head up. "But I think you'd be entertained by watching me squirm as I pay you back, and therefore more likely to give me the money."

His smirk was cocked and charged, like a loaded gun.

I was right. He *was* enjoying this.

"Where's that useless husband of yours now?"

"I don't know. Trust me, if I did, I'd have chased him to the end of earth and back." Made him pay for what he did.

"How are you planning to pay this loan back?" Kill ran the back of his hand over his sharp jawline.

"Slowly." The truth tasted bitter in my mouth. "I'm a pre-K teacher, but I moonlight as a babysitter and tutor first and second graders. I'll work tirelessly until I pay you back every penny. You have my word."

"Your word doesn't mean anything. I don't know you. Which brings me to my final question—why *should* I help you?"

What kind of question was that? Why did normal people usually help others? Because it was the decent thing to do. But Cillian Fitzpatrick *wasn't* normal nor decent. He didn't play by the rules.

I opened my mouth, searching my brain for a good answer.

"Thirty seconds, Persephone." He tapped the hourglass, watching me.

"Because you can?"

"The number of things I can *do* with my money is infinite." He yawned.

"Because it's the right thing to do!" I cried out.

He picked up one of the brochures on his desk, flipping through it. "I'm a nihilist."

"I don't know what that means." I felt the tips of my ears reddening in shame.

"Right or wrong are the same side of the coin for me, presented differently," he said impassively. "I have no morals or principles."

"That's the saddest thing I've ever heard."

"Really?" He looked up from the brochure, his face a stone mask of cruelty. "The saddest thing I've heard recently is a woman who got screwed over by her no-show husband and was about to get trafficked, murdered, or both."

"Exactly!" I exhaled, pointing at him. "Yes! See? If something happens to me, it will be on your conscience."

My lower lip trembled. As always, I kept my tears at bay.

He tossed the brochure across his desk.

"First of all, as I mentioned not two seconds ago, I have *no* conscience. Second, whatever happens to you is on you and the complete and utter buffoon you married. I'm not another item on your pile of bad decisions."

"Marrying Paxton wasn't a bad decision. I married for love."

This sounded pathetic, even to my own ears, but I wanted him to know. To know I hadn't been twiddling my thumbs, pining for him all those years.

"All middle-class girls do." He checked the time on the hourglass. "Very uninspiring."

"Cillian," I said softly. "You're my only hope."

Other than him, my only option was to disappear. Run away from my family and friends, from everything I knew, loved, and cherished.

From the life I'd built for the past twenty-six years.

He adjusted the tie clasped under his waistcoat.

"Here's the thing, Persephone. As a matter of principle, I do not give anything away without getting something back. The only thing separating myself and that loan shark who's after you is a privileged upbringing and opportunity. I, too, am not in the business of handing out free favors. So unless you tell me what, exactly, I could gain for the one hundred thousand dollars you're asking me to kiss goodbye, I'm going to turn you down. You have ten seconds, by the way."

I stood there, cheeks ablaze, eyes burning, every muscle in my body taut as a bowstring. A cold shiver ran down my back.

I wanted to scream. To lash out. To collapse on the floor in cinders. To claw his eyes out and bite and wrestle him and…*and do things I never wanted to do to anyone, my enemies included.*

"Five seconds." He tapped the hourglass. His snake-like eyes sparkled in amusement. *He was enjoying this.* "Give me your best offer, Penrose."

Did he want me to give him my body?

My pride?

My soul?

I wouldn't do that. Not for Byrne. Not for him. Not for anyone.

The remaining seconds dripped like life leaving Auntie Tilda's body.

His finger hit a red button on the side of his desk.

"Have a nice life, Flower Girl. Whatever's left of it, anyway."

He swung his chair to the window, documents in hand, ready to return to his work. The glass door behind me burst open, and two brawny men in suits stomped in, each grabbing me by an arm to drag me outside.

Casey waited by the elevator bank with her arms crossed and shoulder propped over the wall, her cheeks flushed with humiliation.

"It's not every day security takes out the trash. Guess there's a first time for everything." She flipped her hair, cackling like a hyena.

I spent the entire bike ride to North End fighting back the tears.

My last and only chance just went up in flames.

Three

Cillian

"We're pregnant."

Hunter made the announcement at the dinner table. I wanted to wipe his shit-eating grin with a disinfectant.

Or my fist.

Or a bullet.

Breathe, Kill. Breathe.

His wife, Sailor, rubbed her flat stomach. Generally speaking, she was about as maternal as a chewable thong, so I wasn't quite sure any of these idiots were capable of taking care of anything more complex than a goldfish.

"Eight weeks in. Still early, but we wanted to let you know."

I kept my expression blank, cracking my knuckles under the table.

Their timing couldn't have been worse.

Mother darted from her seat with an ear-piercing squeak, throwing her arms over the happy couple to smother them with kisses, hugs, and praises.

Aisling went on and on about how being an aunt was a dream come true, which would have alarmed me about her life goals if it wasn't for the fact she was about to finish med school and start her residency at Brigham and Women's Hospital in Boston. *Athair* shook Hunter's hand like they'd signed a lucrative deal.

In a way, they had.

Gerald Fitzpatrick made it perfectly clear he expected heirs from his sons. Spawns to continue the Fitzpatrick legacy. I was the first in line, the eldest Fitzpatrick, and therefore was burdened with the mission not only to produce successors but to also ensure one of them was a male who would take the reins of Royal Pipelines, regardless of his love for business and/or capabilities.

If I hadn't had children, the title, power, and fortune would all be given to the offspring next in line to the throne. Hunter's kid, to be exact.

Athair—*father* in Irish Gaelic—gave his daughter-in-law an awkward pat on the back. He was big—in height, width, and personality—with a shock of silver hair, onyx eyes, and pale skin.

"Great job there, sweetheart. Best news we've had all year."

I checked my pulse discreetly under the table.

It was under control. *Barely.*

Everyone's heads turned to me. Ever since my father stepped down and appointed me as the CEO of Royal Pipelines less than a year ago, I'd been bumped up to the leader of the pack and took the seat at the head of the table during our weekend dinners.

"Aren't you going to say anything?" Mother played with her pearl necklace, smiling tightly.

I raised my tumbler of brandy. "To more Fitzpatricks."

"And to the men who make them." *Athair* downed his liquor in one go. I met his jab with a frosty smirk. I was thirty-eight—eleven years Hunter's senior—unmarried, and childless.

Marriage was very low on my to-do list, somewhere under amputating one of my limbs with a butter knife and bungee jumping sans a rope. Children weren't an idea I was fond of. They were loud, the boring kind of dirty, and needy. I had been postponing the inevitable. Marrying had always been the plan because producing heirs and paying my dues to the Fitzpatrick lineage wasn't something I'd dreamed of worming out of.

THE *Villain*

Having a family was a part of a bigger plan. A vision. I wanted to build an empire far bigger than the one I'd inherited. A dynasty that stretched across much more than the oil tycoons we currently were.

However, I had every intention of doing it in my late forties and with stipulations that would make most women run for the hills and throw themselves off said hills for good measure.

Which was why marriage had been off the table.

Until this week, when my friend and lawyer, Devon Whitehall, urged me to get hitched to douse some of the flames directed at Royal Pipelines and myself.

"Well, *Athair*," I said tonelessly, "I'm happy Hunter exceeded your expectations in the heir-producing department." The writing was on the wall, smeared in my brother's semen from that time he dragged us all through PR hell with his sex tape.

"You know, Kill, sarcasm is the lowest form of wit." Sailor shot me a piercing glare, taking a sip of her virgin Bloody Mary.

"If you were a selective conversationalist, you wouldn't marry a man who thinks fart jokes are the height of comedy," I fired back.

"Farts *are* the height of comedy." Hunter, who was only half-evolved as a human, jabbed a finger in the air. "It's science."

Most days, I doubted he was literate. Still, he was my brother, so I had a basic obligation to tolerate him.

"Congratulations would have been sufficient." Sailor poked the air with her fork.

"Bite me." I downed my brandy, slamming the glass on the table.

"Dear!" Mother gasped.

"You know there's a term for people like you, Kill," Sailor grinned.

"Cunts?" Hunter deadpanned, pressing two fingers to his lips and dropping an invisible mic to the floor. One of the help poured two fresh fingers of brandy into my empty tumbler. Then three. Then four. I did not motion for her to stop until the alcohol nearly sloshed over.

"Language!" Mother threw another random word in the air.

"Yup. I speak at least two fluently—English and profanity." Hunter cackled.

He also used the word "fuck" as a unit measurement (*as fuck*), engaged in grotesque carnage of the English language (*"be seein' ya," "me thinks"*) and up until marrying Sailor, had provided the family with enough scandals to outdo the Kennedys.

I, however, avoided sacrilege of any kind, held babies at public events (reluctantly), and had always been on the straight and narrow. I was the perfect son, CEO, and Fitzpatrick.

With one flaw—I wasn't a family man.

This made the media have monthly field days. They dubbed me Cold Cillian, highlighted the fact I enjoyed fast cars and wasn't a member of any charities, and kept running the same story where I rejected an offer to be on the cover of a financial magazine, sitting next to other world billionaires, because none of them, other than Bezos, was anywhere near my tax bracket.

"Close, honey." Sailor patted Hunter's hand. "Sociopaths. We call people like your brother sociopaths."

"That makes so much sense." Hunter snapped his fingers. "He really breathes new death into the room."

"Now, now." Jane Fitzpatrick, aka Mother Dearest, tried to calm the discussion. "We're all very excited about the new addition to the family. My very first grandchild." She clasped her hands, looking dreamily into the distance. "Hopefully one of many."

So rich, for someone who had the maternal instinct of a squid.

"Don't worry, Ma, I intend to impregnate my wife as many times as she'll let me." Hunter winked at his ginger bride.

My brother was the poster child for TMI. And possibly pubic lice.

The only thing stopping me from throwing up in my mouth at this point was that he wasn't worth wasting food over.

"Gosh, I'm so jealous, Sail! I can't wait to be a mother." Ash balanced her chin on her fist, letting out a wistful sigh.

"You'll make a wonderful mom." Sailor reached over the table to squeeze her hand.

"To your imaginary kids with your brother-in-law." Hunter threw a sautéed bite of potato into his mouth, chewing. Ash went crimson. For the first time since dinner began, I was faintly amused. My sister nurtured a hopeless obsession with Sam Brennan, Sailor's older brother and a guy who worked for me on retainer.

The fact she was a wallflower and he was a modern-day Don Corleone didn't faze her in the least.

"What about you, *mo òrga*?" *Athair* turned to me. My nickname meant *My Golden* in Irish Gaelic. I was the proverbial modern Midas, who turned everything he touched into gold. Shaped and molded in his hands. Although, judging by the fact I'd given him nothing but bad press ever since I inherited the CEO position, I wasn't sure the moniker was fitting anymore.

It wasn't about my performance. There wasn't a soul in Royal Pipelines who could surpass me in skill, knowledge, and instincts. But I was a soulless, impersonal man. The opposite of the patriarch people wanted to see at the head of a company that killed rainforests and robbed Mother Nature of her natural resources on a daily basis.

"What about me?" I cut my salmon into even, minuscule pieces. My OCD was more prominent when I was under pressure. Doing something ritually gave me a sense of control.

"When will you give me grandchildren?"

"I suggest you direct this question at my wife."

"You don't have a wife."

"Guess I won't be having children anytime soon, either. Unless you're impartial to ill-conceived bastards."

"Over my dead body," my father hissed.

Don't tempt me, old man.

"When are you announcing the pregnancy publicly?" *Athair* turned to Hunter, losing interest in the subject of my hypothetical offspring.

"Not before the end of the second trimester," Sailor supplied, laying a protective hand over her stomach. "My OB-GYN warned me the first trimester is the rockiest. Plus, it's bad luck."

"But a good headline for Royal Pipelines." Father stroked his chin, contemplating. "Especially after the Green Living demonstration and the idiot who managed to break both her legs. The press was all over that story."

I was tired of hearing about it. Like Royal Pipelines had anything to do with the fact a dimwit had decided to climb up my grandfather's statue on the busiest square in Boston with a megaphone and fell.

Athair helped himself to a third serving of honey-baked salmon, his three chins vibrating as he spoke.

"*Ceann beag* has been the media's darling for the past couple of years. Nice, hard-working, approachable. A reformed playboy. Maybe he should be the face of the company for the next few months until the headlines blow over."

Ceann beag meant *little one*. Even though Hunter was the middle child, my father had always treated him as the youngest. Perhaps because Ash was wise beyond her years, but more than likely because Hunter had the maturity of a Band-Aid.

I put my utensils down, fighting the twitch in my jaw while slipping my hands under the table to crack my knuckles again.

"You want to put my twenty-seven-year-old brother as the head of Royal Pipelines because he managed to impregnate his wife?" I inquired, my voice calm and even. I'd busted my ass at Royal Pipelines since my early teens, taking my place at the throne at the cost of having no personal life, no social life, and no meaningful relationships. Meanwhile, Hunter was jumping from one mass orgy to the next in California until my dad dragged him by the ear back to Boston to clean up his act.

"Look, Cillian, we've been facing a lot of backlash because of the refinery explosion and exploratory Arctic drills," *Athair* groused.

Cillian. Not *mo òrga*.

THE *Villain*

"The refinery explosion happened under your watch, and my Arctic exploration rigs will likely up our revenue by five billion dollars by 2030," I pointed out, thumbing the rim of my brandy glass. "In the eight months I've been doing this job, our stock has gone up fourteen percent. Not too shabby for a rookie CEO."

"Not all tyrants make bad kings." He narrowed his eyes. "Your achievements mean nothing if the people want you dethroned."

"No one wants me dethroned." I gave him a pitying look. "The board has my back."

"Everyone else in the company wants to stab it," he roared, crashing his fist over the dining table. "The board only cares about the profits, and they'd vote however *I* wanted them to vote if it came down to it. Don't get too comfortable."

Utensils clattered, plates flew, and wine splattered over the tablecloth like blood drops. My pulse was still calm. My face tranquil.

Keep it together.

"You scare your employees, the media loathes you, and to the rest of the public, you're a mystery. No family of your own. No partner. No kids. No anchor. Don't think I haven't spoken to Devon. I happen to be of the same mindset as your lawyer. You need someone to dilute your darkness, and you need her fast. Sort this out, Cillian, and do it fast. The press calls you The Villain. Make them stop."

Feeling the tic in my jaw, I pursed my lips.

"Are you done being hysterical, *Athair*?"

My father pushed off the table, rising to his feet with a finger pointed at me.

"I called you *mo òrga* because I never had to worry about you. You always delivered whatever I needed before I'd even asked for it. The first perfect eldest Fitzpatrick child in generations since your great-great-*great*-grandfather made his way from Kilkenny to Boston on a rickety boat. But that has changed. You're pushing forty, and it's time you settle down. *Especially* if you want to continue being the face of this company. In case your job is not a strong enough incentive, let me spell it out for you." He leaned toward me, his eyes leveling mine. "The next in line for the throne is Hunter, and right now, the person after him is your future niece or nephew. Everything you've worked for will be handed down to them. *Everything*. And if you fuck this up, I will make sure to dethrone you, too."

He stalked out of the dining hall, ripping a portrait of all three of us Fitzpatrick siblings from the wall.

Mother darted up from her seat, running around to her estate manager to no doubt order them to get the portrait reframed and redone.

I smiled serenely, addressing everyone at the table.

"More food for us."

I spent the rest of the weekend in Monaco.

Just like my loveable idiot of a brother, I, too, had a taste for unconventional sex.

Unlike my loveable idiot of a brother, I knew better than to have it with random women.

I'd made bi-monthly trips to Europe, spending time with carefully selected, discreet women who'd agreed to ironclad arrangements. Sleeping with a woman required more paperwork than buying a spaceship. I'd always been careful, and dealing with a sex scandal on top of the farce that was my public image wasn't in my plans.

I paid them a mouthwatering rate, tipped them well, was always clean, gracious, and polite, and contributed to the European economy. These escorts weren't down-on-their luck single mothers or poor girls who came from broken families. They were top-tier university students, aspiring actresses, and aging models of middle- to upper-class families.

THE *Villain*

They traveled first class, lived in lavish apartments, and were picky about their decamillionaire clientele.

I hadn't used my family's private jet for my trips to Europe since being appointed CEO. Leaving a carbon footprint of Kuwait to get laid was too wicked, even for my conscience.

Fine. I had no conscience.

But if the media ever found out, my career would be as good as dead, and death was a specialty I'd left for Hunter's brain cells.

Which was why I was slumming it in first class on a commercial flight, quietly enduring the presence of other humans on my way back to Boston from Monaco.

There weren't many things I hated more than people. But being trapped with a large number of them on a winged bus and recycled air was one of them.

After settling into my seat on the plane, I leafed through a contract with a new contractor for my Arctic oiling rig, pushing away all thoughts of Hunter's approaching fatherhood and the Penrose sister who barged into my office last week begging for a loan.

I told her I didn't recognize her, which drove her mad and drove me into a state of a constant hard-on.

But I remembered Persephone.

Well and clear.

On the surface, Persephone Penrose ticked all the boxes for me: hair like spun gold, cobalt blue eyes, rosebud lips, and a petite frame wrapped in romantic dresses. A declawed, defanged preschool teacher, easier to tame than a kitten.

Wholesome, idealistic, and angelic to the bone.

She wore handmade frocks, watermelon lipstick, her heart on her sleeve, and that lamb-like expression of a Jane Austen character who thought dick was nothing more than a nickname for men named Richard.

Persephone wasn't wrong with her assumption to come to me. With any other acquaintance of mine, I'd give them the money just to watch them sweat while paying me back.

Only in her case, I didn't want my life tied with hers.

Didn't want to see her, hear from her, and endure her presence.

Didn't want her to owe me.

She'd been infatuated with me before. Feelings did not interest me unless I found a way to exploit them.

"Ouch." A squishy toy squeaked behind my seat. "Cut it out. Swear t-to God, Tree, I-I will—"

"You will what? Tell Mommy on me. *Snitch*."

Tree? The people sitting behind me named their child Tree? *And* decided to travel first class with two kids under the age of six?

These parents were the reason serial killers existed. I popped two ibuprofen, washing them down with bourbon. Technically, I wasn't supposed to drink with the medicine I was taking daily for my condition.

Oh, well. You only live once.

"Quit fussing, Tinder," the mother snapped behind me.

Tinder.

I officially found parents worse than my brother would be. I was ninety-one percent sure Sailor wouldn't let Hunter name their child Pinecone or Daylight Savings. The missing nine percent was due to the fact they were nauseatingly blinded by love, so you could never know for sure.

"H-e he always does this!" little Tinder bellowed, managing to kick the back of my seat even though it was about four feet away. "Tree is a s-stinky face."

"Well, you're ugly and weird," Tree retorted.

"I'm not weird. I'm special."

Both hellions were insufferable, and I was about to break the news to their equally diabolical parents before remembering I couldn't afford another headline of the Cillian-Fitzpatrick-eats-babies-for-breakfast variety.

CEO of Royal Pipelines shouts at innocent children on flight back from his escorts.

No, thank you.

And just for the record, I'd never consumed human flesh in my life. It was too lean, too unsanitary, and entirely too uncommon.

Mentally tapping my foot until takeoff, I cracked my knuckles.

Once we were in the air, I stood and walked around, making notes on the contract with a red Sharpie.

When I returned to my seat, it was taken.

Not just taken but taken by my archenemy.

The man I'd expected to resurface from the shadows the minute I'd been appointed CEO of Royal Pipelines. Frankly, I was surprised it had taken him so long.

"Arrowsmith. What a terrible surprise."

He looked up, beaming back at me.

Andrew Arrowsmith was a good-looking bastard, in a local news anchor sort of way. Identikit haircut, bleached white teeth, each the size of a brick, tall frame, and what I was seventy percent sure was a chin dimple transplant. Once upon a time, he was in my social sphere. These days, all we shared was a rivalry going back to our time at Evon.

We both attended the same schools until we didn't. Until his family went bankrupt, and he fell off the social ladder, so low he entered another dimension, full of trailer parks and canned food.

"Cillian. Thought it might be you." He stood, offering me his hand. When I made no move to take it, he withdrew, running the same hand over his Keith Urban hair.

I hadn't seen the man in over two decades and was perfectly content to spend the rest of my life forgetting his pretty boy face.

"Tough crowd. My family." He gestured to the row of seats behind me, where a bleach-haired woman in full Lululemon attire practiced deep breaths to save herself from a mental breakdown, two snotty kids on her lap, at each other's throats. "This is Joelle, my wife, and my twin boys, Tree and Tinder."

It didn't escape me that Andrew, who was the same age as me, had a wife and kids. The invisible noose was tightening around my neck.

I could lose my job.

My inheritance.

My golden, grand vision.

I needed to start reproducing, and fast.

"Who picked their names?" I jerked my chin toward the little monsters.

Joelle perked up, waving a hand as though I asked who found the cure for cancer.

"*Moi*. Aren't they darling?"

The names or the children? Both were awful, but only the names were her fault. I turned back to Andrew, ignoring his wife's question. I never lied. Lying would imply I gave a damn what people thought.

"Heading back to Southie?" I inquired. Last I checked, he lived in the worst part of Boston where his family barely made ends meet, thanks to mine.

Clearly, his fortunes had changed if he was flying first class these days.

"You'd be surprised to hear I am." He grinned big, his chest swelling with pride. "Bought a house there last month. I'm getting back to my roots. To where I came from."

He came from Back Bay, the rich pricks' area, but I didn't give him the pleasure of showing him I remembered.

"Just took a job with Green Living. You're looking at their newest chief executive officer."

Green Living was a nonprofit environmental organization that was seen as Greenpeace's more violent, more daring sibling. There weren't many companies that hated Royal Pipelines more than Green Living did, and there weren't many men who loathed me as much as Andrew Arrowsmith.

This, in and of itself, wasn't news. I could count on one hand the people who knew me and *didn't* actively dislike me. What made Andrew dangerous was that he knew my secret.

The one thing I'd kept safely locked away since boarding school.

Since Evon.

Now *that* was a game changer.

"That's cute," I said dryly. "Do they know you're about as competent as a napkin?"

That wasn't true. I'd kept tabs on him over the years and knew that not only was he a successful attorney with a flair for ecology and environmental issues, but that he was also the morning shows and CNN darling. Every time climate change popped into the news, he was there with a microphone, either leading a mass demonstration, chaining himself to a goddamn tree, or talking about it on prime-time TV.

Andrew had interfered with Royal Pipelines' business many times along his career. He bullied advertising companies from working with us, had a gaming company drop their partnership with us, and wrote a best-selling book about petroleum lords, essentially blaming companies like mine for giving people cancer.

He had fans, groupies, and Facebook groups dedicated to him, and I wouldn't be surprised to know there was a dildo with his face on it.

"Oh, they know my capabilities, Fitzpatrick." He plucked a flute of champagne from a stewardess's tray. "Let's not pretend we haven't been keeping tabs on each other. You know my credentials. My victories. My agenda. I let my principles guide me just like my old man."

His old man had been fired by *my* old man when we were both boys, thrusting the Arrowsmith family into a life of poverty. Before that, our families had been close, and Andrew and I had been best friends. The Arrowsmiths never forgave the Fitzpatricks for the betrayal even though *Athair* had a solid reason to fire Andrew Senior—the accountant had dipped his hand into the company's honey jar.

"How's your old man doing?" I asked.

"He passed away three years ago."

"Not terribly good then."

"I see being an asshole still runs in your blood." He downed the champagne.

"Can't fight my DNA," I said bluntly. "Now, people who are out for my blood are another thing. I can fight them tooth and nail."

"How 'bout Gerald? Still hanging in there?" Andrew ignored my thinly veiled threat.

"You know Gerry. He can survive anything short of a nuclear blast."

"Speaking of soon-to-be dead things, I hear Daddy gave you the keys to Royal Pipelines since he had to step down because of... what was it?" He snapped his fingers, frowning. "Type 2 diabetes? Gluttony always ran in your family. How is he handling his health issues?"

"Wiping his tears with hundred-dollar bills." I let loose a wolfish smirk. Arrowsmith tried to offend my delicate sensibilities, forgetting I had none.

We were still standing in the aisle when the new reality settled in, trickling into my bloodstream like poison.

Marrying was no longer an option.

It was a necessity to secure my position as Royal Pipelines CEO.

Andrew Arrowsmith was headed back to Boston to bring me down, taking over a company that put ruining Royal Pipelines on its flag.

He had leverage, an appetite for revenge, and was privy to my darkest secret.

I wasn't losing the company, and I definitely wasn't losing my wealth to Hunter and Aisling's future kids.

"Are you going to skip to the good part, Andrew?" I made a show of yawning.

"No part of me believes we bumped into each other accidentally."

"Always such a straight shooter." Andrew leaned forward, dropping his voice low as he went in for the kill. "I may or may not have taken the job to settle an old score. The minute I heard you were on the throne, the temptation to behead the king became too much." His breath fanned the side of my face. "Killing you and your father financially would be easy. With Gerald weak and out of the loop, and you vulnerable after years of bad press, I am going for your throat, Fitzpatrick. The media darling versus the press villain. Let the best man win."

Sauntering back to my seat and making myself comfortable there, I flipped a page of the contract I was working on.

"You always were a silly boy," I mused, flipping another page of the contract I was holding nonchalantly. "I will strip you of all the things you've managed to achieve since I've last seen you. Take whatever is near and dear to you, and watch you pay. Oh, and Andrew?" I looked up, flashing him a smirk. "Let me assure you, I am still the same resilient bastard you left behind."

He went back to his family. I felt his gaze on the back of my head the entire flight.

I needed a bride, and quick.

Someone media-friendly to balance out who I was.

What I represented.

I knew just the person.

Four

Persephone

DAYS DRAGGED LIKE A NAIL OVER A BLACKBOARD.
I was on edge. Jumpy, cranky, and incapable of taking deep, satisfying breaths.

Ever since I returned from Cillian's office empty-handed, I couldn't stomach anything—be it food, coffee, water, or the sight of myself in the mirror.

My mind constantly drifted to a mental video of Byrne and Kaminski throwing my lifeless body into the Charles River. About Cillian's rejection. The unbearable sting of it.

I'd forgotten the words to all the songs during circle time in class, almost fed Reid, who was lactose intolerant, Dahlia's mac and cheese, and mixed kinetic sand with the real one, making a huge mess I had to stay late to clean up afterward.

Gray clouds swollen with rain hovered over me as I headed home, jogging from my bike to my entryway, clutching my shoulder bag in a vise grip. I reminded myself I had both pepper spray *and* a Taser, and that there was zero percent chance Byrne and Kaminski would kill me at my doorstep.

Well, maybe a ten percent chance.

It was probably somewhere around twenty-five but definitely *no* more than that.

THE *Villain*

The minute I got into my building, I reached for the switch. To my surprise, the light was already on. A strong hand gripped my wrist, spinning me around to face the person it belonged to.

Fight or flight? my body asked me.

Fight, my brain answered. *Always fight.*

I threw my bag in the intruder's face, a growl ripping out of my mouth. He dodged it effortlessly, dumping it to the floor and causing the contents of my bag to roll out. I reached up to claw his eyes. He snatched both my wrists in one palm, locking them in place between us before backing me against the entrance door so we were flush against each other.

"Let me go!" I screamed.

To my shock, the dark, mammoth figure did just that, stepping back and picking up the pepper spray that fell from my bag to examine it flippantly.

"*Cillian?*"

I resisted the urge to rub my eyes in disbelief. But there he was, wearing a designer trench coat, pointy Italian loafers, and his signature go-fuck-yourself scowl that made my heart loop around like a stripper on a pole.

"You're here," I said, more to myself than to him.

Why? How? When? So many questions floated in my foggy brain.

"I sincerely hope our children won't inherit your tendency to point out the obvious. I find it extremely trivial." He popped the safety off the pepper spray and screwed it back right, so the next time I tried to use it, it would be ready to go.

"Hmm, *what*?" I swatted away wisps of hair that flopped over my eyes like stubborn branches in a jungle. The five o'clock shadow veiling the thick column of his throat made me want to press my lips to his neck.

His imperfections made him intimately beautiful. I despised every second of being around him.

"Remember I told you I don't hand out free favors?" He rolled the pepper spray between his fingers, his eyes on the small canister.

"Kind of hard to forget."

"Well, it's your lucky day."

"Allow me to be skeptical."

At this point, I wasn't down on my luck. I was six feet *under* it. Somewhere between hapless and cursed.

"I figured out what I want from you."

"You want something from little ole me?" I put my hand to my chest with a mocking gasp while I tried to regulate my racing heartbeat. I couldn't help it. He never missed a chance to belittle me. "I'm speechless."

"Don't get my hopes up, Flower Girl," he muttered.

My nickname didn't escape me. The Flower Girl was traditionally the toddler at the wedding, designed to draw coos and positive attention. The naïve kid whose job was to walk a straight line.

He stepped toward me, invading my personal space. His scent of male, dry cedar, and leather seeped into my system, making me drunk.

"For this to work, you mustn't develop any feelings for me," he warned darkly.

There was no point in telling him I'd never gotten over him in the first place. Not really. Not in all the ways that mattered.

He removed a lock of damp hair from my temple without touching my skin. The way he stared at me unnerved me. With cold contempt, suggesting he was brought here at gunpoint and not of his own free will.

"I will take care of your money and divorce problems. Make them go away. Not as a loan, but a gift."

My body sagged with relief.

"Oh, God. Cillian, thank you so—"

"*Let me finish*," he hissed, his voice cracking through the air like a whip. "I never let a good crisis go to waste, and yours might be very beneficial for me. You won't have to pay me because your form of compensation will be on the unconventional side. You are going to be my wife. You will marry me, Persephone Penrose. Smile for the cameras for me. Attend charity events on my behalf. And give me children. As many as needed until I have a son. Be it one, three, or six."

"Anything!" I cried out, rushing to accept his offer before his words sank in. "I would love to—"

Wait, what?

For a long moment, I simply stared at him. I was trying to decide whether he was making some elaborate joke on my behalf.

Somehow, I didn't think he was. For one thing, Cillian Fitzpatrick did not possess a sense of humor. If humor met him in a dark alley, it would shrivel into itself and explode into a cloud of squeaking bats. For another, more than he was cruel, Kill was terrifyingly pragmatic. He wouldn't waste his precious time on pranking me.

"You want me to marry you?" I repeated dumbly.

His face was resigned and solemn. He offered me a curt nod.

Holy hell, he wasn't kidding. The man of my dreams wanted to wed me. To take me as a wife.

There was only one possible answer for that.

"No." I pushed him away. "Not in a million years. No, nope, nien, niet." I was rummaging through my memory for other languages to refuse him in. "No," I said again. "The last one was in Spanish, not English."

"Elaborate," he demanded.

"We can't marry. We don't love each other." I tilted my chin up defiantly. "And yes, I know love is *so* very working class."

"Middle class," he corrected. "The happy, dumb medium is comfortable enough not to care, and stupid enough not to aim higher. Working and upper classes always take financial matters into consideration. May I remind you the last time you married for *love*," he said the word as you would say *herpes*, "it ended with a massive debt, a runaway husband, and death threats? Love is overrated, not to mention fickle. It comes and goes. You can't build a foundation on it. Mutual interests and alliance are a different story."

But here was the really pathetic part—I didn't want to marry him precisely because a part of me *did* love him.

Putting my happiness in his hands was the dumbest idea I'd ever have.

No matter how much I tried to ignore it, Kill was my first real crush. My first obsession. My unfulfilled wish. He would always hold a piece of my heart, and I didn't want to think of all the ways he was going to abuse it if we were together.

Plus, marrying Boston's most notorious villain was a bad idea, and I was pretty sure I'd filled my quota of asshole husbands for this century.

"Look, how about a compromise?" I smiled brightly. "I can date you. Be your girlfriend. Hang on your arm and take a good picture. We'll have a little arrangement."

He stared at me with open amusement.

"You think your company is worth a hundred thousand dollars?"

"You're offering me a hundred grand to become your live-in escort and bear your children. *Plural*. If I were a surrogate, I'd get that same amount of money for one baby," I burst out.

"Go be a surrogate." He shrugged.

"It's a long procedure. I don't have enough time."

"You don't seem to have enough brain, either." He tapped my temple, frowning as if wondering how much was inside that head of mine. "Take my offer. It's your only way out."

I pushed him away.

"You're a bastard."

He smiled impatiently. "You knew that when you offered yourself to me very willingly all those years ago."

He remembered.

He remembered, and for some reason, that completely defused me.

Auntie Tilda, what the hell have you done?

"Look." I shook my head, trying to think straight. "How about we start dating and I—"

"No," he cut me off dryly. "Marriage or nothing."

"You don't even like me!"

THE Villain

Cillian glanced at that chunky watch of his, losing patience.

"What does liking you have to do with *marrying* you?"

"Everything! It has everything to do with it! How do you expect us to get along?"

"I don't," he said flatly. "You'll have your house. I'll have mine. You will be stunningly rich, live on Billionaires' Row, and become one of New England's most envied socialites. You'll be far enough away from me to do whatever the hell you'd like. I am sensible, fair, and realistic. As long as you give me heirs, give me exclusivity throughout our child-producing years, and stay out of tabloids, you shouldn't see much of me beyond the first few years of our marriage. But no divorce," he warned, raising a finger. "It's tacky, bad for business, and shows you're a quitter. I'm no quitter."

I wanted to burst. With laughter or tears, I wasn't sure.

This is not what I asked for, Auntie, I inwardly screamed. *You missed the best part of my having him.*

"You realize I'm a person and not an air fryer, right?" I parked a hand over my hip, losing patience myself. "Because to me it sounds a lot like you're trying to buy me."

"That's because I *am*." He looked at me as though I was crazy. Like *I* was the one with the problem. "People who vilify money have one thing in common—they don't have it. You have a chance to change your fate, Persephone. Don't mess it up."

"Sorry if I sound ungrateful, but your proposition sounds like a very sad existence to me. I want to be loved. To be cherished. To grow old with the man I choose and who chooses me."

Even after what happened with Paxton, and even though I still had strong feelings toward Cillian, I believed in fairy tales. I simply accepted mine was written eccentrically with too much foreword and scenes I was happy to cut.

He produced a pair of leather gloves from his breast pocket, slapping them over his muscular thigh before sliding his big hands into them.

"You can have all those things in time, just not with me. Find yourself a lover. Lead a quiet life with him—provided he signs all the necessary paperwork. You'll do you; I'll do me. What I do, in case you have any lingering romantic ideas about us, includes an insatiable amount of high-end escorts and questionable sexual practices."

The only thing keeping me standing upright at this point was the thought this was probably a hallucination, due to the fact I hadn't been sleeping or eating well recently.

Carbs. I need carbs.

"You want me to *cheat* on you?" I rubbed at my forehead.

"After you give me legitimate children, you can do whatever you want."

"You need a hug." I frowned. "And a shrink. Not in that order."

"What I need is siring heirs. At least one male. A couple of others for appearance and backup."

Backup.

Were we talking about children or phone chargers?

My head spun. I reached to the wall for support.

I always knew Cillian Fitzpatrick was messed up, but this was a level of crazy that could easily secure him a place in a mental institution.

"Why male? In case you haven't noticed, this is the twenty-first century. There are women like Irene Rosenfeld, Mary Barra, Corie Barry…" I began listing female CEOs. He cut me off.

"Spare me the supermarket list. The truth of the matter is, some things haven't changed. Women born into obscene privilege—aka my future daughters—rarely opt for hectic careers, which is what running Royal Pipelines demands."

"That is the most sexist thing I've ever heard."

"Shockingly, I agree with you on that point." He began to button his coat, signaling his departure. "Nonetheless, I'm not the one making the rules. Traditionally, the firstborn's son inherits most of the shares and the role of CEO in Royal Pipelines. That's how my father got the gig. That's how I got it."

"What if the kid wants to be something else?"

He stared at me as though I just asked him if I should pierce my eyebrow using a semi-automatic weapon. Like I was truly beyond help.

"Who doesn't want to be the head of one of the richest companies in the world?"

"Anyone who knows what a role like that entails," I shot back. "No offense, but you're not the happiest man I know, Kill."

"My first son will continue my legacy," he said matter-of-factly. "If you're worried about his mental health, I suggest you send him to therapy from infancy."

"Sounds like you're going to be a wonderful father." I crossed my arms over my chest.

"They'll have a soft mother. Least I can do is give them the hard facts of life."

"You're awful."

"You're stalling," he quipped.

The nervous knot of hysteria forming in my throat grew. Not because I found the idea of marrying Cillian so terrible, but because I *didn't*, and that made me deranged. What kind of woman jumped headfirst into marriage with the wickedest man in Boston while still married to the most unreliable one?

Me.

That was who.

I entertained this insane idea for many reasons, all of them wrong:

No more money problems.

A sure divorce from Paxton.

Having Cillian's company, and undivided attention, even if just for a few short years.

Who knew? Maybe Auntie Tilda was going to deliver after all. We could start off as an arrangement and end up as a real couple.

No. I couldn't board his train to Crazy Town. The last stop was Heartbreak, and I'd had enough of that in my life. Paxton had already crushed me. But my infatuation with Pax was sweet and comfortable. Cillian always stirred in me something raw and wild that could enrapture me.

I needed to think about it clearly without him getting in my face with his drugging scent and square jaw and cold flawlessness.

I stepped sideways, toward the stairway. "Look, can I think about it?"

"Of course. You have plenty of time. It's not like the *mob* is after you," his rich-boy diction mocked me.

I knew exactly how bad my situation was. Still, if I was going to officially sign the rest of my life over to the man who crushed me, I needed to at least give myself a few days to process it.

"Give me a week."

"Twenty-four hours," he fired back.

"Four days. You're talking about the rest of my life here."

"You're not going to *have* a life if you don't accept. Forty-eight hours. That's my final offer, and it's a generous one. You know where to find me."

He turned around, making his way to the door.

"Wait," I yelped.

He paused, not turning around.

A flashback of myself watching him leave and asking him to stay at Sailor and Hunter's wedding slammed into me. I knew, with certainty that scorched my soul, that it was going to be our norm if I accepted his offer.

I would always seek him out, and he would always retreat to the shadows. A dusky, heady smoke of a man I could feel and see but never catch.

"Give me your home address. I don't want to go to your office again. It makes me feel like we're conducting business."

"We *are* conducting business."

"Your PA is horrible. She almost stabbed me that day I visited you."

"*Almost* is the operative word here." Producing a business card, he flipped it over and scribbled down his address. "I wouldn't have covered her legal fees, and she knows it."

He handed the card to me.

THE *Villain*

"Forty-eight hours," he reminded me. "If I don't hear from you, I'll assume you declined my offer or were offed prematurely, and move on to the next candidate on my list."

"There's a list." My jaw dropped.

Of course there was a list. I was just one of many women who ticked all the boxes for the mighty Cillian Fitzpatrick.

I wondered what said boxes included.

Naïve?

Desperate?

Stupid?

Pretty?

I swallowed, but the ball in my throat didn't budge. I felt about as disposable as a diaper and just as desirable.

Cillian shot me an icy look.

"Go browse through your mail-order brides catalog, Cillian." I narrowed my eyes at him. "I'll let you know my answer."

I watched him go, carrying my freedom, hopes, and choices in his designer pocket.

Knowing it didn't matter whether I refused or accepted his offer—either choice would be a mistake.

The next day, I showed up at work in a coffee-stained dress and with bloodshot eyes. I'd called Sailor, swallowing my pride and doing what I promised not to do—ask her for a loan. But before I could even utter out the request, she told me she'd been feeling suspicious cramps in her abdomen, and I couldn't bring myself to ask.

I spent my lunch break calling every cash loaner in Boston. Most hung up on me, some laughed, and a handful expressed their regret, but said they'd have to pass on my business.

I even tried calling Sam Brennan. I was met with an electronic message asking for a code to get through to him.

I didn't have access to the most mysterious man in Boston.

Though I grew up as his younger sister's best friend, I was as invisible to him as the rest of my friends.

Belle was at work when I got home. I was glad she was because a box waited outside her apartment door. The parcel was addressed to me, so I opened it. There were two pieces of lingerie inside.

I picked up a black lace thong, realizing inside the lingerie waited a bullet.

Byrne.

I ran to the bathroom, throwing up the very little I'd eaten.

Shoving a sleeve of crackers into my mouth, I swallowed a small chunk of cheese, and washed them down with orange juice.

I crawled into Belle's bed, still in my work dress. It was cold and empty. The rain knocking on the window reminded me of how alone I was.

Mom and Dad had moved to the suburbs a couple of years ago. Moving in with them now would invite trouble to their doorstep—*deadly* trouble—and I couldn't do it to them.

Sailor was married and having a baby, running a successful food blog and training young archers as a part of a charity foundation she started. Her life was full, complete, and *good*.

Ash was busy coming up with schemes to win Sam Brennan over, going to med school, and blossoming into one of the most fantastic women I'd ever met.

And Belle was making a career for herself.

Lying still in the darkness, I watched through the window as Lady Night went through all her outfits. The sky turned from midnight to neon blue, then finally, orange and pink. When the sun climbed up Boston's high-rise skyline, inch by inch like a queen rising from her throne, I knew I had to make a decision.

The sky was cloudless.

THE *Villain*

Auntie Tilda wasn't going to help me get out of this one. It was my decision to make. My responsibility.

Silence buzzed through the apartment. Belle hadn't returned home last night. She was probably inside a handsome man's bed, splaying her curves like a work of art for him to worship.

Scurrying out of bed, I padded barefoot into the kitchenette, then flicked on the coffee machine and Belle's vintage radio. The same eighties station that never failed to lift my spirits belted out the last few notes of "How Will I Know" by Whitney Houston, followed by a weather forecast, warning about an impending storm.

There was a vase full of fresh roses on the counter, courtesy of one of the many admirers who frequented Madame Mayhem in hopes to capture my sister's interest.

Flower Girl.

I plucked one of the white roses. Its thorn pierced my thumb. A heart-shaped blood droplet perched between the petals.

"To marry or not to marry Boston's favorite villain?"

I plucked the first petal.

Marry him.

The second one.

Don't marry him.

Then the third.

The fourth.

The fifth…

By the time I reached the last petal, my fingers quivered, my heart drummed fast, and every inch of my body was covered in goose bumps. I pulled the last petal, the snowy color of a wedding gown.

Fate said the last word.

Not that it mattered as my heart already knew the answer.

A decision had been made.

Now I had to face the consequences.

Five

Cillian

"Good session, Mr. Fitzpatrick. You're one of the most talented equestrians I've ever seen. Mad skills, sir." One of the pimply stable boys under my payroll staggered behind me, his tongue lapping about like an eager puppy.

I made my way from the barn back to my car, shoving my bridle into his chest along with a fat tip.

If nothing else, being filthy, immortally, *disgustingly* rich meant people were eager to tell me how I was the best at anything, be it horse riding, fencing, golfing, and synchronized swimming.

Not that I synchronize swam, but I was sure I'd be given a medal for it if I asked for one.

"Thanks for the tip, Mr. Fitzpatrick! You're the best boss I've ever—"

"If I wanted my ass kissed, I'd go for someone curvier, blonder, and with an entirely different reproductive system," I said cuttingly.

"Right. Yes. Sorry." He blushed, opening the door to my Aston Martin Vanquish for me, bowing. I slid into the car, revving up the engine.

The Ring app on my phone advised me there was a visitor at my front door.

Tugging at my gloves, I tossed them on the passenger seat before swiping the phone screen.

THE *Villain*

I didn't have to check my wrist to know I wasn't at my usual fifty beats per minute. I was a highly conditioned equestrian, a born athlete. But right now, it was at least at sixty-two.

I was a certified moron to develop a preference toward one potential bride over the other, considering none of the candidates on my list were going to walk down the aisle happily or willingly.

They all had reasons to say I do, and none of them had to do with my winning personality, wit, or flawless manners.

Persephone Penrose was the first I'd approached. She needed financial relief like I needed a good PR stunt and a couple of kids.

She was, however much I hated to admit it, also my favored contender. Good-natured, of sound mind more or less, with the face of an angel and a body that could tempt the devil.

She was perfect. Too perfect, in fact. So perfect I sometimes had to look away whenever we were in the same room. I averted my gaze from her more times than I could count, always opting to observe her mouthy sister. Watching the train wreck that was Emmabelle reminded me I didn't want the Penrose DNA pool anywhere near mine.

Emmabelle was loud, lewd, and opinionated. She could argue with a goddamn wall for days and still lose. Focusing on her was less dangerous than watching Persephone.

And watching Persephone was something I did discreetly, but often, when no one was looking.

Which was why the fact she hadn't returned to me with an answer was a good thing. Terrific, really.

I didn't need this mess.

Didn't need my heart rate hiking over sixty.

Case in point—as the video of my black, brass hardware double doors came into view, my pulse began strumming over my eyelid. It was the cleaning ladies and my chef, marching into my house to prepare it ahead of the kickback I was hosting tonight.

I threw the phone to the passenger seat, glancing at my Rolex.

It had been exactly forty-nine hours and eleven minutes since I'd presented Persephone with my offer. Her time was up. Timekeeping and reliability were two of the few things I'd admired about people.

She lacked both.

Clicking open my glove compartment, I produced the sticky note Devon had given me with names of potential brides. Next on my list was Minka Gomes. An ex-model who was now a child psychologist. Legs for miles, a good family, and a perfect smile (although Devon had warned me she had veneers).

She was thirty-seven, desperate for children, and traditional enough to want a Catholic wedding. She'd already signed an NDA prior to my approaching her, something I'd made Devon do with all of my potential brides, save for Persephone, who was:

1. My first candidate, and therefore my sloppiest attempt. And—
2. Too good to tell a soul.

I punched her address into the navigation app, rolling out of my private ranch's driveway, where I had spent the past few hours riding my horses, ignoring my responsibilities, and *not* seething over the fact Persephone Penrose needed to think about marrying me when the other option available was grisly death in the hands of street mobsters.

I deliberately wasn't home because I knew Persephone wasn't going to take the bait.

She had too much integrity, morals, not to mention—another flipping husband somewhere in the globe.

"Let's hope for your sake you're not dumb enough to turn down my offer, too," I muttered to an invisible Minka as I took the highway toward Boston.

Bride number two it was.

As if it made any difference.

THE *Villain*

Sam Brennan threw his cards onto the table later that evening, tilting his head back, a ribbon of smoke curling past his lips.

He always folded.

He didn't come here to play cards.

Didn't believe in luck, didn't play for it, and didn't count on it.

He was here to observe, learn, and keep tabs on Hunter and me, two of his most profitable clients. Made sure we kept out of trouble.

"Sally" by Gogol Bordello rose from the surround system.

We were in my drawing room for our weekly poker night. A tasteful, albeit boring space, with upholstered leather incliners and heavy burgundy curtains.

"Don't worry, sons. It'll all be over soon," Hunter *tsked*, attempting his best John Malkovich impression in *Rounders*. "Poker is not for the faint of heart."

"This, from someone who is a Nordstrom membership away from being a chick." Sam slid his cigarette from one corner of his lips to the other, his forearms nearly ripping the black dress shirt he wore.

"You bet your ass I have a Nordstrom membership." Hunter laughed, unfazed. "I don't have time to shop with my stylist, and the ladies at the store know my measurements."

"I see your thirty-five k and raise eight thousand." Devon tossed eight black chips to the center of the table, drumming his fingers over his cards.

Devon was the opposite of Sam. A hedonist lord with a taste for fine, forbidden things, open manners, and zero scruples. Watching money burn was his favorite pastime. Ironically, Devon Whitehall needed a job like Hunter needed more distasteful sexual innuendos in his repertoire. He chose to go to university in America, passed the bar, and stayed far away from Britain.

I was pretty sure he had his own can of worms waiting to be cracked open back in his homeland but didn't care enough to ask.

"All in," I announced.

Hunter smacked his lip, pushing his entire stack of chips forward.

"You're taking the piss." Devon narrowed his eyes at my brother. Hunter flashed an innocent smile, batting his lashes theatrically.

"It's a zero-sum game, Monsieur Whitehall. Don't step into the kitchen if you don't like the burn."

"You're mixing two phrases," I said around the Cuban cigar in my mouth, pushing my chips to the center of the table. "It's don't step into the kitchen if you can't take the *heat*. Burn is what you get between your legs for sleeping with enough women to fill up Madison Square Garden."

"Funny, I don't remember you inviting me to your sainthood ceremony, big bro." Hunter took a pull of his Guinness, dragging his tongue over his foam mustache. "Oh, that's right, it never happened because you bonked half of Europe. 'Sides, this was all in the past. I'm a married man now. There's only one woman for me."

"And that woman is my sister, so you better think carefully about what you say next if you want to get out of here with all your organs intact," Sam reminded him.

Sam had brown hair, gray eyes, and tan skin. He was tall, broad, and had that ragged, hunky look that made women lose their pants and senses.

"Dude, my wife is knocked up. Too late for you to second-guess what we're doing in our spare time. By the way, the abdomen pain she had this week turned out to be gas, thanks for asking," Hunter tutted.

Was I seriously listening to a fart report from Sailor now?

"Not every single conversation must circle back to the fact your wife is pregnant," I reminded him.

"Prove it."

Sam jerked his thumb toward Hunter.

"You realize I will kill your brother at some point, right?" he asked me.

"Won't hold it against you." I spat the cigar out to an ashtray. "But wait until after he reveals his cards."

"Speaking of marital bliss," Devon swirled his Johnnie Walker

Blue Label in its tubmler, "I believe our host has some marvelous news to share."

"Aww, you finally opened an account on OkCupid?" Hunter clasped his hands together, cooing. "Our parents have been riding his ass for being lonelier than a satanist in a Youth for Jesus convention for a while now."

"It'll be a cold day in hell when Cillian Fitzpatrick says I do," Sam drawled.

"Better bring a warm coat, mate." Devon smirked.

"Hell's not ready for me yet. And Cillian likes variety too much to settle for one pussy." Sam speared Devon with a deadly glare.

"Women are like pancakes. They all taste the same," I agreed.

Sam flashed his teeth. "I fucking love pancakes."

The man had bedded everyone in town.

Everyone other than my sister.

It didn't take an astrophysicist to figure out Aisling was stupidly in love with Brennan. Whenever she was in the room with her sister-in-law's brother, she all but drooled on his lap. The minute I'd realized her lapse in judgment, I'd hired Brennan on retainer. I didn't have too much work for him back when we started our professional relationship, but having him on my payroll ensured he wasn't going to touch Ash.

Brennan was an honorable man in his own backward, lethal way.

I cracked my knuckles, my eyes firmly on my cards. I had two pairs. I would bet both my nuts Hunter's cards had alphabet letters and drawings of animals at best. For an Irishman, luck wasn't on his side.

"I'm engaged." I dropped the bomb.

Sam choked on his cigarette, the inch-long ash dangling from it falling onto the table. Hunter cackled. Devon gave me a curt nod of approval.

Me? I felt nothing.

Numbness was a notion I was familiar with, knew how to manage, and did not stir me off course.

Hunter slapped his thigh, his cards raining down on the floor as he laughed his ass off. He fell from his chair, holding his stomach.

"Engaged!" he bellowed, dragging himself up back to his seat. "Who's the unlucky woman? Your blowup doll?"

"Her name is Minka Gomes."

"You named your blowup doll Minka?" My brother wiped a tear from the corner of his eye, downing a bottle of water. "I thought you'd go for something more stripper-y. Like Lola or Candy."

"I don't recall running a background check on her." Sam pinned me with a glare. These days, I had him dig up dirt on everyone I met, from business partners to shoeshiners.

"Just because you haven't heard of her doesn't mean she's not in existence," I bit out. Admittedly, it was hard to explain how I'd ended up engaged to a complete stranger.

Minka was pleasant enough when I stopped by her house with a marriage offer earlier today. Devon prepped her for our meeting. She said she was happy to sign all the necessary paperwork and asked for two clauses to be added during our negotiations. She wanted a cabin in Aspen, and an annual trip to Fashion Week in a European city of her choice, along with a healthy shopping budget. I was content to grant both her wishes.

She was beautiful, polite, and obnoxiously eager to please.

She also stirred absolutely *nothing* in me.

"Please explain to me how you went from corrupting Europe's finest princesses to getting engaged to some random local chick." Hunter scrubbed his chin.

My brother, like the rest of my family, thought I'd spent my time romancing EU's finest royals. That was a story I spoon-fed my family to protect them from the truth. I *did* brush shoulders with duchesses and daughters of earls, socially climbing my way from another rich American man to the kind of person who knew everyone worth knowing on the continent.

But I'd never touched them.

I'd never touched a woman I hadn't paid for, if I was being honest. Which I wasn't, with anyone.

Anyone but Persephone.

Even two days later, I still wasn't sure what made me tell her about my preference to pay for sex. I deliberately left out the part where the women I'd seen weren't prostitutes, per se. Waited to see the revulsion on her innocent face. But she was too occupied with mentally beating me with her purse for ridiculing her feelings to let the small details register.

Paying for sex was my way to give conventional relationships the middle finger. I'd taken care of the women I'd seen, both in bed and out of it, but I'd never offered them more than a good time. Dates, presents, phone calls, feelings—those were off the table.

My partners came with a detailed list of dos and don'ts, and the only thing they expected from our encounters was a large tip, a complimentary orgasm from yours truly.

My first time with a working girl was at age fourteen.

My father had visited me at Evon, not long after Andrew Arrowsmith unearthed my secret.

We held a private dinner at London's Savoy. I wore a long-sleeved shirt even though it was summer to hide the cigarette burns and bite marks. *Athair* asked me how many girls I'd slept with, spooning Royal Beluga on a small toast. I curled my index finger to my thumb, making a zero sign. I didn't think much of it. Not only did I attend an all-boy school but I also had bigger fish to fry than getting my dick wet.

Gerald Fitzpatrick choked on his caviar. The next day, he decided to rectify my dire situation by hurling my skinny ass onto a plane and taking me on a trip to Norway, where he was scheduled to visit one of Royal Pipelines' oil drilling rigs.

Maja, the Norwegian woman who relieved me of my celibate status, was in her early thirties, about a head taller than teenage me, and comically confused when I nearly threw up in her lap. I didn't want to lose my virginity. Not at age fourteen, not to a stranger, and definitely not in a high-end brothel on a side street in Oslo. But doing things to appease my father wasn't a strange concept for me.

It was just another Tuesday in the Fitzpatrick household where *Athair* dangled the kingdom's keys in front of me to get what he wanted.

Don't slouch.

Don't curse.

Do not *misspell a word, fall off a horse, display less than pristine table manners, or look your father in the eye.*

And so, I'd put on a condom and paid my dues.

When I'd gotten out of the room, *Athair* clapped my back, and said, "This, *mo òrga*, is the only thing women are good for. Opening their legs and taking orders. You'd be wise to remember that. Try to upgrade your mistresses often, never get attached to any of them, and when the time to settle down comes, make sure you find someone manageable. Someone who wouldn't ask for too much."

Athair did as he preached.

Jane Fitzpatrick was quiet, coy, and lacked anything resembling a backbone. That, of course, didn't stop her from cheating on her husband. Both my parents committed adultery, often and openly.

I grew up looking at the worst possible example for matrimony, took notes, and was expected to follow in their footsteps.

My baby brother had apparently been absent for the Women are Evil lecture. Hunter married for love. Not only that but he also wedded the most difficult girl he'd ever laid eyes on.

Shockingly, he seemed happy.

Then again, that meant nothing. Hunter possessed the intellect of a Lab puppy. I was pretty sure bone-shaped cookies and licking his own balls would make him content, too.

"Earth to Kill?" Hunter snapped his fingers in front of my face. "I asked why Minka. Why now?"

I opened my mouth to tell him to mind his own business when Petar, my estate manager, stormed into the room. His hair was damp from rain.

THE *Villain*

"You have a visitor, sir."

I didn't look up from my cards even though something weird and unwelcome happened in my chest.

The chances of it being Persephone were slim to none. Even if it was her, she missed her chance, and there was nothing to be done about it now.

"Who is it?" I barked.

"Mrs. Veitch."

I could feel Hunter's gaze darting in my direction, burning a hole through my cheek.

"I'm busy." I motioned to the table.

"Sir, it's late and raining hard."

"I can read the time and look through the window. Call her a cab if you feel so inclined to be a gentleman."

"There's a storm. Lines are down. Taxi apps aren't working," Petar countered, hands behind his back, each word pronounced slowly and measuredly. He knew I did not appreciate being slighted. I was always trigger-happy to get rid of unruly staffers. "She is soaked to the bone and seems pretty upset."

Hunter opened his mouth, but I raised a hand to stop him.

"She has five minutes. Bring her in."

"You want her to come here to this room?" Petar glanced around. A rancid cloud of cigarette and cigar smoke hung above our heads, and the sour scent of stale, warm alcohol soaked the walls. The room smelled like a brothel.

She was a damsel in distress, and I was inviting her into the lion's den.

But Persephone turned down my offer. If my ego took a beating, then hers could use a few spanks, too.

I met Petar's eyes with a vacant stare.

"It's my way or the highway, and as far as my knowledge goes, Mrs. Veitch can't afford a car. *Send. Her. In.*"

Not a minute later, Persephone was ushered into the drawing

room, drenched and tattered. A thin trail of water followed her, her shoes squeaking with every step she took. Her eyes, blue and bottomless as the pit of the ocean, looked feverish. Yellow hair framed her temples and cheeks, and her holed windbreaker was tangled around her willowy body.

She stopped in the middle of the room, graceful as a queen who'd allowed her servants the time of the day. I saw the minute it really hit her. When she took in her surroundings. The soft lighting, refreshments, and charcuteries.

This life could have been yours. You turned it down for love.

She drew herself to her full height—which, granted, wasn't much—took a breath, and honed her gaze on me.

"I accept."

The two simple words exploded in the room.

Watch that pulse, Cillian.

"I beg your pardon?" I raised an eyebrow.

She ignored Hunter, Sam, and Devon, exhibiting balls bigger than all three of them. Petar stood beside her, his stance protective.

Persephone tipped her chin higher, refusing to cower and flail. At that moment, soaked as a rat and well on her way to pneumonia, she was mercilessly beautiful, and I knew exactly why I always chose to look at her older sister whenever we were in the same room.

Emmabelle didn't blind me.

Didn't consume me.

Didn't *move* me.

She was just another woman packed with mannerism and entitlement, existing loudly, unapologetically, desperate to be seen and acknowledged.

Persephone was pure and noble. Bare of pretense.

"Your offer." Her voice was silky and sweet as pomegranate. "I accept it."

She accepts.

I was going to punch a wall.

THE *Villain*

No, not just *a* wall. *All* of them. Reducing my Back Bay Jacobean mansion to nothing but dust.

She is accepting an offer that's no longer on the table.

Her cheeks reddened, but she refused to budge, nailed to my floor, a pool of water forming around her.

Having her felt almost too easy at that moment, yet entirely impossible.

"Persy, I—" Hunter rose from his seat, about to rush over and help his wife's friend. I pushed him back down by his shoulder, pinning him on the chair to the wall with force, my eyes still fixated on her.

"You know why I like Greek mythology, Persephone?" I asked.

Her nostrils flared. She didn't take the bait because she knew I'd tell her, anyway.

"The gods have a history of punishing women for hubris. You see, fifty-five hours ago, I wasn't good enough to be your husband. It took you longer than we'd agreed to get back to me."

Her mouth fell open. I'd outed us in front of all our acquaintances without as much as a blink.

"There was a storm." Her eyes flared. "Trains were down. I had to ride my bike in the rain—"

"I'm bored." Dropping my head to the headrest, I grabbed a shiny apple from one of the fruit assortments and rolled it in my hand. "And you're late. That is the essence of the situation."

"I came here as soon as I could!"

Her shock was replaced with anger now. The two steel marbles of her eyes shimmered. Not with tears, but with something else. Something I hadn't seen before in them until tonight.

Wrath.

My father's words echoed in my head—*marry someone manageable. Someone who wouldn't ask for too much.*

Minka seemed docile, adaptable, and desperate.

Persephone, on the other hand, asked for the unthinkable—love.

"Already proposed to someone else." I sank my teeth into the Envy apple, its nectar trickling down my chin as our eyes remained locked in a battle of wills. "*She* accepted immediately."

The room filled with silence.

All eyes were directed at me.

This wasn't a power trip.

This was a full-blown act of humiliation.

I didn't want Persephone Penrose.

She wasn't good enough for *me*.

Even if she were, what good would come out of it? She wanted all the things I didn't.

A relationship. A partnership. Intimacy.

I wasn't Hunter. I wasn't capable of loving or even *liking* my wife. Tolerating? Possibly, and only if we reduced our communication to once a month. Besides, the day my brother married Sailor Brennan, I'd almost let Persephone die of poisoning just to avoid being in the same room alone with her.

I'd been seconds away from devouring her.

From sinking my teeth into her firm, round ass.

From grinding myself against her tits until I came in my pants from the friction.

And now I was hard in a room full of people. *Terrific.*

My point was, Persephone was too messy, too complicated, and too much a temptation for me to yield to. Minka was the right choice. My mind would never drift to Minka unprompted.

"You proposed to someone else," she echoed, stumbling backward.

"Minka Gomes." Sam stuck his seventh cigarette that hour to the corner of his lips, fully committed to get lung cancer before the night was over. He lit it up, puffing away. "We're trying to figure out where he found the poor thing. Ring a bell?"

"I'm afraid not," she said quietly.

"Dodged a bullet. Kill's too cold, too old, and too set in his ways for a nice girl like you. Not to mention, I have my suspicions about his preferences in the sack. Light a candle for Miss Gomes next time you go to church and thank your lucky stars. They definitely aligned tonight." Sam puffed a ribbon of smoke directly in her direction, making her cough.

I wanted to kill him.

"Persy." Hunter stood. "Wait."

She shook her head, mustering a dignified smile.

"I'm okay, Hunt. Totally fine. Please, get back to your game. Thank you for your time. I hope you enjoy the rest of the evening."

She turned around, her steps brisk and even. Petar shot me a disgusted look, then turned around and chased her.

Hunter was about to run after both of them, but I grabbed the collar of his shirt and nailed him back to his seat again.

"Finish the game first."

"Are you fucking kidding me?" my brother roared. His Guinness tipped over. The black stout hissed as it spread across my Persian carpet. "You went around Boston proposing to women—one of them my wife's best friend—and you want me to *finish* the fucking game? Fine. Here. Whatever Kill wants, Kill gets." He slammed his cards over the table. "Now, if you'll excuse me, I'm going to go fix this shit." He pointed at the door. "The last thing my pregnant missus needs is a pissed-off friend. Swear to God, Kill, if you pulled something on this girl…if you somehow got her pregnant to make sure you have an heir…"

I flipped his discarded cards over, ignoring his hysterics.

He had a full house.

Hunter was wrong. I *didn't* always get what I wanted.

Persephone

He was marrying someone else.

I was a few hours late, showing up at almost midnight, looking and feeling like a rag doll that had been left in the mud for the past century, and he didn't even give me a second glance.

What did I expect?

You expected him to treat you as more than just a womb for hire.

But that was my first and hopefully last mistake regarding Cillian Fitzpatrick.

I made my way from my bike to my apartment building, stomping on puddles deliberately. It was the middle of the night, raining hard, and my windbreaker was torn from the ride to and from Back Bay. My toes and fingers were numb. Maybe they fell off on the way, and I hadn't even noticed. The rest of my body wasn't going to miss them when Byrne and Kaminski finally dismembered me and fed me to the crows.

Wherever you are, Pax, I hope you suffer twice as much as I do.

I opened the front door to my building—*Belle's* building. *I had no home*, I reminded myself. It was dark, damp, and moldy. I took the first step toward the stairway when my head flew sideways. My cheek burned so bad my eyes stung with tears.

A whip-like *thwack!* pierced the air a second later. Before I knew what was happening, I was on my knees, facedown. The sound of gurgling reverberated in the empty hallway. It took me a moment to realize I was its source.

A sharp kick to my stomach followed, coming from the blanket of darkness. I collapsed on my stomach, gagging. Craning my neck to look at my assaulter, I shot my arm forward, patting the floor to find my bag in the dark and reach for the pepper spray in it.

A heavy boot flattened over my fingers. A cracking sound filled the air as my attacker put his full weight on my hand.

"Think again, bitch."

For the first time in my life, fear had a shape and a taste. My attacker kicked my bag away, sending it spinning across the floor until it hit the wall. I took the opportunity to claw my nails onto his ankle. I felt my nails bending backward as I desperately tried to hurt him. I used his leg for leverage, pulled myself up, and sank my teeth into his shin, clamping on it viciously until I felt my gums bleeding.

"Fuck! You whore!"

A dirty green army boot kicked me off. I only knew one man who wore this type of footwear.

Kaminski.

"Tom," I croaked, using his first name as if it would help. Warm, metallic blood filled my mouth. Adrenaline coursed through my veins, and every cell in my body prickled with panic. "Please, Tom. Get off me. I can't breathe."

Another kick found me. This time, he hit my jaw. My face throbbed, and I bit my tongue in the process. More blood filled my mouth.

Kaminski could end me right here, right now, and no one would ever know. The only person who knew about the mobsters after me was Cillian, and between almost letting me poison myself and refusing to help me, it was safe to say bringing me justice wasn't high on his to-do list.

I started crawling up the stairs, frantically trying to get away, but Kaminski grabbed my foot, pulling me down the three stairs I managed to take. He spun me around, unzipping himself.

"Why don't we see what you're worth, huh?" His menacing laughter rattled the air. "Seein' as you'll be sucking a lot of cock in a few days to pay back Pax's debt."

Rearing my body back, I sent a kick to Tom's groin, smacking my sneakers against his heavy erection. He tripped backward, screaming in pain as he cupped his groin. I turned around and climbed up the stairs on my hands and knees, like an animal, guttural screams leaving my lungs. I knew Belle wasn't home, but we had four other neighbors in the building.

A hand wrapped around my hair, pulling my head up with a violent yank. Kaminski's rancid breath skated over my cheek, the scent of cigarettes and plaque hitting my nostrils.

"Saved by the bell. You killed my hard-on, but that just means I'll take you up the ass next time. You've got a week, Mrs. V. One week before I turn all your nightmares into reality. You better believe it."

He let go of my hair. My face hit the floor with a thud. The entrance door slammed behind me.

I lay there, allowing myself a rare moment to break. For the first time since Paxton had left, I cried, pressing my swollen, hot, and bruised face to the floor.

Curling into a ball, I bawled like a baby, the agony rocking me back and forth.

I cried for making all the wrong choices in life.

For being deserted by my husband.

For paying for his sins.

For cycling in the storm, wet and cold and desperate, and for being so freaking, unbelievably, pathetically stupid.

For wasting Auntie Tilda's precious Cloud Wish on Cillian Fitzpatrick, who turned out to be the villain in my story.

For believing her stupid miracles in the first place.

Minutes, or maybe hours had passed before I peeled myself from the floor, slapping the dirt and blood from my scraped knees. I dumped my bag into the trash can outside the building, shoving my wallet into my panties to hide it, then went upstairs to Belle's apartment.

My sister had to believe I had been violently mugged.

I couldn't drag her into this mess.

A week. I wanted to scream.

Seven short days.

Before my life would be over.

Six

Cillian

"Employee compensation within the oil and gas industry is currently on the rise, and we came up with a great plan to preserve key staffers and encourage potential prospects to apply to Royal Pipelines…"

My mind drifted as my HR director, Keith, delivered what was surely one of the most boring pitches I had ever listened to in my lengthy corporate career.

Across from me, Hunter was on his phone, probably renewing his Pornhub Premium subscription.

Devon sat next to me, dutifully fulfilling his role as the head of my compliance department by scowling at his phone and ignoring the out-of-country calls that kept going through to his answering machine.

The man was going to inherit a dukedom in a few years (if he ever bothered to show his face in England), yet he refused to set foot in England.

I tapped my Montblanc pen on the table, staring out the window.

Three days had passed since Persephone had shown up at my door, accepting my offer.

Three days in which I had time to reflect on the fact that, indeed, a storm had paralyzed most of Boston's public transportation that day.

Three days in which I'd completely forgotten Minka Gomes existed.

THE *Villain*

Three days in which I'd imagined Persephone birthing me babies that looked like little replicas of her—with blond curls and cyan eyes and sun-kissed skin—and wasn't half-disgusted with the prospect.

My phone pinged with an email notification while Keith continued boring the room to death.

I slid my thumb over the screen.

From: CaseyBrandt@royalpipelines.com
To: Cillianfitzpatrick@royalpipelines.com

Hiiiiii Mr. Fitzpatrick,

Just wanted to let you know the jeweler was sent to Ms. Gomes' apartment earlier this morning for the ring measurements, and I have them here with me.

Should I proceed to pick the engagement ring on your behalf, or would you like to take a look after all? Please let me know. ☺

Relatedly, Ms. Diana Smith, the PR director for Royal Pipelines, would love to schedule a brief meeting with you this week concerning the official announcement of your engagement to Ms. Gomes to make things official.

I'm enclosing your weekly schedule. The highlighted slots could be secured for the meeting.

*If you need me for anything (and I do mean **anything**, LOL) else, let me know <3*

xoxo
Casey Brandt
Executive Personal Assistant to Cillian Fitzpatrick, CEO of Royal Pipelines.

I glanced up from my phone, frowning at Hunter.

He glared back at me, mouthing *fix it* from across the board desk.

Maybe I did need to fix this.

My brother was pitifully soft and cared not only about his average-looking wife, but also about her hang-ons.

Then there was Aisling to think about. She had a gentle soul and didn't deserve to mourn Persephone if the latter was murdered by some street punks.

Then there was Sailor. If Persephone was found chopped into minuscule pieces, floating in Charles River like stale tofu in a miso soup, she could lose the baby.

Choosing to ignore the fact I'd never previously shown signs of conscience, integrity, or consideration to anyone other than my dick, I'd decided to give Persephone one more chance to redeem herself.

This would be my pro bono.

Marrying a girl to save her from sure death.

Flower Girl was going to owe me so much after the solid I was about to give her that she was going to be indebted to me for eternity. That meant I could shape our relationship any way I chose, and what I chose was to see her three times a year, for important holidays, company events, and an annual sex-a-thon (if I was going to pay for her and her future boy toy's luxury lives, I would make sure he knew who she really belonged to).

My fingers flew over my phone screen.

Cillian: Get my driver ready immediately.

Casey: Mr. Fitzpatrick? Are you texting me?! <3

What was it with people stating the obvious?

Cillian: Heading out of the HR meeting now. If he is not there by the time I exit the building, you're both fired.

I stormed out of the boardroom without so much as an apology. Keith stopped mid-speech, his mouth slacking. Hunter and Devon exchanged looks.

I didn't care.

I didn't want to marry Minka Gomes.

I didn't want to marry Persephone Penrose, either, but at least I knew what I was getting out of the bargain. Namely, photogenic children, a doting mother to them, and a wife who would look good on my arm.

All I needed was to keep Persephone at arm's length and away from me after we tied the knot.

Casey: Your day is booked back-to-back, sir.

Cillian: You mean my day is clear and wide open because you used your three working brain cells to shift things around, which is what I'm PAYING YOU FOR.

Casey: Absolutely, sir. What should I do regarding the engagement ring?

Cillian: Send Ms. Gomes a fat check and an apology note. I will not be marrying her.

Casey: OMG really?

Casey: Sorry, I mean, is the vacancy still open, sir? ;)

Casey: I will make a good wife. I promise. I know how to cook, how to fish, babysat like, a ton of kids in my life. And I also know other things...

I got out of the elevator, my brogues clicking over the marbled lobby. I could see the Escalade waiting at the curb from the floor-to-ceiling window, the subzero blizzard its backdrop.

Sliding in the back seat, I barked Persephone's work address to the driver.

Casey: Never mind. Sorry. That was totally out of order. If you don't intend to marry Ms. Gomes, should I cancel the PR meeting with Diana?

Cillian: I said I'm not marrying Ms. Gomes. She is not the only woman on the planet.

Casey: Sir, I'm afraid I don't understand. ☹

Cillian: Don't be afraid. Ignorance is bliss.

The staff at Little Genius Academy recognized me the second I set foot inside. An eager receptionist rushed to help me find my way to Ms. Persy, accompanying me down a corridor full of drawings, art projects, and squeaky toys.

The place smelled like a warm fart and applesauce. It was a dire reminder of the fact that having heirs required raising them first. I supposed I could do the whole remote-dad gig *Athair* was so good at and limit my communication with my spawns until they were fully formed and didn't require any ass wiping.

"There it is, Ms. Persy's class." The receptionist stopped by the classroom door, swinging the door open for me.

I watched as Flower Girl pranced around a room full of kids. Her hair—honey highlights tangled in bright yellow—was gathered into a Dutch braid, and she wore an ankle-length white dress and flat shoes that looked about a decade old.

She was dirt-poor, in deep shit, and still happy to go to work every day.

Unbelievable.

She held the hands of two shy-looking four-year-olds as the class danced in a circle. Every few seconds, the music would stop, and the kids would freeze in place, a funny expression on their faces, trying not to crack up.

I leaned against the doorframe, hands tucked in my front pockets, and observed. It took her three minutes to notice me. Another two to lift her jaw off the floor, straighten her spine, and turn scarlet.

THE Villain

Our eyes met across the room, and that nagging murmur in my chest happened again.

Get that checked. If you drop dead from a heart attack at forty, you'll have no one else to blame.

She winced, looking like I physically slapped her.

"Mr. Fitzpatrick."

"Miss Penrose."

"Veitch," she corrected, just to spite me.

"Not for long," I noted dryly. "A word?"

"I know many. My favorite one right now is—*leave.*"

"You want to hear me out." I cracked my knuckles. "Now say goodbye to your little friends."

She looked back and forth between the kids and me, then turned and murmured something to the teacher next to her, and hurried my way, dunking her head down.

"What are you doing here?" She closed the door behind her, whisper-shouting.

I've been asking myself the same question since bailing on Keith and his snooze-fest speech.

What the hell was I doing here?

Hunter?

Aisling?

Something about Persephone getting potentially offed by the mafia?

The reasons blurred, but they seemed valid when I sat in the boardroom, considering a future with a woman I didn't know and didn't interest me. A woman who wanted an *Aspen cabin* as if it was the flipping nineties.

"When are you done here?" I demanded.

"Not for another four hours."

"Take the rest of the day off."

"Are you crazy? I can barely afford my lunch breaks." Her eyes widened. "I only take them because I have to by law. I asked the director to stay after school hours to help clean up and get some extra money. I can't bail."

The woman was as stubborn as a mule.

And I was about to marry her.

Marry a manageable woman, Athair said.

It wasn't too late to turn around and walk away but having this moron's death on my conscience made me suspect I had one after all. The thought made me shudder.

No. Not a conscience. You just don't want a big mess.

"Take the rest of the day off, or you will have no job to return to," I gritted out, about to turn around and make my way outside before I got secondhand food poisoning from the smell here alone. I paused, examining her closely for the first time.

"What the hell happened to your face?"

Her lower lip was swollen, her cheek was bruised, and under the thick layer of makeup, I could see a prominent shiner circling her left eye.

She looked away, tilting her face down to hide it from me.

"It's nothing. None of your concern, anyway."

The loan shark had finished with his threats and moved to actions.

My pulse quickened. I cracked my knuckles. I didn't understand my reaction to her face. She was clearly alive and in general good health.

But the idea of someone touching her…hitting her…

"You have ten minutes to wrap this up and meet me outside. You should know by now that I do not like to be kept waiting."

I turned around and sauntered back to the Escalade, already regretting the decision to marry her. There weren't enough painkillers in the world to save me from the headache Flower Girl had in store for me.

She appeared minutes later, wrapped in a cheap coat with holes in two different places. I opened the back seat door for her. She climbed inside, and I followed.

"Drive around," I ordered my chauffeur, clicking the remote to raise the partition.

Persephone fumbled with the seat belt, avoiding eye contact.

I stared at the leather headrest in front of me while I spoke. Looking at her face in its current condition made me angry, and I was *never* angry.

"We will live in separate houses. I'll remain in my estate, and you'll live down the road. There's a new construction on Commonwealth Avenue. A four-bedroom, thirty-five-hundred-square-foot condo. I asked my realtor to secure you the penthouse for a rental. You can discuss your permanent residence with her and tailor it to your preference."

She whipped her head in my periphery, staring at me in shock.

"What?"

"I said, there's a new estate on Commonwealth Ave—"

"I heard what you said." Her brows knitted. "I thought you wanted to marry someone else."

"Want is a big word. I decided to settle for you since the other woman is not on the brink of extinction." Unbuttoning my pea coat, I crossed my legs and lit a cigar, stinking up the entire back seat. The hail pounding on the tinted windows meant she had to sit in the small, confined space and breathe in my poison.

A good exercise for our future.

If she refused me again, I was going to drive us across the Canadian border and pay someone to marry us just to spite her. Never in my life had a woman made me feel edgy, but this assertive little shi...*female* had somehow managed just that.

She folded her arms, smiling triumphantly. "She said no, didn't she? Couldn't stomach being your wife."

I puffed a cloud of smoke directly in her face, not gracing her nonsense with an answer.

"Smart girl." She ignored the screen of smoke skulking between us.

"Judging by the state of your face, turning me down is not a luxury *you* can afford."

She stared at me with her California sky eyes. Her complexion was so smooth and dewy that the need to sink my teeth into the side of her throat just to tarnish its perfection made my fingers twitch.

"Can I try your cigar?" She tucked a stray hair behind her ear.

"I'm offering you a twenty-million-dollar condo, and you are asking me about a cigar?" I shot her a sidelong glance.

"Paxton never let me try them. He said cigars are manly." She licked her lips, her eyes on the thick brown roll of tobacco.

Paxton was an idiot. For more reasons than I could count.

Reluctantly, I passed her the cigar. She clasped her pink lips around it, her heavy-lidded eyes blinking back at me. She inhaled, almost coughing out a lung, and passed it back to me, waving her hand around. I didn't take it, still preoccupied by the way her lips wrapped around the thing. This was an entirely new side of me—a fourteen-year-old one, presumably—I wasn't eager to explore.

"It tastes like burning feet."

"You're not supposed to inhale." A wry blade of amusement colored my tone. "Nor are you supposed to lick burning feet. Now suck on it like it's a dick, not a joint."

She cocked her head sideways, squinting at me in amusement.

"Sounds like an audition."

"Don't flirt," I warned. "It's not your affection I'm after."

My desire normally wasn't directed at a specific woman or individual. Rather, it was a prickly sensation I needed to squash. The women I'd used were merely vessels.

I was not accustomed to gravitating toward a specific human being.

Frankly, I didn't know if I was capable of desiring a woman. If I were, I had no doubt it came with side effects I wasn't going to like.

Persephone tried again, puffing on the cigar gently, then handed it back to me. The tips of our fingers brushed. A zing of electricity shot up my spine in a sensation I could only describe as both horrible and pleasant.

I wanted to kiss her and throw her out of the car, preferably at the same time.

Fortunately for my legal department, I did neither.

"What else would our marriage entail?" She lowered her lashes, licking her lower lip.

"You will be available to me for social gatherings, volunteer at my charity of choice, and play your part as a dutiful wife."

"Hmm." She relaxed into the seat, cherishing the luxurious leather like a spoiled cat. "Anything more?"

"You will have to sign an airtight NDA and a draconic pre-nuptial agreement. But as long as you're my wife, you'll be provided for. Generously so."

"What if you decide to divorce me for someone else?"

I can barely come to terms with one marriage. Two would be a stretch.

"I wouldn't let that worry keep you up at night," I said tersely. "I don't have feelings, Flower Girl, which means I can't give them to you nor can I *take* them from you. I will not develop any toward anyone else."

"Other than our *heirs*," she said the last word in a terrible English accent, peppering it with air quotes.

I suspected my neutrality toward people would extend to my future children. But telling her that seemed counterproductive to putting a baby in her.

"Naturally." I moved on to the other topic on our agenda. "As previously mentioned, sex is not a part of the bargain. I will satisfy my sexual needs elsewhere. The encounters will be discreet and confidential, but they will happen, and I expect no fits of drama from your end."

For all my faults—and hell knew there were many—increased sexual appetite wasn't one of them. Twice a month was enough to keep me sated.

She scrunched her nose. "You mean you'll still go to hookers?"

"They prefer to be called sex workers these days."

"Why?"

"I imagine because hooker has a degrading connotation and implies both criminal and immortal activity. Though I do not engage in deep conversation with the women I hire to suck my cock."

"No, why do you hire escorts? You can have any woman you want."

"And I can have any woman I want because of my bank account. Which brings us to square one—why not pay for the service and skip the dinner and chitchat?"

"What's wrong with dinner and chitchat?" she pressed.

"They require socializing, and I am firmly against the concept."

"What made you the way you are?"

"The way I am?" I snarled.

"Cold. Ruthless. Jaded." Her eyes roamed my face as though the answer was written plainly on it.

"A mixture of crushing expectations, a bad year, and lackluster upbringing."

Everything about my life had been designed to keep me on the straight and narrow. That was the only way for me to run the empire I'd been born to lead. I came into this world with a certain disadvantage, knowing my family frowned upon weaknesses. I had to fight the way I was created to survive and took it day by day.

Her gaze clung to mine. "I don't buy your story."

"Lucky for me, I'm not James Patterson."

"Will we be sharing joint custody of our poor children?"

"We could," I answered evenly, "if you don't mind them growing up with nannies half the time. I'll be busy running Royal Pipelines and expanding the Fitzpatrick empire."

Real estate. Commercial banking. Private equity. I wanted to take over the world.

"Let me get this straight." She rubbed at her forehead, frowning.

"You want to have kids, but you don't want to take care of them or make them with your wife?"

"You seem to be figuring it out well all by yourself." I puffed on my cigar. "That's exactly what I'm saying."

"Well, then I suggest you drop me off right here, go back to Minka, and pick up where you both left off."

Right here was the middle of the highway. Although throwing her out was tempting, it was a headline I was less than eager to explain.

"I can't raise children," I said evenly.

"You will not be a deadbeat dad. You will take care of them half the time. And I mean *really* spend time with them. Change diapers, take them to T-ball practices, and reenact their favorite Disney movies. *With* full-blown costumes."

T-ball? Disney? Flower Girl was clearly planning on raising a state university educated dental hygienist, not the next CEO of Royal Pipelines. Luckily, I would be there to steer my spawns in the right direction.

"Sure," I quipped. "I'll do all of that nonsense."

Twice a year since they'll be in Evon and other European institutions year-round.

She munched on the tip of her hair, which I found surprisingly not disgusting. "I have other conditions, too. I'll be able to keep my job and move around unrestricted. You will not be putting any surveillance or security on me. I want to live a normal life."

"You won't need to work a day in your life."

The girl was slower than an airport Wi-Fi.

"So?" She looked at me strangely as though she wasn't following the conversation. That was fine. Between my Mensa member IQ and her beauty, our kids wouldn't be a complete waste of oxygen. "I don't work because I have to." She narrowed her eyes. "I work because I *love* what I do."

That word again.

"Fine. Keep your job."

"What about security?"

"No security." That would be a waste of my precious resources.

"One more thing—as long as other men are off-limits, so are other women." She raised a finger in the air.

"This is not how it works." I put out my cigar, losing patience. I'd negotiated putting three hundred-foot deep holes in the belly of planet Earth in less time than it took me to close a deal with this woman. "You're the one at my mercy. I make the rules."

"Am I?" She blinked at me innocently. "Because, correct me if I'm wrong, but you seemed to have told me you have another wife lined up, and a nice, long list of potential candidates if she doesn't work out. Yet here you are with me. For a reason I can't fathom, we want each other. Let's not pretend otherwise, Kill."

Kill.

Only my friends called me that. All two of them.

"The only reason I prefer you to Minka is because if you die, the women in my life would be upset, and the one thing I dislike more than humans are distressed humans."

"I don't care what excuse you give yourself for marrying me," she said plainly. "*If* we get married, we'll be equal. At least, you'll pretend we are."

I popped my knuckles in succession.

She was pissing me off. That was a feeling, and I didn't do those.

"Let me put this plainly." I smiled politely. "I'm not going to stay celibate for months or even weeks."

"You won't have to. You'll have a wife."

She was so red at this point, I wondered if she was going to combust in my back seat. That would be a hassle to clean from the brand-new Escalade. Not to mention tricky to explain.

"No." I felt my muscles tightening under my suit.

"No, what?"

"I won't sleep with you."

"Why not?"

"Because I don't want to."

"Why's that?"

"Because you don't attract me," I deadpanned.

I was no longer pissed off. I was sweating now, too. Why couldn't I stick to my Minka plan? Persephone was my idea of hell. I couldn't treat her with the same brashness I handled Sailor and Emmabelle because she was an innocent little thing like my sister, yet I had to remind her who was calling all the shots.

"How, pray tell, do you mean to impregnate me, if you don't want to have sex with me?" She scowled, looking frustratingly adorable while doing so. "You *are* familiar with how babies come to be, right? Because none of the versions include a cabbage."

I began scrolling through my phone, answering emails.

"I know how babies are made, Persephone. That's why I bought a stork," I said gravely.

She looked shocked for a second, before letting out a giggle. It was a cute giggle, too. Soft and throaty. If I had a heart—it would squeeze.

"I didn't know you had a sense of humor, Kill."

"I didn't know you were so hard-pressed to get laid," I volleyed back, still typing an email to Keith, aka Lord of the Sleep. "To answer your question, we'll use IVF. You'll be knocked up in no time, and we won't have to know each other biblically."

"What's wrong with the Bible?" She eyed me.

"False advertisement." I smirked sardonically. "God doesn't exist."

Physically wounded from my last comment, Persephone coiled in her side of the back seat. Apparently, she drew the line at God.

"I really ought to hate you."

"Don't bother. Hate is just love with fear and jealousy thrown into the mix."

"Why me? Why not my sister?" She squared her shoulders, clutching onto the remainder of her defiance with bleeding fingernails.

Because she's probably seen more dick than a train station urinal.

I'd broken many people in my life to know what they looked like a second before submitting.

Persephone was fully bent and on the verge of snapping.

Once broken, she'd be easy to reassemble to fit my lifestyle and needs.

"Because she possesses virtually all of the traits I despise in a person—from being eccentric, entitled, bigmouthed, and opinionated to simply being alive."

"Yet you always ogle her." The quietness in her voice left no room for doubt. Persephone didn't like it when I looked at her sister.

"I looked at her because I didn't want to look at you," I grumbled.

"Why didn't you want to look at me?"

Because you make my pulse beat faster, and that could ruin everything I've ever worked for.

I tossed my phone aside. What was I thinking, marrying this woman?

What was I thinking, putting my silly, unexplainable weakness in my path?

"Does it matter why I couldn't look at you? I'm looking at you now, and I've come to terms with what I see. Speaking of your sister, she would have taken no longer than five minutes of negotiations and a quickie to convince. Yet you're the one I chose."

Flower Girl's face twisted in abhorrence because she knew I was right. Emmabelle displayed the moral compass of a fortune cookie. On paper, she was a better match for my brash personality. In practice, however, Persephone was the one who kept my mind reeling.

"We're done here. Email me your ring measurements." I pressed the button to roll down the partition.

She held up a palm. "Two more conditions before I accept."

My knee-jerk reaction was to advise her to take these conditions and shove them inside her pert little ass. But even I acknowledged that she was about to sign off her entire life to one of America's most hated men. If she wanted a nice Hermès bag and new pair of tits as a wedding gift, I could accommodate that.

"Shoot."

"One—I want us to conceive our children the old-fashioned way. I know you think it's pitiful and pathetic of me, but I don't care. I don't want to go through IVF treatments. I don't want to take someone else's place in my quest for a baby before I tried the natural way. I know I'm not your taste, but if I come this far for you, it is only fair that you will…"

"Come *inside* you," I finished for her. "Got it."

I loathed the idea of sleeping with Persephone. The very concept of touching her made my skin crawl. Not because I didn't find her attractive. The opposite was true. Ultimately, though, between impregnating her and having her killed, I preferred the former. *Marginally*.

"Your funeral," I drawled. "I'm a notoriously selfish man, in bed and out of it. What's the other condition?"

"No escorts until I conceive. You can't hop in and out of my bed and still visit your European girlfriends."

"No."

"Yes," she mimicked my dry, indifferent tone. "When you need satisfaction, you will come to me. We'll service each other until I fall pregnant."

Her pink cheeks implied she was mortified by the situation, but she said those things anyway, which I couldn't help but appreciate.

We were still driving around. I looked down at my Rolex and realized we'd been going back and forth for two and a half hours.

Where did the time go, and how on earth could I claim it back?

I turned to look at her again. Her face was twice its usual size, cut and bruised.

I knew the little idiot was going to walk away from this deal if I said no.

She did it before and would not hesitate to do it again.

A lamb marching straight into Colin Byrne's arms for slaughter.

"You drive a hard bargain. Welcome to the dark side, Persephone. Leave your heart at the door."

Seven

Persephone

THE NEXT DAY, DEVON WHITEHALL KNOCKED ON MY apartment door, looking like sin in a stripy navy-blue suit and a dashing haircut. I, in contrast, was wearing Walmart's finest dress from six winters ago paired with shoes that had seen better days and a discounted windbreaker from Salvation Army.

Carrie Bradshaw, right behind you!

"Mr. Whitehall?" I hugged my door, stifling a yawn.

He shouldered past me, soldiering into the studio apartment where Emmabelle was asleep in our shared bed, clad in nothing but a thin red negligee, one bronzed leg flung over the duvet.

She caught his attention, making him pause and admire the view.

"And who is this foam-born Aphrodite?"

"That would be my sister, Mr. Zeus. Now if you'd be as kind as to peel your creepy eyes off her legs…"

Devon turned toward me reluctantly, shoving a mass of paperwork in my chest. Like Cillian, Whitehall had the uncanny ability to make the air stir around him. But while Kill made me want to die in his arms, Devon sent off a different vibe. A mysterious one.

"I filled out most of it. Sign where indicated with arrow flags and your initials on the bottom of each page. Go through your spouse's

THE *Villain*

details one more time and ensure all the information is correct. There's a list of outstanding documentation I'll need you to hand over before the marriage can be resolved. It's on the last page. Get it to me by tomorrow morning. It'll take the court two business days to process the application, in which you agree not to claim any of your and Mr. Veitch's mutual funds or possessions."

"We have no mutual funds or possessions."

"Precisely."

Asking him how he planned to grant me a speedy divorce was futile.

Cillian Fitzpatrick was a resourceful man and only worked with the cream of the crop. With people like Devon Whitehall and Sam Brennan on retainer, he could do just about anything, short of plucking the moon from the sky just so he could enjoy a bit more darkness.

I clutched the papers to my rib cage, excitement and dread swirling in my gut.

"Thank you, Devon. That's—"

"Bugger, don't thank me, you silly little thing." He lifted a hand, indicating for me to stop.

"I didn't do this out of the goodness of my heart. I did it because your future husband needs a baby-maker, preferably the kind that would bring positive press to his doorstep. Which is why you will also find in this load of legal documents a nondisclosure agreement and a prenup, both of which I advise you to read carefully in the company of a proper solicitor." He plucked a few notes from his wallet, tucking them between my fingers. "Here's some cash in case you can't afford one. Consider this my wedding gift to you. There's a sheet of dos and don'ts attached, some stipulations you verbally agreed to yesterday. No house-sharing, a non-compete clause…"

"Non-compete?" I blinked. "I'm not planning to open a petroleum company anytime soon."

I mean, never say never, but this was a pretty unlikely scenario. Devon smirked.

"Having access to the Fitzpatrick clan means you can spy for the competitors or decide to work for someone who'd pose a conflict of interest."

"I'd never do that."

"Clearly, darling." He patted my head as though I was a puppy he was about to turn his back on before adopting its sibling. "We trust you completely. And by 'completely' I mean, about eighty-three percent. The other seventeen is why we prefer to have it in writing. You'll have to mortgage your inner organs if your *never* turns into a *maybe*."

"How do you live with yourself?" I murmured absently, flipping through the pages. I meant that as a general statement. Devon, Kill, Sam…they were so jaded, I sometimes wondered if they believed in anything at all.

Devon laughed easily, his gaze sliding toward my sister again.

"Considering your face was smashed by mobsters, I wouldn't judge your future husband for wanting to protect his assets."

Future husband.

The words hadn't sank in. Not yet.

"Do you mind?" I jerked my head in Belle's direction. She usually slept like the dead, but I didn't want to take any risks. "My sister doesn't know what happened."

"Is she blind?" He cocked an eyebrow, his eyes zeroing in on my black shiner.

"She thinks I got robbed."

"No offense, but you don't look like the type to carry extra cash." A pause. "Or coins. Or food stamps. You're dreadfully gaunt."

I wanted him out of the apartment, out of this building, and out of my life before Belle woke up. I still hadn't told her about Cillian. By the time I got home yesterday, she'd already left for work and returned sometime after five in the morning, when I was asleep. We were having dinner and drinks at Ash's tonight, and I thought it would be a good idea to break the news then.

I shook my head.

"Look, can I have my future husband's phone number?"

Devon plucked my phone from my hand, inserting Cillian's contact info into it.

"How do you know my code?" I frowned.

"Had to write down your birthdate six hundred times when I filled in the paperwork last night. You seem like the predictable sort. Again, no—"

"Offense. I know." His eyes were still on my phone, his thumbs flying over my screen. "You realize prefacing something with these words makes it automatically offensive, right?"

"The code to get to him is six six six. He only responds to texts. Sporadically."

Shocker.

Devon slapped the phone over the pile of documents I was holding. "Cheers, Persephone."

"Wait!" I called out. "What about Colin Byrne? Can I tell him I'll have the money ready for him?"

He stopped at my threshold.

"Ah, that's the best part of becoming a Fitzpatrick." He opened his arms. "Your problems are no longer yours. I do believe Colin is Sam Brennan's jurisdiction. To that end, I'd say you're all covered, and that Byrne is thoroughly and royally fucked for laying a hand on you. Welcome to the family, Persy."

***

"What do you mean you're breaking the pact?"

Sailor spritzed her pink lemonade across the table and all over my dress, the liquid shooting through both her mouth and nostrils.

She coughed, waving her arms around. Aisling dashed to her rescue, patting her on the back. The liquid must've gone down the wrong pipe.

The unshakable storm knocked on the greenhouse where we'd sat down for dinner, the hail threatening to impale the glass. At twenty-five, Aisling still lived at Avebury Court Manor, her parents' mansion. She said it was because between med school and her charity work, she didn't have time to maintain an apartment, but we all knew she took care of her parents, tended to them like one of their servants, and was not likely to leave before she got married.

The greenhouse was warmly lit with an array of colorful succulents strewn everywhere.

"She is not breaking the pact." Ash hurried to hand me napkins after ensuring Sailor was okay. "She's still married to Paxton. She can't wed anyone else."

I dropped the bomb as soon as I sat down at the table before I'd even had time to help myself to a spring roll.

"I *am* breaking the pact." I took a deep breath, bracing myself for another storm, right here in the greenhouse. "I'm getting married to Cillian. He is working on my divorce certificate as we speak."

"Cillian-Cillian?" It was Emmabelle's turn to choke, this time on a crab rangoon. "Tall, dark, broody. Two little red horns peeking from either side of his head? Possibly a tail tucked between those steel ass cheeks?" My sister grabbed a dumpling with her chopsticks, tossing it into her mouth.

"My brother Cillian?" Ash supplemented.

"Yes." I pressed my forehead to my still-empty plate with a groan. "One and the same."

"Why?" Sailor asked.

"*How?*" Belle demanded.

"Is he threatening you?" Aisling shrieked.

"Look, if it's about money, Hunter and I would be more than happy to help." Sailor reached across the table to dab at my collar, pretending to remove the lemonade stains she put there.

"Me too. I wouldn't be able to live with myself if I knew you only married my brother because you were struggling." Ash put a hand on her chest over her heart. She wore a cardigan and a checked long skirt. Her raven-black hair was carefully tied into a chignon.

They didn't get it. Any of it. The reality of my life. My situation, my commitments, my misfortunes…

"Of course she doesn't want to marry him." Sailor flung her arms in the air. "It's Kill Fitzpatrick we're talking about. He hasn't exactly won any Mr. Personality awards in the last decade."

"Love changes people. You and my brother are prime examples of that," Aisling pointed out.

Sailor shook her head. "Hunter has always been good and lost. Cillian is bad and knows exactly where and what he is. A wolf can never be a pet."

Your husband starred in a sex tape, I wanted to scream. *Who died and made you the moral police?*

I shot Belle a glance. She sipped her chardonnay, studying me intently. My sister was surprisingly quiet. I half-expected her to blaze out the door straight to Cillian's house and extract more info from him at knifepoint. But no. She was just taking it all in. Absorbing.

"Look." I sighed. "Thanks for the offers, but I'm good. I'm marrying him because I want to. I know it's sudden, but Kill and I have gotten close in the past few—"

"You better not finish this sentence," Belle warned coldly, draining her glass of chardonnay. "You're already breaking the pact. At least have the decency not to lie to us. You and Kill don't know each other beyond you being his baby sister's friend."

"If Cillian asked you to marry him, it's for all the wrong reasons." Sailor's voice softened as she tried to change tactics. "Did he tell you he doesn't have any feelings? Like, at all? He takes pride in that."

Slurping a noodle between my lips—my first bite this evening—I nodded.

"I know who Kill is. We've been running in the same circles for years now."

"Kill doesn't run anywhere." Sailor laughed. "He swaggers with a cocky grin and fucks shit up. Just tell me what kind of money you need, and I'll get you out of this. Forget about a loan. Don't pay me back."

She turned to the shoulder bag hanging over her seat, plucking out her checkbook and slapping it on the table. She clicked a pen and began writing me a check.

"For my part, I'll ask *Athair* for a good divorce lawyer," Aisling chimed in brightly. "This is totally fixable. It's not too late to say no. We can make sure you'll still get—"

"You want the truth?" I snarled, shooting up to my feet, shaking with anger. "Fine, here's the truth—I'm not like you guys. Belle is a street-smart, man-eating lady boss who is out to conquer the world and build an empire. Aisling, you were born into royalty. You have more money than some countries, two brothers who would kill for you, and a promising career as a doctor. Sail, you already met your Prince Charming, and you have a father and brother who'd get you out of anything. Me…" I shook my head, laughing bitterly. "I'm different. I wanted to marry for love. And I did. Saying it didn't work out would be the understatement of the century. Now it's time to marry for comfort. It is not the noble or honorable thing to do. Trust me, I'm well aware of that. But it's *my* choice. I choose security. I choose stability. I know he is not going to love me, but he will take care of me, and that's something Paxton failed to do. If I can live with it, then so can you."

A tense silence stretched between us. The only sound audible was Sailor's hard swallow.

"I'm breaking the pact," I whispered, the lie burning on my tongue. I *was* marrying for love. It just happened to be tragically unrequited. "And there's nothing you can do about it."

Eight years ago, Sailor dragged all of us to a charity ball Hunter had invited her to. In it, we saw a girl who went to our high school hanging on the arm of a man thirty years her senior. She looked bored and sad and lost and rich. A beautiful, empty urn where hopes, dreams, and ambition once resided. Watching her expression alone sucked the life out of the party. We promised each other we would never let one another marry anyone for anything other than love.

"Listen, I have options. I do." I grabbed my bag and coat. "I *choose* to be with Cillian. He may not give me love, but he'll give me everything else I'm looking for. I'll be able to start the family I've always wanted, have kids. A place to call my own…" I trailed off. "All I'm asking is for you to support this. It's crazy, and insane, and unconventional, but it is still my choice."

Aisling dropped her head into her hands.

Sailor looked the other way as if I'd slapped her.

Belle was the only one who stood, picked up her own bag, and took my hand in hers.

"Welp. If you excuse me, I have to go scream at my sister, have a mental breakdown, then accept her decision. See you later, ladies."

Belle and I ended up heading home, taking a rain check on dinner.

The mood had soured, and no one was hungry anymore.

Ash said she would always be there for me if I changed my mind, and Sailor threatened to shoot Kill with her bow and arrow and pin him to a wall like a butterfly if he screwed up, something we all knew she was capable of, seeing as she was an archer.

Ten minutes into our ride back home, I finally broke the silence.

"How come you didn't freak out?" I stared out the window, watching the ice-crusted buildings zipping by. Belle signaled onto a side street.

"Sorry, were you expecting a whole production?"

"Expected? No. *Predicted*? Yes."

She laughed. "I'm not Willy Wonka. I don't sugarcoat stuff, sis. You know how I feel about Kill Fitzpatrick, but you're not a baby anymore. You can make your own decisions, even if I think those decisions should land you in a psychiatric ward."

"That never stopped you from being super protective of me before."

Wait, was I mad at my sister for not making a scene? No. Of course I wasn't. That would be ridiculous. Then again, I *was* a bit ridiculous. And it wasn't in Belle's nature not to raise hell when the opportunity presented itself. Plus, she wasn't exactly Cillian's number one fan.

In fact, if Cillian *did* have a fan club, she would probably burn the place down.

And dance on its ashes.

And then post about it on Instagram.

(To her grid, not stories. That's how committed she was to despising him.)

"I'll always have your back. But honestly? I'm half-sold on the idea. Paxton left you penniless and heartbroken. I watched you suffer through the past eight months, trying to hold your head up. If you want to switch tactics and marry a wealthy man who will provide for you, I'll be the last one to judge you for it. Ultimately, we all make choices to the best of our abilities."

She paused, gnawing on her lower lip. "There's also something else."

I turned to look at her, ungluing my eyes from the window.

"I know you've never said anything, but I always kind of knew you had a thing for Kill. It was in your eyes when he entered a room. They changed. They *glittered*," she whispered. "It's never too late to change the name of the prince in your story. Just as long as you don't end up with the villain."

"He can't be the villain." I shook my head. "He's already saved me."

"You know he can't love?" she asked quietly.

"Love is a luxury not everyone can afford."

"Well, if anyone can move mountains, it's you, sis."

She removed one hand from the steering wheel, squeezing my knee.

I wondered how much Belle knew about my situation. Devon was right. I didn't look like the kind of woman to get brutally mugged. While Belle took care of my wounds and fussed over each scratch the day after Kaminski beat me up, she held back on her usual Spanish inquisition and didn't nag me when I said I didn't want to file a police report.

There was an ocean of lies and secrets between my sister and me, and I wanted to swim ashore, fall at her feet, and tell her everything.

About Pax. About the loan sharks. About Auntie Tilda's Cloud Wish.

But I couldn't. I couldn't rope her into my mess. It was mine to fix.

"You're not the naïve little damsel everyone thinks you are." Belle killed the engine, and I realized we were parked outside her building. "You have nails and teeth, and a spine to go with them. Persephone wasn't only a floral maiden. She was also the queen of death. Your groom's in for a rude awakening. But know this—if Kill ever tries to play Hades, I'd descend to the underworld myself to rip his balls off."

Eight

Cillian

"All there?" Byrne sniffed. He peered into the open black duffel bag. Kaminski stood behind him, arms crossed over his chest, watching us like The Mountain, Queen Cersei's killer guard.

"Count it," Sam ordered, spitting his cigarette on the floor.

Byrne began to sift through the money, which was bonded in hundred-dollar notes. His posture eased for the first time since we walked into his house. We were in his office, delivering our part of the bargain. Byrne had insisted we come to his place, probably because his office had more weapons in it than a tactical shop.

"Kam." Byrne snapped his fingers as he counted, separating the notes by licking his fingers. His soldier leaned forward. Byrne used the opportunity to smack the back of his assistant's head.

"Count with me, you useless sack of meat."

It took them twenty minutes before they were satisfied all the money was there. They zipped the bag, Byrne smiling at us politely.

"I'm pleased to say we have no outstanding debts between us, gentlemen. Thank you for your business."

Sam nodded, stood, and turned around. I followed suit. We reached the door. Instead of opening it, Sam turned the lock on the door, the soft click signaling we weren't done after all.

THE Villain

"Actually," Brennan hissed, "we do have one outstanding matter to resolve."

We both put on our leather gloves.

"What would that be?" Byrne gulped.

Sam smiled manically. "Your fucking bones."

An hour later, I finally felt I was getting my money's worth.

"Can I tell you a little secret?" Sam's lit cigarette hung from his lips as he tied a thoroughly beaten up Colin Byrne to his own bed, cuffing him to the rails, tugging hard. "I've always had a weakness for numbers. Don't know what it is about them, Byrne, but they calm me down. They make *sense*. My son of a bitch sperm donor was good at nothing but numbers. Guess I got the knack from him."

"Please," Byrne sputtered, teeth chattering, chest caving. "I already told you, I didn't know she was under your protection. I had no idea, man—"

"Stop begging, unless you want me to cut you a nice smile to remind you how cheerful you were when you paid her your weekly visits." Sam dumped a towel over Byrne's head. The heavy fabric muffled his desperate pleas. "Now, here's what *this* math enthusiast wants to know. Why would a loan shark inflate his interest by two hundred percent when the market standard is fifty? Is it possible you took advantage of the lovely creature Paxton Veitch had left behind and decided to whore her out, knowing she could make you a fast buck?"

Before Byrne could answer, Sam grabbed a bucket of water and slowly poured its contents over his face, waterboarding him.

Bracing the top of the doorframe with both hands, I watched Brennan handling Byrne while his assistant, Kaminski, hung by his arms from a hook in the ceiling where the chandelier had been. Kaminski looked like a skinned pig with his head covered in a burlap sack.

Sam dropped the empty bucket, tipping the cigarette ash on Byrne's bare stomach. He removed the towel from Byrne's head, who took a greedy gulp of air.

"Veitch wanted to whore out his wife all by himself before he fucked off!" Byrne coughed, desperately trying to unchain himself from the bedrails. "He wanted to kidnap her and give her to me. I told him not to bother. That I didn't want the FBI on my tail. Human trafficking will get you a shit-ton of jail time. I even gave the bitch extra time to pay me back."

Sam *tsked*, turning his head in my direction. "Are you thinking what I'm thinking?"

"We're dealing with a patron saint," I deadpanned, strolling into the room. I'd asked Sam to allow me to be present during this job even though I knew better than to accompany him to any of the other errands he usually ran for me. This felt personal. Not because I had any feelings toward my future wife, but because Kaminski and Byrne had defaced my property, and for that, they needed to pay.

Sweat, blood, and tears were my preferred currency.

Grabbing a fire poker hanging by the mantel, I brought the tip to the dancing flames in the fireplace, heating it up before swinging it in my hand like a golf club as I approached Kaminski.

"I just can't help but think that, despite your devout intentions, you could have done without beating the shit out of the poor girl." Sam dumped the towel back on Byrne's face and emptied another bucket of water on it. Brennan was definitely in his element. He was in the business of inflicting pain.

Kaminski whimpered at the sounds in the room, dangling from the ceiling.

"It was Kaminski!" Byrne gurgled through the towel. "He did it! I told him to threaten her, maybe slap her around, but no more. He was the one who hurt her!"

"Where'd you hurt her, Kaminski?" I asked the hanging man in front

THE Villain

of me, my eyes leveled with his stomach. He flinched, realizing how close I was. Neither man was going to rat me out. Crossing Sam Brennan was something very few people in Boston did, and those who were stupid to go that route didn't live to tell the tale. Even if Byrne and his brawny assistant *did* run their mouths to the feds, I had half the judges in Boston in my pocket.

"I...I..."

"Her eye?" I asked serenely. "Why, yes. I do remember my fiancée sporting a nasty black shiner."

I swung the poker to his face, crashing it above his nose. The hot metal hissed against the burlap fabric, melting it into his skin. He let out a carnal snarl, twisting violently like a worm on a hook.

"I also remember you got her cheek." I struck his cheek blade through the sack. "Her brow."

Smack!

"The ribs."

Smack!

"Her knees, too."

Smack! Smack! Smack!

I beat Kaminski while Sam drowned Byrne in his own bed. Ten minutes later, when both F-grade mobsters were barely conscious, Sam threw in the towel. Literally. On the floor. I wiped the tip of the poker on Kaminski's pants, then returned the stick to its place.

"Keep the money." Sam stubbed the cigarette butt he threw on the floor with his boot on his way out.

"And don't ever go near my future wife again." It was my turn to address the room. The air was heavily perfumed with sweat, blood, and violence. I tugged my leather gloves as I looked around. "If I hear you so much as breathed in her direction, there will be hell to pay. In fact, I'll be checking in to see you keep your distance from her. If I find you in her zip code..." I trailed off.

I didn't need to finish the sentence.

They knew.

An hour later, we were at a local Irish pub down the road from Colin Byrne's apartment.

"Red Right Hand" by Nick Cave and the Bad Seeds ricocheted through the paneling. Sam flirted with the two busty waitresses, helping one of them fill out a tax document.

Not for the first time, it occurred to me that Brennan was definitely on the spectrum of sociopathy. I'd been smart to keep him away from my sister. I, too, reserved a spot on that scale but somewhere in the middle.

But Persephone was not my sister. I had zero obligation to save her from myself.

At any rate, my plan was to avoid her at all costs as soon as she was with child. Sooner, if I could help it. She had no room in my day-to-day life.

Hurting the men who hurt her left me oddly satisfied. Peculiar, seeing as getting a hard-on from violence was more of Sam's thing.

"What's crawled up your ass?" Sam eyed me over the rim of his Guinness pint, poetic as always.

"Just thinking." I sprawled back in the old wooden booth, scanning the mixed bag crowd of young professionals and blue-collar workers.

"My least favorite pastime." Sam palmed a handful of salted wasabi peas, throwing them into his mouth. "What about?"

"Marriage."

"More specifically?"

"The inconvenient necessity of it. What are *you* waiting for?"

Sam thumped his red Marlboro pack on the table. One cigarette slid up obediently. He raised the pack and caught the cigarette between his teeth.

THE *Villain*

"Nothing." He lit up. Sam was notorious for breaking city council rules. Smoking inside restaurants was among the least offensive things he did. "I have no plans to get married. It's a surprisingly easy decision to make when you have no duty to continue a lineage and your biological parents are a back-stabbing asshole who deserved to die and a whore who left you on her ex-boyfriend's doorstep when you were old enough to know what it meant to be abandoned."

"Who'll inherit everything you own?" I asked. Sam Brennan was rolling in it. I didn't know exactly *how* wealthy he was. He probably declared no more than fifteen percent of his income to the IRS, but I would guess he was in the double-digit millions club.

Sam shrugged. "Sailor. Her kids, maybe. Money means nothing to me."

I believed him.

"But you grew up with Troy and Sparrow Brennan," I pushed, knowing nothing was going to come out of this conversation. The man was cagier than a zoo. "Boston's golden couple."

"Han Solo and Leia Organa on steroids." Sam took a swig of his Guinness, smirking bitterly. "But that means jack-shit. I have neither Sparrow's DNA nor Troy's. I'm an orphan. An elaborated mistake born from vengeance. I have no plans of reproducing. Besides, what good would it be to have a child, knowing I could get locked up for life any day?"

He had a point.

"Now"—he tilted his pint in my direction—"back to business. Byrne and his puppet are out of the picture for good. The next step is to find Veitch. See where he's hiding. What he's doing. Put him on a leash. Maybe bring him back and throw him into Byrne's claws. Kill two birds with one stone."

"Leave him." I waved him off. "Byrne is paid. Kaminski will be in a wheelchair for life. Veitch is probably dead. It's done."

"Dead? I don't think so. I bet you Veitch is alive, and that as soon as he hears his wife got hitched to a billionaire, he'll be back, making demands."

"Not possible," I insisted. "The divorce certificate should arrive tomorrow morning. He wouldn't be eligible for a penny. I don't need to know where Veitch is or what he's up to."

"He can contact Persephone and play on her heartstrings. He's her husband."

"*Was*."

"She chose him."

"She chose *wrong*," I retorted.

"If anyone's prone to take mercy on the asshole who left her behind, it's your future wife," Sam warned.

I cracked my fingers under the table. "Precisely. Better knock her up before she runs off with her ex."

I didn't want a fugitive bride. I didn't trust Persephone not to run in slow motion into her ex-husband's arms and break our contract the minute I dragged him back from the hellhole where he'd been hiding. Besides, the more time that passed without him knowing about me, the more chance I had to knock Persephone up without his interruptions.

Sam examined me coolly.

"It's an unfinished job," he cautioned. "I don't do those, Fitzpatrick."

"You'll do whatever I tell you to do for your salary, *Brennan*." I grabbed my whiskey, tossing it back and slamming the glass on the table. "And I'm telling you to forget Paxton Veitch ever existed."

Nine

Cillian

"THE MEDIA IS ALL OVER THIS SHIT LIKE A HOOKER ON A senator." Hunter took a sip of his coffee, blowing a chef's kiss. He sat in front of me in my office.

"Can't blame them. The bride looks like proper royalty. A modern Cinderella." Devon skimmed through the press release he was reading on his iPad, perched next to my brother.

I snatched the iPad from his hand, taking a look. I didn't know how this Diana chick from PR had gotten her hands on this picture of Persephone—clad in a powder blue dress, her golden hair cascading down to her narrow waist, her pink lips puckered with a faint smile—but she was in for one hell of a Christmas bonus.

Royal Pipelines did a good job announcing my nuptials to Boston's sweetheart: a preschool teacher, a churchgoer, and a woman of good faith, pedigree, and morals.

"Persy's hotter than a Carolina Reaper." Hunter tapped his lips, monitoring my reaction to the divine creature I was about to marry. "You've done well."

"She's done better." I handed Devon the iPad back. "Her beauty will fade. My Forbes status will not."

Persephone had been texting me nonstop for the past two weeks since we broke the news to our friends and family. Apparently, it was not enough to dump a budget more fitting to feed a medium-sized state in her hands and ask her to plan the wedding. She wanted to *talk* about things.

What venue I favored.

Which flowers I liked.

If I had any recommendations for a reputable catering company.

I didn't have the heart to tell her I didn't care if we married at the city hall, a church, or in a ditch. That, in fact, I didn't have a heart at *all*. So I opted for ignoring all her messages. The strategy worked well. I fully intended to adopt it after our wedding.

"Still can't believe she agreed to wed your ass. If I didn't see her saying she accepted your offer with my own eyes, I'd think you shanghaied her." Hunter rubbed his knuckles over his cheekbones. He and his wife handled the news as though we'd just told them one of us was dying. My parents, however, nearly pissed their pants. I wished it were a figure of speech.

Mother burst into tears, and *Athair* gifted me an entire drawer of vintage watches.

I was back to being *mo òrga*.

Golden, brazen, and cunning. Always six steps ahead of the game.

My father was specified, and my CEO position was saved. At least on that front. Hell knew what Arrowsmith had in store for me.

"I don't give a toss what made her say yes. All I care is that she did. We needed that win. Especially with Andrew Arrowsmith back in town." Devon tucked his iPad back into its leather case, glancing at me curiously.

I curved an eyebrow.

I didn't tell Devon Andrew was back. I did not want anyone making the mistake of thinking I cared. Plus, I paid people enough to keep track of what was happening around me.

"He's the new CEO of Green Living," Devon filled me in. When he realized I wasn't surprised, he frowned. "Bollocks. But you already knew that. When were you going to tell me?"

THE *Villain*

"I wasn't. It's your job to keep yourself informed. I'm not your secretary."

"Could have fooled me. You'd look ravishing in a pencil skirt." Hunter snapped his jaw in a biting motion, contributing absolutely nothing to the conversation, as per usual.

"Andrew spent the morning hopping from one morning show to the other," Devon pointed out. "He's cooking something up."

"No doubt," I agreed.

"Is Sam on the case?" Hunter asked. My baby brother had no idea who Arrowsmith was or what history we shared. But like all Fitzpatricks, he could smell trouble from miles away and had the natural-born killer instinct to squash it.

"Not yet." I glanced at my watch. "I want him to make the first move. See what he's got before I destroy him."

My PA knocked on the door. She entered gingerly, wearing a hot pink blazer over what looked like a bra, her platinum hair reaching her calves.

"Mr. Fitzpatrick?"

"Ms. Brandt. Is it Halloween?"

She sloped her head in confusion. "No."

"Then don't dress like it. What do you want?" I laced my fingers together.

She blushed, clearing her throat. I had to admit Persephone had a point. Casey looked like a corporate secretary like I looked like a One Direction dropout.

"Sorry to interrupt, it's just that you haven't answered my last six emails regarding the engagement and wedding rings."

The rings.

I had to choose wedding and engagement rings. Naturally, I had more pressing issues to deal with, such as Andrew Arrowsmith and finding a new edgeless pool for my Palm Spring property.

I speared my brother with a glare.

"What kind of diamonds does she like?"

"How the fuck should I know?" Hunter laughed. "I hang out with the chick. I don't choose pantyhose and earrings with her at Bloomingdale's."

"Ask your wife."

"Ask your fiancée," he countered, kicking my shin under the desk.

"That would require me to talk to her." I pressed my foot over his, applying enough force to hear his toes crack. "I have no desire to do that."

Hunter stared at me like I was clinically insane.

"How am I supposed to answer something like that?" He turned to Devon, waving a hand in my direction. "I can't believe he's marrying my wife's best friend. What's gonna happen if I have to murder him? Will representing me be a conflict of interest for you?"

"Yes," Devon said simply, smoothing his tie. "Regardless, I don't practice criminal law. Don't like to get my hands dirty. May I make a suggestion?"

"No," I said, at the same time Hunter crowed, "For the love of God, please do."

"Go with the most expensive option," Devon instructed. "The answer to every question concerning a woman's taste in jewelry is to go with the expensive option. Works like a charm every Christmas." He snapped his fingers.

"Not with Persephone." Hunter shook his head. "She's picky and particular. Both Penrose sisters have strong personalities. That's why they get along with my wife."

He said that like it was a *good* thing. Christ.

Casey was shifting her weight from one impossible stiletto heel to the other, glancing among the three of us, waiting for an answer.

Deciding we'd spent enough time pondering the matter, I sealed the deal.

"Get all of them."

"Sorry, sir?"

THE *Villain*

"The rings the jeweler has sent. Get her all of them. She can choose, alternate, gift some to her annoying friends, donate to charity, wipe her ass with them. I don't care."

"You mean buy her all eight rings the jeweler has flown here from Mumbai overnight?" She blinked, staring at me as though I grew an extra head and attempted to cover it with a decorative fruit bowl. "They cost half a million apiece."

"And…?" I screwed my fingers into my eye sockets. Peopling was by far more exhausting than running a marathon.

"And nothing. It will be done, sir."

With Stripper Barbie out of the way, I turned back to my brother and lawyer, ready to continue our conversation about Arrowsmith. They both glared at me with a look not much different than the one I saw on Ms. Brandt's face.

"What now?" I barked.

"You could've just gone with any ring," Devon muttered. "Yet you chose *all* of them."

All and nothing were the same things. Essentially, I *still* didn't make a choice.

"What's your point?" I demanded.

"His point"—Hunter grinned, snatching his coffee from my desk and standing—"is that you, my dear brother, are about to get punched right in the feels. Bubble-wrap that black heart of yours because shit's about to get real, and I'm going to grab a front-row seat when you finally realize you are not the soulless bastard you think you are."

"Save me a place next to you." Devon fist-bumped my brother.

I kicked them both out.

Idiots.

Ten

Persephone

AFTER A MONTH OF BEING IGNORED BY THE GROOM EVERY time I called and texted him, I showed up to my wedding tucked in a black limo with Belle and Sailor in tow.

It was a surprisingly sunny day. Especially considering winter bled into spring, and the persistent rain refused to relent in what the local weathermen described as Boston's longest and gloomiest winter to date.

Since I was the one doing all the planning, I made sure the wedding was tailored to my personality and preferences alone.

Despite the fact Aisling had told me Cillian hated fruit in his dessert, the cake was a six-tier chiffon sponge cake frosted with white chocolate and decorated with pomegranate. The venue was St. Luke's, the Protestant church I'd attended since birth even though I knew Cillian was raised Irish Catholic.

I wore a sheath, pearl-hued gown and had enough hairspray to put a dent in the ozone layer. I felt ridiculously flammable and gave myself a mental memo not to get close to smokers and candles.

With the clear intention to signal my future husband I was not to be tamed, I chose wildflowers for my bouquet.

I decided on having a church service only. No party. No big

THE *Villain*

hurrah. My feelings toward Kill were as strong as ever, but I wasn't going to do all the work for him. If he wanted a successful marriage—which I doubted he did—he was going to have to put in the effort, too.

A part of me doubted Cillian would even show up to the wedding. After all, he went back to ignoring my existence quickly after I accepted his offer. If it weren't for Devon, or the realtors, bankers, jewelers, and personal shoppers he sent my way, fawning over me, I'd think he'd gotten cold feet.

Should've known better.

Cillian Fitzpatrick never got cold feet.

It was everything else about him that was made of ice.

I sat in the limo in front of the church. Mom and Dad came from the suburbs. They were disoriented by my shotgun wedding but happy, nonetheless. They knew how hurt I'd been over Paxton and figured I decided to marry my good friend Aisling's older brother because we'd always had this amazing, nurturing connection.

That was the story I fed them, anyway, and that was the version they chose to eat up. Dad, who had just recovered from a knee surgery, couldn't walk me down the aisle.

I'd found it to be an omen more than a coincidence. I'd asked Hunter to do the honor of giving me away ("Personally, I'd prefer to hand you over to Vlad the Impaler, but I'm too scared for my life to deny Kill anything").

"Knock, knock." Ash's thin, church bells voice rang in the air. She flung the door to the limo open and slid in, wearing a blood-red bridesmaid dress.

"Hey." I mustered a smile, realizing I was clutching Belle's hand in mine a bit too tightly. I let go before my sister's hand needed amputated due to gangrene.

Ash handed me a crown of wildflowers.

"A good luck charm for the bride. A Fitzpatrick tradition."

"Is this from Kill?" My eyebrows shot up. I thought about the poisonous flowers he'd plucked from my hair all those years ago. Ash shook her head, turning a shade of maroon that went well with her dress.

"My bad. I should've clarified. *I* made it for you. It's an Irish custom that the bride braids the crown in her hair on her own. Brings good luck to the marriage."

"My hair is harder than a rock right now," I pointed out.

"Is this bitch for real?" Belle snatched the flowered tiara from Aisling's hands. "Sis, you need all the luck you can get. You're putting this thing on if it's the last thing you do. And while you're at it, here." Belle dropped the tiara in my lap, rummaging in her clutch. She found an orange bottle of pills, took one, and shoved it into my mouth.

"What's that?" I murmured around the tablet.

"A little pick-me-up."

I swallowed, weaving wisps of my hair into the crown of flowers while Belle put a glass of champagne to my lips.

"The church is jam-packed. All the pews are filled to the brim." Aisling crawled into the back seat as we waited for the event coordinator to call us out. "Sam locked the church doors on Kill, another Irish tradition to make sure the groom doesn't run away, and Hunter slipped a sixpence into his shoes. Kill *wasn't* happy."

"When is he ever?" Sailor sassed, making the three of them burst into laughter.

I glanced out the window up at the sky. There was only one lonely cloud.

Auntie Tilda.

I grinned. My late aunt worked in mysterious ways, but she couldn't pass up coming here today.

"I can't believe I'm getting married again," I whispered to her more than to anyone else.

"It's not too late to change your mind," Sailor reminded me. "Really. Ask any Julia Roberts movie out there."

"Cut it out," Belle warned our redheaded friend. "We're going to give the asshole the benefit of the doubt, at least for today."

THE *Villain*

"You're right." Sailor rubbed at her nose. "Sorry, Pers."

The event coordinator shoved her head past our open window.

"We're all set. My God, you look like a movie star, Persephone. Hunter is waiting for you by the church's doors. He is the person giving you away, correct?"

"Actually," Belle piped, lacing her arm in mine, "we're *all* going to give her away."

"Reluctantly." Sailor laughed.

And so I walked down the aisle with a herd of my friends and family, feeling loved, cherished, and protected.

Just not by the man I was marrying.

After weeks of not seeing him, his presence hit me like a wrecking ball.

Everything about Cillian standing in a full tux in front of a minister reminded me why I'd been pathetically obsessed with him before Paxton.

Why giving him up had been the hardest thing I had to do.

He was tall, dark, and commanding, dripping untamed power and magnetism money couldn't buy. He stared directly at me as I walked down the aisle, clutching my bouquet in a death grip. A live band began playing "Arrival of the Queen of Sheba" by Handel. The guests stood, whispering and murmuring. Aisling was right. There were hundreds of people in this place, and most of them, I didn't know.

That was when it hit me.

Cillian didn't ignore the wedding.

He simply ignored *me*.

He sent out invitations promoting the idea of him being a family man.

Bastard even chose a song for me to walk to the chapel.

In other words, he was involved in all the parts that mattered to him, and I wasn't one of them.

My heart jackhammered, and my mouth dried around the rich tang of champagne.

My eyes flicked to his golden-specked ones. He looked calm, serene, utterly unaffected.

"Did he tell you he doesn't have any feelings? He takes pride in that."

Sailor's voice drifted back into my memory.

He did. Multiple times.

Still, I wanted to whack him with my bouquet and yell at him to feel something while swearing his alliance to me.

I stopped in front of him, certain the imprint of my heart could be seen through my dress every time it slammed against my rib cage.

Minister Smith began the ceremony. My eyes dropped to Kill's lips, which were pursed in mild displeasure.

Those lips were going to meet mine in a few moments for the first time.

A dream come true for eighteen-year-old Persy.

A travesty for twenty-six-year-old me.

Minister Smith finished his part, then paused, clearing his throat. "Before we proceed, the groom has a few words he wants to say."

He does?

Never had I wanted to throw up more than the moment Kill Fitzpatrick gazed down at me with an easy smile, producing a dove-white ribbon from his breast pocket.

"Love is a fickle emotion, Persephone my dear. Fortuitous, unreliable, and prone to changes. People fall in and out of love at the drop of a hat. They get divorced. They cheat. They get cheated *on*."

My eyes bugged out of their sockets. Was my soon-to-be husband aware he was standing in a *church*? I half-expected him to burst into flames in front of my eyes, swirling into dark smoke, descending straight to hell where he belonged.

Kill began fastening the ribbon over both our right hands with confident expertise.

"The thing is, you can't rely on love. Which is why I intend to offer you something far more consistent. Commitment, friendship, and loyalty. I promise to give you my protection, no matter the price." He proceeded to tie our left hands together with the same ribbon, locking us to one another tightly. His words sounded genuine yet reticent. Dry, but somehow real. "I will never turn my back on us. We will fall in and out of love many times, but I promise to find my way back to you. To put us back together even when the temptation to break things off is too much. And when love feels far away…" He pressed his forehead to mine, his lips moving over mine. "I will bring it right back to our doorstep."

Our hands were firmly tied together. We stared at each other.

Too close.

Too intimate.

Too exposed.

Our guests stared, wide-eyed, in shock and awe. My mouth hung open, a mixture of fascination, surprise, and most dangerous of all—sheer bliss swirled in my chest.

"This is…beautiful." The reverend let out a breath. We said our vows. I didn't puke, despite wanting to, bad. "I pronounce you husband and wife. You may now kiss the bride. God knows you want to." He chuckled, making everyone in the church erupt in wild laugher.

Cillian tugged me using our bandaged hands, jerking me into his firm body. He dived down with eyes that turned from calm, rich gold to smoldering, molten lava. My breath caught in the back of my throat as he crushed his lips over mine with devastating warmth, bringing our hands to his chest and lacing our fingers together. His lips were possessive, demanding; his almost-familiar fragrance of dry cedar and shaved wood made my knees weak.

"Kiss me back," he growled.

He pulled our tied wrists, righting me back up to my feet. I slid limply over his body, too dazed to function. Kill deepened our kiss, devouring me, opening his mouth and connecting his tongue with mine. It was deliberately rough, and heated, and sexy, and *new*. I'd never been kissed this way before. The claps, whistles, and cheers drowned under the white-hot desire washing over me. I forgot where we were and what we were doing. All I cared about was the demanding pressure from his delicious mouth, and the way our hearts rioted in unison, beating wildly against one another.

I felt his smile on my lips as he withdrew slowly. Calculatingly. I blinked, still drugged from the unexpected kiss that screamed things I didn't dare whisper. But when I looked up, he was the same cold and detached monster.

Icy, poker-faced, and completely out of reach.

I glanced unsurely at the pews.

The entire back row was full of photographers, journalists, and cameramen, recording the tender moment we shared.

The speech.

The hand-fastening.

That *kiss*.

They weren't for me. They were for *them*. Lies, carefully designed to fit Kill Fitzpatrick's new narrative: a loving husband. A changed man. A reformed villain.

I stumbled backward, twisting my wrists around the tight knot, trying to escape him.

"Now now," he whispered under his breath. "You're not going to get the fairy tale, Flower Girl, so you might as well sell it to other people. Smile big."

"You're not my Prince Charming," I blurted out, my thoughts going back to the conversation I'd had with my sister in her car the night I told her about my engagement. "You're the villain."

"Fear *is* my greatest asset." He tipped his head down, pretending to nuzzle my throat, his hoarse, low baritone reverberating deep inside me. "But what are villains, my dear wife, if not misunderstood heroes?"

THE *Villain*

Even though I decided against throwing a party, there was a grand dinner hosted at Avebury Court Manor in honor of my sham marriage.

I'd met Jane and Gerald Fitzpatrick countless of times before. I'd been to their mansion practically every week for my takeout night with the girls. But save for the dinner in which we broke the news, this was the first time I was there as their eldest son's bride and not the timid, polite friend of their daughter's.

I could tell by the courteous smiles and awkwardness that they knew this wasn't a love match. Jane glanced at me almost apologetically while Gerald kept checking on me as though he was sure I would bolt out of their house the minute they looked away.

My own parents were dazzled by the luxury the Fitzpatricks lived in. Dad drooled over the fifteen-car garage, and I was pretty sure Mom was on the verge of making sweet love to the kitchen tiles. Both were awestruck by the butterfly garden Gerald had created for his wife, probably to remind her she was trapped in this marriage forever.

Conversation between the families was stilted. Gerald, my dad, and Cillian did most of the talking, filling the uncomfortable silence with safe topics such as the Boston Celtics, street food, and past legendary athletes. I shoved my food around on my plate, occasionally answering a question aimed my way.

Being ignored by Cillian while he wasn't mine was devastating.

But being ignored by him when I was his wife was going to be soul-crushing.

In the past few weeks, I'd been pampered beyond belief. Had a stylist arrive at my apartment with three sets of wardrobes. I'd received an obnoxious number of engagement rings, was moving into a brand-new apartment, and had my Paxton and debt problems taken care of.

But nothing—other than having Byrne and Kaminski off my back—was worth the sacrifice of my freedom to someone who didn't truly want me. Only wanted my womb and my ability to raise his children.

When dinner was over and we kissed and hugged everyone goodbye, Cillian led me by the small of my back to his Aston Martin, opening the door for me while everyone stood at the door, waving goodbye. He was the image of a perfect gentleman.

During the drive, I kept silent. I wasn't sure what pissed me off more—the fact he acted like he cared in front of the cameras and our families, or that I was stupid enough to buy it.

Probably the latter.

"The wedding went smoothly," Kill observed, his eyes on the road as the vehicle skidded through the pastoral neighborhoods of Back Bay. The evening frost bit at my skin; the sunny weather of the morning was replaced with dark gloom.

A chill ran down my spine. He was my Hades, and I came to him willingly.

"I'm glad you think so." I looked out the window with my arms folded over my chest. I hunted the sky for a cloud, desperate to see Auntie Tilda again, but all I saw was a consistent blanket of black velvet.

"Is the apartment to your satisfaction?"

"Tonight will be my first night there," I answered curtly. "I'm sure I'm going to love it."

Why wouldn't I? It was in the most exclusive building in Boston. With five-star hotel amenities, a chef's kitchen, Subzero appliances, heated flooring, and Italian-imported furniture.

And…I couldn't care less.

About any of it.

If anything, I was bummed I couldn't stay at Belle's, where at least I'd have her body heat against mine every morning when she crawled into bed. Where I had conversation, and happy moments, and weekends making food in the tiny kitchenette with a glass of wine.

I hated everything about this conversation with my husband.

The clinical politeness.

The lack of intimacy.

How I now knew what his lips felt like.

"Why did you ask the orchestra to play 'The Arrival of the Queen of Sheba?' Why not 'Bridal Chorus?'" I blurted out.

"I don't like Wagner."

"Because he is loved?" I teased.

"No, because he was a Nazi," he answered plainly.

I shot him a sidelong glance, surprised.

"Interesting."

"Not particularly. You may want to broaden your pool of interests."

Turning toward him fully, I smirked.

"So you don't consume products that are loosely connected to racism. By that logic, you don't drive a Ford, wear Hugo Boss, or use Kodak products."

"I drive an Aston Martin, wear Kiton and Brioni, and no to using Kodak."

"Careful, hubs, or I'll suspect you have a soul."

"Nobody has a soul. What I have is a few working brain cells and loose principles."

"Nobody has a soul?" I echoed, dumbfounded. "I know you don't believe in feelings, or God, but you don't believe in *souls*, either?"

"Do you?" He took a smooth turn into our neighborhood. We lived only a few blocks away from each other.

"Of course," I said, incredulous.

"Where is it then?" His amber eyes were still on the road. "Your soul. Anatomically."

"Just because you can't see something doesn't mean it's not in existence. Take air, for instance. Or intelligence. Or *love*."

"The fact you shove the L-word into every conversation says a lot about you, you know."

"There are no facts, Cillian my dear. Only interpretations."

It was his turn to shoot me a disbelieving look.

"Nietzsche."

"I married a nihilist." I ran a hand over the soft satin of my gown. I'd spent the past few weeks reading everything Nietzsche and Heidegger like my life depended on it. "The least I could do before saying I do was to take a tour in that mind of yours. Understand your moral compass."

"I have no morals. That's the point of being a nihilist."

You boycott companies and people because once upon a very long time, they stood for something you strongly disagreed with. You are nothing but morals.

Of course, pointing that out was only going to make us argue more. It was best to make him find out for himself that he wasn't the asshole he thought he was.

He took a turn to my street and parked in front of my apartment building. A doorman stood at the entrance. I put my hand on the door handle, drawing a breath before shoving it open.

"*Persephone.*"

I whipped my head around, my eyes clinging to his face.

"We still haven't discussed the conception part."

"There's nothing to discuss. You can start taking my calls. Better yet—call *me* when you're ready to start trying. We can hit the road running and get pregnant by summer."

I wanted children with all my heart. Was always the girl who tucked her dolls into little plastic strollers while her sister climbed on trees and skateboarded with the boys.

All I ever wanted was a family of my own. Babies and matching plaid jammies and elaborate Christmas trees with handmade decorations.

"What are my chances of convincing you to go the IVF route?" Kill asked, businesslike.

"Nonexistent," I said flatly. "We have a deal."

THE Villain

"Fine. I'll have someone send over ovulation tests. Call me when you're ready."

"That's a no from me."

"Excuse me?" He whipped his head in my direction. Did I finally manage to anger him? Probably not, but at least he didn't look his cool, dead self for a moment.

"I don't want to take tests. I like the element of surprise." I shrugged, deliberately provoking him.

"Is there a point to having sex if you are not ovulating?" To his defense, he tried. Tried to cling to the remainder of his calm with everything he had. But I intended to snap it.

"There is," I replied sunnily.

"Do share it."

"I'll orgasm."

For the first time in my life, I saw *the* Cillian Fitzpatrick blushing. I could swear it. Even in the dim light cast by the streetlamps, I noticed his face turning a shade I'd never seen on him before. His mouth pressed in a hard line.

"Sexual favors weren't a part of our negotiation."

"Sue me." I threw the passenger door open but didn't get out just yet. "Look, if you don't want to touch me this much, don't bother. You don't *have* to sleep with me, Kill. But if you want me to give you a baby, that's the route you'll have to take. And another thing." I turned to him. I could tell he was shocked by my bold behavior. He was counting on a watered-down version of his sister. And to an extent, I was exactly that person—romantic, sweet, always willing to help.

But I knew damn well that with Kill, I had to fight back if I wanted to earn his respect, his trust, and a place in his life.

He stared at me, cracking his fingers under the stirring wheel.

"You, my darling husband, kiss like a hungry Rottweiler."

No response.

"You really need to work on your tongue-to-lips ratio. And you use way too much saliva."

He *continued* staring at me, ridiculously unmoved.

C'mon. Feel something. Anything. Anger! Wrath! Disgust! I'm insulting you.

"I guess I can teach you." I let out a sigh.

"Hard pass."

"But you—"

"Drop it, Persephone. In order to insult me, I'll first have to value your opinion, and as established five minutes ago, I don't value *anything*."

"Your loss."

"Never heard any complaints."

"Of course you haven't!" I got out of his car, slamming the door in his face. "You don't pay them to grade you. Good night, hubs."

Turning around, I walked away, feeling his eyes on me the entire time.

I entered my new golden cage, knowing full well that for all its gilded beauty, it was, after all, still a cage.

Eleven

Cillian

THE THREE WEEKS AFTER MY WEDDING DAY WERE LITTERED with *almosts*.

I *almost* called Persephone when the urge to go to Europe and satisfy my needs torched my blood. It was nothing short of a miracle I'd managed to take care of business in my shower with a hand propped over the mosaic tiles, rubbing one out like a crazed teenager.

I *almost* drove straight to her apartment when I spotted Sailor prancing around my office with her tiny baby bump, bringing Hunter lunch and finally looking like an expectant mother and not like a six-year-old scrawny boy who had an extra serving of Brussels sprouts.

I *almost* texted my wife when I saw a paparazzi picture of her in a local gossip column Devon had sent me in which she headed to a hot yoga class with her sister clad in tight yoga pants and a sports bra.

And I *almost* used her as a consolation prize this morning when I arrived at the office to find a billboard the size of a goddamn building—one that was directed to my office window—with my face on it, fake blood dripping from the corner of my mouth.

The #1 Western World Villain is here to kill the polar bears
And your planet.

Goddamn Andrew Arrowsmith.

Every time I was about to make a move, I remembered how she deliberately tried to anger me the night I dropped her off at her new apartment.

Everything about my wife was messy, annoying, and inconvenient. The worst part was that somehow the docile little creature had managed to put me at a spot of disadvantage.

In order to impregnate her, I needed to see her.

Which I very much didn't want to do.

The ball was in my court, and I wanted to kick it across the world where I wouldn't have to see or hear her. Where I wouldn't have to *taste* her.

I was struggling to remember what made me agree to stay celibate.

I was even more puzzled by the fact I had kept my word.

With a trip to my mistresses firmly off the table, I drowned myself in work while trying to think of loopholes of how to impregnate her without touching her. She and I had very different ideas of what sex should entail, and tarnishing her with my filthy hands and mind was not something I was willing to entertain.

My phone danced across my office desk.

"Devon." I hit the speaker button. "To what do I owe the displeasure?"

"I'd say to being a world-class cunt and collecting enemies around the globe like they were Royal Mail stamps."

"I pissed someone off," I concluded.

"Correct."

"You'll need to specify."

"Look out your window."

"Already did. Not my best picture, but I just redirected three mill to PR and advertising to buy this spot—and all the others in the city—and replace it the moment Andrew's lease is done with positive ads."

"The sodding billboard is nothing. Your old mate, Andrew Arrowsmith, went for a grander gesture to profess his hate for you. Look *down*."

THE *Villain*

I sauntered to my floor-to-ceiling window. There was a demonstration outside the Royal Pipelines' building.

No. Not a demonstration. Complete chaos, consisting of hundreds of activists waving Green Living flags and holding *Strike for the Climate* signs and giant cardboard prints of the melting Arctic.

Some of them marched with enlarged printouts of penguins standing on melting icebergs, starving polar bears with ribs poking out of their fur, and various dead oceanic animals smeared in oil.

I took a deep breath. I knew my pulse would stay in control. It always did.

"How did I not know about this?"

"It's a spontaneous demonstration. They didn't clear it with the police. It'll disperse in the next hour or so. I already made some calls."

"And where is Arrowsmith?" I gritted out.

"Town hall." The soft click of Devon's smart shoes told me he was walking somewhere and fast. "He's filing a public lawsuit against Royal Pipelines for drilling exploratory wells in the Arctic. He wants them shut down."

"How worried am I?" I grabbed my laptop, getting ready to go down to the fourth floor and rip my legal team a new one for not smelling this from a hundred-mile radius.

"Considerably. You own the land, but Andrew is suggesting some amendments to international laws," Devon admitted. "What's your game plan?"

"Make him lose his pants by prolonging the trial until Green Living won't be able to afford a package of lettuce," I said right off the bat.

"That'd stall him, not stop him." Devon sounded thoughtful. "I'm on my way. Meet me on the fourth floor."

I stormed out of my office, passing a desperate Casey, who flailed on her heels, trying to chase me down to figure out what I wanted for lunch.

Andrew's head on a platter.

"Kill?" Devon asked on the other line as I punched the elevator. "Arrowsmith made a bloody good move. We might need to negotiate."

"I don't negotiate with terrorists."

Besides, I knew Andrew didn't give two damns about the polar bears or fluffy snow foxes. If anything, he must've known drilling the Arctic wasn't half as dirty and controversial as hydraulic fracking, also known as Royal Pipelines' method of choice until I came into the picture.

He was after the Fitzpatricks.

Me, specifically.

Unfortunately for him, I had two rules:

1. I never shied away from a good, gory war.
2. I always won.

After an urgent meeting that bled into late afternoon, I took the elevator back to the management floor.

Devon and my entire legal team had advised me to bide my time, stay silent, then release a public statement in a few weeks' time, indicating Royal Pipelines would cease its exploration in Arctic water due to insufficient quantities of petroleum.

In other words, I was asked to retreat and wave the white flag on the grounds that going to war made my knees look bloated as opposed to because I was afraid of losing to Andrew Arrowsmith.

Little did they know, I *never* lost.

I wasn't angry or unruffled, but I definitely wasn't in a giving mood. Just because I didn't feel didn't mean I was immune to a bad temper. Andrew was trying to screw me over, and I did not appreciate the way he went about it.

THE *Villain*

I sauntered past Hunter's glass office, pausing when I realized he had company.

Sailor sat on his desk, throwing her head back and laughing. Emmabelle was there, too, in heels more fitted for a drag show and a red leather skirt. She probably frequented the same shops as Ms. Brandt.

Then there was my *wife*.

Persephone wore a designer black chiffon dress with silver stars, swinging a new pair of Gucci boots as she sat on the edge of Hunter's desk, sucking on a lollipop.

She moved like a siren gliding out of the water. Healthy, radiating, and happy. At least a few pounds heavier than she was at our wedding. The extra weight gave her curves and arches that would make the Pope's mouth water.

My wife was glowing, content, and gorgeous.

And it made me want to *strangle* her.

She was living the life while I picked up the tab. New apartment, new wardrobe, cleaners, and meal kit services, plus a full staff waiting for her to snap her fingers and tell them what to do. She still hadn't fulfilled her part of our bargain.

I got a raw deal, and if there was one thing I wasn't—it was a bad businessman.

Smoothing a hand over my waistcoat, I walked over to Hunter's office and opened the door without knocking.

"Hey, bro." Hunter looked up from something he showed the women on his phone, still smiling. "'Sup? You look like someone pissed in your soup."

Ignoring him, I moved toward Persephone, who stiffened the minute I entered the room. I leaned down and kissed her cheek, watching the color rising on her porcelain-grained complexion.

"Kill," she said, bizarrely surprised by bumping into me in my *own* office building. Was she expecting me to run my meetings at the local Chuck E. Cheese?

"How have you been?" I asked coolly.

"Great."

I bet, sweetheart.

"May I have a word?"

She looked around us, hesitating as though I'd pounce on her. We both knew we had the opposite problem.

"Is the honeymoon phase over?" Sailor raised a ginger eyebrow. "Oh, that's right. Kill didn't take Persy on a honeymoon."

"Don't make me take off my earrings." Belle stepped toward me, folding her arms. "Kill will *get* killed if he messes with my baby sister. I've already told him that."

That's right. Emmabelle paid me a visit shortly after news of my engagement to her sister broke. I still mourned the ten minutes I had to listen to her rambling.

First, she'd offered herself as a bride if I'd let her sister go. It had obviously been a test, meant to see if I'd wanted Persephone specifically, or any woman with a uterus and of good health. When I'd told Emmabelle my interest in touching her rivaled my desire to step on every piece of Lego in North America barefoot, she'd proceeded to make idle threats and flex her nonexistent biceps, bullying me with bodily harm.

I'd stared at her impatiently for the duration of her speech, then sent her back to where she came from.

However much I disliked both my sisters-in-law, they seemed completely unaware of what went on in my marriage, and that was good news. It meant that Persephone had kept her mouth shut. Sure, Hunter, Sam, and Devon were privy to the truth—I uttered it aloud in front of them that poker night—but they were my allies.

My wife hopped from Hunter's desk, sticking the red lollipop back into her mouth.

"All right, hubs. Make it quick."

I led her to my office, then continued into the private en suite, where the walls weren't glass, and no one could see us.

I closed the door behind us, then fixed her with a look.

"What are you doing here?"

"Having lunch with friends." She popped the sucker out of her mouth. The scent of watermelon filled the air, making my dick stir. "Having a good day, hubs?"

"Not particularly."

"Yeah, I saw in the local news about the demonstration." She scrunched her little nose, which I sincerely hoped my future kids were going to inherit. "That billboard up there isn't your best angle, either."

I stared at her, not sure why I called her in here. I had nothing to say to her. Yet the need to monopolize her time burned in me. *I was the one who deserved her attention.*

I got her out of trouble.

I paid for her newly indulgent lifestyle.

I was the one she should be spending time with.

You don't want any of these things, you moron.

"What you're doing in the Arctic is…" She put a hand to her chest.

"Terrible?" I finished for her with a smirk.

"*Monstrous.*"

"Cry me a river."

"You'll probably find a way to pollute it, too."

"A bit of loyalty wouldn't kill you, Flower Girl. I'm your husband. Although that's not saying much, considering you divorced the previous one without his consent." I leaned over the granite wall, crossing my legs at the ankles.

Her eyes widened.

"Are you kidding me? You're comparing my divorcing my runaway husband to what you're doing?" The same blaze of fire I saw when we negotiated our terms returned to her eyes, making my semi a full-blown erection. "You're ruining our planet for financial gain. The Earth is not your wasteland. Not to mention, you're driving entire animal groups into extinction. The polar bears and the penguins come to mind."

"I'm sorry you feel that way," I said robotically. A well-rehearsed reply to the same thing I'd heard over and over again.

"No, you're not."

"You're right. I'm not sorry at all. You can't run your car on adorable."

"But I can run it on batteries, thanks to Elon Musk," she dished back, her tone sweet.

"I know women are fond of battery-operated devices, but they're never as good as the real thing."

She choked on her lollipop. I wondered if she had an oral fixation. First the cigar, and now this. It was hard to concentrate when her pink lips were always wrapped around something. Especially when it wasn't my cock.

I could have told her the truth. That the Arctic wasn't a long-term plan. That I had a greener environmental plan to put my hands on natural gas. A futuristic, twenty-second century invention that was in the works. But I didn't much mind to be known as the man who was responsible for ruining the world.

"Why are you really here, Persephone?" I pushed off the wall, advancing in her direction, not stopping until we were flush against one another. While emotions were a liability, getting my wife pregnant was a calling.

The faster we could get it done, the sooner we could cease communication.

Her delicate throat bobbed with a swallow. She was plastered to the wall, cornered like an animal. She licked her lips, her blue eyes dropping to my mouth.

"Lunch." She stuck to her version. "Why else would I be here?"

I put my arm over her head, crowding her, meeting her eyes. I had a few good inches on her, even with her new heels.

"I think you're here because you owe me something."

"I'm giving you everything I signed on for. I live in the apartment you've designated for me. I'm available to you. I don't remember you picking up the phone and asking to consummate our marriage." She arched an eyebrow.

She had delicate eyebrows. Another thing I wouldn't mind my children getting from her.

In fact, I'd be glad if they took everything from her.

Everything but that bleeding heart.

And that showed you exactly how highly I thought of myself.

"I don't beg," I drawled.

"No one asked you to. But if you want to get into my bed, you'll need to make the required arrangements. It's not too much to ask."

She made sense, and that worried me because usually, I was the pragmatic person in the conversation. *Any* conversation.

"You're here now," I noted.

I wasn't in the mood for sex, but I supposed I had to get it over with at some point.

She beamed around the lollipop, her lips swollen and achingly kissable. "We're not having sex in your bathroom. I have more self-respect than that."

"Are you sure?" I asked, half-sardonic, half-hopeful. "So far, you've acted like a glorified mail-order bride. Bending over the vanity would be well within your typical behavior."

She laughed.

She actually *laughed*.

Flipping her hair to one shoulder, my wife spun on her heel.

"Goodbye, *hubs*."

She strutted her way to the door, all fire, sugar, and temptation. She knew exactly what she was doing, and she did it well. No part of her was meek and naïve now.

Not accustomed to having women leave before verbally excusing them, I watched with fascination mixed with annoyance. I'd never had to figure out how to keep someone close. Usually, my status, power, and fat wallet did it for me.

Watching her leave made me feel as though I'd been robbed of something.

"Persephone," I barked.

She stopped.

"Turn around."

"No."

"Don't make me teach you a lesson."

"Why?" she asked brightly. "I'm a good student. Although I think I'm the one who is giving you a valuable class today. If you want me to stay, you're going to have to ask nicely and not order me around."

My instincts urged me to disregard her. Put her in her place. But that would be acting out of emotions, and I didn't do those. Normal Cillian—*sane* Cillian—would humor her to get what he wanted and then discard her.

Quarreling with her wasn't going to bring me a step closer to triumph. Or to having an heir.

Swallowing down a juicy curse I couldn't believe I *thought* about, let alone could utter, I took a breath.

"*Please* turn around."

She did, slowly. And for the first time, I realized how awful it felt to be at someone else's mercy. The humbleness in my situation made me borderline nauseous.

Knock her up and get rid of her. You'll be the last one to laugh when she is changing diapers and raising your future heirs while you're deep inside a French socialite.

"Would you like to have dinner with me?" I spat out.

"Yes." Her smile was warm like the sun, full of promise. "Tonight okay?"

"Tonight's fine."

"Why don't I cook for us?"

Because it will probably taste horrible.

But these were thoughts I needed to filter at least until my objective was achieved. Not being unbearable was a learning curve.

"I have a private chef. We can also order in."

She shook her head. "Nothing beats a home-cooked meal."

"Where do you think my chef cooks my meals? Not the bathroom," I bit out.

Definitely a learning curve.

She laughed. "Your chef doesn't cook with their heart."

"Fortunately," I scowled, "that would be unhygienic. Any preferences?"

Her eyes traveled down to my crotch. Heat rose up my spine. It was the celibacy. I wasn't used to being dependent on someone else's availability.

Was this what monogamy felt like? No wonder the divorce rate in Western countries was through the roof.

"Don't worry about my preferences. Just let me do the cooking. I have one stipulation."

There were always stipulations with this woman.

But no matter how much I wanted to regret marrying her and not sticking to my Minka Gomes plan, I had to admit Persephone was an aphrodisiac the carnal side of me couldn't refuse.

Her biting beauty, easy wit, and warm personality gave her a regal shine. Like all rare jewels, I wanted her for myself for the sake of having her.

Tucking my hands into my front pockets, I shot her a look.

"Well?"

"I want it to be at your place."

"Done."

I wasn't a sentimental man. Bringing her to my bed wouldn't make me associate said bed with her in it. She wasn't a goddamn safety blanket.

If she thought she was tricking me into developing feelings toward her, she was gravely mistaken.

"See you at seven." She turned away, leaving me with a hard-on, a bad mood, and the uneasy sense I'd just made a terrible mistake.

Getting rid of her just turned from a plan to a necessity.

I needed to remove my wife from my life before she trickled into my system.

Twelve

Persephone

M Y MAIN ISSUE WAS, I DIDN'T KNOW HOW TO COOK.

My second issue was, I actually hoped fixing Kill a home-cooked meal (which was very likely to taste like mothballs) was going to make a difference.

But my third and most pressing issue was the one I concentrated on right now—I was pretty sure I was setting my husband's kitchen on fire.

Maybe it was Karma bitch-slapping me for playing dirty.

Once it had become obvious that Husband Dearest wasn't going to make the first step to see me, I'd decided to drop by his office and milk a dinner date out of him.

I was desperate to form a connection while he was determined to protect my virtue. In many ways, it felt like having an impotent sugar daddy—I got all the perks but not the dick.

The problem was, I *wanted* the dick. The shoes were great, but not so great I wanted to moan their names.

I'd asked that it would be at his place because I wanted to invade his space, rip out his walls, and claw my way into his life. Being married to a man who didn't want me—who actually actively sought ways to get *rid* of me—felt like swimming against the stream. I was

THE *Villain*

exhausted but determined. Because failure meant heartbreak. And because no matter how much Cillian was trying to prove everyone otherwise, I genuinely believed that deep down (and I meant *very* deep, as deep as the rigs he drilled), that thing in his chest was a ferocious monster. Locked, chained, and heavily sedated but very much alive.

"Holy fu...what's that smell?" Petar jogged into the kitchen, grabbing a towel from the counter and flapping it around to clear out the smoke in his path.

Even though we'd agreed on meeting at seven sharp, Kill wasn't around when I got here. Petar, his estate manager, said he was swimming, getting his daily exercise, and would join me shortly.

Despite the fact I prided myself in not having a temper, I had to keep my irritation in check.

"I'm trying to make lemon chicken and risotto." I staggered away from the hissing pot in front of me. "I guess trying is the operative word here."

Petar rushed to my side, turning the stove off. He withdrew the sizzling pan from the stovetop, dumping it into the sink and turning on the faucet. Black smoke rose to the ceiling, setting off the fire alarm around the ginormous kitchen.

The shrieking sound pierced my eardrums, shaking the entire mansion. Petar proceeded to turn off the oven, then open all the windows and the door leading to the backyard. I apologized profusely while he got the small fire under control.

"Remind me why you insisted on making dinner?" Petar waved a kitchen towel in the air, trying to get rid of some of the smoke.

Explaining that ridiculous things found their way leaving my mouth every time I was next to his boss wasn't an acceptable answer. So I went a different route. "I wanted to have a special evening."

"It's special, all right." Petar snorted as he produced his phone from his back pocket.

"I'll call the maintenance guy. See if he can start working on the kitchen tonight if I throw in a few extra bucks." Petar scrolled through his contacts. "Although I gotta say, the boss is not gonna be happy."

"Why am I not going to be happy?" A chilling voice rang behind my back. I turned around, sucking in a breath. My husband stood at the doorway, not even a foot away from me, freshly showered and shaven, his dark chocolate hair damp and tousled. The simple white V-neck and sweatpants clung to his lean body like eager fangirls, and his biceps and forearms were still flush and taut from his workout.

The twinkling golden band on his finger, which I noticed he hadn't removed since our wedding, caught the light in the room, reminding me that at the very least, he was legally mine.

"I burned down your kitchen." I tilted my chin up.

Better not to mince words. Besides, the huge black stain on his ceiling above the stovetop was visible from Africa. Chances were, he didn't need me to spell it out for him.

He studied the stain, his cold, dead eyes returning to mine.

"Deliberately?"

"No."

"Are you hurt?"

The question caught me off guard. I felt my brows bunching. "No."

Kill sniffed the air. He had the maddening ability to do the most mundane things in a sexually charged way. He raised his arm, snapping it in Petar's direction, still looking at me.

"Out."

"Yes, sir."

Petar scurried out, shutting the door behind him. The fire alarm stopped, and the chill from the evening breeze replaced the suffocating smoke.

My husband took a step toward me. A hot whip of pleasure struck my skin at his proximity. I wore something sexy tonight. A champagne-colored pleated dress that barely made it to my thighs paired with Louboutin heels—one out of thirteen new pairs I'd been gifted by my husband.

THE *Villain*

He clasped my chin in his fingers, angling my head up, his eyes honing in on mine.

"What was on the menu?"

"Lemon chicken and risotto."

"What the hell were you thinking?"

I wasn't. I wanted to impress you.

"Maybe I wanted to poison you." I narrowed my eyes.

A ghost of a smile passed his lips.

"The only person you're capable of poisoning is yourself, as demonstrated a few years ago. Even then, you botched the job."

"*Hey*, I did a great job. It's not my fault you saved me."

"I still have my regrets." He gave me a playful shove. I took a step back, my eyes never leaving his.

"Here's the thing. You had your stab at cooking dinner, and you blew it. I have a poker game in a couple of hours. Which means we'll have to skip the first course and get straight to the entrée."

"You scheduled a poker game tonight?" I felt my eyes flaring.

He took another step forward, and I instinctively stepped back. He was cornering me. Trapping me into his cobwebs while I desperately tried to think straight.

"You weren't planning on spooning in front of *When Harry Met Sally*, were you, Flower Girl?" he asked, giving me a mocking pout.

I wanted to tell him to go to hell and stay there for the foreseeable future, but just as I opened my mouth, my back crashed against the kitchen island. Kill grabbed me by the waist, hoisted me up, and balanced me over the marble. The cold surface hit the back of my thighs, and I sucked in a breath, waiting for him to kiss me, to touch me, to do something wild and raw and uncontrolled, the way he did at our wedding.

Instead, he produced a small satchel from his back pocket, tearing it open.

I frowned.

"A condom?"

He *tsked*.

"Lube. As I mentioned before, getting you off is not a part of my job description."

"I'm not a whore." I pushed him off.

"*Sex worker*," he corrected blandly. "Trust me, no one mistakes you for one. If you were an escort, I'd flip you over and plow into you by now."

My face flamed. "You're getting your paid company off?"

"Unfailingly."

"Why?"

"Because it's the right thing to do. And because there is absolutely zero chance of my forming any attachment to them or vice versa. It is not too late for IVF, Persephone. Do the right thing and leave the dirty fucks for the mistresses. You're better than that."

The way he said that dryly with the satchel of lube still dangling between his fingers made me realize he'd planned this all along.

He lured me in here, kept me waiting while I made dinner, then took out the lube to humiliate me. He angered me like I angered *him* at his office. Threw me off balance to put me off the idea of having sex with him.

Cillian wanted me to leave here untouched with a promise to try IVF.

I couldn't help but notice his reason for not wanting to touch me.

I was too good.

Not a mistress.

Not an escort.

A spark of hope ignited in my chest. I was determined to beat him at his own game even though he changed the rules so often he made my head spin.

"Fine." I shrugged, trying my best to appear calm. "You win."

He nodded, stepping back from between my thighs. "I know an excellent fertility expert. Dr. Waxman. I'll see that—"

"No. I meant I'm fine with the lube. Hand it over." I opened my

THE Villain

palm, stretching my arm in his direction. He paused, eyeing me as though this was a test.

When he didn't make a move, I wiggled my fingers. "Go on."

"You won't come," he hissed.

I rolled my eyes, shimmying my panties down my legs. "Let me tell you a little secret, Kill. We women often don't."

"You're stubborn."

"So are you," I answered. "How far are you going to take this thing?"

"A mile further than you will," he assured me. "I never lose, Flower Girl."

"There's a first time for everything."

"Not with me."

"I guess only time will tell. Hand me the lube," I repeated. "Rules are rules, and we had an agreement."

Reluctantly, he disposed the lube in my hand. I squeezed it on my fingers and slid the cold, wet thing into my channel, sucking in a breath at the sudden intrusion. It felt like an OB-GYN exam, and the fact that secretly—*stupidly*—I'd been dreaming about this moment for years, of being with Cillian intimately, made me swallow down a lump of tears.

I spread my legs, allowing my dress to hike up my thighs, exposing myself to him. My husband snuck a quick look between my thighs, his throat bobbing. He looked away, color rising on his sharp cheekbones.

This adamant, fearless creature in front of me told me he was incapable of feelings, but he did feel something now—discomfort. Excitement. Dread.

He stepped forward, settling between my legs, still fully clothed. The air crackled between us, and the fine hair on my arms prickled with anticipation.

I leaned back on my forearms, biting the corner of my lip. He pushed his sweatpants down, his eyes transfixed on an invisible spot behind my head. He was determined not to be present when it happened. Refusing to touch or look at me. He released his cock from his underwear. He was painfully hard and engorged, a pearl of cum on his tip.

At least now I knew our problem wasn't physical attraction.

He angled himself toward my entrance, his wry expression making him look like he was a man on death row, then slid in all the way in one go, filling me to the hilt. His eyes rolled, his gaze drifting to the ceiling as he suppressed a hiss.

I was not only wet—I was *soaked*. My center hot and inviting. I grabbed his cheeks, slanting his face so he'd look at me. His nostrils flared, his lips pursing into a thin line. He didn't move inside me. We both knew it felt too good. Too right. We fit perfectly, and I struggled to maintain control when every muscle in my body shook, threatening to surrender to the acute pleasure rolling through me.

I reached behind my back, tugging at the string that kept my crisscross dress fastened, and let it loose. The fabric fell at the front, exposing my heavy breasts.

Cillian's breath hitched. He looked away again at the wall, pulling out, then driving into me once.

Thrust.

Thrust.

Thrust.

His movements were measured, controlled, designed to hold back. He wasn't here. Not really.

"Nice kitchen," I commented, making idle conversation. I refused to allow him to forget I was in the room as he sank into me. As my muscles involuntarily squeezed around his heavy hardness, begging him for more. Tremors danced along my skin. "Did you get it remodeled recently?"

He grunted, squeezing his eyes shut and driving into me again with more force. I let out a moan. I didn't *mean* to take pleasure in this, just as I was pretty sure Cillian didn't *mean* to hit my G-spot.

Regardless, both those things happened, and I felt my thighs quivering around his narrow waist. The hot, pressed-silk of his cock drove me mad, and my mouth watered.

Thrust.

Another whimper escaped me.

"We fit so good," I purred.

He covered my mouth with his palm, looking pained and disgusted with both of us.

Thrust.

I threw my head back, pressing my eyes shut as I felt my breasts bouncing to the pace of his jerks. I hated that I enjoyed it. Hated that I was going to come apart completely unprompted. But I couldn't blame myself. Cillian was a fantasy, and having him inside me was enough to ignite my world and detonate it into a different galaxy all by itself.

Thrust.

"Kill." I licked his palm on my mouth, inserting my tongue between his fingers.

Another exasperated groan from him. He picked up the pace, and I knew he was losing it. Losing the precious control he valued so much. The thing that kept him from taking his own wife to bed. I grabbed one of his hands, putting it on my breast, and clutched the wrist of the hand he still used to shut me up, licking his fingers one by one like the lollipop I had in my mouth earlier today, sucking each of them individually.

Thrust.

Thrust.

Thrust.

The orgasm uncurled in the pit of my stomach, warm and sweet. It slithered down to my legs, up to my chest and arms. Desire licked every inch of my flesh. My muscles tightened. Then he let out a harsh growl, grabbed the back of my thighs, and began plowing into me so hard and fast, I thought he was going to tear me apart.

"Cillian," I cried out, clawing at the marble. He flattened me against the surface, threw my legs over his shoulders, and pounded into me harder, penetrating me deeper, the hand that lay dormant on my breast trekking up to my neck, grabbing it in a vicious hold.

Finally. Out of control.

He invaded me like a Roman army with a ruthlessness that robbed me of my breath, his hold bruising my neck, his hatred toward both of us at that moment scorching my soul.

I felt his hot cum shooting inside me, the violent ripples rolling through his muscled body between my legs.

His head flopped down, his face nestled by his shoulder, turned away from me like a wilted rose on a stem. I let my head drop back to the granite, laughing drunkenly.

I did it.

I made him feel.

Pleasure at the very least, but also anger and frustration and disgust.

A cold whoosh of air stroked the damp spot between my legs. I popped my eyes open, realizing my husband was no longer in the kitchen.

He left.

Straightening up and sitting down, I blinked.

"Cillian?" I looked around.

Mortified, I tied the back of my dress, put on my jacket and panties, and stumbled out of the kitchen, hunting for my husband.

His house was massive, boasting curved hallways, dozens of doors, and a stairway leading to a second floor. It was only my second time inside. Naturally, I'd never gotten an official tour.

I spotted Petar by the entrance, talking to a guy in khaki pants and a blue hoodie with a maintenance company name on it. They were heading toward the kitchen. Feeling like a thief, I tiptoed up the curved stairway before Petar spotted me. The second floor was wide and tall like a cathedral. Cillian's house, much like his parents', was more old-world luxury than the modern, kitschy pads you saw on *Selling Sunset*.

I worked my way through the rooms, pushing each door open halfway until I reached a pair of double doors that were presumably his room. I pressed my palm over the oak, not wanting to intrude, but hating to leave without a sense of closure, either. This was huge. We just had sex.

"Kill?"

No answer.

"Are you okay?"

It occurred to me that maybe he wasn't. Maybe I pushed him too far, too fast.

Maybe you shouldn't have laughed like a nut.

Pushing the doors open, I wandered into the room. It was gorgeously designed with off-white floors and beige walls covered with fantastic art. A balcony bled into an elaborated reading area and an office space with a strategic view of the back garden.

I noticed another set of closed doors. The bathroom. I walked over to them.

I was about to call his name again when I heard it. Pounding. A different kind of thrashing. Nothing like the pounding that happened downstairs, in the kitchen, with both of us sweaty and angry and desperate.

It sounded like a head smacking against the wall rhythmically. Labored breaths seeped from the crack under the doors.

Pressing my forehead to one of the doors, I closed my eyes, taking a deep breath.

"I'm sorry I pushed you," I croaked. And I was. But I was also thrilled that I'd managed to pull something out of him that wasn't indifference.

There was no answer.

"Would you like me to get you a glass of water? Maybe call Petar?"

The *tap-tap-tap* stopped. A second later came his voice.

"Leave."

"I don't want to leave like this." I wringed my fingers in my lap. "Your friends are about to be here, and I—"

"Leave!" he roared like a beast.

Taking a step back, I glared at the closed doors. In the eight years I'd known my husband, he'd never raised his voice to anyone. Not even once.

He threw the doors open, stalking outside, looking like the devil himself. His eyes were dark and hard, the snarl on his face making chills roll down my spine. He had a busted lip, blood gushing out of it.

Since he didn't let me touch him—kiss him, embrace him—I deduced I wasn't responsible for it.

He did that to himself.

He hit himself.

He advanced toward me, quick and efficient. I tripped, nearly falling twice while trying to escape him.

"You got what you wanted. Now get out of my house and don't come back until I call for you. If you don't get out of here in the next five minutes, I'll assume you want to see your husband's true colors and get fucked in front of my friends on the poker table, slowly and all evening, while they watch."

He stopped when I was cornered, flat against his wall. We were so close I could smell the sex on both of us. Cillian grabbed my neck. I felt the tender rings that had already formed around it from when we had sex.

"You think you escaped a bad relationship by marrying me." He flashed me his Lucifer smirk. "You have no idea, Flower Girl. I pay them because fucking me is not a pleasure, it's a job. Now"—he leaned close—"*run.*"

I did.

I fled before he caught me and did all the things he threatened to.

Bolting down the stairs, I took them two at a time. I crashed into Petar on my way out, clutching his shirt breathlessly.

"Can you call me a cab? Please?" My fingers shook around the collar of his shirt. "I'll get the driver." His eyes bulged out.

He was surprised and a little flustered by my state, shoving me out the door as though he, too, was afraid my husband would get to me.

It was only when I was tucked in an Escalade on my way back home that my heart slowed and my mind started working again.

My husband had a deep, dark secret that could ruin him.

Something he was ashamed of.

A weakness I'd almost unveiled.

And tonight, I got very close to finding out what it was.

I tossed and turned in my bed for the rest of the night, going through every emotion in the feelings book. I was angry, scared, worried sick, and vengeful. I hated Cillian for acting the way he did, but I also knew I played a big part of it. He'd always been mean and snarky with me but never cruel. I pushed him, and he felt hunted.

An injured animal thrown into fight-or-flight mode.

A text message lit the pitch-black bedroom. I reached for my nightstand, grabbing my phone. It pained me that I didn't even consider it could be from him.

Hunter: Your husband is an asshole.

Me: Tell me something I don't know.

Hunter: All polar bears are left-handed. Bet you didn't know that.

Hunter: Also, and relatedly, your husband is an asshole who checks his phone every five seconds. Are you guys texting?

Me: No.

Hunter: Weird. He always logs off during poker nights.

Me: Can you do me a favor?

Hunter: What kind? I'm a married man. I know Kill is nowhere near the realms of my perfection, alas, you missed the train.

Me: A—delusional. And B—not even if you were the last man on earth.

Hunter: What's the favor?

Me: Keep an eye on him. See that he is okay.

Hunter: And you care because...?

Me: He is my husband.

Hunter: I thought that was only on paper.

Me: You thought wrong.

Hunter: Other than the phone shit, he looks like the same old Kill to me. Chain-smoking, drinking devil who needs a good hug and a great fuck.

Me: Night.

Hunter: Obvs, silly. x

Cillian had managed to overcome whatever it was that happened to him in less than an hour. That was peculiar. And alarming. But at least I knew he was remorseful enough to check his phone for a message from me.

Guilt was a feeling, after all.

Unless he is checking it for work-related stuff.

When dawn broke over the sky, I padded to my terrace barefoot, relishing the heated floorboards and extravagant French doors. Looking outside, I spotted a lone cloud sailing north.

"What do I do, Auntie Tilda?" I whispered.

She didn't answer.

I picked up my phone to type my sister a text. Ask her if she remembered the days when Auntie took us to the carnival. How delirious with joy we were.

To my surprise, there was a message waiting for me.

A message from a number that had yet to answer all twenty-seven text messages I had sent it while I planned our mutual wedding.

Cillian: It won't happen again.

Even though I knew exactly what he meant, I decided to press where it hurt. Lure him out of his cave a little more.

Me: The sex part, or the part that came after it?

Cillian: The part I'm not proud of.

What was he doing awake at five? Maybe he had trouble sleeping after last night, like I did.

I sat on a recliner on the balcony, rubbing at my forehead.

Me: Still doesn't answer my question.

Cillian: My outburst was out of line.

Knowing he'd been pushed far enough—I'd never heard my husband apologize to anyone—I changed the subject.

Me: My Auntie Tilda, the one who chose my name, told me that every time I see a lone cloud in the sky, she is watching me. There's only one cloud outside now.

After putting my phone on the table by the recliner, I stood and went about my morning. Brushed my teeth, curled my hair, and got dressed, knowing there was no chance my husband was going to grace me with an answer.

When I returned to the balcony table, after flicking the coffee machine on, I noticed my cell screen was lit with an incoming message.

Cillian: Are you on drugs? Sobriety was not a part of our contractual agreement only because I assumed it was a given.

Snorting out a laugh, I typed back.

Me: Look outside. Do you not see it?

Cillian: Your dead aunt on a cloud? No.

Me: She is not ON it. She IS it. Let me send you a pic.

I raised my phone to the window, snapped a picture of the perfectly fuzzy cloud, and sent it over to him.

Me: Well?

Cillian: Nice to meet you, Persephone's aunt. You two look nothing alike.

Me: Who is being cute now?

Cillian: Me, apparently.

Me: Don't worry, I know you're incapable of anything good and moral. Having a sense of humor won't tarnish your wickedness.

Cillian: Is that a hint?

Me: What do you mean?

Cillian: The Arctic drilling.

Did I hate the idea of him drilling holes inside the Arctic to see if he can find oil, ruining an already fragile part of the world? Of course I did. It made me sick to my stomach, to think the man I loved and directly profited from did that. But I also recognized talking about it with him now, when we were starting out, wouldn't make him move an inch. If anything, he'd probably drill in a few more places just to spite me.

Me: It's not a hint. I think my position on the matter is clear.

Cillian: Batteries over SUVs.

I grinned, remembering the sex toys innuendo he'd made at his office yesterday afternoon.

Me: Correct.

Cillian: Look at your garage, Flower Girl.

I made my way downstairs to the building garage.

Sure enough, there was a brand new red Tesla sitting on my apartment's allotted spot.

He bought me a car.

An *electric* car.

The type of vehicle that was supposed to put him out of business eventually.

Not missing what it meant, I typed my husband a reply with shaky fingers.

Me: Thank you.

Cillian: Batteries are for pussies.

Thirteen

Cillian

I managed to successfully avoid my wife for the rest of the week.

That did not stop her from sending me daily text messages about her dead aunt hiding in clouds every time the sky was clear.

The messages, like my prayers to have a sane wife, remained unanswered.

She had suggested we meet up a few times, despite the radio silence on my end.

The thought of seeing her again disgusted me, so I decided not to consider it until I cooled down.

But seven days in, and my traitorous body made no sign of settling down.

The memory of her writhing beneath me burned hotter at night.

Statistically speaking, limiting our encounters to once a week would still ensure a pregnancy within the next few months.

To be on the safe side, I'd created a chart with her potential ovulating dates and decided to alternate the days in which I saw her each week in order to cover all the bases. But I knew next time we met, I would have to do a better job at reeling in the monster inside me.

No part of me had meant to lose control the first time we had sex, but when I saw her naked tits bouncing to the rhythm of my thrusts

THE *Villain*

and her pink, O-shaped mouth hanging open in desire, I'd lost the self-possession I'd clung to like a desperate Belieber meeting her tattooed, acne-ridden hero and came apart.

I blamed her for the mishap. She was the one who insisted I stop visiting my side pieces and deprived me of a chance to rid myself of my animalistic nature.

Luckily (and I used that term very loosely), I had no time to think about my bride. I had a shitstorm to prepare for in the form of Andrew Arrowsmith.

Upon filing the lawsuit, Arrowsmith had sent me a formal letter through his lawyers, accusing me more or less of single-handedly ruining planet Earth. He had made sure the letter would leak to the press, and all the positive news I'd garnered since marrying Persephone, aka Little Angel Baby Jesus, went down the drain.

Andrew didn't stop at that. Blind items about a powerful, Boston-based CEO visiting European prostitutes began to pop up like mushrooms after the rain in the tabloids, and I had no doubt he was the one who fed the journalists these pieces.

He had me followed.

Did his homework. Uncovered my secrets. All of them.

Which was why I'd decided to gather Devon, Sam, and Hunter on my ranch for a weekend of brainstorming, horse riding, and planning the demise of my archnemesis.

Bonus points: going to the ranch would put some mileage between Persephone and me.

We were in my car, heading out of Boston, when Devon said aloud what Sam and I were thinking.

"I'm surprised Hunter agreed to spend an entire weekend away from his missus." He was in the passenger seat next to me while Hunter and Sam sat in the back.

"What can I say? I'm full of surprises." Hunter slouched back, grinning.

"And shit," Sam spat out.

"And yourself." Devon smirked cockily.

Frost covered the narrow, winding road, the same shade as my wife's eyes.

"Dev, can you check Kill's temperature?" Hunter nudged the back of his seat. "He just missed a chance to slag me off, as your people call it. It's unlike him."

"Very few things would make me touch your twat of a brother, and you are *definitely* not on the list," Devon quipped.

Once we parked outside the ranch, my stable boys shot out of the barn like bullets to help us with our suitcases.

Ignoring their toddler-like blabbing, I removed my leather gloves as I made my way into the main cabin. I stopped dead in my tracks when I noticed Sailor's Porsche Cayenne parked in front of the door. I shot my brother a dirty look.

He raised his palms in surrender.

"In my defense, you shouldn't have trusted me. I can't stay celibate for an afternoon, let alone an entire weekend. Everyone knows that."

Sam flicked the back of Hunter's head as he marched in my direction with his duffel bag slung over his shoulder.

I didn't have to ask Hunter if he extended his invitation to his wife's friends and our sister. These women were attached by the hip.

I was glad I didn't care what Persephone thought about my performance in the sack because she was sure to share her final score with her BFFs.

Disinterested in coming face-to-face with my wife, I disposed my bag with Hunter and headed straight for the stables.

Checking on my horses, I fed and brushed their coats, then took them out, one by one, and cleaned their hooves. I sat on a barrel, my back facing the cabin, and got right down to it, still in my pea coat and eighteen karat *F* cuff links.

The air turned chilly by the time I heard the soft sound of hay crunching under boots.

THE *Villain*

Seconds later, she stood in front of me, next to the horse I was tending to, wearing a yellow dress that complemented her blond hair.

She looked like a swan with her long, delicate neck, and her head tilted down in elegant resignation.

My gaze hardened on the horse's hoof.

"What's his name?" She put a gentle hand on its back. The sweetness of her skin drifted into my nostrils, even under the overwhelming stench of the stables.

"Washington." I raised the hoof pick, pointing it at the stalls behind him. "The rest of these rascals are Hamilton, Franklin, Adams, Jefferson, Madison, and Jay."

"The Founding Fathers." She sashayed to the barn, leaning against its wall with her hands tucked behind her back, watching me.

"Congratulations, you just passed a third-grade history exam." I patted Washington's thigh, signaling him to raise his other leg.

"*Fifth*," she corrected with a grin. She was always happy to spar with me.

"I studied abroad," I muttered. All my American history studies were given to me by tutors.

"I know," she said softly. "Unlike our children, who will be staying right next to us until they are old enough to make up their minds about where they want to study."

Uh-huh. You keep telling yourself that, sweetheart.

"Over your dead body, huh?" I groaned, digging deeper into the hoof with the pick.

"No," she said calmly. "Over yours."

My gaze shot up to hers, before returning to my work.

"That's a lot of horses for one man," my wife commented. "They're beautiful, but some of them seem quite old. Gray-faced. Do you ride all of them?"

"Yes. They're all in pristine condition."

I dropped the pick, then grabbed the brush and moved it over Washington's hoof.

"My father gifted me a horse for every year I finished top of my class, starting in middle school."

She strode over to me.

"Isn't being perfect all the time tiring?" Her hand was on my shoulder now. My muscles flexed. I focused on my task.

"What kind of question is that?"

"One I'd like an answer to."

"Is being average boring?"

"No," she replied, no trace of bitterness in her voice. "Then again, I don't think I'm boring at all. I think I'm exactly who I was supposed to grow up to be, flaws and all. My parents always encouraged me to pursue my dream, and my dream was to raise children. Other people's as well as my own."

"Well, I enjoyed the opposite treatment. Everything about my arrival in this world was carefully planned. I came first, and I was male, which meant the expectations from me were complete and utter perfection in all aspects of my life. I knew I was going to carry the Fitzpatrick bloodline, take over Royal Pipelines, continue the lineage. My existence has always had a purpose, and nothing short of excellence will do."

"You're not perfect with me."

"What you witnessed last week was lack of discretion." I cracked my knuckles. "It wasn't pretty."

"No. But we're all ugly in certain parts, and I'm still here."

Because I paid for you.

"Come inside." She ran a hand over my hair, like a mother would. If nothing else, she was going to be good for our children. Better than Jane ever was. "Food's ready."

I took her hand and dropped it gently.

"Not hungry."

"Where are you going to sleep tonight?"

"The master bedroom."

"Where am *I* going to sleep tonight?"

"Any of the six guest rooms. I own this place, so you get first choice."

"I choose your bedroom," she said without missing a beat.

"First choice *other* than my bed," I clarified.

"Our friends will talk," she warned.

"They have the irritating tendency to do that. Everyone knows ours is a sham marriage. No one's going to buy your charade." I stood, leading Washington back to his stall.

After locking the stall behind the horse, I turned around, watching her.

Despite what she thought, I was doing us both a favor. Entertaining her need to make this relationship feel normal would only cause disappointment in the long run. Even if I yielded to the temptation of sharing a bed and the occasional meal with her, she would eventually outgrow the detached arrangement I had to offer her and resent me even more.

"I made a mistake coming here." She tilted her face up, staring at the moon under a star-filled sky. She was so gorgeous at that moment, so uniquely Persephone, that I wanted to ignore all the facts, scoop her in my arms, and fuck her all night.

Watching her from a safe distance—far enough to prevent breathing in her drugging scent or touching her velvet skin—I agreed.

"You did. I will only have you on my terms, Flower Girl."

My wife turned her head to face me.

"That wasn't a part of our contract."

I hitched up a shoulder, giving her the same answer she gave me when I complained about our agreement.

"*Sue me.*"

"The lawsuit is airtight. I read through it several times." Devon passed me a stack of papers the next day over coffee, omelets, and pastries. We sat on the back porch, watching the horses gallop in the field, warming up ahead of the day.

I put my coffee to my lips, skimming through them.

"I've spent an unholy amount on money on the Arctic offshore development. I'm not canning this project because Arrowsmith has a hard-on to see me go bankrupt."

"We won't go bankrupt," Hunter interfered, spooning fig jam to smear it over a warm croissant. My clown of a brother had agreed to leave his wife behind for the duration of the breakfast so we could talk shop. "I looked at the numbers. Stopping the drilling in the Arctic is going to hurt our pocket, but we can take the blow. The capital growth will stop for the next four years, but we will still be making money."

"I'm not here to make money. I'm here to take over the world." I put my foot down.

"You might not have a choice," Devon pushed. "If you lose the lawsuit, you'd have to stop anyway. And have plenty of legal bills to pay, another PR disaster on your hands, and a father who'd kick you out of the CEO position, turn the board against you, and appoint Hunter to run the show. No offense, Hunt."

"None taken." Hunter shrugged. "I don't want to be CEO. You know what this kind of pressure can do to my skin?" He rubbed his knuckles over his jaw.

"We can always think outside the box. And by that, I mean put Arrowsmith in one." Sam lit up a cigarette, not touching any of the food. I doubted he could digest something that wasn't meat, beer, and nicotine.

Devon smiled politely. "I've a feeling I don't want to be here for *this* conversation. Allow me to excuse myself, gentlemen." He stood and walked back into the cabin.

Sam shot me a sidelong glance. The bloodthirsty bastard was always in the mood for breaking spines.

"Regretfully, you can't kill Arrowsmith. The blowback would be huge, all arrows would point at me, and the media would have a field day. Not to mention, Arrowsmith has children."

"When did you grow a conscience and start caring about children?" Sam asked.

"You haven't met the little devils. If something happens to their parents, no one would want to adopt them."

"Fine. He can live. I can still throw my weight around."

"Physical extortion won't get you far." I dropped the papers on the table. "He's got something on me, and I'm waiting to see how he's going to use it. We need to play this carefully."

"What does he have on you?" Hunter leaned forward. "You're disgustingly perfect. Dad's fucking *mo òrga*. What could it possibly be?"

I smiled. "We have to keep it clean. Let's leave it at that."

"In that case, I'm with Whitehall on trying to squash that beef," Sam admitted, tossing his lighter on the table. "He is going ahead with the lawsuit. You can get him in a few months when things calm down. In the meantime, your best shot is finding common ground with Green Living."

"Cillian will never cower." My brother shook his head.

"Retreating is not submitting." Sam stood. "If Kill wants to win this thing, he has to play it smart. This is round one out of many. History doesn't remember the battle. Only the name of the man who threw the final knockout."

Sam wasn't wrong.

What he didn't know was that Andrew Arrowsmith was the last man to throw the punch before we parted ways many years ago.

And this time? I wasn't going to stop until he saw stars.

Fourteen

Persephone

MY HUSBAND DID AN ADMIRABLE JOB OF AVOIDING ME FOR the entire length of our first day at the ranch.

He dodged our meals together, escaped the walk we all did on the trail, and spent long hours with his horses.

Was I disappointed? Yes. Was I going to let it ruin the weekend for me? Hell no. I hadn't gone on very many trips outside of Boston in my twenty-six years, and this was a golden opportunity to have fun with my friends.

For the first time since I'd married Paxton, I wasn't broke. I didn't have to look over my shoulder on the street for fear I'd be ambushed. My life took a turn for the better, no matter how empty it had still felt without Cillian fully in it.

The last day on the ranch, Belle announced she wanted to horseback ride with just us girls.

"But you don't know how to ride." Aisling tilted her head, forever the voice of reason.

Belle shrugged, popping a cherry into her mouth over the breakfast table.

"So? You can teach me. Besides, I've done my fair share of riding in my life, just not bareback." She winked. "Safety first."

"Thanks for ruining breakfast." Sailor saluted to Belle with her orange juice.

"Seriously, though, who goes to a ranch without riding?" Belle wondered.

My sister had a point.

"Cillian won't like it if we use his horses," Ash warned.

"Cillian doesn't like anything," I snapped, a little too harshly.

Sailor snorted into her orange juice. "Preach. I actually think it's a great idea. Not only because it would piss off Persy's husband, but also because an opportunity to ride horses like Cillian's doesn't come often. Each of them costs like 300k or something. Unfortunately"—she patted her rounding belly—"riding is off the table for me. But I'll cheer you on with a bag of Cheetos in hand. Live vicariously through you."

My need to stick it in Kill's face was greater than my fear of mounting a 2,200-pound beast that could break my neck with one wrong move.

"Actually, I agree. I think we should ride," I chirped.

"*Really?*" Everyone at the table turned to me in surprise. I wasn't exactly known for my rebellious streak. I nodded. It was high time I tried new things. And since having a genuine relationship with my husband wasn't going to be one of them, why not take up horseback riding?

"But Cillian—" Ash started.

"I'll handle him." I raised a hand to stop her. "Tell him I held you at gunpoint if it comes to it."

"Well, then." Aisling clapped her hands together. "Let's get changed and meet at the stables in an hour."

I went through the motions of getting changed, then met Ash and Belle outside the barn. Aisling, who'd learned to ride like her two older brothers from infancy, led Hamilton out of his stall by his bridle, patting his brown coat with a smile.

"He's the sweetest out of the bunch. He was my training horse after I graduated from ponies."

"Dang, Ash. That's the whitest thing I've ever heard." Belle checked her ass in her tight riding trousers with her phone camera.

Ash led Hamilton out of the stables and cantered with him. She explained to us the basic anatomy of the horse, the signals, and what they indicated. We bumped into Hunter, Sam, and Devon on our way out of the barn to the trail. The track wrapped around the smoky mountain like a ribbon.

The men strode into the stables just as we got out.

"You're riding, too?" Aisling asked, turning tomato-red as soon as she noticed Sam. True to his Sam-ness, he ignored her existence as he breezed past her.

He wasn't rude to his boss and best friend's baby sister. But there was no doubt he considered her off the menu.

"Bet." Hunter fluffed her hair, popping his gum. "Where's my better half?"

"In the cabin, reading."

"Bomb. The only stud she should be hanging out with while preggers is me. Dev, can you help Belle get on a horse? I'll do Persy."

"I don't need any help," Belle protested.

Devon's eyes ran over my sister as though she was his favorite dessert while a sinister smirk tugged at his lips.

"I like her fire, Hunt." Devon jerked his thumb toward my sister.

"Great," she chirped, "because you're about to get third-degree burns if you keep objectifying me."

"He's not objectifying you." Hunter shook his head. "He's trying to keep you alive. Your ass has never ridden before."

"We have Ash to help us." I squatted down, adjusting my riding boots.

Ignoring my words, Hunter picked me up from the ground like I was a milk crate, carrying me to Hamilton. He untied the reins on the horse, put my boot in the stirrups, and helped me swing onto the saddle, holding my waist.

"Ash is good, but she's not a professional. If I bring you back with as much as a scratch, your husband will make me bleed from places that aren't even on my body."

"He is right." Aisling smiled apologetically. "Both about my horseback riding abilities and about Kill."

"Cillian ignores my existence."

"You're still his," Sam cemented, businesslike. "I don't need to be physically present in my car in order not to want someone to scratch it."

"Tell me he did not just say what I think he said." Belle pointed at Sam, scowling.

Sam stood tall, nonchalant as ever. "So dramatic, Penrose."

"So chauvinistic, Brennan."

After much bickering, we headed to the trail. I shook with anxiety and exhilaration even though Hunter was riding close to me on Jay and often leaned over to pat Hamilton and give me visual and verbal instructions.

Behind us, Belle was on Washington, Sam on Madison, Ash on Adams, and Devon on Jefferson. Devon and Belle seemed to overcome the initial frostiness. They were bantering like old friends, hitting it off instantly, while Aisling tried to strike up a conversation with Sam and got slammed each time.

Twenty minutes into ascending the trail to the mountains. I heard the gallop of a horse behind us. Hunter turned his head and groaned, pointing his finger to his temple like it was a gun, cocking it and shooting himself with a comic *poof!*

"Don't tell me you didn't tell your husband you're riding."

"I didn't tell my husband I was riding." I stared ahead, ignoring the prickle of fear pinching my spine.

Hunter dragged a hand over his face, tipping his head back. "God-fucking-dammit, Pers."

God-fucking-dammit indeed.

Within three seconds, Cillian was riding by my side on Franklin, pushing Hunter out of the way, forcing him to ride behind us.

Everything, from his good looks to his flawless posture, bothered me. His easy movements put us all to shame.

He didn't wear any riding gear. Not even a helmet.

He *did* wear an expression of someone who was dangerously close to committing a massacre.

"The hell do you think you're doing?" His eyes tapered, zoning in on me like a weapon.

"What does it look like I'm doing?" I used the sweetest, most innocent voice in my arsenal.

"Pissing me off."

"Thought you were above human emotions."

"This one seems to be reoccurring every time you're around. You found your calling."

"Ha," I gasped, "so I *am* good at something. And here you thought I was average."

"Hunter." Kill snapped his fingers behind him, his hard stare giving my cheek frostbite. "We're splitting. Lead the group to another trail. I'll help Persephone get back to the ranch."

"No, you won't," I countered, feeling abnormally irritated. I was the mellowest woman in Boston—voted Most Likely to Replace Mother Teresa in my high school yearbook—but somehow, my husband made me feel angrier than Pax ever did even though Pax had screwed me over so hard I'd almost died.

"Last I checked, it's a free country. I'm allowed to ride a horse, *hubs*. Whether you like it or not."

"The country is free, but the horses are not. Hamilton belongs to me, and I don't want you riding him. *Ceann beag.*" Kill turned to his brother again, snarling, "Beat it before I beat *you*."

"Sorry, doll. There's a reason he has a demon in his garden fountain and not a cherub or a fawn. You married Satan, and I don't want the fucker to assign me a room in hell. He'll probably put me in the same cul-de-sac with Hitler and the dude who invented berry-flavored La Croix. I deserve better neighbors. Just following orders."

Hunter pushed two fingers into his mouth and whistled, redirecting our friends to a side trail, leaving Cillian and me on the main one.

Lava simmered in my belly. Every inch of my body charred with humiliation.

How dare he scold me publicly after avoiding me the entire weekend? Our entire *marriage*?

In the back of my head, something else also bugged me. Something completely trivial.

Cillian had a demon-shaped fountain in his garden, but I hadn't seen it before. Not even the day Petar snuck me into the house for a tour when Kill wasn't home.

"I'm getting you off this horse," he said matter-of-factly.

"Why don't we start with you just getting me off? You seem to be having trouble in that department," I hissed out.

"The first and last time I touched you, you came so hard I was worried my dick would have to be removed from you surgically."

"That was accidental." All the blood rushing to my face made me hot and sweaty.

"So was my giving you an orgasm."

"You really want me to hate you, don't you?"

I didn't know what I expected when I married him, but it definitely wasn't this. The hermetic resistance no one could pierce.

"Sailor is not riding," he pointed out.

"Sailor is pregnant."

"As far as we know, you could be, too."

His temper was frayed, and I couldn't figure out why. I'd stayed well away from him the entire weekend. What else did he want? He seemed to be put off by my existence, and I was growing tired of it.

"If I am pregnant, it's at a very early stage."

"All the more reason to be careful."

"Oh, for *fuck's* sake, Kill. Don't give me this bullshit as though you actually care about my well-being." My voice cracked, and I turned to face him, momentarily forgetting I was on a horse.

His nostrils flared, and he let go of his rein to pop his fingers. "Do *not* curse."

"Or else?" My chin felt wobbly, much like my insides. My grip on the reins tightened. "What're you gonna do about it? You're already the worst possible husband a woman could have."

That wasn't exactly true, seeing as Pax was the reigning champion of Worst Husband for this calendar year, but I wanted to hurt him back. To make him feel the way he made *me* feel.

"By the way, are we going to have sex once a month and pray I get knocked up? How're we going to do this thing? Please let me know because I'm starting to realize you haven't thought your genius plan through!"

My voice carried with an echo that ricocheted on the treetops, shaking the ground beneath Hamilton's hooves.

Hushed murmurs seeped from the parallel trail our friends were taking.

"...*my sister!*"

"...*can hold her own.*"

"*I swear to God, if he hurts her...*"

"*She'll hurt him back. You said it yourself, Belle. She's not a kid anymore.*"

Our friends were arguing whether to step in or not.

Now everyone knew we were a mess, and whatever was left of my hope to make this marriage resemble normalcy flew out the window.

"You're being a brat," Cillian said coolly, regaining his composure.

"You're being a *coward*." My teeth chattered with fury.

Hamilton stirred beneath me, his strides jerky and uneven. I ran a hand over my face. "Seriously, if you're going to ignore me for the rest of our lives, just grant me a divorce. I'll pay you back the money, and we'll forget this ever happened."

"Never." His tone turned steely. Punishing. "I'll give you a lot of things, Flower Girl, but divorce won't be one of them."

THE Villain

"That so? I'll tell Sailor, Belle, and Hunter. I'm sure they'd love to know what you roped me into."

"Go ahead." He tapped the side of his boot to his horse, making it go faster. "See how much power other people have on me. You'll find the exact amount is absolutely none."

"So you won't have me, but you won't let me go. Do you just want me to be miserable like you?"

His nostrils flared. He looked like he was about to say something, but of course he didn't. He never did. He never explained himself to me.

"I *hate* you," I screamed, and without thinking, stomped my foot to the horse's side. Hamilton bolted forward in a rage. Before I knew what was happening, I was flailing above the horse, my body suspended over the saddle, bumping against his sides as he sprinted. I yelped, trying to grab the reins, my fingers grasping air.

Shit, shit, shit.

I looked back. My heart was in my throat. I'd ascended the mountain far enough that I knew if I fell from Hamilton, I'd roll down a few dozen feet and get seriously hurt. Break a bone or two, at the very least.

Kill rode beside me, fast and furious, barking instructions at me, but I couldn't hear him over the wind and the adrenaline buzzing between my ears.

Hamilton halted, sloping on his rear legs with a neigh, throwing me off his back.

I tipped over and flew in the air, squeezing my eyes shut and bracing myself for the fall. A sudden, harsh jerk threw me back up and over a horse, my midriff smashing against a saddle.

For a second, I thought I managed to climb back on top of Hamilton, but when I opened my eyes, I saw I was perched on Franklin, my body slung across his back like a potato sack.

Cillian wasn't on Franklin anymore.

I heard a hiss and craned my neck sideways. Kill was behind me, sitting on the ground. He got up, not bothering to clean himself as he darted in our direction, putting his fingers in his mouth and whistling for Franklin to stop.

Cillian limped but picked up his pace in order to reach us.

The horse slowed to a gradual stop, dutifully waiting for his owner. Kill stopped when he reached us. He grabbed my waist and hoisted me down, making sure both my feet were on the ground before he eased his grasp on me.

I collapsed against my husband, shivering uncontrollably.

"Oh God, oh God, oh God," I kept mumbling.

I gathered Kill's face, examining him. His entire left cheek, including the temple and neck, was scratched and bloodied. He hit the ground face-first when he threw himself off his own horse and flung me over it in order to save me.

The realization slammed into me.

My husband saved me.

Put my safety in front of his own.

Without giving it a second thought.

He was bleeding, limping, his expensive clothes ruined and torn.

He looked at me as though he was taking inventory and making sure I was okay. His smoky, amber eyes darted from my face to my shoulders, down my body, then up again to my neck, arms, and fingers.

After everything that happened, *he* was checking on *me*.

Instead of thanking him—the sane, grown-up thing to do—I burst into childish tears, dropping my head to his shoulder, clutching his shirt like he was going to fade into smoke.

"*Fuck*," he said gruffly. It was the first time I'd heard him curse, and for some stupid reason, it made my heart sing. He patted the back of my head awkwardly.

"Now, now…uh."

He didn't know what to say. He wanted to comfort me but had never done it before.

"You're not hurt," he said steely. Robotically. "I checked."

THE *Villain*

"But *you* are." My tears kept rolling.

"I'll survive, much to some people's dismay." He brushed my flyaways with his thumbs, wiping my face clean before resting his bloodied cheek on top of my head. His other hand ran along my back. "Shhh. It was just a little scare. You're fine."

"That's not the point! You're not fine!"

I was wailing—full-blown wailing—and there was nothing he could do to stop me. So he didn't. He let me fall apart in his arms, holding me together.

"I-I don't even know what I did wrong. Ash said Hamilton is your best horse for rookies."

Realizing I wasn't in a state to ride back, he sank down to the grass, taking a seat while I was in his lap, my arms looped around his shoulders.

Franklin stood by our side, eyeing us curiously while grazing.

"You didn't do anything wrong. Hamilton has had a bad couple of years. He had swelling in his rear legs and didn't get much riding time. When winter hit, he was down for the count. I knew I needed to re-break him come spring. He wasn't ready for riding. When I saw you on him without a helmet…" He shook his head, closing his eyes as he took a ragged breath. "I'm going to dismember Hunter and feed him to the polar bears he is so desperate to save."

"Hunter doesn't like the Arctic drilling, either?" I hiccupped, surprised.

"Don't start," he warned.

"Fine. But you should know it was my idea to ride." I put my hand on his chest, feeling his heart rioting in contrast to his carefully blank stare. He held me gently as though I was a precious thing he didn't trust himself not to break.

"Hunter screwed this up. He didn't give Hamilton enough time to get acquainted with you. Smell you. Feel you."

"He was by my side the entire time." My tremors were subsiding, but I still held onto him tighter. "It's not his fault. It's no one's fault."

Well, I mean…it was kind of *my* fault.

And by *kind of* I meant totally.

But I wasn't going to admit that and give my husband ammo against me.

I trailed my thumb along the cut on his forehead. While he didn't need stitches, he definitely should sterilize the area to make sure it didn't get infected. Mud and blood caked his temple.

"You saved me," I said quietly. "*Again.*"

The first time was the bleeding heart flowers.

The second was Byrne and Kaminski.

This was the third time Kill kept me alive, despite my unfortunate talent to find myself in life-threatening situations.

"You're my wife." He tapered his eyes as though the reason was obvious.

"You don't act like I am," I whispered. "We're not a normal couple."

"No," he agreed. "We're not."

I waited for him to elaborate, but apparently, that was the sum of it. I looked around, changing the subject.

"Where's Hamilton?"

"A question of the ages. I'll give you a ride home, then go look for him. You stay with Sailor and try to stay alive while I'm gone."

He got up swiftly, helping me back on my feet.

The ride back was silent. I texted Sailor that we were on our way and asked her to have a first-aid kit ready. When we got back, Sailor was waiting for us outside with water bottles and a medi-kit. Cillian ignored her, dismounting Franklin and putting me down back on the ground gently.

"You look like shit." Sailor eyed my husband.

"You aren't exactly my type, either," Kill drawled dryly, placing me in front of her like a piece of furniture. "Make yourself useful and draw her a bath. Don't let her out of your sight. She's easy to forget and hard to keep alive."

He got back on the horse, riding away without sparing either of us a glance.

Sailor directed her green eyes at me, biting back a smile.

"Nothing about this situation is funny." I dropped onto a nearby rocker, flinging an arm over my eyes with a sigh.

"Oh." She sat on the arm of the rocker, rubbing my arm. "But of course it is."

"Please enlighten me."

"You made your husband shit bricks, dude." Sailor slid into my lap, pulling me into a crushing hug, giggling uncontrollably. "You should've seen the asshole when I told him you guys went riding. He looked ready to smash some skulls. Someone's got it bad for you. Kill and Persy are sitting in a tree. F-U-C-K-I-N-G."

She was wrong.

Kill didn't want me.

He wanted what I could *give* him.

I laughed, letting the sting of the truth roll off my shoulders.

I tilted my head up to the sky, praying to find Auntie Tilda.

It was full of clouds.

Two hours later, Belle, Aisling, Devon, and Sam were back.

My friends hurried to my room, gushing about my banged-up husband ("Cowboy Cunt-sa-nova," as Belle referred to him). How he found his horse on the top of the mountain and rode it back to the ranch.

"Let me tell you, I think cowboys are libido repellents, but somehow, watching Kill riding an unruly stallion changed my mind." Belle fell onto my bed, sighing.

I elbowed my sister. "Watch it. It's my husband you're talking about."

Ash rolled her eyes, plopping onto the mattress beside us. "Don't worry, Belle is too busy trying to figure out how to drag Devon Whitehall into her bed to think about your husband."

We group-hugged, me squeezed in the middle. I turned to my sister, popping my eyebrows.

"Oh, yeah? I don't think you'll need to sweat it. The man was all over you like a rash."

"He's such a delicious flirt," Belle groaned, throwing her head down on my pillow.

"What about you and Sam?" I turned to Ash. "Any progress?"

"If it's not going to happen this year, it's not going to happen at all." Ash smiled sadly.

I rubbed her arm. "I'm sorry."

The dinner before we drove home was delightful. It consisted of bacon-potato corn chowder, fried chicken, and cornbread, all cooked from scratch by Sailor. For dessert, she served rhubarb tart and a peach cobbler.

"Anyone else wants to complain about how I invited the girls over?" Hunter wiggled his brows behind his coffee cup. He had three servings of the cobbler alone and shoved enough food down his throat to last a week.

"How'd you learn to cook and bake like that?" Devon sucked on a teaspoon, regarding Sailor with newfound respect.

"Our mom is one of the best cooks and bakers in the world."

Sailor put her hand on Sam's forearm.

"*The* best," Sam corrected.

I sat next to Cillian, smiling and nodding. We both stared at our friends as they drifted in and out of easy conversation, first talking about the Brennans' many restaurants, then about sports, and the disastrous stormy weather that still tore into Boston with its sharp talons.

I knew I had to put my big girl pants on and thank my husband properly, not just for today, but for everything else he'd done for me.

THE Villain

I was walking the tightrope between wanting to ignore his existence and restore my wounded ego, and taking a metaphoric hammer to his walls, demolishing them one by one.

"Thanks, by the way," I said under my breath, squeezing his hand under the table.

He slipped his hand away from mine. My heart bled.

This is going nowhere, and you are letting him lead the way, blindfolded.

"What for?"

"Taking care of Byrne. Paying my debt. Getting me a divorce. Saving me from Hamilton's wrath. I never said thank you, and I should have."

"It's a part of our agreement."

"You taking care of me or avoiding me?"

"Both."

I opened my mouth to tell him something. I wasn't even sure what, when Hunter threw a poker chip in our direction, hitting my husband's shoulder.

"*Mo òrga*, are you in or are you out?"

"In." Kill drew a cigar from a box, clipping its cap before lighting it up.

Hunter began shuffling. "And the missus?"

"She's out," he answered on my behalf.

"Holy shit." Belle checked her phone. "Look at the time. It's the twenty-first century. That means women can do whatever the hell they like without asking their husbands."

Devon grinned, watching my sister with open admiration.

"You needed the phone to check what century you're in?" My husband puffed on his cigar calmly. "I think it's time to lay off the mimosas, sweetheart."

"My sister is going to play." Belle stubbed the table with her finger, breathing fire.

"Wanna bet? We're already in a gambling mood."

Cillian was arranging his chips neatly, not even sparing her a look.

I didn't even *know* how to play poker, so they were both being stubbornly dumb.

"I swear to God, Kill—"

"*Drop it.*" My husband raised his gaze from his chips. "Her ex lost her entire worldly possessions in poker. Think she wants to relive that, Einstein?"

Silence fell over us.

He gathered the cards Hunter dealt for him with a shake of his head.

"Yeah. Thought so."

"If I were her, I'd play just to spite you," my sister persisted, the fire absent from her voice now. Everyone at the table played other than Ash and me.

"That's why you're *not* her. Why she's married to a billionaire and you're running a strip club," Cillian said dispassionately, his yellow-rimmed hawk eyes scanning his cards.

"Madame Mayhem is a respectable institution. Burlesque is not the same as stripping, assface." Belle blew a raspberry.

"I do love burlesque," Devon groaned, shifting in his seat.

"You'd love genocide if Emmabelle did it," Kill deadpanned.

"Stakes?" Sam asked around a lit cigarette. "Not that I'm not entertained by watching you all bickering like a flock of old hens."

"Same as always," Kill said.

"Like hell they are. Not everyone at this table can afford throwing a bunch of money on a poker game." Belle slapped her cards over the table. "I'm not playing for thousands of dollars."

"We can play for less," Sailor suggested mildly.

"Or strip poker." Hunter grinned.

"Unfortunately for Emmabelle, strip poker would also put her at a point of disadvantage, considering she's wearing nothing more than a napkin." My husband threw another jab at my sister.

THE Villain

Belle wore a flimsy mini dress, but dousing the argument between them seemed counterproductive. Besides, did he really think I'd let him talk to Belle like that?

"Cillian," I warned pointedly. "*Please*."

"You're an asshole." My sister darted up on her feet, pointing at Kill.

"And you're stating the obvious." Kill yawned, ignoring me. "How about we make this interesting? The stakes stay the same as always, seeing as you're the only broke person at this table. If you lose, I'll foot the bill. And if I win," Kill paused, puffing his cigar smoke in her face, his taunting eyes holding my sister's, "I get what I want from *you*."

My heart plummeted to the pit of my stomach with a thud that reverberated inside my body. The green claws of jealousy wrapped around my neck.

He wanted something from Emmabelle.

Why wouldn't he? She was the interesting, worldly, firecracker one.

What was he after?

Her body?

Her *heart*?

I stiffened, focusing on my breaths, telling myself not to kill him. Not now. Not yet.

"And what is it that you want from me?" Emmabelle asked slowly, lowering herself back to her seat.

"The most precious gift of all," Cillian said. "Silence. More specifically, if I win, you will stop treating my wife like a helpless lamb I'm about to annihilate. I hear and see everything. You're not giving my marriage a fair chance. You badmouth me every step of the way. It is disrespectful to Persephone, and it stops today. That applies to you, too." He pinned Sailor with a glare. "Same stakes. Same terms. Either of you win—you get the money. I win—I pay your debt, and in return, you hop off the Cillian is Satan train. If my wife wants to ride it, she'll buy her own ticket and travel solo."

Belle and Sailor exchanged glances.

Since when did Kill care what *anyone* thought of him?

"Are you saying what you have is real?" Sailor probed.

"I'm saying what we have is *ours*," he countered. "It's between Persephone and me. Didn't hear any objections when Sailor was on babysitting duty to make sure Hunter's dick wasn't going on a world tour in their shared apartment." Kill gestured to his younger brother. Hunter winced.

When Sailor and Hunter fell in love, we all knew he was a playboy yet still supported their relationship. Kill had a terrible reputation, but so far, he proved himself to me more than Hunter did to Sailor before they went steady.

"I'm a good poker player." Belle bowed a silky eyebrow.

She wasn't good. She was the *best*. And she knew it.

"Me too," Sailor said.

Kill smirked. "I'll take my chances."

Fifteen minutes later, everybody was engrossed in the game. Sailor, the most competitive woman on the planet, kept wiping at her brow every time she pulled a card. Belle refused to lose focus, not taking part in the conversation in the room. My husband lounged in his chair, his body language bored and lax, occasionally throwing an idle remark about the stock market, which Hunter and Devon discussed at length.

"So. You want a divorce." His smooth baritone trickled deep into my body. He picked up our conversation from the afternoon when I asked him to set me free if he was going to continue ignoring me.

"If I'm destined for a life chasing after my husband begging him to get into bed with me, then yes, I want a divorce. You never should've married me if you don't find me attractive."

"I do find you attractive." He frowned at a card he drew from the pack, businesslike. "The problem is I find you *too* attractive."

"I'm confused," I said even though I was anything but. I just wanted him to tell me something reassuring. Boost my shattered ego.

THE Villain

"So am I. Every time I look at you. Which is why I've been avoiding you."

"I have needs." I shook my head.

"And I have skills," he quipped back, putting his cards down, picking an orange chip and tapping it on the oak surface. He dropped one arm under the table casually. A moment later, his heavy, hot hand settled on my inner thigh.

My breath hitched. I wore an off-shoulder emerald-green dress that barely reached my knees. He hiked his fingers up until his hand nestled in the crook between my thigh and groin.

"Your move, Kill." Sam threw one of his cards into the pile.

My husband pushed a stack of chips to the center of the table. The players looked around, gauging each other's reaction. Kill took the opportunity to graze his fingers over the cotton of my panties, nudging the fabric sideways.

He trailed two fingers over my exposed slit, exploring lazily, teasing my flesh without entering me. I shuddered, feeling my nipples hardening.

Belle frowned at her cards. "He's bluffing. I raise."

She dragged more chips to the center of the table.

"So brazen with other people's money." Kill smiled idly.

"I'm always brazen," Belle corrected. "But when it comes to putting assholes in their place, I'm also gleeful about it."

"I fold." Sailor tossed her cards, wincing at my sister. "Sorry. You know it physically hurts me to lose."

"Me too, dammit." Hunter smacked his cards on the table.

Devon, whom I gathered from our few interactions was a total snake, chuckled, his eyes moving between Belle and Cillian.

"Is this a who's-got-the-biggest-cock competition? Because Emmabelle, my darling, I would be sorely disappointed if you win."

"But not undeterred," Sam muttered. "Roll your fucking tongue back into your mouth. You're drooling into the tortilla bowl."

My sister stared at my husband expectantly, but Cillian hadn't bothered noticing anyone in the room. His expert fingers were now playing with my clit, his thumb rubbing my slit under the table, unaffected by the fact everyone's eyes were on him. Every muscle in my body tightened deliciously, begging for release.

I liked that we had an audience even though they weren't aware of it.

"Show us your cards," Emmabelle snarled.

"Ask nicely," he schooled her.

"Goddammit, Kill, read the room. You're about a snarky remark away from getting stabbed." Hunter laughed.

Cillian turned his cards with his free hand. Everyone leaned over the table to examine them just as he slipped a finger into my core, curling it, his thumb pushing against my clit.

I gasped, twisting my fingers over the edge of the table.

Mother of dragons.

"Are you okay, Pers?" Sailor turned to me.

"I don't know about her, but her husband sure isn't." Belle revealed her cards in triumph, making everyone wheeze. "You've got nothing, American Psycho. I, however, have a full house."

Using both her arms, she collected the chips in the center of the table.

"I'm fine, just…just…" I panted, trying to string a sentence together, but Kill pushed another finger into me, now pumping in and out, the pad of his thumb still circling my sensitive bud. I was soaked, shamelessly trying to arch my back and grind against more of his hand. I was also pretty sure if people around us shut up for a second, they could hear the slurps that erupted when he played me like an instrument.

"You what?" Sailor pressed.

"I pulled a muscle in my foot." I reached for my drink, forcing myself to swallow down a sip, my fingers shaking so bad the water sloshed over.

"Oh, shoot." Ash scrunched her nose, pushing her chair back. "Let me have a look, maybe I can…"

"No!" I cried out. My husband fingered me deeper, faster, more possessively than he'd ever touched me. He was knuckle-deep inside me now, spreading me wide, making me feel deliciously full. "I-I'm fine now. Thanks."

Cillian's expression was empty as he examined Belle's hand calmly.

"Beginner's luck," he decided.

Obviously disappointed by his lack of emotional response, my sister snorted.

"Don't worry, Kill, I'll clean out your chips by the end of the next game."

"And my house, if that stripper club gig doesn't pan out."

Devon started dealing again.

I was panting hard, grasping the edges of my seat now, chasing his touch under the table. I'd never felt so hot and bothered in my entire life. Paxton and I had never had sex anywhere worth mentioning. What made everything a million times hotter was no one suspected what we were doing. My husband was the vision of everything elegant, golden and proper, wearing his icy, unapproachable mask while he did filthy things to me.

Kill picked his new cards when I reached my peak. I wrapped my fingers around his thick wrist under the table as I angled him where I wanted him and began riding his hand in a wave-like motion. My climax shook me to the core. Every muscle in my body clenched, my breath stopped, and my mouth fell open, an earthquake rocking me head-to-toe.

"My Gosh, Pers, you sure everything's okay? You look in pain," Ash lamented behind my eyelids. I blinked, drugged and satisfied.

"Another cramp. Sorry." I knew my cheeks were flushed. Kill threw a card in a pile, drew another one with frigid disinterest. His hand retreated from between my legs, outside my panties.

He stopped to wipe my juices on my thigh, rearranging my dress above the smears of my climax.

"I better walk a little, stretch my limbs." I shot up to my feet. "Anyone want anything from the kitchen?"

"Cognac," Kill said, not withdrawing his eyes from his cards.

"Guinness," Hunter gruffed.

"Cyanide." Sam raised his hand. "Make it a double. This game is boring me to death."

"That's because you don't enjoy money and always fold early." Hunter snorted. "Why do you do that?"

"I don't play to win or lose," Sam explained.

"Then why *do* you play?"

"To study my opponents, find their weakness, and use it against them."

"Ah." Hunter nodded. "Remind me to never get on your bad side."

"You got my baby sister pregnant," Sam scowled. "A little late for that."

I locked myself inside the kitchen to steady my breath and wipe away any suspicious stains. I came back with a tray and distributed the drinks. Afterward, I loitered around the room, studying the artwork on the walls. Rustic paintings of the woods, lakes, and snowstorms. One of them drew my attention. It was of a moonlit cabin, but there was a thick, big cloud in its backdrop.

Aunt Tilda?

"Flower Girl," Cillian clipped, using my nickname in front of everyone. All heads looked up in unison as though he'd spoken in another language. He pointed at my seat. I whipped my head from the painting.

"Show your sister which side you're on."

"You sure? It wouldn't be yours." I put on a sarcastic smile, but I was honest. Belle was my sister. I'd always have her back.

Belle laughed. "Ouch."

My husband moved the remainder of his chips to the center of the table, unfazed.

THE Villain

"All in."

Sailor and Belle looked at each other. Over the course of the evening, the games were pretty even, with Cillian, Sailor, and Belle ending up with about the same amount of chips.

Hunter, Devon, and Sam all folded, too entertained by the prospect of seeing Kill going against two women who wanted him dead to interfere.

"Me too." Sailor pushed forward her pile of chips, turning to Belle. "You?"

"Goes without saying." Belle dumped all her chips, rubbing her palms together.

Sailor was the first to put her cards down. "Say hello to my two pairs."

Belle patted Sailor's shoulder smugly, revealing her own cards.

"That's all nice and dandy, but you're formally invited to my second *full house* in a row. Gee, I wonder what I'll do with all this money." She smiled at my husband, tapping her lips. "I'm thinking a vacation in the Bahamas or maybe get a new car. Whaddaya think, Fitzpatrick? Will I look good in a Mercedes?"

Please don't tell my sister she'd look good in a coffin, I inwardly prayed.

It was such a Cillian thing to say.

Kill's face remained blank. He dropped his cards lazily, revealing a hand that made everyone in the room suck in a breath.

"Royal flush!" Belle bristled, jumping up. "There is a one in a half-million chance of getting a royal flush, and you're not that damn lucky. You tampered with the cards. Admit it."

It was Kill's turn to stand. He didn't collect the chips, just stared at Belle with a look that made me realize he never liked her. Whatever made him look at her every time we were in the same room together was not lust. He told me he never wanted her, and I finally believed him. Kill was cruel, decadent, and bad to the bone, but lying and cheating were beneath him.

193

"If you're going to throw around accusations, you better back them up with some facts." He raised an eyebrow.

"How the hell would I do that?" She laughed bitterly. "Fine. Whatever. Just so we're clear, I think you're the most corrupted man on the planet."

"Just so we're clear," he mimicked her tone, causing stifled giggles to rise from the table, "I don't care. Keep the change. And to your question of what to do with said money, I suggest you buy some common sense. In the meantime, I remind you that you've agreed not to interfere with my marriage. No brainwashing my wife or giving her a piece of your mind about me. She's a big girl and can make her own decisions. Same goes to you." He snapped his fingers at Sailor.

With that, he walked away, leaving the room.

The men were the first to chuckle and get up, trickling back into their rooms.

We women sat in companionable silence for a few minutes, digesting.

"What just happened?" Aisling asked, finally.

"I think," Belle rolled one of the poker chips between her fingers, "Pers just managed to put the first chip in Satan's icicle heart."

"And it hurt him." Sailor laughed. "Like a bitch."

Fifteen

Cillian

Devon: We need to buy time. Sit down with Arrowsmith and compromise.

Me: Wrong number.

Devon: You pay me to give you solid advice. My advice is to sign a backroom sweetheart deal and figure out your long-term plan after you dismantle this ticking bomb.

Me: The only backroom thing Arrowsmith will be getting from me is going to send him into anal reconstructive surgery.

He broke me once. This time, I'd be doing the breaking.

Devon: I respect that you loathe him, Kill, but we were young lads. Throw him a fat donation, make him feel pretty, and move on with your life. You could lose your CEO title, millions of dollars, and face jail time if you tamper with this trial.

Me: He was a monster who shaped me into becoming a better monster. Now we are both carnivorous beasts. It is time to see who can shed more blood.

I tossed my phone onto the leather seat, frowning out the Escalade's window.

Andrew Arrowsmith wasn't going to rest until he saw me filing for bankruptcy.

It wasn't about the money. Never was for me.

It was becoming better than my father at being a CEO because he was better than *his* father.

Back when my great-great-great-great-grandfather incorporated Royal Pipelines, you could shoot a bullet in the ground and oil would spill. By the time my father inherited the company, he had to do some serious fracking and squeeze the natural resources available to him to continue the monstrous growth of our company.

Me? I didn't want to simply increase our capital. I wanted to triple it. To go down in history as the best CEO the company had ever known.

I had Sam digging up dirt on Andrew as I decided which angle I wanted to attack him from. In the meantime, I made sure Green Living threw a lot of money into the lawsuit, losing their pants and their funds quickly.

For all I cared, by the time I was finished, Andrew wouldn't have a job, a company, or a roof over his head.

The Escalade came to a halt in front of my wife's apartment building. I fired her a text to come downstairs, scrolling over the unanswered message from earlier, supplemented with a picture of the sky.

Flower Girl: Look outside. Auntie Tilda came out to say hello this morning. ☺

Auntie Tilda was a pain in the ass and was responsible for my wife's unfortunate name. Persephone was only marginally better than Tree and Tinder.

I continued ignoring my wife's daily texts. It was bad enough I'd spent the last week haunted by the memory of the poker night on my ranch. The game was a bore, punctuated by mind-numbing commentary from Sailor and Emmabelle, who became two of my least favorite things about Boston. My wife, however, was another story. No matter how much I tried to deny it, she pleased me.

In the way she looked at me.

In the way she smiled at me.

In the way she called me *hubs* as though this was real and not a life sentence born from the crappy cards she'd been dealt by her previous husband.

She'd already gotten her debt paid, her divorce granted, and the means to live like a Kardashian. She didn't have to pretend to tolerate me but still had the courtesy to do so.

My eyelids dropped as I tried to bleach out the memory of her clinging to my hand under the table, riding my fist, her thighs clutched around my knuckles in a vise grip. She burned like a blood-red rose, her petals curling and twisting around the flame, and I was glad I couldn't watch her openly while we were in company because I had no doubt I'd have come in my pants.

I wanted to purge my wife out of my system. To relocate her somewhere far away—maybe to her parents' new house in the suburbs. To pluck her from obscurity only when the mood struck me on special occasions.

She was dazzling, kinetic. Too loud, too much. Marrying her was the worst and best decision I'd ever made.

"Power-napping, huh?" Persephone's throaty voice filled the Escalade. "I read somewhere that catnaps are more effective than eight hours of sleep. Did you know that?"

She scooted next to me, wrapped in a gown that clung to her curves like I would if I wasn't a hundred and one shades of messed up.

I produced a cigar from a box next to me, lighting it up. "Nice number."

"Is that a compliment I'm hearing?" She pressed the back of her hand to my forehead, teasingly checking my temperature. "Nope. No fever."

"Your beauty was never in question," I puffed.

"What is, then?"

"Its ability to disarm me."

She shot me a look that said she wasn't happy with me. A look that, for reasons unbeknownst to me, I couldn't stand. She produced something from her Valentino clutch. A piece of paper. She unfolded it. A ten-dollar note rolled out of it. Also a pen. She handed me all three.

"This is for you, by the way."

"What am I looking at?" I scanned the paper in her hand without taking it.

"I saw this on a TV show. *Billions*. It's a contract in which you sell your soul to me."

I really should've made her take a drug test before I put a ring on her finger.

The amount of nonsense spewing out of that pretty mouth could keep the entire Senate busy for a century.

Then again, deep down, I knew even if the results came back saying she was hooked on meth, cocaine, heroin, and every homeless dick downtown, I still would have married her, and that was a problem.

A *huge* problem.

"Sign it." She released the ten-dollar bill in my lap like I was a B-grade pole dancer. I didn't make a move to pick it up.

"What's the problem?" She frowned. "You already told me I can never have your heart and mentioned you don't believe in souls. That means selling yours to me shouldn't be too hard, right?"

The fact she was trying to philosophically challenge me made her cute enough to eat. Then again, I didn't need much incentive to want to eat her out. Wondering how my wife's pussy tasted was something I did often.

I'd licked my fingers after the card game on the ranch. Her scent hitting my system alone had made me painfully hard.

"It's okay if you don't want to take any chances." She withdrew the contract, about to tuck it back into her purse.

"There's no such thing as a soul," I repeated dully.

THE *Villain*

"In that case, I'd like to buy yours."

"How'd it end on that TV show?" I sat back, twirling the cigar between my fingers.

"*Billions*?" She frowned. "The girl—who has a similar set of beliefs and views on the world as you—signed the contract, proving she truly didn't believe in her soul's existence."

"Amateur mistake." I clutched my cigar between my teeth to free my hands, adjusting the necklace on my wife's neck so the clasp wouldn't show. "First rule in business is supply and demand. You put a price on something in accordance to how other people value it. My set of beliefs is irrelevant. *You* think souls exist, and therefore *I* will sign mine over to you for the highest price."

"What would that price be?"

"Your full submission to our arrangement." I plucked the pen and paper from her hand, tucking them into my breast pocket. "More on that when I figure out what that exactly entails. Subject closed."

The need to own, conquer, banish, and discard her made me lose sleep.

It didn't even make sense, and sense was the compass I could always count on.

Persephone made me swear, and *nothing* made me swear. Yet when we were on that trail, I said the word *fuck*. Not because I cracked two ribs—which, by the way, happened—or because I was bloodied and wounded, but because she looked scared, and I never wanted to see that emotion on her face again.

She smoothed her dress, examining me under a thick curtain of lashes.

"I'm glad we're going to this charity event. We haven't gone out as a couple since we got married. Paxton and I used to have date nights all the time. I miss that."

"Where did Paxton take you?" The question slipped out before I could shove it back into my throat and choke on it. Which was what I deserved for even *thinking* about it.

She blew a lock of sunflower hair that flopped over her eye.

"We had an annual Disney pass. I love a good fairy tale. We used to go to restaurants, dance clubs, football games. Oh, and have picnics, sometimes. Our dream honeymoon was to go to Namibia, but we were too broke to do it."

"Why Namibia?"

Why ask her more questions?

"I once saw a picture of the Namibian desert in a journal. The yellow dunes looked like velvet. I became obsessed with lying on one of those perfect dunes and looking up at the sun. It looked like the height of being alive. So poignant. So pure."

So stupid.

She had the good sense to blush.

I turned back to the view zipping through the window, having heard enough about her previous relationship.

"We had a good run."

An unfamiliar needle pricked my chest. Maybe I was having a heart attack. Spending a night in the ER would still beat Arrowsmith drooling over my wife like a horny tenth grader publicly.

"A man named Andrew Arrowsmith is going to be at the charity ball. He's the one filing a lawsuit against Royal Pipelines." I changed the subject.

"I know him from TV. He does morning shows and environmental panels."

"I expect you to be on your best behavior. He'll examine us closely, look for cracks in the façade."

She flashed me a curious look. "Why do I get the feeling there's more to this story than a lawsuit?"

"We go back. We grew up together, went to the same schools for a while. His late father worked for mine."

"I'm guessing his departure didn't include any employee of the year awards."

"*Athair* made him do the walk of shame and blacklisted

him from working at any reputable company on the East Coast. Arrowsmith Senior had a knack for embezzling."

Persephone crossed her legs. "So this lawsuit is personal?"

I offered her a curt nod. "Arrowsmith Senior died recently."

"Which opened the old wound, making Andrew take the job at Green Living."

She caught up quickly. Flower Girl had been a lot smarter than I gave her credit for before I asked her to marry me.

"How come the media hasn't picked up on it?" She readjusted my tie. This time, I didn't move her hand away. "His hidden agenda, I mean. He's a highly public figure."

"I haven't leaked it yet."

"Why?"

"Arrowsmith's got something on me, too. We're hanging our sins over each other's head, waiting to see who blinks first."

"Let's make him flinch then, *hubs*."

"There isn't a *we* in this operation. You worry about giving me heirs, and I'll worry about Arrowsmith."

She studied me; her blue eyes tranquil. I could tell she was no longer fearful of me, but I wasn't sure if that satisfied or annoyed me.

"I mean it, Flower Girl. Don't butt into my business."

She was still smiling.

"What are you looking at?" I glowered.

"You held my hand in yours the entire length of the drive. Since you took the contract from me."

Dropping my gaze, I immediately withdrew from her.

"Haven't noticed."

"You're handsome when flustered."

"I swear, Persephone, I'm going to relocate you to your precious Namibia if you don't stop grating on my nerves."

"So now I annoy you constantly." Her blue eyes shone. "That's one, steady emotion. Twenty-six more to go!"

There were twenty-seven emotions? That seemed completely unmanageable. No wonder most humans were categorically useless.

The driver opened the back door. I slid out first, taking my wife's delicate hand in mine as the cameras clicked, devouring us, wanting more from the woman who had decided to lock her fate with The Villain.

I tucked my wife behind me and marched past them, blocking the blinding flashes with my body so she wouldn't trip and embarrass me.

It was showtime.

The charity ball reminded me why I didn't do people.

Out of the bedroom, anyway.

A rancid cloud of perfume hung over carefully sprayed hairdos. The checked marble floor of the nineteenth century hotel twinkled, and the aristocrats immortalized on the paintings framing the ballroom glared at the guests disapprovingly.

Everything about the event was fake, from the conversation, to the veneer teeth and crocodile tears over what we were raising money for—clowns for kittens? Ant sanctuary? Whatever it was, I knew I stood out like a sober guy at a frat party.

I led Persephone inside, ignoring the few people who were dumb enough to approach me.

That was the beauty in being Boston's most hated businessman. I didn't need to pretend I gave a damn. I wanted a private word with the man who was suing my company, so I came here with a check the organizers couldn't refuse. But my willingness to socialize or play the game was below zero.

I snatched a flute of champagne from a waitress's tray for Persephone and a cognac for myself, snubbing a hedge fund manager

THE Villain

who came to introduce himself with a boring-looking woman I assumed was his wife.

Something fast and hard bumped into my leg. It stumbled backward, landing at my wife's feet in a tangle of pudgy limbs.

Persephone lost her grip on the champagne, spilling her drink all over her dress. She let out a breath while I grabbed the stupid thing and scooped it in the air. It was kicking and screaming.

"What in the—"

"*Let him go!*" my wife cried out, swatting my hand away. She crouched down, giving everyone in the room a front-seat view to her cleavage, and righted the thing—fine, *child*—who'd crashed into us, helping him to his feet.

"Are you okay, sweets?" She rubbed his arms.

The child looked vaguely familiar, but since I wasn't acquainted with any kids, I figured they all looked the same. Like squirrels or Oreo cookies.

The little boy screwed his nose, shaking his head. His right eye ticked twice…no, six times.

Tick. Tick. Tick, tick, tick, tick.

My gut twisted. I stepped back, popping my fingers one after the other.

"Are you lost?" My wife put a palm on the snotty thing's cheek.

Yes.

The boy cast his eyes down, twitching and buzzing.

"Y-y-yes."

"Let's go find your parents."

She offered him her hand. He took it, when another identical-looking kid sailed on his sneakers in our direction, bumping into the twitchy kid. They both knocked Persephone down. Instead of pushing them out of the way, she laughed her throaty laughter that seemed to have a direct speed-dial connection to my groin and collected them in her arms as if they were eager puppies. They stuck their sticky fingers into her blond curls and fingered her diamond necklace.

"Easy there, little ones." She laughed.

"I'm not little. I'm a big boy. Tinder!" the second boy cried. "Mommy and Daddy are looking for you."

"T-Tree. Look what I found. A real princess." He motioned to my wife.

Tinder?

Tree?

Oh, for fu…

"Fitzpatrick. Fancy seeing you here. What are you doing raising funds for For the Love of Cow?" Andrew Arrowsmith strolled behind his children, leading his wife by the small of her back.

I glanced at one of the posters in the room, certain he was testing me. Sure enough, the words *For the Love of Cow* were plainly there. Apparently, I'd slid a fifty-thousand-dollar check at the door to support research on how to decrease methane's effect on depleting the ozone.

Cow's shit just got a whole new literal meaning.

I stole another glance at Tinder. He was jerking around in my wife's arms, his throat producing feral sounds I doubted he controlled.

"Don't tell me you grew a conscience." Andrew smirked. I had to admit, he wore his newly earned aristocracy well.

"What conscience?" I asked nonchalantly. "I heard the word *cow* and figured there'd be steak."

"That sounds more like you." Andrew's eyes drifted to Persephone, who was still on the floor, *ahh-ing* and *aww-ing* over something his children said.

"She is lovely."

"I have eyes."

"Aren't you going to introduce us to her?"

"No," I deadpanned.

Unfortunately, part of why I was mildly obsessed with Persephone was due to her impeccable manners. She rose to her feet, extending her hand to my nemesis with a warm smile, introducing herself anyway.

THE *Villain*

"Persephone Fitzpatrick. It's a pleasure to meet you."

"Andrew Arrowsmith, and this is my wife, Joelle. I believe you've already met my sons, Tinder and Tree."

"Oh, they made a grand entrance." Persephone brushed brown locks from Tinder's pasty forehead, laughing.

Do not touch his kid.

"I-I-I-I'm b-b-bored. C-Can you play with me, princess?" Tinder tugged at my wife's dress, still damp from the champagne he made her drop.

I was not jealous of a five-year-old.

I simply wasn't.

Even if the awe in which my wife regarded him grated on my nerves.

"This place is boring, huh?" She winked at him conspiratorially. "Let's see what trouble we can find around here."

"No, thank you. We still have a few people to greet." Joelle pulled her kids back to her side, struggling to control them. She looked pitifully average, especially next to my wife. Her features boring, her hair too stiff.

Flower Girl gave her a pointed look.

"I think Tinder needs the fresh air. We'll stay on the balcony, where you can see us. You're welcome to join us."

"Sweetheart." I put a hand on my wife's arm. "You're off-duty. Let his parents deal with him."

She shook away from my touch. "Not everything is a chore."

I pinned her with a look but kept my opinions to myself. What could I say? That the kid was broken, and hopeless, and any kindness she was going to show him was going to give him cruel and unjustified hope he could one day be normal? Accepted? Loved?

"Please, Mommy." Tinder fell on his knees. "Please, we really want to have fun for a change."

"*Fiiiiine.*" Joelle laughed nervously. "Tree and I will tag along."

"You never let us play during stuff like this." Tree looked up at his mother suspiciously. "Why now?"

Joelle snorted, waving her hand around.

"Of course I do, honey."

The women left with the children. Andrew and I stayed behind, leaning against the bar, watching them. A couple of people who passed us shook his hand and waved at him, ignoring me.

"She really is something." He scrubbed his chin, following my wife's elegant movements, undressing her with his eyes.

"Something you better avert your eyes from," I hissed. "Unless you don't mind my scooping them out with a dessert spoon."

"Don't pretend you are capable of forming an attachment to anyone or anything other than money, including this delectable little creature."

He turned to smile at me, satisfied. "Does she know?"

There was no point in pretending I didn't know what he was talking about.

"Yes," I lied.

He chuckled. "Nice try. She doesn't, but she will. And once she does, she'll dump you."

"Tinder's an interesting kid," I poked back.

"Yeah." Andrew propped his elbows on the bar, still watching our families. Persephone wrapped her lean arm around a column on the balcony, spinning and laughing. Tinder followed suit, and Tree joined them. Joelle looked on, a grim smile on her face. "I give him all the support and help he needs."

"Your love and support can't fix his nervous system." I tilted my head back, downing my cognac.

"I'm having a real good time fucking up your business, putting billboards next to your office, arranging demonstrations, suing your company for all it's worth. What do you have to say about that?" He grabbed a drink from the bar and took a sip. "Oh. That's right. You never curse. How is that working for you?"

I turned to him. I could count on one hand the things that managed to pierce through my armor these days.

Andrew Arrowsmith was one of the few.

So was my wife.

"Let's cut to the chase, Andrew. Drop the lawsuit, or I will make you lose your job, then your home, then your reputation, exactly in that order. The Arrowsmith fingerprints are all over Royal Pipelines from decades ago. All it takes is one dig inside the company's records"—I snapped my fingers—"and everything you've built will crumble like a stale cookie. The apple doesn't fall too far from the tree," I assured him. "My father left you penniless and forced you to scale back on your dream and potential, and if you push me to it, I will make sure your kids won't be able to afford the clothes on their backs and the bread in their stomachs."

Andrew took a step forward, getting in my face.

"Don't forget I have something on you, too, buddy-boy."

"A condition, not a scandal," I cemented.

"Condition or not, I bet your father still doesn't know his golden boy is anything but precious metal. Doesn't know the extent of embarrassment you've caused the Fitzpatrick name. You touch Green Living, and I will make sure everyone in the world knows your story. Your history. The ugly lies and uncomfortable truths. It's either economic carnage or a private bloodbath, Fitzy. Your pick. But I've a feeling you already came to terms with the fact I'm going to destroy Royal Pipelines."

The women appeared in our periphery before I delivered a comeback. Andrew took a step back, bowing in Persephone's direction.

"Mrs. Fitzpatrick. May I have a dance?"

If she was uncomfortable, she didn't let it show. She placed her hand in his. I used every ounce of my self-control not to pounce on him and rip her from his hands.

It was just a dance. Besides, it was great practice for seeing her in someone else's arms. Which was something I was destined to go through in a few years, after she gave me heirs and officially threw in the towel on my sociopathic ass.

We would turn into my parents.

Civilized strangers, linked by commitments, common interests, and social ties.

I was left alone with horsey Joelle and her unbearable twins.

It was Joelle's turn to drape herself against the bar, a cunning smile smeared on her ill-fitted lipstick.

"She's a darling."

"She will do."

I should peel my eyes away from Persephone in Andrew's arms, but I was fascinated by what it did to me. To my insides. My head throbbed.

Mrs. Arrowsmith's eyes ignited with curiosity.

"That's not a glowing review for a wife you can't seem to stop staring at. How's being a newlywed treating you?"

My gaze glided down her face. No wonder Andrew couldn't take his eyes off my wife. *His* looked inbred.

"I thought shotgun marriages were a thing of the past," Joelle continued, tapping her lips, ignoring her children, who were off running between the legs of the couples on the dance floor. "Everyone is wondering if you two have a little bun in the oven."

I wish.

Jackson Hayfield, an oil baron from Texas, caught my eye from the other side of the room and saluted me. I saluted back, treating Mrs. Arrowsmith as if she were air. For all I cared, that was exactly what she was.

"It is my understanding that this is Persephone's second marriage."

"Do you enjoy talking to yourself?" I wondered, checking my phone for emails. "You seem to be holding this one-sided conversation well. A telltale of your marriage dynamic?" I knitted my eyebrows together.

Her smile faltered, but she didn't back down.

"I'm sorry, I didn't mean to come off as forward. I just think it's so brave, what you're doing. My husband told me about your condition, and well…" She trailed off, playing with the necklace on her neck.

"And what?" I turned, finally taking the bait.

"And it is clear she is still with her ex-husband. I mean, why else would she be visiting her grandmother-in-law at a retirement home every weekend?"

Joelle flipped her dyed, straw-like hair to one shoulder, going in for the kill.

"I mean, it makes sense. She was penniless with no prospects. And it was high time you got married. The pressure was on, I'm sure. If you ask me, arranged marriages have their merits. So how does it work, exactly? Are there three of you in this marriage, or does Mr. Veitch pop in every few weeks for a visit…?"

The look on my face must've told Joelle she needed to rewind. I had no idea how she knew about Persephone's ex-husband. He wasn't a society man. Sam told me Paxton was a D-list errand boy for Byrne.

Joelle read the question on my face, waving a hand around.

"Please, Cillian, people talk. The minute the country club folks in Back Bay heard about your nuptials, tongues started wagging. Paxton Veitch was my tennis mate's student in high school, so she volunteered the information. Apparently, she still visits his grandmother, too. Poor thing has no other relatives in Boston, and she's in quite a state. I'm told your wife hasn't missed a visit in three years, not long after she started dating him. *Familia primum*, huh?"

Family first in Latin.

So Joelle was one of *those* women.

Fluent in Latin, mingling, and designer brands.

Gently bred to become the wife of men like me.

"Here's the thing." I inclined my head toward her, bulldozing into her personal space as she did into my business. "My marriage may be a sham, but at least my wife and I are upfront about it. Your marriage is a farce, and I bet you're dumb enough to believe it's the real deal. Let me guess—you come from money, don't you, Joelle? Never worked a day in your life. You have a nice, albeit useless bachelor's degree from an Ivy League university, a prestigious lineage, and trust funds coming out of every hole in your body?" I arched an eyebrow. By the way she flinched, I'd hit a nerve. I plowed through it, gutting it with a pitchfork. "Everything Andrew Arrowsmith has done from the moment he was born was to try to make up for the fact he wasn't born into the Fitzpatrick family. He ate from our plates, played in our backyard, and attended the same extracurricular classes I took part in. His family went as far as to send him to the same schools as me. But make no mistakes—the Arrowsmiths never sliced through the airtight seal of Boston's upper crust. He is our hang-on, and you, my dear, are his meal ticket. While it is true that I, too, stand in your position of feeding an ambitious, good-looking go-getter of the world, at least I married a woman I'd like to take to bed every night. You married a social climber who wouldn't touch you with a ten-foot pole given the chance. When was the last time he ate you out?" I leaned down, my lips brushing her ear. Her body responded with an excited shiver. "Ravaged you like you were a precious prize and not a check he needed to deposit? Your husband is cheating on you, isn't he, Mrs. Arrowsmith?"

She paled under her makeup, staggering backward. I shot out a hand to clasp her arm and help her to her feet, a polite smirk on my lips.

"That's what I thought. Tell anyone about my wife visiting her former grandmother-in-law, and I will make sure everyone in America knows your husband has side pieces. Enjoy the rest of your evening, Mrs. Arrowsmith."

"Mrs. Fitzpatrick will be spending the night at my place. There's no need to stop at her apartment," I announced to my driver when we slid into the back seat of the Escalade.

Persephone took off her heels with a joyous sigh, dropping

THE *Villain*

her head to the cool leather, too exhausted to discuss this new development.

She'd danced with every man worth knowing in the ballroom tonight. Was handed from one pair of arms to the next. A dazzling, shiny toy that belonged to the most closed-off man in New England. Everyone wanted to see who had managed to tame The Villain, and since most people had long given up on approaching me directly, Flower Girl was the next best thing.

"I see I'm growing on you." She rubbed her swollen, red foot, propping it on my knee in hopes I'd give her a massage.

"You might be needing glasses." I patted her wiggling toes, ignoring her pleas.

"How can you be so unhappy when everything went smoothly tonight?" She blinked at me. "Are you programmed to be miserable or something?"

I paid my dues in this marriage and with a healthy interest rate. Not only keeping my wife alive—which turned out more challenging than I'd expected—but also showering her with everything a twenty-first century woman could dream of.

If Persephone thought she was going to run around, visiting her ex-husband's family, and keeping in touch with the Veitch clan—maybe even with Paxton himself—she was sorely mistaken. She was mine now, and if I had to close the deal by impregnating her this week, I was up for the job.

Once we arrived at my house, Petar dashed from his room to see if I needed anything.

A loyal wife would be nice.

"Out of my way." I waved him off. Persephone and I headed to my study on the second floor, ascending the Tuscan staircase.

I closed the door behind us, strolled over to my desk, retrieved the stupid contract from my breast pocket, and slapped it on the table. Producing my own pen from a nearby drawer—one without a goddamn plumbing company's name—I signed the contract, handing my soul over to my wife, then held the paper between my index and middle fingers in the air.

She lifted her arm to snatch it. I tilted my arm up, shaking my head slowly.

"I found a price for my soul."

"Let's hear it." She folded her arms over her chest.

"Stop visiting your ex-husband's grandmother. It is inappropriate, ungrateful, and sends the wrong message."

There was a beat of silence in which she tried to digest how I'd known about this to begin with.

"No," she said, point-blank. "She has no one. She is senile, and lonely, and in desperate need of companionship. She doesn't have much longer to live. I'm not going to turn my back on her."

It surprised me she didn't deny visiting her ex-relative.

Although it shouldn't have. I was always under the impression Persephone was easier to handle than her friends and sister—aka the PMS Brigade. In practice, my wife simply had an unconventional approach to things. Instead of standing her ground, she perched on it cutely with a sweet smile on her face.

But she was still, technically, *on* her ground, not moving an inch.

"She's not your responsibility anymore." Bracing my knuckles over my desk to stop myself from popping them, I leaned forward, feeling the threads of my cool unraveling.

"I'm not buying your soul for the price of tarnishing mine." She erected her spine. "Sorry, hubs, you'll have to think of something else."

"I'll hire a nurse for her."

Was I really negotiating with this woman? *Again?*

"No," she said flatly.

"Two nurses," I gritted out.

She shook her head.

"The woman is *senile*." I bared my teeth. "She is not going to know the difference between you and a professional."

"But *I* will." She unfastened her hair clip, her golden locks spilling like waterfalls on her shoulders. "And I'll know I turned my back on someone helpless just because of my husband's whim."

I wanted to…wanted to…what the fuck did I want to do to this woman?

And why the fuck did I think the word *fuck* in my head just now?

I did it again.

God-fucking-dammit.

She ambled toward me, putting her hand on mine from across the desk.

"Cillian," she whispered. "Listen to me. The two most important decisions in our lives are not ours to make. Our creation and our death. We don't choose to be born, and we don't choose when or how we die. But everything in-between? That's our jurisdiction. We can fill in the blanks as we please. And I choose to fill mine by doing the right thing. By being a good friend—a good human—according to my standards."

Calmly, I retrieved the contract between us and shoved it into my office drawer. I locked it, disposing the key in my front pocket. I wasn't going to get my way—not tonight, anyway—but negotiations were my playground, and the small print was where I thrived.

She was going to stop seeing the old hag, if I had to work full-time at making it happen.

I rounded the desk, leaning against it and crossing my ankles.

"Come here."

She closed the space between us without hesitation, willing and responsive. *Perfect.* I'd never met someone so agreeable yet so stubborn.

We were flush against each other, her flowery scent invading my nostrils.

"Seen your Aunt Tilda recently?" My hand slid to her cheek, palming it. She took a ragged breath, her entire body trembling to my briefest touch.

I wondered how receptive she was to her ex-husband.

How hard she quivered when pressed against someone she'd actually chosen.

Someone whose arms I sent her directly to.

"Yeah, I did, in fact, the other day…" She stammered, letting me tug her into position. Her thighs straddled my right leg. I angled her so her clit pressed against my muscled quads. "Uhm, which, I guess, was Tuesday?"

She wasn't thinking straight.

Unfortunately, neither was I.

I dipped my head down at the same time she tilted hers up, her lips parting for me. I took her mouth in mine, pressing my knee between her thighs, feeling her muscles sealing against me. A moan fell from her mouth. She pushed her breasts to my chest, rubbing against me everywhere, craving friction. My tongue danced with hers, and I gathered her face in my hands, deepening the kiss, trailing my mouth down her chin, then her neck, stopping to draw a lazy circle around her racing pulse with the tip of my tongue when I reached the sensitive part of her throat.

Her fingernails dug into my shoulders. She was close to climaxing from kissing alone. We were electric together, and I wondered when she was going to draw the line. To realize the things I wanted from her weren't things she was willing to offer.

"Oh my God, Kill," she yelped.

Rather than pointing out God didn't exist, my mouth continued its journey south, to her collarbone, then to her tits, which I cupped, my tongue sliding like an arrow between them. She grabbed my head and pushed it to one nipple. I suppressed a chuckle, peeling off the side of her dress, slipping her pink, erect nipple into my mouth and sucking it. She sighed into my hair, her little talons grazing my shoulders as she dragged her hands down my back, claiming my ass cheeks like she was trying to squeeze water out of them.

"Give me everything." She lolled her head back and forth, her lips against my hair, mumbling, "Every inch of you. I want everything you give them and more."

Them.

The women I'd paid.

The women I was going to continue paying because Persephone wasn't born, prepped, and meant to fulfill my dark fantasies. That was out of the question.

She was too good.

Too innocent.

Too precious.

And besides, I had to be the dumbest man on planet Earth to deliberately tangle my life with hers any more than it already was.

I moved to her other nipple, lapping, pulling, and biting. Teasing her with my mouth, I brought her to the brink of an orgasm, to a point she was humping my leg shamelessly. I knew she was close. The tremors in her thighs told me so.

I chose that moment to rip my mouth from hers and step away.

She nearly fell on the desk. I clutched her waist and tugged her back to me, tilting her chin up. "Do I still kiss like a hungry Rottweiler?"

I was pleased to find my voice was the same dry, bored rumble.

She cleared her throat, boneless against me.

"You're improving. This one was better."

"Better, but not perfect?" I arched an eyebrow, amused.

She shook her head, grinning mischievously while working my zipper. "Sadly, we still have to practice. *Often.*"

I couldn't help it.

I laughed into our kiss.

It was the first time I'd laughed in years.

Maybe decades.

And it felt…new. *Good.*

"Now show me why you put a continent between you and your mistresses. What could you do to them that is so kinky?"

She didn't give me time to answer. With my zipper undone, she tugged at my hand and dragged me to the hallway, glancing around, waiting for me to lead the way to my bedroom. I did even though I knew she knew.

Knew she took a tour of my house when I wasn't home. I saw her in the cameras when Petar showed it to her.

I shut the door behind us, locking it for good measure, and she stepped in front of me. Wiggling out of her dress, she let it pool on the floor around her like a frosted lake.

She snatched my hand, wrapping it around the front of her snowy neck.

"Is this your jam?" Her chest rose and fell to the rhythm of her frantic heartbeats, her eyes zinging with exhilaration. "You did it the day…that time…"

I kicked her out screaming.

"Or…" She trailed off, sliding my hand down her body, all the way to the curve of her ass until I reached the crack. "Maybe this? I don't mind doing things to you, either. I don't mind anything, Cillian. As long as it's with me."

My resolve was dissolving faster than edible thongs in a seedy bachelor's party in Vegas.

The devil on my shoulder told me it wasn't my job to warn her off sleeping with me.

The angel on my shoulder was…well, currently duct-taped and gagged in the devil's trunk.

"I don't fuck fair," I warned.

My hand was still in her palm. She moved my fingers into the folds between her legs, spreading her thighs for me. I dipped my index finger inside her. She took my finger and sucked it clean.

I died. The end.

Fine. I did not die. But I was getting close to it, and all the reasons I shouldn't sleep with her—my control, my condition, how she was entirely too good for me—were starting to sound like more of the same BS.

"Show me your true colors," she croaked, her voice breaking with emotions.

"They're ugly," I said flatly.

She shook her head. "Not to me. You'll never be ugly to me."

That was all it took to melt my determination into a puddle of nothing. Grabbing her hair from behind, I brought her lips to mine in a punishing kiss.

"Do I need a safe word?" She sucked in a breath.

"Your mouth will be too occupied for talking. Tap any surface twice, and I'll stop."

I thrust her against the window overlooking my garden, butt naked, tits and pussy smashed against the glass, shoving my dress pants down my hips and freeing my cock. She whimpered, wiggling her ass in my direction, arching, begging, pleading. She was so wet her juices made her thighs stick together. I kicked her legs open and kneaded her ass so rough, I left pink marks all over it. I watched down on my wife's angelic face from behind as reality sank its claws into her.

She was pressed against a window overlooking my yard—but also someone else's private garden. She was naked as the day she was born, about to get fucked so hard women in neighboring zip codes were about to get secondhand orgasms. Persephone gulped but didn't stop me when I leaned down, picked up her drenched panties, rolled them into a ball, and stuffed them into her mouth.

Flower Girl gagged on her sensible cotton underwear, her eyes watering. I stayed still, waiting to see her fist rising in the air, tapping it out. Sensing I was testing the water, she splayed her fingers over the window, giving me a nod.

Bring it on.

I plowed into her in one go.

She cried out, her panties muffling her moan. My neighbor came trotting out to his patio holding a beer, wearing a wifebeater and smart dress pants as I knew he would. Every night at ten sharp, Armie Guzman, a Wells Fargo banker, came out to water his rosebushes.

Persephone's eyes widened as I began to move inside her. He was standing directly in front of us with a full view of her being hammered against a window.

She whimpered when I drove into her again, smacking her ass, leaving an imprint.

"Tap twice." My teeth sank into her neck, reminding her she had a way out. The way she responded to my thrusts with her back arching told me she wasn't the innocent little thing I'd made her out to be in my head.

I wanted her to tell me it was too much. Too soon. Too perverted. To prove to me we didn't fit in all the ways I suspected we did. If she were cold and unresponsive, walking away from her once she was pregnant would be easy.

Fine. Not easy. *Doable.*

She shook her head, meeting me halfway, grabbing my hand from behind and putting it on her ass again.

I spanked her again.

And again.

And again.

And again.

She turned her head to stare at me, eyes half-lidded, drunk on what we were doing. To make matters worse, each time I drove inside her, I left a small part of myself I wasn't prepared to let go of.

A shard of self-control.

I grabbed her jaw and redirected her face to the neighbor's backyard.

"Play with your tits for him," I ordered. "Make it worth his while."

I was trying to push her as far as she could go, in hopes she'd tap out, turn around, agree to the IVF, and leave me the fuck alone.

She did as she was told, playing with herself for him, pinching, tugging, caressing the shape of her heavy breasts. The middle-aged man looked up from his rosebushes and halted, his face tilted up to my window.

Persephone Penrose was good.

Proper.

Sweet.

…and fucking depraved, just like me.

That made her a very powerful drug.

"That's it," I growled into her ear, pumping harder as gooseflesh prickled on every inch of her skin. "Open your thighs and smear your juices on my window to show your new neighbor what your husband does to you, my sweet, beautiful slut."

Surely, she was going to throw in the towel.

She couldn't…

Wouldn't…

She did.

Obeying, she parted her thighs and played as I slammed into her from behind.

The man was still glaring, his face carefully expressionless as my wife rubbed her pussy against the window while I was fucking her from behind, the friction on her clit wreaking havoc through her body. Her inner muscles clenched around me, so I knew she was close. I bent her over, L-shaped, in a position that allowed for deeper penetration. Then I grabbed both her ass cheeks and pounded her mercilessly. Her palms raked the window, leaving sweaty handprints.

We were both soaking wet. I glanced down at her jiggly, bruised ass, hating how much I loved the view.

The power she had over me disgusted me. She would never know how much I craved her. How much I preferred her above all others.

How it felt like her glorious yellow hair wound and looped around my wrists and feet, like a creature out of a Greek mythology, chaining us together.

She spat her underwear out. "Holy shit, I'm coming."

Her legs shook, and she fell on her hands and knees to the carpeted floor, spent and thoroughly screwed.

I wrapped an arm around her lower stomach, massaging her clit to milk another climax out of her. Still driving into her, I chased my own release, doggy-style.

A minute later, my balls tightened, and I felt the euphoric release of a carnal fuck emptying inside my wife just as she found her second climax.

The moment I was done, I pulled out, wiping my still-hard dick on her ass cheek. I stood, a little woozy from the orgasm, quickly dressing and regaining my control.

"God. I can't believe he saw us." Persephone collapsed, burying her face in the carpet, her red and pink ass staring back at me. "I'm never leaving this house."

"Yes, you are, and soon," I quipped.

I wasn't done parading her like a winning horse.

"I'm mortified."

"Don't be."

"Why?" She moaned into my carpet. I supposed it was a bad time to comment it cost more than her sister's entire studio apartment and ask her not to stain it.

"The window is tinted from the outside," I said dryly, buckling myself up, hoping to hell she was going to fall pregnant tonight. Not only would it help me get rid of my nagging fixation with her, but it would kill any potential ex-husband drama. Something I sincerely didn't want to deal with. I didn't envy the bastard if he came back for what was now mine. I was never in a sharing mood.

She whipped her head, her eyes flaring.

"Are you kidding me?"

"I don't have a sense of humor, remember?" I buttoned my shirt, which was halfway undone, though I didn't recall taking it off.

"What was he looking at, then?" She sat up, turning around to face me, still buck naked.

"The flowerbeds on my balcony. My landscaper grows superior roses. Drives him mad."

"Why didn't you say so?"

THE Villain

"Watching you squirm turned me on." I leaned down to pat her messy blond hair like she was a pet before walking over to my recliner and opening my cigar box next to it.

"Excuse me?"

"Gladly. You are excused. Have been for the six minutes since we finished." I waved her off.

Her tits were fantastic, especially when she stood suddenly, in a jerky movement. Full and pear-shaped, with pink nipples like two small diamond studs. My wife grabbed her dress from the floor, sliding back into it with a shake of her head.

"Petar'll call the driver for you." I tucked the cigar to the side of my mouth, texting my estate manager while she jammed her feet into the nasty pair of Manolo Blahniks that gave her blisters.

"Screw you, Kill."

"Sounds like a plan. How about tomorrow? I have an opening at lunch. If that doesn't work, you'll have to wait until I'm back from work at around nine thirty."

She turned around without a word, stomping to the door. She stopped at the threshold, her hand touching the wall as she peered at me from behind her slender shoulder.

"I'm the same as you, you know."

"Highly doubt it." I didn't look up from my phone, already answering an email from my legal department. Not my finest show of gentlemanly character, but I knew if I looked at her, I'd ask her to stay.

"I like to see you squirm, too."

A smirk touched my lips.

"That's adorable. Aim high, Flower Girl."

"That's why, when I danced with Andrew Arrowsmith tonight, I agreed to his proposal," she explained calmly.

My eyes flew up from the phone in an instant.

"What proposal?"

"Oh, lookie here." She smiled sweetly. "Now I have your attention."

"*What* proposal?" I repeated, my tone lower.

"To tutor his children."

I saw what Arrowsmith was doing there.

Putting my wife close to my secret. To my shame. To the loaded gun in the room. Making her realize what I was, what it meant, how inferior I was to her blatant perfection.

I darted from my seat, about to give her a piece of my mind.

She lifted a hand.

"Save it, hubs. You have your conditions, and I have mine. One of them was I wanted to keep working."

"As a pre-K teacher, not my archenemy's au pair. This goes against the non-compete contract, which, by the way, *you* signed."

"You can't tell me what to do with my career."

Her voice was peaceful, like the sailing clouds she loved so much.

Red-hot anger slithered in my veins. My pulse quickened.

Not good.

"I just did." I flashed my teeth, smoke seeping from my mouth. "And I'm saying it again, for the brain cells in the back: you're not working for Andrew Arrowsmith. See? Easy."

She clasped her hands together, all sugar and honey. "In that case, you're not drilling in the Arctic."

And just like that, I was no longer in danger of asking her to stick around.

"Sorry, sweetheart, your job is riding my cock, not giving me business advice."

She nodded. "Then yours is knocking me up, not telling me who I can visit during my weekends and who to work with."

"This is a violation of our contract," I warned.

She pretended to think about it, then hitched a shoulder up.

"Leave me then."

"You know divorce is not an option," I gritted out.

She winced. "It does take the sting out of the contract, doesn't it?"

THE *Villain*

The little sh…

She had a point.

"I'm going to make your life very miserable if you defy me, Persephone."

My wife waved her hand around as she slipped through my door. "Been there, done that. Night, hubs!"

Sixteen

Persephone

THE NEXT DAY, I LOITERED IN THE TEACHERS' LOUNGE DURING my lunch break, clutching the leftover Trader's Joe enchilada, shifting from foot to foot like a punished kid.

The welts on my butt were sore, but it was the scars Cillian left on my soul that scorched painfully.

Sex with Kill wasn't good. No.

It was mind-blowing. Earth-shattering. Like nothing I'd experienced before.

But the swiftness in which he pulled out of me and regained his composure made me so lightheaded I couldn't breathe. Not because I expected hours of spooning and pillow talk, but the switch from responsive to harsh gave me whiplash. The ferocity of my feelings toward him frightened me, and the need to protect him from harm's way made me seasick.

Not just seasick, deranged. *Immoral.*

I'd never sacrificed my morals for Pax.

I got it now. Why Cillian paid for sex. It wasn't that his tastes ran so much on the unconventional side. He lost control when he was with a woman. He came alive, he cursed, he let go. The layers of inhibition he wrapped himself in shed like a snake's skin, leaving him exposed and raw. He writhed, and trembled, and growled, his heart racing erratically against my back when he entered me.

I'd gathered my belongings and scurried out of his house before he had the chance to kick me out. I couldn't risk another rejection. Couldn't let him walk all over me like I was the *Unwelcome* rug outside his mansion's door.

I just hoped the plan I weaved at the charity event was going to work.

"Surprise!" two familiar voices screeched from behind me, pulling me out of my reverie.

I turned around to find Belle and Ash at the door, holding bags of takeout food. I discarded the half-eaten enchilada on one of the round tables.

"What're you doing here?" I flung my arms over their shoulders, gathering them into a group hug.

"Well, Madame Mayhem doesn't open until this evening, and staring at the wall at home got old about, let's see"—my sister checked her Tory Burch watch—"two and a half hours ago." She strutted in wearing a leather mini dress and an oversized, puffy sweater. Taking a seat at a free table, she unpacked her takeout bags.

"And I had a break in-between classes, so I thought I'd check in on you. You missed our weekly hangout last week, and I got worried. I love my brother, but I also wouldn't trust him with a plastic spoon." Aisling laughed.

That's fair, considering he'd probably try to shove it up my privates.

The scent of meatballs, pasta, fettuccini Alfredo, and garlic bread made my stomach grumble. They both sat down, staring at me expectantly. Right. Guess I needed to join them.

Heaving a sigh, I slid into a chair, hissing when my butt made contact with the plastic.

Cillian, you son of a gun. The minute I pop your heir out, I'm naming him Andrew. Andrea, if it's a girl.

"So how's life with Lucifer?" Belle stabbed a meatball with a plastic fork, tossing the whole thing into her mouth.

I spun spaghetti around, giving it some thought. My friends and sister knew Cillian and I lived in separate places, but chalked it up to my wanting to take things slow.

I was too embarrassed to admit the idea to live apart came from him.

Begrudgingly, I had to admit Kill ticked every box on the good husband list, even if on technicality. He spoiled me with a lavish wardrobe and state-of-the-art apartment, paid my debt, kept the bad guys at bay, and worshipped my body in ways I didn't know were possible, introducing me to things I'd never done before.

He was only stingy with what I craved the most.

Passion. Emotion. Devotion.

Demanding those from Kill wasn't only breaking our contract but it was also smashing it into minuscule pieces and throwing the dust in the air like confetti.

Not only was it foolish but it was futile, too. Cillian didn't have the word *emotion* in his vocabulary, much less an idea of how to feel one. I'd yet to see him sad, hurt, or hopeless. The closest he'd ever gotten to feeling something was annoyance. I irritated him often. But even then, he gained control over his mood with record-breaking speed. Otherwise, my husband reduced his heart to nothing more than a functional organ. An empty, white elephant.

Chewing, I said, "It's okay, I guess. Every couple has its ups and downs, right?"

Belle's eyes zipped to my half-open shoulder bag hanging from my seat. A drawing one of my students, Whitley, had made for Greta Veitch peeked from it, with the elderly woman's name on it, surrounded by flowers and hearts.

"Does he know you still see Pax's grandmother every week?" Belle asked.

"He found out yesterday." I sliced a meatball with my plastic fork.

"Snap." My sister winced. "How did you break the news?"

"I didn't. Someone else did."

THE *Villain*

"Who?" Ash's cornflower eyes widened.

I didn't know for sure, but it didn't take a genius to put two and two together. The Arrowsmiths.

I shrugged. "Not really sure. But it's out in the open now. He demanded I stop visiting her."

"Bastard has no right to demand you flush the toilet after taking a dump at his place." Belle narrowed her eyes, clearly ignoring her vow to stop trash-talking my husband after losing a poker game. "Your marriage came with a hefty price tag, and every feminist bone in your body ain't one of them."

"I refused him," I said calmly.

Ash reached to rub my arm. "At least you tried."

"And *succeeded*." I brought another forkful of spaghetti to my mouth. "He backed off."

"*What?*" both Belle and Ash squealed.

"Are you sure?" Aisling looked between my sister and me, her mouth hanging open. "I've known Kill since the day I was born and can count his losses on one hand. One finger, actually. Maybe half a finger. A pinky."

"Positive," I said, leaning forward and dropping my voice to a whisper. "Can I ask you a few questions, Ash?"

"Goes without saying."

"Does Cillian have a demon fountain in his garden?"

I'd thought about that fountain since the day Hunter had pointed it out during our time at the ranch but couldn't find it. Yesterday, while Cillian took me from behind, my eyes searched every point in his garden. My only bet was the fountain was in the small courtyard behind the garden. There was an ivy-laced door with high timber walls that seemed out of style with the rest of the garden.

"He does," she said. "At least, he did."

Did.

Of course.

Maybe he just tore the fountain prior to the wedding ceremony.

Either way, I knew asking Cillian was futile. I was never going to get a straight answer.

"Thanks. Next question." I cleared my throat. "Do you know what his beef with Andrew Arrowsmith is about? There seems to be buckets of bad blood between them, but your older brother isn't the most forthcoming man of our generation."

"Criminal understatement. You could extract more information from a garlic press." Belle unscrewed a bottle of water, rolling her eyes. "Hashtag fact."

"I know *of* Arrowsmith." Aisling frowned, weighing her words. "There's an age gap between Cillian and me. I was still in diapers when he and Arrowsmith were friends, but from my understanding, they were inseparable at a point. The way the story goes—mind you, I picked scraps and pieces of it from different sources and puzzled it all together in my head—Kill and Andrew were best friends from birth. They were born on the same day, at the same Boston hospital, both a little underweight. My father had met Andrew's father while both of them were watching their newborn sons through a glass window. Shortly after, *Athair* had hired Andrew's dad as an accountant for Royal Pipelines. Cillian and Andrew did everything together, and when it was time for Kill to go to Evon as per our family tradition, *Athair* footed half the bill and sent Andrew along with him. Kill and Andy were like brothers. Spending their summer vacations together. Riding together, having sleepovers, planning world domination side by side. Until *Athair* fired Andrew's dad and sued him for all the money he'd stolen from Royal Pipelines, leaving the Arrowsmith family penniless and struggling to make ends meet. *Athair* cut off the cash flow to Andrew's education, punishing the son for his father's sins. Andrew's dad refused to admit defeat and pull his son out of Evon the first year. He wanted to save face. The family resorted to begging their relatives for loans. Some say Andrew's mother, Judy, became some rich guy's plaything to keep their heads above water. Andrew's parents divorced not long after. He dropped out of Evon the following year and moved into a tiny apartment in Southie with his

THE Villain

mother and sister. Their lives fell apart, and so did the close friendship between Andy and Kill. The families drew an invisible line in Boston, splitting it down the middle, avoiding one another at all costs."

Andrew knows my secret, Kill had said.

I couldn't think of one thing that would embarrass the immaculate, flawless Cillian Fitzpatrick. But if Andrew used to be his best friend—he had access to his soul, too.

Back when he had one.

"Did Andrew try to retaliate for your father's decision through Kill?" I asked.

Ash shook her head, hitching a shoulder up, in a beats-me kind of way.

"Mom said the one year Andrew and Cillian spent in Evon together almost cost her a son. My older brother lost a lot of weight, quit playing polo, and withdrew completely from the world. My brother has always been cold and different, but after that year, everyone agreed he'd become, well…" Ash took a deep breath, dropping her gaze to the scarred table in front of us. "*Soulless.*"

The word slammed into me, bursting like acid. I wanted to flip the table and its contents over and scream, *he has a soul. So much soul. More than you'd ever know.*

Belle passed me a drink of water, sensing the threads of my poise tattering. Andrew did something terrible to Cillian. That much I was certain of.

And Cillian, in return, became who he was today.

"Thanks for sharing this with me, Ash." I reached to squeeze her hand.

She sealed my hand in hers. "That's what sisters-in-law are for, right? Just please don't tell Kill. He'll never forgive me."

"Your secret's safe with us," Belle assured her.

The question was, was my husband's secret safe with Andrew Arrowsmith?

One thing was for sure: I wasn't about to wait to find out.

Later that day, I walked into an empty apartment.

The nakedness of it didn't register at first, maybe because I never considered it fully mine.

The furniture remained in place, shiny, futuristic, and cherry-picked by the interior designer. The kitchen appliances twinkled, the quirky family pictures and scented candles I'd brought with me when I moved in were still perched over the mantel.

I strode into my walk-in closet to get ready for a yoga class and realized it was empty.

My clothes were gone. So were my shoes, my toiletries, and the few personal belongings I'd stashed in one of the guest rooms. I tiptoed through the apartment, my pulse stuttering against my wrist. Had I been robbed?

It made no sense. Byrne and Kaminski exited my life, leaving skid marks in their wake. I knew I was under Sam Brennan's protection for as long as I was Cillian's wife, which had added a perverse sense of invincibility to my existence.

Besides, burglars would have taken the expensive Jackson Pollock paintings and flashy electronics I hadn't even bothered to learn how to use.

I padded barefoot to the kitchen and found a note on the granite island.

In the spirit of trying to knock you up and get rid of you as soon as possible, I am moving you to my estate until you are with child.

Faithlessly,
Cillian

THE *Villain*

My initial instinct was to pick up the phone and inform my husband, in decibels more fitting to an Iron Maiden concert, that the pigs called—they wanted their chauvinism back.

I bit my tongue until warm, thick blood filled my mouth, then drew a ragged breath and decided—*again*—to beat Kill at his own twisted game.

Cillian was concerned about his position in my life and wanted to keep me close. Whatever bullshit excuse he gave himself for moving my stuff into his mansion—the Arrowsmiths, my visiting Mrs. Veitch, the shape of the moon—didn't matter. The bottom line was, he was breaking his own rule—no living under the same roof—to keep me close.

It surprised me that he had let me get away with breaking the non-compete clause. When I'd told him I was going to work for Andrew Arrowsmith, and that if it didn't suit him, he was welcome to file for a divorce, I was almost certain he'd kick me out of his mansion and life.

It had also surprised me how he seemed to accept that I kept in touch with Greta Veitch. Not that he had any say in the matter, but I figured he'd put me through hell once he'd realized I wasn't going to cater to his whims like everyone else did.

I probably should have told him about my weekly visits to Greta. Then again, Kill never gave me a chance to talk to him. Since he hadn't asked me about my relationship with Paxton even once, I hadn't offered any information.

In truth, Pax and I were done before I'd even found out that he lost all our money.

Before I'd set eyes on my ex-husband for the first time.

Before I'd tugged Paxton behind a living sculpture for a make-out session, frantic and full of vengeance, in a pathetic attempt to forget how Cillian rejected me.

Move on.

Marry someone boring, like you.

Paxton had worked at the wedding as a part of the security staff and enjoyed my attentions the entire night. Every time I bumped into Kill, with his frosty detachment, I ran back to Paxton's arms. By the time the sun rose the next morning, with Sailor and Hunter off to their honeymoon, Paxton was tucked inside my bed, arm flung over my naked back, snoring contently.

He'd stuck around, and I'd never questioned his existence in my life.

I just thought Auntie Tilda had worked her magic and sent me a love to help me forget the one I was never meant to have.

Grabbing my bag, I slid into my Tesla and drove the short distance to Cillian's house. Petar opened the gate and directed me to my new parking spot. He led me to a room on the second floor, right next to the master bedroom, blabbing happily about the home theater system, jogging trail that framed the property, and indoor pool like an eager realtor.

"Petar, can you show me the demon fountain?" I asked him when we climbed up the stairs.

He froze, then shook his head. "Mr. Fitzpatrick wouldn't want me to. No."

Dang it.

I wasn't surprised to find all my things in my room. My possessions were unpacked, and my clothes folded, hung, and arranged neatly in a walk-in closet.

"Anything you need, just let us know." Petar bowed his head, an impish beam on his face. "Seriously. A home-cooked meal, extra pillows…the name of a good shrink. I'm at your service, Persephone. On call twenty-four seven."

Chuckling, I gave him the thumbs-up. "Thanks, Petar. You're a star."

He turned to leave while I pulled out my laptop. My yoga class had already started, so I might as well prepare new material for next week's school lesson plans.

"May I say something?" Petar stopped at the door.

I looked up from my laptop, surprised. "Of course."

"I can't tell you how happy everyone in this place is to have you here. I'm not sure *how* exactly you managed to persuade Mr. Fitzpatrick into moving in—I've never seen a woman who wasn't an employee, his sister, or his mother set foot in this house—but I'm glad nonetheless."

My smile stayed intact, but something rattled in my chest. Something very close to maternal wrath I couldn't completely understand. How lonely was Cillian that he hadn't entertained any women in this place before?

The fact Kill had broken so many of his contract clauses with me had planted a seed of hope in my heart. I knew if I watered it with wishful thinking and faith, it would grow and blossom into expectations.

And expectations from a man who swore to never love you were a dangerous thing.

"I intend to stick around." I kept my voice neutral.

"I hope you will." Petar nodded. "And if there's anything I can do to make you stay, please let me know."

As soon as he spun on his heel and left, I made my way into Cillian's room.

I had some homework to do if I wanted to learn who my husband really was.

I ended up dozing off on Cillian's bed, the mixture of adrenaline, heartache, and anger making my systems crash. I should have gone back to my room, but his linens were drenched with his scent, and the temptation to nuzzle into them was too much. Besides, pissing off my new husband had become something I was dazzlingly good at—why break a tradition?

It was hours later, after the sun had already set, when a nudge to my foot stirred me awake. I stretched on the king-sized bed, blinking the world into focus.

Kill sat on the edge of the mattress, clad in a sharp navy suit, complete with a gray tie and a pea coat. His aroma—of ice, the crisp night, and cedar wood—told me he just got home. Didn't even stop to take his coat off.

"That's not your bed," he announced.

"If I'm good enough to warm it, I'm good enough to sleep in it."

I pushed up on my elbows, blowing my hair out of my eyes.

"No one said you're good enough to warm it. I took you on the kitchen counter and against the window, *not* my bed."

"Keeping track and cherishing every moment, I see." I batted my eyelashes.

"Don't be ridiculous."

"Aww, but you started it, hubs. What's the time, anyway?" I looked around. My stomach growled, begging to be fed.

"Nine thirty."

Jesus Christ and his holy crew.

"Do you always work this late?"

He undid his tie with one hand, shrugging off his coat at the same time.

"My social calendar is—by choice—wide open. As your legs should be every night when I come back home, by the way. It is not my job to undress you to candlelight and Frank Sinatra."

"I prefer Sam Cooke and incense."

"I don't care what you prefer."

"Rectify that," I said dryly. "Today. Or live a life of celibacy. I'm not your blowup doll. If you want me to fulfill my marital duties, you better believe you are going to fulfill yours. You will never, *ever* touch my things without my permission again, move me around like I'm a chess piece, or make a decision about our lives without consulting me first. Additionally, you will be home every evening not a minute after seven, so we can have a meal together *before* we have sex. Like a normal couple."

"What part of our relationship gave you the illusion of a normal couple, the fact I bought your ass like you were a discounted bread maker on Black Friday, or had you sign a thirty-seven-page contract, an NDA, and a waiver before putting a ring on your finger?" He tossed his tie and coat on an upholstered recliner in the corner of the room.

I ignored his words. The scar tissue Andrew had wrapped around this man made it hard to pierce through and touch his core.

Tough, but not impossible, I hoped.

I wasn't a quitter, and I sure as hell wasn't going to quit on a man who I was pretty sure had been let down by everyone else in his life.

"*Furthermore*," I drawled in my teacher tone, ignoring his words, "during dinner, we'll perform the taxing task of small talk."

I could swear my husband actually paled. He looked like he was going to gag. I continued, undeterred.

"You'll tell me about your day, and I'll do the same. Then, and only then, will we make love."

His eyes nearly popped out of their sockets at the mention of the L-word.

"The answer is no."

"Fine. Let's go through the whole routine where I refuse you a few weeks in a row, and you march back to your bed unsatisfied, then go to the office, see Hunter waving around 3D ultrasound pictures of his future child, *then* do it my way." I smiled sunnily. He opened his mouth, about to say something snarky, but he knew I was right.

He needed an heir.

I needed more time to prove to him we could be more.

"Careful, Flower Girl." He wrapped his cold, strong fingers around my jaw, drawing me close to his lips with a snarl. "Run with scissors and you'll get hurt."

"I've been cut deep before."

"Whatever you're trying to do won't work."

"Humor me, then."

"Humor me first." He tugged at my leg, one hand still on my neck, and hoisted me into his lap. I straddled him, wrapping my arms around his shoulders. My core landed straight on his erection, and when I looked down, I saw it nestled on the side of his leg. Swollen, hard, almost too much to handle.

His fingers trailed the delicate spots on my throat.

"I can give you anything your heart desires, Persephone. Jewelry, lavish vacations, every Hermès bag ever produced." He brushed a lock of hair from my cheek, his voice so menacing it almost sounded demonic. "But I can't give you love. Do not ask me for something I am incapable of delivering."

I pressed my cheek to his palm, kissing it softly, refusing to let his words sink in.

"My heart is a terrible place. Nothing ever grows there."

"Stop." I shut him up with a kiss.

Maybe it was because he'd moved me here, into his kingdom. Dragged me to the underworld. Because he wanted to prove to himself that my being here meant nothing.

"Ever step on artificial grass, Flower Girl?" he murmured into my lips.

"Yes," I growled, kissing him deeper.

"It's shinier than regular grass but feels awful."

You don't feel awful to me.

His lips demanded my surrender. I yielded, riding his muscled thigh, all concerns for my still-sore butt flying out the window. He broke the kiss, his forehead dropping to mine.

"I'm going to ruin every good thing about you."

"I'd like to see you try."

I produced what I'd found earlier that evening on my treasure hunt in his room. I'd rummaged through his drawers, using every piece of information I could find to piece together the puzzle of who he was. My husband left much to be desired. He kept his room blank and impersonal.

THE *Villain*

Having seen his closet, I'd had no doubt Cillian was incapable of anything *but* an arranged marriage. His clothes were organized not only by season, but also by color, brand, and cut. He wasn't exactly a fan of surprises.

Kill's eyes narrowed at the white ribbon I pulled out of my bra. It nestled between my breasts while I was asleep.

"Where did you find this?"

"Your cigar box."

"You were going through my things."

"Your talent at deduction is staggering." I curved an eyebrow, willing my heart to stop somersaulting like a reckless kid in the sun. "You took *my* things out of my apartment without consulting me. Consider it me getting even. Why did you keep the fastening band?"

"Tradition."

"Please." I snorted. "You're not the sentimental type."

He pushed off the bed, seizing the ribbon from between my fingers.

"Good point. It's not too late to throw it out."

He galloped to the bathroom, presumably to the trash can.

"Shame. You were so good at tying us with it," I purred from his bed.

He stopped midway, turning around, staring at me in annoyance.

At that moment, all my energy was channeled into not having an orgasm based on that exchange alone. It was fitting that Cillian couldn't feel anything and I was a puddle of feels. I was angry, depraved, lustful, and desperate. Every sense was heightened, every cell in my body raw with carnal hunger.

"You noticed." A devilish smirk curved on his face.

I noticed everything about this man, so this wasn't exactly breaking news.

"Why are you doing that?" I wet my lips.

"Doing what?" His dark eyebrows furrowed in mock innocence.

"Looking at me like I'm your next meal."

"Because you are," he deadpanned. "That's why you're here, isn't it?"

Something sizzled between us. I couldn't look away from him.

He advanced toward me. I scooted to the center of the bed. Kill flipped me over on my stomach and pinned me to the mattress. Pressing his knee between my thighs to pry them open while my butt was in the air, he grabbed my wrists and locked them behind my back. The satin of the ribbon fluttered around my wrists, making me shiver. He wrapped the ends of the ribbon, reversing the direction to secure me in place. He did it quickly and expertly, cinching and completing a second loop to ensure I couldn't move my arms.

"So this is how you knew how to tie us both with one hand," I panted.

"It's called a hogtie." He gave his work of art a tug. "Lift your feet up."

Next, he tied me by the legs, connecting the ribbon between my wrists and ankles. Like a little piggy about to get barbecued in a fire. I laughed breathlessly, partly because I was aroused and partly because there was something thrilling about giving up control. The bed dipped as Cillian leaned back, examining his work behind me. I couldn't see his expression, which somehow made things ever hotter.

"Should've undressed me first," I muttered into the linen, frustrated.

I wanted out of my clothes so bad they burned against my skin.

My desire scared me. It was foreign, overwhelming; I enjoyed sex with Paxton, but it was also something I could go without. The famished, depraved notion that came with being with Kill was new and frightening.

"Do you trust me, Persephone?"

His voice sounded so far away, he might as well have been on another planet.

"Yes."

The speed and conviction in my answer startled me. I didn't

THE *Villain*

know why I trusted him, or even if I should. I just knew I *did*. That he would never hurt me. That he would stop if things went too far for my taste.

He got up from the bed and walked to a small desk facing one of his windows. I craned my neck to watch him from my position, tied on his bed, still in my conservative teacher dress. He opened a drawer and returned with a letter opener. My entire body blossomed with goose bumps.

"Sure about that, Flower Girl?" He ran the edge of the letter opener over my calf, so gently and teasingly I wanted to push myself into it.

"I'm not scared." I trained my voice to sound as bland as his.

I was carefully bowed like a gift—his gift—and I wanted him to unwrap and ravish me.

"Why?" He sounded curious. Almost…hopeful?

No. It couldn't be.

Hope was an emotion, and Kill didn't do those.

"Because I know you would never hurt me."

"That's an optimistic assumption to make."

"You saved my life three times, and counting," I said. "That's optimistic. I'm realistic."

The next part happened so fast my head spun. One minute, I was in my dress, and the next, it was ripped from my body by the letter opener in one clean movement. Kill grabbed the fabric so it didn't cling to my skin and ran the blade through it, all the way down my butt. The dress pooled beneath me while my husband got rid of my panties, clipping them from each side, boomeranging the letter opener back to his nightstand.

I wormed, pushing my ass upward, toward him. It was so brazen that I didn't recognize myself in the act. I wasn't that girl. At least I didn't *think* I was. But I guessed a dormant part of me was wild all along. I simply never let myself explore it.

Cillian paused. For a moment, everything was so quiet, I

half-suspected he wasn't in the room anymore. Maybe it was a part of the game. The waiting. The suspense. The anticipation.

"Your ass," he said finally, pulling away from me. "It's…"

Red as hell. I know. I peed squatting in the air all day.

"Oh, that." I laughed it off. "My skin is super sensitive. Welsh heritage, and all."

"I did that to you," he said gruffly.

"It's nothing," I protested. And it was. Yes, he spanked me last night, but it wasn't something I hadn't heard about from friends or seen on HBO shows. Heck, I'd been spanked worse by my own mother growing up. And it wasn't like I hadn't wiggled my butt in his direction, asking for more.

His hand went to the bondage, and I felt him unfastening it, letting me loose.

"Don't you dare." I used my firm teacher voice. "Mr. Fitzpatrick, you did *not* ask for permission to untie me. You will not do so until I explicitly request it. Am I clear?"

The air was scorched with sex, bloated with endorphins.

"I don't normally see them the morning after," he admitted tersely. "I've never stopped to wonder what it looks—"

"Don't tell me about your whores while we're in bed!"

I was screaming at this point. I was so deep in teacher mode that he was lucky I didn't send him to time-out. He said nothing, and I was annoyed I couldn't see what was on his face. "Actually, don't tell me about them out of it, either."

"There are no whores anymore," he barked back. "You made sure of that."

"*Good.*" I felt supremely authoritative for someone who was tied naked on a bed. "I hope your mistresses go bankrupt now that you are not there to pay them, and get a real job to support themselves."

"You're insane," he offered, his voice as calm as ever.

"Well, lucky for me, *hubs*, you're not charting high on the sanity spectrum, either. Now do what you want to do to me. And make it worth my while."

THE *Villain*

Cillian pulled the knot between my wrists and ankles, one gentle hand on my butt cheek. He slipped two fingers between my folds. The sound of my wetness against them filled the room.

I closed my eyes, hissing. "*Yes.*"

Kill fingered me, the slurps of my want for him drowned by my moans. He curled his fingers when he was inside, hitting my G-spot.

He was a generous lover, something he omitted from our conversation during our negotiations.

He snuck his free hand to my lower belly, propping me up and supporting my body as his mouth joined the party, feasting on my dripping pussy from behind, his tongue lapping between my folds.

Groans of pleasure and delight escaped both our mouths, and I mentally yelled at myself that it meant nothing. That this wasn't intimacy. It was sex. Foreplay. Nothing but a means to an end for him.

I dropped my head to the black satin pillows, breathing in his singular scent, a white-hot thrill zinging through my spine. The electric currents of an impending orgasm chased one another. I quaked, losing control, mumbling incoherent things into his pillows.

The minute the climax hit me, he withdrew his tongue and fingers, ripped the bondage on my ankles off, and slammed into me in one go. I didn't know if this was a trick, but it sure made my peak feel twice as violent as it rippled through me. His entire body pressed against my back, his heavy arousal sliding in and out of me from behind.

I groaned, adjusting to his weight on me.

Cillian went very still while he was inside me.

"Tell me to stop."

"Go harder." I pushed myself against him.

He did.

We were endless together. One searing entity without a beginning or an end.

He brushed a curtain of hair plastered to the side of my neck, pressing his lips to it as he rode me hard and deep.

"You please me, Persephone."

I sank my teeth in his skin, not even sure what I was biting. He let me.

Allowed me to touch him, to mark him, to claim him.

Progress.

He came to his release, and I found mine again, in his words.

Once he was done, he untied my wrists, kissed the top of my head, and left the room. His unspoken words were clear and cutting as blades—we were done.

I slipped back to my room, feeling miserable and elated and confused and frustrated and defeated and victorious.

His words echoed inside me like flashes of light through the dark.

You please me, Persephone.

His soul bled all over me tonight.

Now I was expected to fall asleep smeared in his pain.

Cillian and I fell into a routine after that night.

He showed up for our daily dinners obediently, but made it a point to walk through the door three or four minutes after seven, even if it meant waiting in his Aston Martin, scowling at the front door like it was an ingrown hair he couldn't get rid of.

He defied me like an unruly child, waiting to see how his mother would respond to his pushing the limits. This was a man *without* limits. A tycoon who had spent his life demanding and receiving everything he'd ever desired, in quick fashion. He was raised in the arms of nannies, private boarding schools, and au pairs who had taught him Latin, table manners, and how to tie a tie four different ways.

No one had taught him love.

Patience.

THE *Villain*

Compassion.

How to live, laugh, and enjoy the sensation of raindrops on his skin.

No one had shown him *humanity*.

Maybe that was one of the reasons he was so fond of bondage. It allowed him to remain in control, even in a situation where letting go was required.

Dinners at the Fitzpatrick household were, to put it mildly, a pain in the butt.

I'd tried to spice them up, no pun intended. I'd invited Petar, Emmabelle, Hunter, Sailor, and Aisling to join us a few times each week, since the cook had made enough food to feed the entire neighborhood. One time, I even took it upon myself to invite his parents.

Cillian accepted his new reality with quiet resignation. He was clearly unhappy with the socialization I injected into his life, but he suffered through it, knowing our nights together were worth it.

Not only did we have daily dinners together, but I made sure to fill them with stories about my day. Funny anecdotes about the kids I taught, and things they said and did in the classroom. Most of the time, he answered with monosyllabic groans. He volunteered next to nothing about his days at work and refused to address the Green Living lawsuit.

I knew he wanted to ask me if I ever heard back from Andrew Arrowsmith about that job.

The answer, by the way, was a big, fat, disappointing no.

But I didn't volunteer any information. Waited for him to ascend from his underworld kingdom and play with his little mortal wife. Take interest. Make conversation.

Something compelled me to still send him pictures of lone clouds whenever I found them in the sky, even though he'd failed to respond. Maybe to remind him miracles did exist, and so did magic.

We made love every night.

Sometimes, it was depraved and rough, and sometimes, it was

slow and taunting. It was always a wild exploration. A symphony of new notions and tastes and colors I'd never experienced before.

Three weeks after I moved in, I got my period.

I cried when I saw the first spot of blood on my panties. I wiped my tears, took a shower, threw the underwear in the laundry basket, and drank two glasses of water to calm myself down. It was my second period since I'd started sleeping with my husband.

I wasn't sure what hurt more—my wanting a baby so much and not getting my wish, or letting Cillian down, which I was undoubtedly going to do.

"Aunt Flow is in town," I announced during dinnertime. It was one of the rare occasions where it was just the two of us.

"Better than Aunt Tilda, I suppose." Kill didn't look up from his plate.

"Is this supposed to be funny?" I asked in a thin voice. He patted the corners of his lips with a napkin, still staring at his plate.

"Thanks for letting me know. I'll plan my evening accordingly."

"Have fun," I gritted out, this time not bothering to hide my disappointment.

"I intend to."

I didn't expect a visit from him that night.

To his credit, he managed to hold himself off until half past eleven. I'd listened to him through the adjoining wall of our rooms, going about his evening. Typing on his laptop. Flipping sports channels. Taking business calls.

Finally, there was silence. A knock on my door sounded a few seconds later. I loved that he always asked to come in, never assuming, never demanding.

I opened the door.

We stared at each other for a beat.

"Did you call me?" He frowned.

I suppressed a smile. "No."

"I thought I heard your voice."

My chest filled with something warm.

All I did was shake my head. This time, he had to work for it.

"I came for…" He broke off, running his fingers through his silky brown hair, furious with himself. "I don't know what the hell I came for."

"Yes, you do," I said softly.

I wanted to hear it from him. That he enjoyed it. *Us*. That he didn't only do it because we were supposed to, but because it made him happy.

God knew it made *me* happy.

Too happy, maybe.

He leaned down to kiss me. Letting him off the hook was tempting, but for the sake of his synthetic grass heart, I put a hand on his chest, pushing him away.

"Say it."

His downturned lips flattened, and his eyes hardened. He snapped his knuckles, something I'd noticed he tried not to do when there were other people in the room. He was hanging onto his control. Barely.

"I came here to make out with you middle school style. Happy?"

"Very." I pulled him by the white V-neck of his shirt into my room, closing the door behind us.

On that night, and the four nights after it, all we did was kiss and fondle and explore. He sucked my nipples until they were too raw and sensitive for me to wear a bra the next day, and I gave him hand jobs while we both stared at my small hand wrapped around his cock in awe.

When my wrist started hurting, I graduated from hand jobs to blow jobs. At first, Cillian was skeptical.

"I like your hands and mouth where I can see them," he drawled.

"I'm not a rabid animal from the wilderness." I laughed.

He gave me a jury's-still-out-on-that sort of look, which made me laugh even harder. I bit down on my teeth.

"*Sree*?" I asked, my voice was muffled. "*Nrro teeth*."

Grinning down at me, he got up from the bed, standing up and lowering my head with his hand until I was on my knees in front of him.

"Fine. But we'll do it my way. I've got requirements."

"Shocker!" I gasped. We both laughed. Then I said, "I'm listening."

"Lick it first. Thoroughly."

He released his cock, velvety, throbbing, and impossibly hard. I captured it in my fist, my fingers barely creating a full circle, and began licking it shaft to tip. He groaned, fisting my hair and tugging on it roughly.

"Faster."

I obliged.

"More tongue. More saliva. *More*."

He ordered with that sharp, princely twang he had that made him sound like the ruler of all things. I did as I was told, getting so wet, I selfishly wished he'd choose not to come, toss me into bed and enter me, Aunt Flow be damned.

"Well," he said calmly, even as I was doing my best to drive him nuts with my tongue and mouth. "I was going to keep the line between respectful wife and my flings firmly drawn, but I suppose…"

I groaned, continuing to suck and bobbing my head back and forth eagerly.

I want to be your everything. Your sexy nymph and virginal bride.

"I suppose the line has already been crossed. Choke on my cock, you beautiful slut," he finished his musings by grabbing my hair harder and began to fuck my mouth ruthlessly. Each time, his tip hit the back of my throat. And each time, I almost came when it happened. My eyes got teary, but only because my gag reflex was on high alert.

"Tap my thigh twice if you want me to stop." His voice hovered above my head. I didn't want him to stop. I sucked harder, more greedily, taking him all in, moaning like I never had before. I could tell he was getting close to his release. His thighs began to quiver, and that male scent of sex hung thick in the air.

THE *Villain*

Though he seemed like the type to finish in the mouth, my husband pulled out of me, came into his fist, then tenderly—almost longingly—used his cum-covered fingers to wipe my hair from my face, tilting my chin up.

"That was good," he said. "You get an A+, Flower Girl."

"Then why didn't you come in my mouth?" I tried very hard not to whine and, in my opinion, almost succeeded.

"Instinct, I suppose." He was already getting dressed. "Escorts have been known to steal billionaires' sperm. My ground rules are I always bring my own condoms and never leave my cum unattended." He lowered himself to his knees, so we were almost eye to eye. "Now, how about I return the favor and eat that sweet pussy?"

My eyes widened. "On my period? Never."

"I don't care."

"*I* do."

"Fine. Nipples it is."

He didn't stop until he made me come.

It was the first time I came like this.

One of many firsts my husband introduced me to.

While my home life was still far from blissful, it was resembling normalcy more and more every day. My husband was mine, at least for the time being.

I knew he wasn't seeing other women.

That he was faithful and desired me.

Even Ash, Belle, and Sailor backed down from badmouthing Kill. Maybe it was because of the poker game they'd lost to him, or maybe they had noticed I'd been happier since moving into my husband's house, but they seemed accepting of my new relationship.

Some nights, I would look out the window at a lone cloud and talk to Auntie Tilda. I'd tell her about my life. My job, my plans, my new marriage.

She always stuck around until I got sleepy.

Never sailed away before I said my goodbyes.

And so, I'd forgotten a very important lesson Auntie Tilda had taught me when I was younger.

I believed I could change my husband.

I was wrong.

It took a full month for Joelle Arrowsmith to pick up the phone and give me a call.

She explained her husband gave her my phone number and asked if I could help the twins for a few hours under her supervision. Trace letters and numbers with them.

"They fell a bit behind on the material. As you know, there are certain milestones they need to hit by the time they go to first grade," she huffed over the phone.

I knew this well. As a pre-K teacher, my job was to teach children age four and five to use training scissors, know their letters and numbers, and sharpen their intellectual and physical skills so they'd arrive at public school equipped.

We agreed I'd come to their house the following Saturday. It worked well because Saturdays were my day to visit Greta Veitch, something I did religiously despite my husband's disdain. I could easily slip out early and use the extra hours to spend time with Tinder and Tree.

It wasn't like Cillian was at the house during the weekends.

He went to his ranch to spend time with his horses and never invited me. My husband always made his way back from the ranch to our house in time to consummate our marriage, but woke up extra early the next day to leave before I woke up. God forbid we'd have breakfast together.

I arrived at the Arrowsmiths' house first thing Saturday morning. Joelle opened the door, her hair sticking out in every direction and bloodshot eyes, and waved me in.

"God, you look fresh as a daisy." She sounded disappointed.

I laughed. "Well, I try to get eight hours of sleep every night."

"The twins wake up several times a night to go to the bathroom and ask for water."

"You need to sleep train them," I said. "I can help you with that."

She led me through a narrow, modern hallway painted in scarlet red. The Arrowsmiths lived in an up-and-coming, trendy Southie neighborhood. Their house resembled an actual home from the outside—deliberately humble—but inside, it still reeked of wealth. With granite flooring, crown moldings, and all the other eye-popping things the Fitzpatricks were so fond of.

Tinder and Tree jumped on me in unison, tackling me to the floor, excited to have a playmate.

"Children, please calm down. I apologize." Joelle wove a hand disapprovingly at them. "The nanny is a middle-aged woman from France. See, we really wanted them to be bilingual. But she didn't know what I meant. My eyes traveled to her designer shirt, which was not only stained, but inside out.

"Very."

"Then I suggest you drop the French lessons and hire someone young and fun to do daily activities with them. Take them to swimming lessons or do cartwheels at the park. Teach them how to ride a bike and a scooter. Do things that would build their confidence."

These kids looked thirsty for attention, conversation, and exploration. A second language was the last thing they needed. I got up from the floor and headed to the kitchen with the twins and Joelle following me as though they were the guests.

"Maybe you can do all those things with them," Joelle mused, quickly losing her reservations. It took her a full month to come to terms with the fact she needed my help. After all, I was her husband's enemy's wife. Now that she took the leap, she figured she'd squeeze the hell out of the arrangement.

"I can do three times a week. Do they go to school?" I asked.

"Yes, but only until noon. Andrew works nonstop, and I am on the panel of three different charities and on the county board of supervisors. Not to mention, Andrew just signed another book deal. There'll be a grand tour…"

I eyed her in disbelief. She gave her hair a toss.

"Don't look at me like that. Andrew wants to run for mayor."

"I see."

I didn't see anything, other than how this couple had their priorities all wrong.

"What's your rate, anyway?" she asked primly.

"Twenty-five per hour," I answered. She tilted her head, taken aback.

"Really? So little?"

I smiled. "It's not so little for me."

Not that I did it for the money. In fact, I'd already decided I would donate every penny given to me by the Arrowsmiths. It felt morally wrong to spend Cillian's enemy's money.

"I take it you and your husband have separate accounts."

Joelle scanned me in new eyes, her face lighting up.

"We do."

It was technically true. Kill and I did have separate accounts. But that didn't mean I didn't have access to his money. Money I'd refused to spend. I still only used whatever I was paid every Friday by Little Genius, letting the astronomical amount of dollars Kill transferred pile up in my checking account, untouched.

"All right. Three times a week. Including full Saturdays. I have to catch up on admin work." Joelle stretched her arm in my direction. I shook it.

THE Villain

"Half a Saturday. I visit my former grandmother-in-law on Saturdays."

"Oh, that's right." She gave herself away. So she was the one who told Kill. "You got yourself a deal."

Turning around to the twins, I exclaimed, "Guess what? We're going to make letter-shaped cookies today! I brought all the ingredients. You ready?"

"Yes!" Tree pumped the air with his fist.

Tinder nodded, eyeing me shyly. He was obviously more reserved than his brother. I herded the boys to the bathroom to wash our hands, rubbing between their fingers as we made funny hygiene songs that included a lot of fart jokes. Meanwhile, Joelle set up her laptop in the kitchen so she could see us. I appreciated that, if nothing else, she was concerned enough to keep an eye on us.

I set bowls with flour and sugar on the kitchen counter and dragged two chairs for the boys to stand on. We cracked eggs, added oil and water, then battered, sang, and whistled as we worked.

Every now and again, I'd catch Joelle watching us with longing mixed with envy and fascination.

Andrew wasn't at home. I had the feeling he rarely was, which made spying on him a little harder.

We poured the batter into letter-shaped cutters. While we waited for the oven to heat, I emptied a mixed bag of colorful sprinkles into a bowl and asked the boys to separate the colors. It was a great exercise in patience, self-soothing, and teamwork.

"Don't forget to save me all the reds," I sing-songed. "Red is my favorite color."

The color of pomegranate.

"I love blue." Tree exploded into giggles. "Like Sully from *Monsters, Inc.*"

"And I love pink," Tinder said. "Like flamingos."

"Pink is for girls." Tree blew a raspberry. "Tinder likes Elsa, too." The boy stubbed a pudgy finger at his brother's chest, leaving a cloud of flour on his shirt.

"So do I." I high-fived Tinder. "Isn't she cool? She has awesome superpowers."

"Catboy from *PJ Masks* is cooler," Tree said defensively, pitching the idea to me. "He is as fast as lightning and can hear anything. Even ants!"

"B-But can he freeze someone?" Tinder grinned, gaining confidence with me by his side.

The differences between Tree and Tinder were staggering.

Tree was talkative, animated, and naturally curious. Tinder stuttered, and his left eye twitched frequently. His jerky movements and low-hanging head told me he was extremely insecure. He also chewed on the collar of his shirt until a pool of saliva formed around it.

"*Moooooom.*" Tree narrowed his eyes at his brother. "Tinder ruined his shirt."

"Jesus Christ, Tin, *again*? You're really something, aren't you." Joelle darted from the table, advancing toward us.

She grabbed Tinder by the shoulder. I put my hand on hers, stopping her.

"Please don't," I said. "It's totally natural. I have a few kids in class who do it, too."

"He goes through dozens of shirts a week!" she burst, her lower lip trembling.

"Let him," I whispered under my breath. "If it's his way of coping with stress, making a fuss would only escalate the issue."

We held each other's gazes for a second. Luckily, the oven dinged, signaling it had reached our desired temperature.

"Excuse me." I grabbed the trays.

I sent the children to wash their hands again, asking them to sing the songs we'd made up together from the top of their lungs while I tidied up the kitchen. That gave Joelle and me a few minutes alone.

"Joelle," I started cautiously. I didn't know how much time I was going to have with this family, but I knew they needed me. "Tinder is—"

THE *Villain*

"I know," she cut me off, fidgeting with her necklace. "His therapist said it is too early for an official diagnosis. We are monitoring him closely, but I feel completely in the dark as to what his condition entails."

"Criticizing him won't help." I put my hand on her arm. "Every child is different in personality, progress, and needs. French is the very last thing these kids need. Tinder, especially, needs a lot of love, and affection, and attention. He needs to know you love him unconditionally. If you're confused, think about what he is going through. He is starting to realize he is different."

Her shoulders sagged with a deep sigh. By the exhausted look on her face, I could tell she'd been wanting to talk about this with someone for a long time.

"I'm at a loss. My family produced happy-go-lucky kids. We don't have a history of anything outside the norm. Tree reminds me so much of my brothers and me when we were little. Independent and athletic. While Tinder is—"

"Other great things. And not even a pinch less treasured than his brother," I completed for her curtly. "Different kids require different sets of rules and techniques. You were blessed with two healthy children. That's more than so many women dare to dream of."

Me, for example.

I hadn't told Kill but getting my period despite having unprotected sex with him for a couple of months unraveled me from the inside.

It shouldn't have. Two months meant nothing in the grand scheme of things.

I read somewhere that it takes between eight to eleven months for the average couple to get pregnant if they actively try. But other couples weren't on a deadline. I knew if I failed to give him heirs, Cillian would get them elsewhere.

The thought made me want to throw up.

"You're right." Joelle straightened her spine. "You're so right. I need to stop this self-pity. Tinder's a great kid, you know? A little behind on the letters and numbers, but he can paint like nobody's business. And he is so imaginative!"

The light in her eyes was back, and that was when I realized I'd never seen it on in the first place.

"Tell you what. I'm about to read them a few stories while the cookies bake. Why don't you stick around? Spend some time with us?"

"You think it's a good idea?" She seemed uncertain. "They don't seem to like me all that much."

"You're their mother." I snorted. "They're bound to adore you unconditionally."

"I come from a family where parenting is done by others. I'm not very good with kids," Joelle admitted hoarsely.

"You're better than you think you are," I assured her.

"How do you know?"

"Because you made them."

We spent the rest of the afternoon together. By the time I got out of the Arrowsmiths' house, I knew I was in deep trouble.

As much as I hated Andrew Arrowsmith for what he did—and was still doing—to my husband, I couldn't help but like his family.

Ultimately, I was going to hurt them.

For now, I tried to heal them.

Seventeen

Cillian

Three months had passed since Persephone moved in.

Three months of irritating daily dinners, text messages full of pointless cloud pictures, and an unholy amount of sex.

Physically, I'd never been this satisfied in my life. Mentally, my disposition and ideologies shriveled into themselves and shut the windows every time I stepped into my house.

If Flower Girl thought we were making progress on our way to marital bliss, she had another thing coming.

I wasn't an inch more in love with her than I was three months ago and didn't care for her an ounce more than I had the day she burst into my office, asking me to be her knight in shiny loafers.

Yet.

Yet.

My new lifestyle had a price, and I was not happy to pay it.

I cracked my knuckles behind closed doors so frequently I was surprised my fingers were still attached to my hands, and I spent double the time at the gym taking my energy out on a punching bag to blow off steam.

It didn't help matters that Sailor was sporting an impressive belly.

She'd stuck it out every weekend when we'd all gathered at my parents' house, patting it to make sure no one forgot she was with child. My parents' initial euphoria with my nuptials had died down, and they were back to cooing and fawning over Sailor's stomach.

I needed an heir and fast. My sole motivation was to lead the Fitzpatrick clan and sire someone who would do the same. I didn't want to see Hunter's spawn hijacking my hard-earned company and with their DNA, pissing it away on flashy cars, drugs, booze, and a spaceship full of sorority sisters.

Having said that, each month my wife informed me that she had gotten her period, I found myself content.

A baby did not fit into my world.

Not yet, anyway.

I needed to get rid of the Andrew Arrowsmith problem, make sure Royal Pipelines was lawsuit-free, and ensure the exploratory drillings in the Arctic were fruitful.

Besides, knocking Flower Girl up meant I no longer had an excuse to keep her around, and having a steady lay turned out to be convenient. So much so, that I was toying with the idea of taking a local side piece after this was all done and dealt with.

Not *too* local, but local enough to be on the same continent as me. Someone I could stash close enough for comfort and too far away for dinner dates.

There were other merits to getting rid of Persephone, of course.

Namely, the fact that sometimes (although not very often, and in a completely manageable way) she made me feel like I was falling through an endless abyss full of glass ceilings.

Next time I chose a mistress, I'd do my due diligence. Get Sam on the case. Find someone less attractive than my wife, and not half as stubborn. Chances were, I'd never have to deal with the discomfort of wanting someone physically so much again, simply because Persephone had always stirred in me what no other woman had.

Now, I played the memory of last night in my head while I entertained my friends during our weekly poker night.

Of my wife in her lacy white nightgown. How we met halfway

THE Villain

in the hallway as we often did. I was coming to see her, and she was coming to see me, neither of us in the mood for that tug-of-war, who-caves-first game.

We exploded on the carpet, fabric ripping, teeth nipping, moans drifting downstairs to the staff quarters.

"*My favorite wish,*" she had rasped into my mouth when I came deep inside her. "*My miracle.*"

"Is that a smile on Cillian's face?" Hunter scratched his head, dumbfounded.

It had only been forty minutes since they'd arrived, and already I wanted to kick them out with my shoes still deep in their ass cracks. Flower Girl was upstairs, having a Zoom conference call with her friends, and my mind was deep in the gutter as to what I had planned for her tonight.

"A smile? Surely not." Devon squinted at his cards, taking a sip of his brandy. "Perhaps he is having a stroke."

"Maybe something got stuck in his teeth." Hunter tapped his cards against the table. "Like, you know, feelings or something."

"Zip it," I warned.

"No. They're right. You're beaming." Sam frowned at me in abhorrence. "It's disgusting. People are trying to eat here." He dropped his sandwich onto his plate.

"Leave him alone. I think it's cute." Hunter took a pull of his beer. "Kill caught a case of the feels, and there's no vaccine for what he's experiencing."

"Are you really one to talk about being pussy-whipped?" I plucked a card from the stack in the middle of the table. "Your balls have been MIA since your wife came into the picture, and no search unit in the world can find them."

Every head in the room snapped in my direction.

"*What?*" I bared my teeth.

"You said pussy-whipped." Devon's forehead creased. "You never curse."

"*Pussy* is not a curse word."

"I have a gay joke on the tip of my tongue." Hunter squirmed as though he was trying hard not to pee.

"Swallow it," I snapped.

"That's what he said." Hunter couldn't help himself. I shot him a look. He zipped his lips with his fingers, making a show of throwing the key across the room.

"Sorry. Had to get it out of my system. I'm done now."

Jokes aside, I knew I'd have probably not used the word six months ago. The necessity to utter profanity did not appeal to me, but how else could I direct my wife to park her pussy on my face? To ride my cock? Bend down and let me rope her ass?

Calling what she had between her legs a vagina would make me one. I wasn't her OB-GYN. I had no business calling pussy anything other than pussy.

"Anyway, point is, you say you're immune to feelings, and I call bullshit on it." Hunter laughed.

"I'm not immune to feelings," I countered. "I have two: pleasure and pain."

"Your wife's pussy gives you pleasure," Devon, who had assumed the role of Captain Obvious for the night, supplied. "But when was the last time you felt pain?"

"Very soon, when Persy finally realizes she married a robot and kicks him to the curb." Hunter chuckled, tossing his cards at the center of the table. "I fold."

"Kill," Sam lit up a cigarette, "I need a word in private."

"Perfect timing. Game's over." I threw my cards.

"We've only just started." Devon frowned. "I have a good hand going."

"Mine's about to snap your neck if you don't get out of here." I smiled politely. Hunter and Devon left. Now all I needed was to get rid of Sam, and I could visit my wife's bed.

"What's up?" I leaned back in my chair.

THE *Villain*

"It's about Andrew Arrowsmith."

I'd lawyered up since I'd heard about the lawsuit, did my due diligence regarding Green Living, and made sure to show my face at charity events with my wife on my arm and sign fat checks to nonprofit organizations.

I'd also paid some local media outlets handsomely to run less than flattering items about Andrew, lured potential donors from investing their money in Green Living, and made sure I choked Andrew's workplace financially the best I could.

I did everything by the book ahead of the court date, which was scheduled for September twenty-third, still a couple of months away, but I knew Arrowsmith had a strong case and the public's sympathy.

Taking a dump on one of the world's most delicate natural resources was apparently severely frowned upon.

"I did some digging. Spoke to one of his lawyers." Sam handed me his iPad from across the table. "One of the angles they're going to use in court is defamation. Specifically, the poor state of your marriage. They're going to imply your character is flawed through your estranged relationship with Persephone. Basically, they're going to heavily suggest you're an abusive husband. Your wife is employed by them and receives a salary from them. She visits their house three to four times a week, which I'm sure you are aware of."

I'm not, goddammit.

What did you do, Persephone?

"Not only is Persy spending most of her time with the Arrowsmiths, but you don't have a family life to speak of. It looks bad. The apartment you're still renting for her, your separate bank accounts..."

I held up a hand to stop him. "Rewind. Separate accounts?"

Persephone signed an NDA and was definitely in no position to tell anyone about that.

Sam puffed on his cigarette, eyeing me wryly.

"Don't tell me you were dumb enough to add her to your bank accounts, Kill."

"No," I gritted out. "But I deposit a sixty-thousand-dollar monthly allowance into her checking account. Seeing as she lives under my roof, eats my food, and generally lives at my expense, I figured this would be a sufficient amount for her not to look for any side gigs."

"Well, that's what she told the Arrowsmiths. You *did* know she works for them, correct?"

I did, and I didn't.

Persephone told me months ago that she was planning on doing so but never followed up. I assumed—fine, *hoped*—her declaration to tutor Tinder Arrowsmith was just another way to get on my nerves. Trying to milk a human emotion out of me was her favorite hobby.

I didn't think she would actually follow through.

That Tinder kid was a pathetic excuse for a...

"Cillian?" Sam slanted his head. I cleared my throat, tucking my hands under the table and cracking my knuckles.

"I knew," I lied.

"Why didn't you stop it?"

"Because I don't care much what she does in her free time as long as she doesn't nag me to spend time with her."

"Well, start caring if you want to win the case against Arrowsmith. Tell your wife to drop their asses, pronto. If there's one thing you don't need right now, it's for Persephone to give Arrowsmith ammo."

"How much does her word really weigh?" I snarled. "She is just a stupid kid."

"A stupid kid you're married to," Sam reminded me. "Dismantle her."

"I will."

"Why don't we tail Goldilocks?" Sam flicked his cigarette straight into the ashtray, scanning my face for a reaction. "See what she's up to."

Because I contractually promised her I would never have her followed, and even though she enjoys taking long shits all over the contract she signed and break it time and time again, I've a feeling I won't be able to get away with doing the same.

"Why would I waste my precious resources on my wife?" I asked dryly.

"Don't you want to know if she still visits Mrs. Veitch?"

"She does."

"And you don't care?"

"For all I care, Persephone can go back to her loser ex after she's done having my children." I stood, collecting my phone and shoving it into my back pocket.

"Remind her you will drop her ass if she breaks your agreement," he warned, his arms hooked behind the back, his thighs spread.

"Anything else?" I checked the time on my watch.

"Yes." He stood, pointing at me. "Get your shit together. I've never seen you lose a poker game unintentionally. These assholes ripped you a new hole today, and it hasn't even been an hour. I've never seen you at home before nine o'clock in the evening before, either. Guess what? Last week, I dropped by your office at half past six and was told you'd gone home early."

I wouldn't call six thirty early, exactly, but Persephone sent me a text with a picture of her wearing nothing but a nightgown the peachy color of her clit, and my dick all but signed Royal Pipelines over to Arrowsmith in a bid to go home early.

It infuriated me that Sam had a point, even if I was sure it was nothing but a phase to get my wife out of my system.

"I said I'll talk to her. Know where the door is?"

He shot me a confused look. "Of course."

"Use it."

With that, I turned around and stomped up to the second floor.

It was time to teach Persephone that in the underworld, everything outside the narrow scope of what I found acceptable was bound to perish.

I fucked her first.

I knew the conversation was going to turn things sour between us and didn't want anything to hinder my attempts to impregnate my wife.

Since she was senseless enough not to use fertility tests, I had to do it every day.

I tied my wife to the bedrails, ate her out, then ravished her several times until she was sore and tender everywhere.

I'd waited until we were both spent and lying on her bed before I opened the cigar box, which I had moved to her room, seeing as I'd spent most of my time there, and lit one up.

"You're going to stop tutoring the Arrowsmith kids starting tomorrow morning," I announced.

Persephone was still wrapped in her blankets, her golden hair fanned over both of us, her skin dewy like a spring morning.

She rolled toward me, her big blue eyes settling on my face.

"Excuse me?"

"I know you've been tutoring them. It stops right now."

"Have you been following me?" Her voice turned from sweet to cold in seconds.

I flung the blanket off me and sat up, jamming my legs into my briefs.

"Sweetheart, let's not pretend I care enough to have you followed. Sam follows Andrew, and he saw you going in and out of his house."

"Sam's an asshole." She jumped off the bed as though she'd been burned.

I pulled a V-neck shirt over my head, ignoring her hysterics.

"What Sam is and isn't is not my concern. I'm not married to him. You, however, are currently breaking a contract you signed. The non-compete clause. You went and ran your mouth to my enemy like the little idiot that you are, telling him we have separate accounts. Now Andrew is going to use your employment in court to show that I am an unloving, neglectful husband in order to establish my bad character."

THE Villain

"You *are* an unloving husband." She threw her hands in the air, laughing bitterly.

"Love wasn't in the contract."

"Screw your contract!" she screamed, losing her usual, saintly patience.

"Why? Screwing you is so much more enjoyable." I was already making my way to my room. I was pleased with myself for not allowing us to sleep in the same bed since we'd gotten married. It gave me some semblance of control.

I stopped by the door.

"Quit tomorrow morning. I won't ask twice. This is non-negotiable."

"Or else?" She jutted her chin out. "What are you going to do if I decide to continue tutoring these kids—Tinder especially, a boy who needs me, who relies on me, who is *attached* to me?"

I turned around. Stared her down with the same, cold disdain I'd used with everyone else in my life.

She was just a warm hole.

A distraction.

A means to an end.

Getting attached to someone who'd been *bought* to save her life was a special kind of stupid. The type of cautionary tale I was supposed to pass on to my own son as my father had done to me.

"Disobey, and I will give you what you've been begging for."

Divorce.

She'd been throwing the word around often enough. Like I was the one at her mercy.

"Say it," she hissed, her eyes challenging me. "Tell me what you'll do. Tell me I mean nothing to you."

I gripped the back of her neck, feeling my dick hardening in my briefs as I did. I couldn't allow it to turn into makeup sex. The daily dinners were enough. Her constant presence pushed me to my limits.

"If you continue to ignore our contract, I'll have to break my part of the bargain, too. If you still work for the Arrowsmiths by midweek, I'm putting Sam on your ass to tail your every movement. Next, I'm taking a flight to Europe, to fuck every abled body in my vicinity. Then—without taking a shower to wash them off—I'll come back to put a baby in you, *with* ovulation tests." My lips touched hers as I spoke, and I felt her trembling against me, both with anger and lust. "Their smell and juices inside you. To remind you that you are nothing but a plaything to me. The sad part is that we both know you'd let me, Flower Girl. You've been hot for this dick since the day you saw me. But you'd hate yourself for it, and every time you would look at our child, you would see what I've done to you. Know your place, Persephone. You are not here to co-rule the kingdom by my side. Merely to help me continue it."

She ripped her mouth from mine, pushing my chest as hard as she could, her teeth chattering.

"You wouldn't touch someone else." She pounced forward, pushing me again. "You wouldn't."

"Really?" I raised my eyebrows, feigning interest. "What makes you say that?"

It was bad enough I couldn't spit the word *divorce* out of my mouth. Now I had to stand here and listen to why I was apparently in a monogamous relationship.

My life certainly took a turn for the worse since our genitals became acquainted.

"You will never find what we have elsewhere," she seethed. "And you're the stupidest smart man alive to think that you can."

"Are you done being dramatic?" I leaned a shoulder over the doorframe of her bedroom, crossing my arms like an exasperated father.

"Are you done being heartless?" she countered.

"No. Which brings us to the only reason you're still here—you're not pregnant yet."

THE *Villain*

"Have you considered I might not be able to have children at all?" She began putting her clothes on. Panties first, then an oversized shirt.

"I have," I said. "The minute I came up with this plan, I made a list of pros, cons, and potential complications. Possible infertility was at the top of the cons list."

"And?"

"And everyone is replaceable."

She froze, not moving an inch.

"I see," she said carefully. "In that case, don't let me waste your time."

She had already taken months of my time but telling her so would be counterproductive to us reproducing.

"I'll be continuing my employment with the Arrowsmiths. You can find another suitable candidate to have your precious children," she said matter-of-factly, plucking a brush from her nightstand, running it through her hair.

Perhaps I misheard. No one was as stupid as to throw away wealth, mind-blowing sex, and freedom for a stupid principle. What we had was different. It was…

What? A voice inside me chuckled. You just told her you were going to visit your paid-for flings if she doesn't comply, then added that, by the way, if she can't get pregnant, you will replace her with a 2.0 version.

I knew I needed to turn around and walk away, but something told me I wasn't going to get a good night's sleep if we left things as they were, which was absurd. I'd always slept like a baby. Came with the territory of not having any regrets, worries, or a soul.

"You're still here." She flung her magnificent hair to one shoulder, parting it into three sections and braiding it as she got ready for bed. "Why? I told you my decision."

"Don't be stupid," I warned her.

"The only stupid thing I did was marry you." She stopped mid-braid to lunge forward, pushing me the rest of the way out of her room, then slammed the door in my face.

I trudged back to my bedroom, too angry to think straight. I said divorce wasn't an option, and I'd meant it. If Persephone wanted out of this marriage, it'd have to be in a coffin. Whether I was the one inside it or her was the real mystery.

Once I got to my room, I noticed my phone was flashing with new text messages.

Sam: Stop her before she costs you this fucking lawsuit.

Sam: Don't let anything fuck it up. Least of all a woman.

Cillian: Have her followed, tracked, and surveyed at all times starting tomorrow morning. Track her phone and text messages, too. I don't want my wife to take a piss without knowing about it.

Sam: Whatever happened to not giving a shit?

Cillian: Business is business.

Sam: Finally, you got your head screwed right. Consider it done.

The next day, I emptied all of Andrew Arrowsmith's British Virgin Islands accounts. The money Sam told me he'd stolen from his father-in-law. The sum came up to a little less than eight million dollars.

Andrew showed up at my office door less than an hour after I moved all the money to numerous charities across the globe, making anonymous donations.

"So this is how you chose to play this?" He stormed into my domain, running his fingers over his hair, nearly ripping it from his skull.

I swung my chair around, ripping my gaze from a monthly report concerning my new drillings.

"Play what?" I asked innocently.

THE Villain

"You know exactly what went missing."

He advanced toward my desk, crashing his palm over it, expecting a reaction.

He got one, all right. I yawned, wondering what caused my restless stupor last night.

It was probably the linguini. I should never have eaten carbs for dinner.

The alternative to what had caused my restlessness was too ridiculous to consider.

"Where is it?" he fumed.

"Where's what?"

"The thing you stole from me."

Of course, uttering the words aloud was admitting misconduct.

I rubbed at my chin. "Still doesn't ring any bells. Care to be specific?"

"Cut the bullcrap, Fitzpatrick. Where's my money?" He tried to grab the collar of my dress shirt, leaning over my desk, but I was quicker. Pushing back in my seat, I made him dive headfirst onto my desk, his eyes landing on the mouthwatering numbers that came back from the monthly report.

I stood, buttoning my suit.

"What's money in the grand scheme of things, Andy my friend? You have the Arctic to save."

"You won't be so smug when I knock on the FBI's door and tell them how much money you stole from me." He scurried to his feet, straightening his tie.

"Please let me know when you do that, so I can pay a visit to the IRS and inform them you've been keeping undeclared millions in offshore accounts. A sure way to kill your nonprofit career faster than a fish out of water."

He stiffened, knowing damn well I had a point. Andrew would have to take the financial hit. No one was supposed to know he stashed millions where no one could see or touch them.

He narrowed his eyes at me.

"You think I care?" he hissed. "You think that'd stop me from sending Tinder and Tree to Evon? To give them all the things your family *stole* from me? You can never touch my personal wealth. My wife is a millionaire."

"No, her parents are," I pointed out, striding along the floor-to-ceiling window, watching the human dots going about their day on the street. "Real estate, right? Her daddy is a property tycoon type? Bet there's a whole can of worms to explore there, too," I tutted. "Never met a New York real estate mogul who liked to pay his taxes."

At this point, my arm was shoved so deep inside Joelle Arrowsmith's family fortune, on the lookout for any transgressions, I could tell Andrew things about his in-laws I doubted *they* knew about one another.

Andrew realized the noose around his neck was tightening.

"Remember one thing, Fitzpatrick. Your wife visits our house frequently. She talks."

I could only imagine what things Persephone said about me. She wasn't a fan unless we were in bed. I had no idea why she tried to burst through my walls so persistently only to ruin my defense against Andrew.

So she can have power over you.

Arrowsmith had used that tactic before. Why wouldn't she?

"Watch your back, Cillian." He pointed at me. "I broke you before. I intend to do it again."

I smiled. "Give it your best shot, Andy. I sure as hell am going to do the same."

The rest of the week was an elaborate torture.

Sam sent two of his investigators with the combined IQ of a cucumber to track Persephone. He promised they'd do their best to remain unnoticed.

THE *Villain*

The days following our fight, I received hourly text messages about my wife's whereabouts. Her predictable routine was the only thing keeping my pulse from exploding.

She was either at work, at yoga class, tutoring the Arrowsmith kids, or with her friends and sister.

One place she was notably missing from was my bed. Even though I couldn't fault her for not crawling in my lap at night to offer me her sweetness, I hated that she wouldn't let me in her room, either.

The evening after our fight, I arrived at our moronic dinner as if nothing happened and was even charitable enough to offer a piece of information about my day. I told her I had fired three people that morning—didn't she say she wanted me to *share* things with her?—but after I got out of the shower and knocked on her door, she didn't open it.

I'd knocked again, thinking she hadn't heard me the first time.

Nothing.

"I know you're there," I'd grumbled, loathing myself for pushing it.

I'd never sought out a woman before. All of my companions expressed prior attraction to me before I took them on. I could have gotten what they offered for free. I simply didn't want to have them on their terms—only on mine.

"I'm not trying to pretend I'm not here," Persephone had answered from behind the door.

Cracking my knuckles and reminding myself that she had every right to be angry after I declared I would replace her with someone else, I'd rested my forehead on her door.

"You have marital duties to perform."

"If you think you're walking through that door, you're not just a cold fish, Cillian. You're a dumb one, too."

Cillian. Not Hubs or Kill.

She also called you a dumb, cold fish. Perhaps that's the part you should focus on.

I felt my nostrils flaring and my lips thinning as I uttered, "I'll be quick about it."

"No."

"*Please.*" The word tasted funky in my mouth. I couldn't have said it more than a handful times in my lifetime.

"Go to Europe, Cillian. Have fun with your little girlfriends. Maybe they'll give you the child you want so badly."

My pulse was through the roof now.

I could feel the tension and pressure curling around my neck, and for the first time in years, I knew they were going to win.

Being turned down by my wife wasn't even one of the worst things that happened to me this *month*, yet the idea she rejected me made me want to tear off my skin and cannonball it all over Sam Brennan's house.

It was his idea I throw my weight around with her. Now not only did I have Arrowsmith as a problem but I also had a wife who refused to get knocked up.

I turned around, storming down the hallway, zipping past the master bedroom like a demon, continuing all the way down the hall, to the farthest room on the second floor. My fingertips itched. My eyelids ticked. I could no longer hold it inside.

Could no longer rein it in.

For the first time in years, I was going to let the beast come out.

I flung the door open.

It was an old study room I converted into a spa. Whatever BS excuse I could give the builders to soundproof the room and fill it with soft, unbreakable things.

I slammed the door behind me and let the monster in me take over.

Hoping the bruises and cuts it would surely leave would be gone by tomorrow.

THE Villain

On my seventh day of celibacy (but who the hell was counting?), we met for poker again.

Sam was watchful, Hunter was in his usual devil-may-care mood, and Devon looked like he was trying to work out what crawled up my ass.

Exactly one week from the moment I'd told Flower Girl she couldn't tutor the Arrowsmith kids anymore, and she proceeded to piss all over my demands and continue about her life, banishing me from her bed in the process.

I'd been on edge all week, channeling my simmering anger toward Arrowsmith. Each day, I found a new way to poke him.

One time, I sent paparazzi cameramen to take pictures of Andrew picking his nose at a restaurant. The other, I had a PI sit in front of his house all night just to mess with his head, and on another occasion, I had an editor of one of the local newspapers run a story of that time Saint Andrew himself was caught in a three-way during his frat years at whatever community college he'd attended.

The issue with my secret was, revealing it would be damaging to Andrew, too. I wanted to push him to a point where he had nothing left to lose. To go to my father and tell him. Expose me. Turn me from the golden child to the fraud he thought I was.

Today, I was particularly sour. So much so I hadn't even gone to the ranch to visit the horses. It started in the morning when it occurred to me that something was amiss. That something was the lack of cloud texts I'd been receiving (and ignoring) for months.

I couldn't believe I missed Auntie Tilda.

The old hag never ceased to create problems for me.

Persephone was taking things too far.

I knew I had two choices—either I was going to back down and throw my wife a bone, tell her if she couldn't get pregnant, or I was infertile, or both, that we could adopt—which I was genuinely open to.

Or I could flex my muscles and kick her out.

I had the decency to pretend to debate the two options for the sake of my ego as we played.

Hunter kept checking his phone. Sailor wasn't anywhere near ready to pop—she wasn't even half-close to delivery—but he acted like she was the first human to give birth to another one.

Earlier today, Sam's spies had texted me at nine a.m. that Persephone had arrived at the Arrowsmith household. She spent a whooping six hours there before going straight to a nursing home on the outskirts of Boston to visit her former grandmother-in-law. She was still out, probably bathing and dressing Greta Veitch, putting her to bed.

My wife, I had to admit, was either the most naïve or disloyal person alive. Possibly both.

One thing was for sure: for all her traits, she wasn't the pushover I expected her to be. Not by a long mile.

Snippets of conversation sliced through the air, unable to penetrate my thoughts.

"…ripping him a new one. You have to calm down, Kill. You've been going so hard at Arrowsmith. You're lucky people haven't noticed yet."

"Kill thinks luck is just lazy math."

"Kill is not thinking *at all*. Check out his face. He looks like he is about to kick all of us out again so he can have a snuggling session with Wifey Dearest."

Speaking of the she-devil, the door to the entertainment room burst open, and Hurricane Persephone thundered in. Raindrops scattered about her face and lips like tiny diamonds, a telltale sign of the showers pouring outside.

Tiny diamonds.

One premium cunt and I was down for the count.

It had been getting warmer and nicer recently, but this week, it'd been pissing rain.

The strong resemblance to the scene of Persephone accepting my

THE Villain

proposal in front of my friends licked my gut, and I grinned, watching her with an air of amusement.

Finally, she'd come to her senses.

My wife slowed to a stop. By the time I realized she was clutching something in her curled fist, she tossed it at my chest. A soaked, heavy cloth slithered down my dress shirt.

I could almost hear Sam's, Devon's, and Hunter's jaws as they slammed against the floor in unison.

"You've been following me!" Persephone thumped her open palms on the table and in one movement, wiped it clean of cards, glasses, and ashtrays. The contents of the table flew to the floor. "I found your stupid soldiers waiting by my car when I left Mrs. Veitch's nursing home, so I decided to chase them. Got one guy's beanie. The other was too fast."

"Which one did you manage to catch?" Sam asked conversationally. "So I'll know who to fire."

Her gaze bolted in his direction. She pointed at him. "Shut up, Brennan. Just shut the hell up!"

I removed the now identified beanie from my abs, dumping the thing on the floor with a sneer. I knew an apology wasn't on the table right now.

A Fitzpatrick never bowed down or cowered to his wife.

He married an agreeable woman who sired other agreeable women, and sons who were as impossible as they were awestruck by their fathers.

That was what I'd been taught.

That was what I'd lived by.

That was how I was going to die, too.

Hunter might have been an exception marrying for love, but he wasn't the eldest. The leader of the pack. The man who'd been burdened with the task of carrying on all the family traditions.

Besides, I had a reputation to uphold.

"Back to hysterics, I see," I commented blandly, smoothing my shirt. "Care to tell me something I don't know? I told you about my plans last week. One of them was to have you tailed. Did you think I wasn't going to follow through with my threats? Did you think you were...*special*?" I pouted sarcastically, feigning sadness.

Her eyes widened. We were both thinking the same thing. My so-called plans also included visiting my mistresses and humiliating her publicly.

"You're following through on *all* your threats," she said hoarsely. There wasn't a question mark after the sentence. I knew I should back down. Every bone in my body told me to, but I had to seize the opportunity to prove to myself she didn't mean anything to me. That she was nothing but a toy.

I smiled cruelly. "*All* of them."

"Following me was against the contract," she reminded me, having too much pride to mention the other thing I promised not to do.

"Actually, I found a loophole. Sam did the following. I only gave the order." I winked.

"The devil is in the details." Sam slouched in his seat, thoroughly entertained.

"Now, that's just bad manners, Brennan. Show some respect to the mistress of the house." I snapped my fingers in Sam's direction, still staring at my wife. "Apologize."

"My sincere apologies." Sam bowed his head theatrically, laughing, enjoying ridiculing her. He wasn't capable of loving a woman and didn't want me to, either. "My heart bleeds for you."

It was a peculiar choice of words, considering I'd taunted Persephone about her bleeding heart. I'd never told Sam—nor any other living soul—about the time I'd spent in the bridal suite with her.

The day I couldn't stop thinking about for years afterward.

But Flower Girl didn't know that.

Her face reddened, and she clutched the sides of her dress in her fists.

Now was a good time to tell her I did not tell Sam what happened.

THE Villain

That he didn't know she poisoned herself.

Before I could do any of these things, Persephone turned around and disappeared like a fleeting ray.

All eyes were on me.

"Ready for my monster hand?" I leaned forward on the now empty table, fanning the cards I still held in my hand.

Hunter groaned.

Devon rolled his eyes.

But Sam...Sam knew.

He looked at me with his calm, gray eyes that didn't miss anything, big or small. Important or mundane.

I plastered my kings on the table and sat back.

Hunter and Devon choked.

"Goddamn." Hunter smacked his cards on the rich oak. "You always win."

Not always.

I glanced at the empty doorway.

Not this time.

Three hours later, my friends were finally gone.

I climbed up the stairs, taking them two at a time. I was forty-five thousand dollars richer and a million times more likely to stab Sam Brennan in the face for his bad advice.

What on earth made me put surveillance on my wife? I already knew she was going to do as she pleased. And what did Sam know about women, anyway? He loathed the very idea of them unless they were his stepmother and sister.

I didn't bother to go through the whole pretending-to-get-ready-for-bed-in-my-room routine. I went straight to Flower Girl's room and knocked on her door.

After three knocks and radio silence, I pushed the door open a few inches.

The room was empty.

"Petar!"

My roar nearly tore my vocal cords and likely caused the windows some damage. My estate manager was there within seconds, having never heard me raise my voice before.

I was sorting through her closet, trying to see if she'd left some of her essentials here. The things she loved and cherished the most.

She hadn't.

Dammit.

"Sir, do you need anything?" Petar said from the doorway.

I turned to him.

"Yes. I need to know where the *fuck* is my wife?"

By the look on his face, I wasn't done shocking people with my recent use of profanity. He snapped quickly, shaking his head.

"I…ah…she…she didn't say. I figured she was going on a weekend somewhere?"

"And why would you figure that?" I asked through gritted teeth.

"Well, because she took several suitcases with her and didn't want any help with them."

"Did she say where she was going?" I demanded.

"No, sir."

"How many suitcases did she take with her?"

"Quite a few."

"Do you know how to count, Petar?"

"Yes, sir."

"Now's the time to use those math skills and give me a fucking number."

He gulped, doing the math with his fingers.

"Seven. She took seven suitcases, sir."

"And you thought she was going for a weekend," I lamented. I was surrounded by idiots. He swallowed hard, about to say something, but I wasn't in the mood to hear it. I stormed into my room. A part of me wanted to chase her ass and bring her back home, where she should

THE Villain

be, but another acknowledged that I'd done quite enough of twisting her arm to my will, and that she could very well decide to testify against me in the Arrowsmith case if I continued pushing her.

The thought shocked me.

The idea of Persephone sitting on the stand telling people how I'd mistreated her sickened me.

I grabbed my oak desk, looking out the window, digging my fingers into it so hard, the wood broke into splinters. I clutched the surface until my fingers were bloodied and shaking with exhaustion. Until the tremors in my body ceased.

Don't lose it.

Don't lose it because of a woman.

Don't lose it at all.

I grabbed my phone out of my pocket, about to text Sam.

He had to tell his men to stop following her.

Then I had to tell *her* I wasn't sleeping with anyone else.

I slid my thumb over the screen just as I got an incoming message.

Persephone: You refuse to let me go, but you won't have me. If you won't get a divorce, I will. You can't keep me against my will. Don't call me. Don't text me. Don't come anywhere near me. Don't worry. I won't file until after the trial against Green Living is over. Your secret's safe with me. You wanted to marry a stranger. Congratulations. You just made me one.

Eighteen

Persephone

"I'M GOING TO KILL MY BROTHER," SAILOR ANNOUNCED.

She was standing in the middle of Belle's studio, cradling her baby bump.

My sister, Ash, and I were tucked on the couch inside a giant throw, sipping wine in glasses the size of fishbowls. I called the girls for an emergency meeting the minute I'd left my house.

My *husband's* house.

Our marriage wasn't real, and neither was our partnership.

Right now, both seemed in real jeopardy of surviving the latest blow.

"You'll off Sam, I'll murder Kill," Belle talked to Sailor, rubbing my arm reassuringly. "I'm leaning toward castrating him and letting him bleed out. Not necessarily using a blunt object. Something that would make the process slow and painful."

"Medically speaking, I don't think there's a non-painful way to castrate a man to death," Ash murmured into her wine glass, her eyes flying in my direction. "Was it really *that* bad?"

"Yes, it was," Sailor retorted before I had the chance to answer. "You know Pers, she'd never breathe a bad word about someone if her life depended on it. Hunter was there, and he told me himself. Said he was shocked by Kill's behavior. Recently, he was under the impression Cillian and you had a good thing going."

"Honestly? I was dumb enough to think the same." I burrowed into my sister's neck. Now that I didn't have to be strong and resilient anymore, all I wanted was to break down and cry in the arms of the people I knew would never judge me.

Aisling wrinkled her nose, placing a hand on my knee.

"You know I think Kill having private investigators follow you is deplorable, but you never actually told us what the nature of your relationship was. Again, I'm *not* trying to make excuses for my brother. I grew up seeing him at his best and his worst, so I know both versions of him are frightening to the average person. But your relationship was never explained," Ash said gently. "I just want to make sure we're getting the entire picture so we can advise you accordingly."

"Ash's got a point." Belle peered down at me. "You just told us you're getting hitched one day, then *poof!*" She snapped her fingers. "You were a married woman. Every time we see you with your husband, he looks at you like you're the brightest star in the sky. At the same time, we all know you did not go the usual couple route. Tell us how you became Mrs. Fitzpatrick."

The question wasn't unwarranted. What we had looked bizarre to outsiders.

Heck, it was weird from the inside, too.

My friends rolled with the punches because that was what we did—we had each other's back unconditionally—but nothing about my marriage made sense.

I grabbed a handful of tissues, dabbing my nose and eyes. My head hurt from all the crying. Taking a breath, I started.

"When Paxton left me, he didn't leave me with nothing. He left me with a hundred thousand dollars of debt. It was the worst eight months of my life. The loan sharks he'd been indebted to chased me around, lurked outside my workplace, patrolled Belle's apartment…it got real bad. They even physically attacked me one time."

A shiver that felt awfully like Kaminski's finger ran down my backbone.

Belle's hold on me tightened. Aisling held her breath, and Sailor stared at me with open horror. I turned to my sister.

"It was the time I told you I got mugged. I didn't want to ask Hunter, Sailor, or Aisling for the money. It wasn't a small sum. It was a straight up fortune."

"We wouldn't have minded!" Aisling cried out.

"Don't be stupid." Sailor rolled her eyes. "Of course you could've asked us for it. You're family."

I shook my head. It didn't matter that I almost did. All that mattered was that I hadn't.

"When things went from bad to worse with the creditors, I went to Cillian's office and asked for a loan. He said no. A few days later, he came back with the marriage proposal. He said all my problems would go away if I said yes, and…well, he kept his promise."

I told them about our contract. About my hesitation, stemming from how much I'd always liked him. How my crush on him never fully wore off. How I convinced myself marriage would come first, but that he would grow into loving me back as time went by.

I took a shovel, dug into the ugly parts, and dumped them on the coffee table for my friends and sister to dissect and interpret. By the time I was done, there was only one more confession to make in order to feel completely liberated.

"Wanna know what the worst part is?" I grabbed the cheap bottle of wine—was it our fourth or fifth?—pouring a generous helping into my glass. "That I still love him. I've always loved him. The first time I saw him at that charity ball Sailor dragged us to because she didn't want to be alone with Hunter and I set my sight on Cillian, I knew. I knew one day he would take my soul, set it on fire, and walk all over my ashes when it was all done and dealt with. I'd known it from the very moment I found myself staring at him while he was watching Emmabelle from across the room. He was lost in my sister, but I found myself—everything I'd ever wanted—in him."

"Kill never looks directly at the things he wants." Ash squeezed my hand. "He says desire is a weakness. If he wanted Belle, he wouldn't have looked at her."

"I don't know what to do." I dropped my head to me knees, sighing. "I told him I want a divorce after the Green Living lawsuit is over. I need to leave. Leave before he breaks whatever's still left in me. Leave before he leaves *me*."

The last sentence robbed me of my breath. There was a good chance Cillian was going to come to the conclusion I wasn't worth the drama. Cut his losses and move on to the next wife on the list. Nothing went smoothly between us. I wasn't pregnant yet. I was working for his enemy, still keeping in touch with my ex-husband's grandmother…

It was not what he wanted, and Kill Fitzpatrick *always* got what he wanted.

Not to mention, I couldn't live like this anymore, either. Straddling the line between real and fake.

Belle was the first to speak.

"My mind and my heart are at war right now. I can't believe I'm saying this, but I'm about to give you my heart's advice. Remember at the cabin, all those months ago? When Cillian bet his ass in poker and left the money for Sailor and me to take? The only thing he asked was for us not to badmouth him to you. It was very telling, mostly because Kill's name is being dragged through the mud on a daily basis in the news and he doesn't seem to give a shit. I think he cares for you. I think he doesn't *want* to care for you, but he does. He doesn't want your loved ones to tell you not to be with him. I lost a bet, and I intend to respect it. I can't tell you to leave him, Pers. Not now. Not yet."

My gut twisted.

"Sam always says, a child who is not loved by his village will burn it down to feel its warmth," Sailor said quietly. She took a seat on the edge of the coffee table, raking her fingers through her fire-red hair. "I think Cillian has been watching everything around him burn for far too long. The Fitzpatrick men are wounded, but they hide it very well, and from what I gather, very differently. If anyone can stop him from destroying the rest of the world, it's you. Give him time," Sailor whispered. "It's the most precious gift of all."

I turned to Aisling. She was the only person to remain quiet. She was also the only person who didn't lose the bet with Kill.

"I think"—she bit her lower lip—"my brother wants you. I think he cares for you. But I also know he was the same man who blackmailed you into marrying him. He knew your life was in danger, and he took advantage of you. I don't know if this is the kind of environment you want to raise your child in." She rubbed at her forehead, struggling to let the words out. "I grew up in a dysfunctional family, and I don't have it in me to recommend you go the same route. I don't think you should stay."

We were split down the middle now.

Stay or walk away?

My heart said one thing; my brain said another.

In the end, it was my body that won.

I fell asleep in the arms of my best friends.

My estranged husband did not contact me for two weeks.

I'd spent every single day with Tinder and Tree, ignoring Cillian right back. Just because I didn't truly leave him, didn't mean I was going to actively seek him out. Something had been broken the day I'd found out he had me followed—maybe even *cheated* on me—and I needed time.

I moved back to the apartment he'd set up for me. Just a little F-you to my husband, letting him know I intended to make use of all the plush amenities he'd offered me.

When Saturday rolled around, I showed up to my tutoring

THE *Villain*

session with Tinder and Tree bearing gifts. I wasn't Gerald Fitzpatrick. I couldn't fault the two nuggets for their father's sins, and I'd grown to love and care for them.

Especially Tinder, who needed every ounce of love he could get.

"Guess who is here, and with presents!" Joelle announced when she opened the door for me that morning. I marched in carrying bags of goods. Tinder and Tree descended the stairway, squealing in delight. Tree slid down the bannisters making pirate noises while Tinder bounced on his toes all the way down. They both tackle-hugged me. We fell on the floor in a heap of breathless giggles.

"Auntie Persy, look what I made for you." Tinder shoved a drawing in my face. The title gave me pause. He thought of me as family, and I wasn't family. I was, in fact, just the opposite. Still, I plucked the paper between his pudgy fingers, gasping and asking questions.

"It's a map. If we follow it, we'll get to heaven, and in heaven, everyone is nice, and no one hits you!" Tinder exclaimed.

I whipped my head in his direction, about to ask him who, exactly, hit him, when Tree pounced on me.

"What'd you get us?" Tree grabbed my cheeks, squashing them. "Is it a truck? I told Mommy I want one for Christmas. Red. It has to be red. It *must*. Your favorite color, right, Auntie Persy?"

"Tree, my gosh, why would you say that? Any gift is welcome. The fact she thought about you is enough." Joelle scoffed. Our eyes met, and we shared a smile. In the past few months, we'd built a tentative friendship, based on our shared love for her sons. I knew it wasn't easy for her to open up to me. Especially seeing as she had to slam her door in the faces of journalists and cameramen on a daily basis every time my husband leaked an unflattering piece of news about hers.

Andrew Arrowsmith was no longer the media's sweetheart thanks to my husband.

Now they were both bad men who hated each other and stopped at nothing to destroy one another.

I wanted to give her the tools to be there for Tinder and Tree.

Especially now that I'd been with the family long enough to know Andrew's presence in the boys' life was almost nonexistent.

"You're here," Andrew's steely voice rumbled, and we all looked up to the top of the stairways.

The timing of him being here made my heart leap. "Andrew."

"How're you doing, sweetheart? Is that savage husband of yours still giving you trouble?"

"Andrew!" Joelle yapped, blushing.

I raised my hand up.

"It's okay." I turned to smile at her husband. "Actually, I moved out."

The words felt bitter on my tongue. What an incredibly traitorous thing to say. But I had to throw my plan into high gear. I didn't know how much time I had with the family. How much time I had with Cillian. I was working against the clock.

"You did?" His eyebrows jumped to his hairline. "Why, if I may ask?"

I was still sitting on the floor, the twins in my arms.

"I'm not so sure it's going to work out after all."

"I see. How unfortunate."

I smiled politely. "Well, I have a day full of activities with the kids. I better get started."

He nodded distractedly. "Yes. Of course. I won't keep you. I have some…some phone calls to make."

To his lawyers, no doubt. He probably wondered if it was the right time to ask me to testify against my husband.

"Thank you for sharing this information, Persephone. It means a lot to us to have your trust. You'd tell us if Mr. Fitzpatrick mistreated you in any way, wouldn't you?"

And there it was.

The bottom line.

The master plan we both had for my being here.

"Of course. You guys are like family to me."

THE Villain

The Lannisters, but whatever.

Andrew turned around and made his way back to his office. I proceeded to hand Tree and Tinder their gifts, with Joelle standing next to us. I motioned for her to come join us. She did.

"Thank you, you shouldn't have." She crouched down. "I know you save every penny."

"I love the boys."

Tinder unwrapped his first gift. A chewing necklace. Shark-toothed shaped. He yelped in delight, thrusting it in his mother's hand.

"Can y-you put it on m-me, Mommy?"

She stared at him for a moment, shocked. I had a feeling she didn't have many moments like these with her children.

"I...of course. Turn around, sweetie."

I watched them as Tree unwrapped his present—a bike helmet—blabbing happily about how he wanted a motorcycle when he grew up. Joelle's hands shook as she wrapped the toddler necklace around her son's neck. Tears pricked my eyes. Somewhere along the way, Joelle had forgotten how to mother. Or maybe she never got the chance to be one at all, always helping her husband chase his dreams.

Tinder twitched, curling and uncurling his fists, making animal noises, which he did often.

"I was raised by au pairs," Joelle said grimly, her eyes still on the necklace she was putting on Tinder. "I thought that's the way things were supposed to be. I never planned on having a son who is..."

"Special?" I finished for her softly. "It's a blessing. It makes you grow. Find your strength. There's a lot we can learn from children. Things we'd already forgotten but shouldn't have."

"Like what?"

"Like what's important in life. Family. Friendship. The beauty of a lone cloud sailing across a perfectly blue sky. Kids have their priorities straight. It's us adults who sometimes forget the meaning of life. Now come." I stood, offering her my hand. I was forming an unlikely friendship with a woman who fantasized about destroying my husband no less than I wanted to topple hers. "Let's make new memories with the boys. It's not too late. It's never too late."

I led everyone to the two bikes I'd purchased earlier that week. I used my own paycheck, refraining from touching Kill's allowance. The money continued piling up in my account, like a mountain of broken promises and cracked dreams.

We spent the rest of the afternoon in the backyard, teaching the boys how to ride a bike with no training wheels. Tree got the hang of it quickly while Tinder clung to me and made me promise not to let go of his bike the entire time. It took four hours and a hundred attempts before Tinder managed to ride a zigzagged line, but he did it, and my heart was ready to burst when I saw his face light up.

"I'm doing it! I'm riding!" He laughed. Tree followed behind on his bike, making racecar noises. Joelle and I looked at them, laughing.

"I never thought he'd learn." She giggled. "Thank you so much."

"I'm-I'm-I'm going to-to-to tell D-D-Daddy I can ride a bike. Maybe he'll come downstairs and s-see us?" Tinder tugged at my blouse. I looked down and smiled, ignoring Joelle, next to me, whose smile turned into a grimace.

"That's a great idea, Tin! I'm sure he's going to be over the moon."

Tinder padded back into the house through the glass door, making happy noises, his arms jerking about.

"Mommy! Look! No hands!" Tree bragged, stretching his short arms on either side of the bike. Joelle hurried to her son in a mixture of awe and anxiety. I wondered what it felt like to watch your own child spread their wings and take their first flight. The horror of knowing everyone falls, gets hurt, gets *scarred*. That you cannot shield your child from the ugliness of the world forever.

Not wanting to interrupt their moment, I turned around and entered the house. I'd been wanting to check if they had ingredients for a sponge cake. The boys loved baking in the afternoons, and even though Greta didn't remember who I was anymore, she always appreciated a good cake.

THE Villain

The minute I walked into the house, I noticed the walls rattled with a piercing scream coming from upstairs.

"Just fucking say it. Don't stutter it. *Say. It!*"

I tore up the stairs in a flash, the sounds of Andrew's shouts drowning the thuds of my feet hitting the wood.

"I can't fucking listen to you anymore, you no-good piece of… piece of…*crap*! You remind me of him. You're just like him. A little, stupid loser."

I screeched to a halt on the threshold of Andrew's office, panting. It was the first time I'd ever been there. He was crouching down, shaking Tinder's shoulders, spraying spit all over the poor kid's face.

I didn't think.

I didn't even stop to digest what was happening.

I stormed inside, scooping Tinder in my arms, ripping him from his father's hands. Andrew stood and staggered backward, his face morphing from anger to shock. He didn't think he'd have an audience.

"*Persephone.*"

My name fell from between his lips like a curse. Like he wanted to shake me, too. How often did he do this to him? Tinder's words vibrated in my body, making it hum with rage.

"It's a map. If we follow it, we'll get to heaven, and in heaven, everyone is nice, and no one hits you."

The better question to ask was how many more outbursts could Tinder expect in his lifetime—many, I suspected—and how many more victims were out there in the world who suffered under Andrew Arrowsmith's wrath?

The last question hit me hard.

It hit me hard because deep down, I knew there was at least one other person close to me who was shattered by Andrew.

Traumatized enough to swear off the entire human race afterward.

"Look, I know what it looks like…" Andrew made a move toward me, his voice soft and soothing.

I jerked Tinder to my chest.

I shook my head. "I'm not ready to talk about what I witnessed here before I talk with your wife."

"What's happening here?" Joelle's voice drifted from the hallway. I turned around to face her. The look on my face said it all. The hopeful, open smile that graced her lips the entire afternoon collapsed into a glare.

"Oh, no. What did you do now, Andy?"

Now implied there were a lot of *befores*.

"I just told him to speak clearly." Andrew tried to laugh it off and tousle Tinder's hair, but the boy buried his face in my shoulder, sniffing.

"He shook him," I said quietly, not wanting to add any more details to avoid embarrassing Tinder. Kids were much more perceptive than adults gave them credit for. "I'm going to take the boys downstairs to make a sponge cake. I'm sure you have things to talk about."

I offered my hand to Tree, who stood behind his mother, and went downstairs still holding Tinder.

"Can we make triangle sandwiches first and cut off the crust? I *hate* the crust." Tree giggled.

"Of course. What about you, Tin? Would you like anything for a snack?"

"A-A-Ants on a log, please. S-S-Sorry I made Daddy upset with my stut-stut-stuttering. I didn't mean to."

He coiled into himself in my arms. I shook my head briskly.

"Nonsense. I want you to remember something very important, okay, boys? Something I want you to carry with you everywhere, no matter where you go, like the necklace I gave you."

We reached the bottom of the stairs. I put Tinder back on the floor and crouched to their eye level.

They nodded, their big, innocent eyes clinging to my face.

"Whenever Daddy loses his temper and yells at you, it's not your fault. We are not responsible for other people's actions. *Only* for our own. That is not to say we are never wrong. It is our job to try to do our best to become better and always hold ourselves accountable for our own actions. But *never* blame yourself for what Daddy or Mommy is doing, okay? Promise me."

"Scout's honor!" Tree put two fingers up.

"I-I promise, too!" Tinder jumped.

My heart rattled in my chest like a rusty, empty cage full of feelings I didn't want to face.

The family I was trying to build was a threat to these children.

And their parents were a threat to mine.

But I couldn't turn my back on them.

Not anymore.

I dropped my half-full duffel bag to the floor, scowling at Petar.

"Really, dude? You promised he wouldn't be here."

The sound of the front door being thrown open was enough indication my husband walked into the house even though I'd specifically called Petar to make sure the coast would be clear so I could pick up the small stuff I'd left here and move it back to my apartment.

Petar hitched a shoulder up helplessly.

"He wasn't supposed to come until ten or eleven, I swear. Ever since you left the house, he's only come here to sleep. Sometimes not even that. Three times I had to send a courier to the office with a new set of suits for him this week."

Though it was tempting to feel bad for Kill, I pushed the emotion out of my heart.

I threw the duffel bag on my bed, stuffing the knickknacks I'd forgotten in my haste to leave two weeks ago.

"Where is she?" I heard Cillian's rumble from downstairs. Petar did the sign of the cross, looked up, and dashed out of my room. It didn't take a rocket scientist to know where I was, so I left the question hanging unanswered.

Sure enough, not five seconds later, Cillian was standing at my bedroom door, dark and surly as Hades holding uneaten pomegranates.

"Back so early?" I huffed, stuffing one of my one hundred thousand flowery self-help journals into my bag. "What would Daddy say? I thought you were born to work."

He walked in, closing the door behind him.

"Shouldn't you be at work?" I made idle conversation, knowing how much he loathed it.

"Shouldn't you be living with your husband?" he shot back.

"No," I said evenly, zipping the bloated bag, tugging at the stuck zipper. "You spent the past few months cementing the fact that we aren't a real couple. All I'm doing is finally listening to you. You did a great job convincing me we're nothing more than a contract."

I avoided looking at him directly. The hornet-sting that came with laying my eyes on his magnificence was too much on a normal day, and completely unmanageable when we were estranged.

A stranger or an ally, Cillian always had the talent to make my heart sing and my soul weep.

For a long beat, he just stood there, drinking me in.

He took a step forward, putting a hand on my arm.

I wanted to break down and cry.

To tell him what I saw Andrew do.

To confess I couldn't eat or sleep well.

"I told Sam to pull the surveillance," he said.

I looked up at him, through a curtain of unshed tears.

"And?"

"And I haven't touched anyone since I put a ring on your goddamn finger." His lips barely moved, his jaw was so tight.

"*And?*" I arched an eyebrow.

Give me an emotion.

THE *Villain*

Any emotion.

"And I shouldn't have broken the contract," he said gruffly, looking away from me. "I trust you."

"Bullshit," I choked on a dry laugh.

He said nothing.

I was beginning to see nothing I could say or do was going to change his mind about people. About *me*. He was incapable of feelings and pushing him to love me would achieve nothing other than to make him resent me. Even now, he didn't want me because he liked me.

Only because I was a comfortable arrangement. A means to an end.

"You're not leaving," he said simply.

I pulled the bag, hoisting it over my shoulder and turning to face him.

"I'm sorry."

He stepped toward me, snarling.

"Sorry for what?"

"For changing the rules on you. For breaking the contract. For asking for more. I realize that I was out of line. I want you to marry someone who gives you what you want. Who is happy with what you're willing to give back. And I'm not that person. I meant what I said. As soon as your legal/PR issues are over and everything quiets down, we can get a divorce."

I sidestepped him, but he matched my step, getting in my face again.

"All this because of one mistake?" He scowled. "I already told you I haven't touched anyone else. You were watched exactly one week, Persephone."

I threw my head back, laughing. "You think that's the only problem? One mistake? Get real, Kill. You never treated me as your wife. Never spent the entire night in my bed. Never took me on one date that wasn't a fancy event. No honeymoon. No meaningful conversation. I was never your equal. The only thing that's changed is that now, I finally realize I never will be."

His eyes thundered. I bet his precious pulse was skyrocketing. I didn't think he realized I even knew about it. How he put his fingers to his wrist discreetly to keep himself in check.

How he cracked his knuckles every time he got ruffled.

"I dined with you every evening. I fucked you every night. I took you to balls. To family dinners. I bought you jewelry. What more do you want from me, Persephone?"

"A *relationship*." I hurled the duffel bag on the floor, growling.

"I don't know how to have one!" he screamed back in my face.

Kill began to pace, shaking his head.

"I don't know what that even means. I never had a relationship. You request something, and I make it happen. Is that not what a relationship is about?"

How could I even answer that question without sounding like a complete bitch?

"How did you know I was here?" I asked.

"This house is wired more than a police informant in a bad cop show." He rolled his eyes, stopping to examine me.

"So you left everything and came here?"

He parked a hand on his waist. "You talk like I don't give a damn."

"You don't."

"Well, newsflash." He took a step forward, plastering me to the wall, his hand coming to the back of my neck, grabbing it as he tilted his head down. "I do. I'm not fucking happy about it, to be sure, but that doesn't make it any less true."

It was everything I'd wanted to hear since the day I met Cillian Fitzpatrick, yet at that moment, it was too late.

If life taught me anything, it was that giving your all to someone who only agreed to return a fraction of themselves to you was a bad idea.

"Come home, Flower Girl." His eyes fluttered shut, his mouth moving over mine. The sensation was like a roller coaster, when you tip over the edge and your stomach dips. The rush of warmth flaring in my chest made my body buzz. Kill's words drifted through my clouded brain. "Let me fuck you. Be the wife I need. You just need a bit more training. A few more months and we can fuck each other out of our system."

Months.

We had an expiration date.

We would *always* have an expiration date.

I ripped my mouth from his.

He didn't get it, and I was tired of explaining.

"Give me one reason to stay, Cillian. I'm not asking for many. Just the one. Something to hold onto."

"Because I want you to."

"No. Something else. Something that's not completely selfish."

"I can't be anything other than selfish," he said brusquely.

I picked up my duffel bag, pushing at his chest.

"As soon as the lawsuit is over, we're getting a divorce."

This time I didn't look back.

I pushed through the pain.

Numb, prideful, and only half-alive.

I finally knew what it meant to have your heart broken.

Understanding—finally—that Paxton didn't as much as put a dent in mine.

I got back to my apartment, threw myself into the shower, and shoved a few dry rice cakes down my throat. My improvised version of dinner.

I hadn't even unpacked the bag I retrieved from Cillian's house. Just fell on my sofa in my living room and flipped through channels, battling a headache.

All the local news headlined the same story, about Cillian and Andrew going head-to-head in the trial that would take place soon. The news anchor cut to a video of the oil rig in the Arctic, an ugly black thing sticking out like a sore thumb in the middle of the infinite blue. Crushed shards of ice scattered around it like broken glass. My heart bled for the piece of nature that fell victim to Cillian's cruelty.

You and me both, Arctic.

I picked my phone up and typed my husband a message.

Me: Stop the Arctic drilling.

Me: You want heirs so much, have you ever stopped to think about what kind of world you are leaving for them?

His response came promptly.

Cillian: Yes. One where they'll be filthy rich.

Me: Does being rich make you happy?

Cillian: Happiness is a feeling, ergo...

Me: You can't feel it. Gotcha. What did Andrew do to you?

Cillian: He made me.

Me: And what are you going to do to him?

Cillian: Undo him.

My doorbell rang, nearly making me jump out of my skin.

It wasn't Kill's style to show up where he wasn't invited. But I knew there was zero chance of it being anyone else. My parents didn't know I lived in this apartment and not my husband's house, Emmabelle worked nights, Sailor was probably off sneaking into archery ranges—only to be chased down by her worrisome husband—and Aisling very rarely raised her head up from the medical books these days.

Rolling up from the couch, I padded to my door.

"You really have some nerve coming here after the conversation we just had." I opened the door, ready to give my husband a piece of my mind.

My heart dropped as soon as I saw who it was on the other side.

Paxton.

THE Villain

Cillian

Just because I called off Sam's private investigators didn't mean I let go of my unhealthy obsession with my wife.

No. That would be the normal, sane thing to do.

Not my fucking style.

In my defense, I set my phone to receive notifications each time her apartment door opened, not because I suspected she'd cheat, but because I wanted to know she'd made it home safely.

Why I still gave a damn about her well-being was beyond me.

The piling evidence against her should have, in and of itself, made me drop her like a mic after an amateur rap night.

Persephone worked for my nemesis on a daily basis.

Visited Paxton's grandmother.

What on earth made me believe she'd be faithful?

Nothing. The answer to that was nothing. And as I watched the blond, broad-shouldered man in the Next Door app shifting from foot to foot on her doorstep, head bowed, fingers tapping the side of his legs, waiting for her to open the door, I realized I'd been played.

Ridiculed and undermined.

Betrayed to the highest degree.

Sam warned me he was unfinished business, and I didn't listen.

Now here he was, in the flesh.

Paxton Veitch.

Nineteen

Persephone

"WHAT THE *FUCK* ARE YOU DOING HERE?"

The F-bomb was a guest of honor in my vocabulary. I rarely used it but felt the urge to spit it out for this special occasion. My body shook so badly I had to grab the door handle to stop myself from collapsing.

My ex-husband stood in front of me, looking appallingly healthy for someone who'd been on the run for the past year. Tan, muscled, and at least as far as I could tell, still in full possession of all his teeth. His blond curls scattered about his head playfully, his soulful eyes blinking back at me.

"Babe." His lips twisted in a relieved smile, and he let out a sigh. "Fuck, you look just as gorgeous as I remember. Holy shit, Persy. Look at you."

He gathered my hands in his, bringing them to his mouth, laughing. Tears coated his sparkling eyes. I was too shocked to shove him away.

Paxton was here.

In the flesh.

After hundreds of unanswered phone calls, emails, and sleepless nights.

My head swarmed with questions. Where had he been hiding? When did he come back? How did he find his way into my building? There was a doorman at the entrance.

Mostly, I wanted to know *why*. Why did he leave me to deal with his mess?

And if I meant so little to him, why come back and stand at my doorway?

My hands were still in his, scorching with his betrayal. I snapped out of my reverie, pushing him away.

"I'll repeat myself." I took a step back. "What're you doing here, Paxton? And how did you know where I live?"

"Dropped by Grandma Greta's nursing home. Your name and address were listed as an emergency contact."

"That's right because you, her only living relative, were MIA."

"I know." His voice broke. "I'm here to make amends. Let me? *Please*?"

He kissed my cheek hastily, worming into my apartment uninvited.

I closed the door, knowing I was going to blow the rooftop with screams in about half a second and not wanting to get evicted or causing Cillian any embarrassing headlines.

"Give me one good reason not to tell Byrne and Kaminski you're back in town." I crossed my arms over my chest.

Paxton gave himself a tour around my living room, whistling as he drank in the expensive fixtures, gourmet kitchen, and quartz countertops. His neck craned as he studied the lighting, one hand brushing over a floor-to-ceiling art piece that cost more than the apartment we'd rented together while married.

"Wow. Okay. Nice digs."

When he saw I was still standing by the door, fully ready to throw him out, he poked his lower lip out.

"C'mon, babe. It's been a minute. We need to iron things out, but there's a lot to talk about, don't you think?"

No, my mind screamed.

Sam had told me I'd dodged a bullet the night of the storm, when I tried to accept Cillian's proposal and found out he'd already withdrawn it. But the deadly bullet I'd escaped was the day Kill took me as a wife.

He made my problems disappear.

Put me out of harm's way, no matter the price.

"I'm not buying your charade," I said pointedly.

"Fine." His voice dropped to a low growl. "Then let's get real. I'm glad your bouji ass is living the good life. Got yourself a sugar daddy and found your sass, huh?" Paxton winked, his charming, dimpled smile on full display. He jerked my fridge open, taking out a glass bottle of juice. The kitchen had been stocked thrice a week by Cillian's people.

The thought of Paxton being here, drinking an organic pressed juice at Kill's expense made me want to punch him into a wall.

I hadn't been fair to my husband.

He fulfilled his end of the bargain, providing me with everything he'd promised and more. In return, I pushed him into giving me things he was incapable of providing. Love, sympathy, and tenderness.

Kill deserved to know everything.

About my plan to destroy Arrowsmith.

About Paxton being here.

"The word you are looking for is a *husband*. My husband does well for himself, yes," I corrected. "But even more important than his deep pockets, he was kind enough to get me out of the trouble you got me into. Knowing Cillian, he won't appreciate you being here, so I suggest you get out of here before he does the job Byrne couldn't finish."

Paxton snapped his head toward me mid-sip, his eyes bulging.

"Don't tell me you fell in love with him. That's such a sap move, Pers. Rich boys don't have hearts."

"Neither do poor ones from Southie, apparently."

He collapsed onto a barstool, groaning as he scrubbed his face.

"Look, I know I haven't been the man you deserve, babe. But I needed a way out. I knew you were going to get us out of trouble. I couldn't keep in touch while you were working on getting us out of this, but I stood on the sidelines and watched, ready to pounce if they actually did something to you. I *always* had your back, Pers. I did this to protect you. Protect *us*."

The lie was so half-assed, that I felt hysterical laughter bubbling in my throat. He continued, undeterred.

"Our goodbye was temporary. I always planned to come back. You were smart, resourceful, and responsible. I just needed you to do me this little solid. When I saw the article about your marriage to Cillian Fitzpatrick, I wanted to kiss you. I thought, 'that's my girl.' I was beginning to worry Byrne would follow up on his threat to pimp you out. I was about to step in."

He put a hand to his chest. He looked like a bad soap opera actor. The type to win a Razzie award every year and be arrogant enough to walk the red carpet to accept it.

My blood buzzed. I was on the brink of smashing his nose in with my fist, and I *never* hurt so much as a fly.

"You knew they were following me?" I gritted out.

He nodded. "I kept an eye on you the entire time. Made sure you were okay. I was worried sick, Pers."

"I wasn't okay."

"You really need to give yourself more credit, babe. You did great."

"How did you keep tabs on me?" I demanded.

"Friends."

"*Which* friends?"

"C'mon." He waved his hand around as though I was missing the entire point.

"Where were you, Paxton?" I pressed, taking a step toward him.

No part of me was unsure or ambivalent.

No disappointment.

No sorrow.

No pang of that wild heartbreak that tore at me each time Cillian left my bed at night.

All I felt was disgust.

"Here and there," Paxton sulked, averting his eyes from me to his shoes.

The idiot thought he could waltz into my life and reclaim me.

He mistook my bleeding heart for a dumb brain.

"You either answer my questions or I'm calling security." I raised my phone in the air.

He shot me a tired smile.

"How'd you think I ended up here? The security in this place is trash."

"In that case"—I swiped my finger over my phone's screen—"I'll call my husband. Don't let his rich-boy reputation confuse you. He is very good with his hands, beyond just making me come."

Paxton's jaw constricted, his eyes darkening.

"*Don't*," he bit out. "Fine. Whatever, Persy. You wanna play? I'm game. What do you wanna know?"

"Who told you about Byrne and Kaminski following me?"

"Mitch." Mitch was the guy he was paired with by Byrne for assignments. "He was still hustling for Colin a few months after I bailed. Still shoots the shit with Kaminski every now and again."

"Where were you all this time?"

"Costa Rica was my first stop. The day word got out that Byrne knew I blew all our savings and couldn't pay him back, I bought a one-way ticket. I laid low there. Worked in construction. Saved up whatever I could. At first, I'd hoped I could come up with half the money, then pay the rest in Boston. I always wanted it to work between us, Persy. I just knew keeping in touch with you was going to put you in a whole lotta risk. Then the news of you marrying Fitzpatrick broke the fucking internet. There were *memes* about it, dude. I picked up the phone and called Mitch. Asked if it was true. He told me your husband made sure Kaminski could never take a piss standing up again he trashed him so bad. Byrne wasn't doing so hot, either. I realized I was probably next on your husband's shit list. That he was going to unleash Sam Brennan on me. Brennan has eyes and ears everywhere, so I moved up to Mexico. Cancun. Stayed with a friend."

"A friend?" I asked with a snort. The only piece of information to make my heart stutter was Cillian beating up Kaminski. I had no idea he did that.

"A chick from high school. She's running a spring break resort there. It was always crowded, lots of people moving in and out. I knew Brennan would have a bitch of a time catching me there. I cleaned her pool."

"Platonically, I assume." I rolled my eyes. He was such a cliché.

He laughed humorlessly.

"Please, Pers. Let's not pretend you haven't been sucking Fitzpatrick's cock every night the better half of this year. We both did what we had to do in order to survive."

"In my case, I enjoyed the task *immensely*," I lamented. "You haven't even picked up the phone to check in on your grandmother."

I knew because I asked at the nursing home if they'd heard from him each time I visited.

Paxton flopped his cheek over his fist, sighing.

"I knew you would take care of her. I'd trust you with my own life. You always do the right thing. Listen, we're out of the woods now. Mitch told me the debt has been paid. Byrne's out of the picture. We can be together, Persy. Start over fresh. Pick up where we left off. He didn't make you sign a prenup, right?"

My ex-husband wasn't only insane, he was also as dumb as a shoestring. I tried to remember what I saw in him in the first place, beyond his Instagram model looks. The answer was clear as it was embarrassing—he was the designated rebound. The antidote to Cillian's refusal. The untried vaccine that ended up nearly killing me.

"We're happily divorced. I married someone else." I erected my wedding finger, an engagement ring with a diamond the size of his face sparkling back at him.

I never took it off. Even when I knew I should.

Paxton jumped up to his feet, hurrying over to me. Maybe it was because he wasn't built like Cillian—not quite as tall, as broad, as commanding—or maybe it was because he simply *wasn't* Cillian, but his very presence annoyed me.

"I get it, babe. You're angry. You're hurt. You have every right to be. But you're not fooling anyone. Your marriage isn't real." He stood before me now, grabbing my arms, itching to shake me.

"Ours wasn't, either. In the spirit of being candid, I, too, have a confession to make." I broke out of his grip, taking a step forward, my breath fanning his face. "You were always nothing more than a distraction. It was always Kill. *You* were on borrowed time. But Cillian? Cillian is my forever."

The words settled between us, an invisible barbed-wire barrier.

By the way Paxton stared at me, I knew he wanted to rip it apart.

The hunger in his eyes alarmed me, even if I knew it wasn't for me, but for all the things I represented now: wealth, power, and connections.

"All right," he rustled. "You win. I'll be the side piece. But it's gonna cost ya."

"I don't want a side piece. Even if I did, you would be the last person on the planet I'd consider. You are mean and selfish, Paxton. Get out of my apartment before I speed-dial Sam Brennan and throw you out myself."

"*Babe*," he groaned, seizing me by the jaw, walking me backward until my back hit the door. "I know you're pissed, but we were good together."

His lips spoke over mine. He was kissing me. Half-kissing me, anyway. His breath and heat and body pressed against mine. His tongue rolled over my lower lip.

"I don't want good," I spat into his mouth. He tripped backward, his eyes wide.

THE Villain

A slow, vicious smile spread on my face. I didn't recognize myself in my behavior, and for the first time, I was fine with it. "I want divine, and I found it. Get the hell out, Veitch."

"You're crazy if you think I'm letting you go."

It was promise, a warning, and a declaration. He stepped away, giving me a once-over, assessing me before he made his next move. "I'll change your mind. I won you once, and I can do it again. Whether it's the easy way or the hard way, you'll be writhing beneath me in no time, and when you are, I promise you, Persephone, I will make sure your husband knows it."

"*Out!*"

He shouldered past me with his tail tucked between his legs.

I closed the door, locked, and bolted it, then pressed my back against it, letting out a ragged breath, feeling rather than thinking a word that'd been pulsating against my skin from the moment I said "I do" to my new husband.

Saved.

Cillian

"You dumb piece of cock-sucking shit." I raised a fist to Sam Brennan's face the minute he walked through my door, slamming it against his thrice-broken nose.

I'd texted Brennan at five in the morning to let him know if he didn't show up at my doorstep in fifteen minutes, I was going to buy every building in Southie—federal and private—and bulldoze through each childhood memory in his neighborhood just to shit all over his day.

He made it to my house in nine minutes and didn't even look ruffled.

I, on the other hand, moved from no profanity to nothing *but* profanity.

"Good morning to you, too," he said calmly, readjusting his nose back to its place without as much as a wince as blood spurted out of his nostrils. The crack the bone made alone would make anyone but the two of us gag. "To what do I owe this greeting?"

"To being a bullshit private investigator and a terrible fucking friend. You slacked off. Guess how my wife spent her night yesterday?" I plastered him against my front door, swinging my fist again.

I jabbed his ribs, feeling and hearing at least two of them crack.

"With your dick in her ass?" he asked flatly, tapping the pocket of his leather jacket, taking out a pack of cigarettes and lighting one up. He really was immune to pain. "I suggest you try other holes if you're interested in knocking her up."

"You're a sick human."

"Thank you." He dropped his Zippo into his front pocket.

"It wasn't a compliment."

"To me, it was. Most people don't consider me human at all. So what was your wife up to yesterday?"

I stepped back from him, realizing his lack of fear and pain made it pointless to beat him up. I walked over to the bar cart. It *was* five o'clock. Sure, it was in the morning, but I never let semantics get in my way.

"Paxton Veitch paid her a visit." I poured a finger of cognac into a goblet, training my eyes on the golden liquid.

Sam limped in my direction, his expression unfathomable. "He's in town?"

"You should've known that."

"You told me not to check on him. You were fucking specific about it, too." He leaned against the wall, watching me.

He had a point. I'd rejected the idea Paxton Veitch posed a threat

THE Villain

to my marriage for so long, being proved differently wasn't on my radar.

"You need to tail him," I instructed. "Find out why he's here. What he wants."

"I can tell you right now why he's here—he's here because his ex-wife just married into one of the wealthiest families in the country, and because he is a money-grabbing scumbag. Do you need me to deal-deal with him?" He raised his eyebrows.

My instincts told me to say yes.

Have Sam off him, chop him up, and throw him into the ocean.

Not necessarily the Atlantic. That was too close. The Indian Ocean sounded good.

I'd never made such a request before, but in Veitch's case, I was ready to make an exception. I'd refused to give my wife the only thing she'd ever asked from me—love—and sent her right into the arms of her ex-husband, who was probably waxing poetic at her all night.

I pretty much wrapped her up in a bow and handed her over to him.

Yet I couldn't, for the life of me, do this to her.

Have her idiotic ex-husband killed.

No matter how much I wanted him out of the picture.

I shook my head, clutching the goblet so hard, it dented out of shape, the liquid raining down to the floor. Sam's face remained unmoved, as if I hadn't just bent a gold chalice with my own fist. I dumped it to the floor, turning to the bar and plucking a napkin. I patted my palm clean of alcohol and blood.

"Don't touch him. Just find out as much as you can. Where he lives, what he's doing, what's his angle. I'll deal with him myself."

Sam nodded.

"Do it now. Drop everything else."

Another nod. "Anything else you want to know?"

Yes, I wanted to know if I was truly losing Persephone, but that was beyond Sam's scope.

"Just do your fucking job." I turned around, ascending the stairway back to my office.

I cursed again.

But this time, no one was surprised.

I was beginning to unfurl, break, crack, and shatter.

I was *changing*.

Feeling.

And I hated it.

I spent the rest of the day pretending.

Pretending to be present, pretending to work, pretending not to give a damn.

I attended meetings, scolded employees, went through our quarterly reports, and grabbed lunch with Devon, in which we strategized our defense in court against Green Living.

"I should not have eaten the sashimi. It upset my stomach," I complained when we parted ways at the entrance of the restaurant.

Devon barked out a laugh. "The sashimi was fine. The queasy feeling in your gut is longing. Is Persy still living in her Commonwealth flat?"

I didn't even grace that with an answer. Longing was something teenage girls did with Armie Hammer. The only long thing about me was between my thighs.

At six o'clock, I called it a day. I drove back home, parked, then spotted Persephone's Tesla at the front gate.

Killing the engine, I got out of the car, something weird and warm rattling in my stomach.

Food poisoning. Fucking raw fish. I saw a documentary about it. I probably had maggots the size of shits inside my intestines.

THE *Villain*

Taking measured steps to the front door, I glanced through the window. I spotted my wife standing by the stairway, her delicate hand perched on the bannister.

She wore a white dress, her blond hair tumbling down her shoulders all the way to the small of her back. A dirty angel with a golden crown for a halo.

Imaginary ants traveled up my toes, all the way to my skull.

I rounded the front entrance, trying to get a better angle of her. I saw her talking to Petar, her back to me. Petar was standing directly in front of the window I was standing behind. He spotted me. His face went from distressed to surprised in seconds. I wasn't known for hiding behind bushes and watching people. Especially people who were inside *my* goddamn house.

His mouth opened, probably to tell her I was there. I shook my head. He clamped it shut.

Why was she here?

Take a wild guess, asshole.

She was here to thank me for the money, divorce, and enthusiastic dick, pack the remainder of her possessions and ride off with Paxton into the horizon in the Tesla I was dumb enough to purchase for her.

Unfortunately for Flower Girl, playing into her hands wasn't in my plans. Not anymore. If she wanted to destroy this marriage, she was going to have to do it the long, slow, excruciating way. I wasn't giving her the chance at a clean kill.

The memory of my visit to Colin Byrne stirred something violent in me.

"Veitch wanted to whore out his wife all by himself before he fucked off. He wanted to kidnap her and give her to me."

I remembered his words, verbatim.

I'd never wanted to kill a person more than I had wanted to put a bullet in Paxton Veitch's skull.

All I needed to do was walk inside the house and tell her.

It was that simple.

But I knew it'd hurt her.

Break her spirit.

Show her that the man she chose to spend the rest of her life with wanted to sell her.

It was a terrible time to grow a conscience.

I turned around, walked back to my car, and called Sam.

"Give me Paxton's address."

I wasn't going to break Persephone.

But I sure as hell wasn't going to let the *real* villain get the girl.

Paxton Veitch's temporary residence was nothing more than a shack in the back room of an illegal poker joint in Southie. Judging by the exterior of the decaying two-story building, he was probably sleeping in a cot made solely of garbage, pubic hair, and STDs.

Rather than announce my arrival with a knock, I kicked the flimsy screen door down, barging in.

Three round tables full of men with oil and dirt stains on their faces looked up at me, their eyes snapping off their cards.

"Paxton Veitch," I grumbled. No other words were necessary.

Silence rang in the room.

I knew dangling my sharp suit and expensive haircut in front of them was inviting trouble, but I welcomed it. Sighing, I took out my wallet and raised a hundred-dollar bill between my index and middle fingers, waving it around.

"I'll ask again, where's Paxton Veitch?"

This time, the men shifted in their seats, glancing at each other.

"Oh, for fuck's sake, we don't even know him, why are we protecting him? He's in the back room!" one of them piped up, banging his cards over the table. "Take the stairs up. His is the second door on the left."

THE *Villain*

I dropped the bill to the floor, proceeding as a few men rushed to the floor, fighting for the money.

When I got to the door I was looking for, I took a few breaths to calm myself down. I'd imagined going head-to-head with the bastard longer than I'd like to admit. Before Persephone and I were on speaking terms.

The memory of her kissing him at Hunter and Sailor's wedding still made my blood boil.

I'd walked along the hedge garden, inwardly convincing myself I wasn't a complete moron for rejecting the Penrose girl I wanted so much. The topiary assaulted my eyesight. A tacky mixture of angels, animals, and heart shapes. The sound of panting made me slow next to a cloud-shaped shrub.

"Oh, Paxton," a throaty, sweet voice had moaned.

My blood ran cold.

I took a step aside, pretending to read a sign explaining the design of the garden. From my position, I could see strands of white-blond hair woven in the shrubs, a delicate, snowy neck extended, and a male mouth peppering kisses all over it.

"God, you're so fucking sweet. What's your name again?"

"Persephone."

"*Persy-phone-ay.*" His hands were everywhere as he mispronounced her name. "What does it mean?"

I'd strained my neck, developing perverse satisfaction in making myself watch her in another man's arms after snubbing her. His head trailed down her breasts, disappearing from my line of vision. She was panting hard and fast.

Take a good look at what you did. She is in someone else's arms now.
Someone normal.
Who deserves her.

Now, Paxton's door taunted me.

I pushed it open, unbothered about stomping into his territory unannounced. He did that twice to me. It was time he got a taste of his own medicine.

He was in the room, having an intense phone conversation, standing in front of a small, dirty window with his back to me.

"You think I'm not trying? It's not as easy as I thought. She's changed, man. Probably all that dough and gold-plated cock." He snickered, snorting. "I'm not gonna hurt her. I still love Persy, you know. She's always been my girl. I just want in with her ass, so I can get my way, too. There's too much money in that pot for me not to get my share."

At least now I knew she hadn't fucked him yesterday.

Silver linings and all that jazz.

I grabbed the phone from behind him and killed the call, tossing the device onto his bed. He whipped his head around, his mouth hanging open.

"Shi—"

I shoved him toward a wooden desk pushed against the wall, shutting him up.

He sagged onto it, plopping down.

"Time for a little talk, Veitch."

"You're the Fitzpatrick guy." His brows furrowed. "The dude she married."

"And here I thought you were just a pretty face."

We examined each other. He was a good-looking kid. Light hair, soft features. Clad in a broken-in leather jacket and saggy jeans that made it look like he needed his diaper changed.

Paxton folded his arms over his chest.

"Look, man, I don't want any trouble."

"If you didn't want trouble, you wouldn't chase it across the planet. Do you really think I'd let you touch what's mine?"

He shook his head. "I don't know what to think. All I know is that Persy and I had a good thing going. I fucked up, but she's a good girl. She could still forgive me."

That meant she hadn't yet. My heart slowed for the first time since I saw him enter her apartment. I tugged at the leather gloves in my back pocket, slapping them over my thigh and putting them on. His throat

THE Villain

bobbed with a swallow. *Good.* He needed to know I wasn't above getting down and dirty to get my point across.

"Don't mistake Persephone's goodness with naiveté," I warned. "She is past forgiving you."

"You don't know her like I do." He shook his head.

"What I *do* know is that you tried to pay Byrne with her as currency, which is why I'm here. Now, you're going to listen carefully and follow my every instruction, and I will spare your miserable, pointless life. Veer off the lane I put you on, and I'll make sure you slam into a ten-ton semi-trailer and feed whatever's left of you to the hyenas. Are you following me so far?"

He clutched the edges of the table behind him. I reached over, grabbing the gun I noticed was tucked in the back of his jeans, cocked it, and pushed the barrel against his forehead.

"You're going to write a ten-page letter to Persephone, in which you apologize profusely for being the shittiest husband in the history of civilization. In this letter, you will take the entire blame for the fallout of your marriage and excuse her from any wrongdoings. I will read and approve the letter before you send it. *After* you send it, you will pack a bag, drive to the airport, and buy a one-way ticket to Australia. Once there, you will drive to Perth, where you will settle down. Perth, in case you're wondering, is the farthest point geographically from the US of A, and therefore exactly where I want you to be, at least until Virgin Galactic offers flights to Mars, to which I would be happy to relocate you. You will not, under any circumstances, contact my wife. You will not, under any circumstances, write, call, or meet her again. If I hear you as much as breathed in her direction, I will unleash my three-headed hounds on you—a Hades reference, in case it escaped your bird-sized brain—no matter where you are. I will make sure you experience the most painful death known to man. Tell me you understand."

I pressed the barrel harder to his forehead. Paxton groaned, closing his eyes, dripping sweat.

"I understand."

"I will provide your flight ticket, accommodations, and a work permit. The rest is for you to deal with."

"I don't…"

"This is not a conversation." I held up my free hand. "This is me feeling uncharacteristically charitable and not blowing your brains out, mainly because blood makes my wife feel queasy."

He nodded again, gulping.

"Forget she's ever been a part of your life."

Another nod.

"Oh, and Paxton?"

I slid the gun down the bridge of his nose, tucking it into his mouth. His eyes widened, a drop of sweat trailing down the same path the barrel had made, exploding on his neck.

"How'd you end up here? We both know you don't have a penny to your name."

"Arruw Arrameeth," he said around the barrel.

"Andrew Arrowsmith?" I pulled the weapon from his mouth. He wiped his mouth with the back of his hand.

"He found me in Mexico. Paid for my flight back here. Got me this apartment and told me to get my girl. Said she was in trouble. That you were hurting her. Good guy. Nothing like *you*."

Andrew knew Persephone and I had been estranged and tried to take advantage of it.

I wiped away a stray tear that slipped from his eye using the gun. "That, I agree with. Do as I say, and nobody will get hurt. Other than Arrowsmith, but I suppose that's not your problem, is it?"

He shook his head.

I emptied the gun of bullets, put them into my pocket, then threw the weapon onto the cot he'd used as a bed, next to his phone, walking away.

"Have a nice life, Veitch." I saluted with my back to him.

He didn't answer.

He knew there wasn't a chance of that ever happening.

Twenty
Persephone

"My goodness, Tin, how did you get this boo-boo?" I leaned down, brushing a nasty, open wound on Tinder's knee.

We spent the day together, just the two of us. Joelle and Andrew attended a charity event and decided to only bring Tree, the "normal" child, along. The one who didn't make any funny noises or made heads turn. Joelle looked guilty when she asked if I could tutor Tinder alone today. I knew the idea to leave him behind didn't come from her. I couldn't help but resent her for not fighting for her principles. For her son.

If I could go against one of the most formidable men in Boston—a man I *loved*—why couldn't she demand her boy be treated as his brother's equal?

I vowed to make it a memorable day for Tinder. A treat, rather than a punishment. We went to Sparrow Brennan's high-end diner for breakfast, where we shoved pancakes and waffles down our throats, then lounged by Charles River, watching the clouds as I told him Greek mythology tales, just as Auntie Tilda used to do with me.

Tinder chewed on the shark necklace I gave him, sniffing as he pointed at an almost identical injury on his other knee.

"T-This one, too," he stuttered.

I kissed both knees better.

"Let's go to Walgreens and get super cool Band-Aids for them. What do you say?"

"Y-Y-Yes! Maybe they'll have *Puppy Dog Pals*." His nose twitched. I slipped my hand in his. We walked past the green bannisters, kayaks, and pedal boats. The sun pounded on our faces.

"So what happened?" I asked. "Did you fall off your bike? I hope you know it happens to everyone."

"No," he answered quietly. "It wasn't t-the bike."

"What was it, then?"

The silence that followed was crammed with the thoughts teeming in my head. Like that weird letter I got from Paxton, that sounded *nothing* like Paxton, and his mirage-like disappearance, that happened as quickly as his reappearance.

Or how my husband had been avoiding me the entire week, not only refusing to accept my house calls every time I dropped by, but also dodging my text messages. I was days away from showing up at his office and embarrassing us both. The only thing keeping me from doing so was I understood his need to be fully focused on the Green Living lawsuit against Royal Pipelines ahead of the trial.

But I needed to tell him about Paxton. About Andrew Arrowsmith and my plan.

"It was Daddy."

The words hit me in the chest, cracking it open and spilling a feeling I'd never felt before. Not even to Byrne. Or Kaminski. Or Paxton.

Pure, consuming hatred.

I stopped in the middle of the busy street. A woman walking a French bulldog bumped into us, making a cyclist who whizzed by swear. Ignoring them, I crouched to my knees, holding Tinder's arms, my eyes leveling with his.

"How did he do this to you?" I asked, in a voice I just barely managed to keep steady.

THE Villain

Tinder looked down, drawing a circle with the tip of his shoe in the sand. He flinched, his movements jumpy.

"I-I-I-I…" He tried, then stomped his foot and bit his tongue. "*Oof!* I can't get the words out. N-N-No wonder he hates me."

"Tinder," I whispered. He was having a tic attack. The first I'd witness him having. He recoiled in the same manner every few seconds, a repetitive movement, pinching his shoulders together and thumping his head. He couldn't stop.

"I'm not your father. I'm your friend. You've got all the time in the world to tell me what happened. I just want to know so I can help you. You are not in trouble."

I let him ride the tic out, taking a step back to allow him as much space as possible. The tics subsided after a few minutes, melting into small, familiar nose twitches. I scooped him in my arms, stopped at a street vendor, bought him apple juice and a soft pretzel, and sat him on a bench.

"Tell me everything, Tin-Tin."

"He used a ruler."

Saying nothing, I waited for more while my heart looped around itself, rolling into a pile of painful knots.

"He-He-He-He said that it works. He said he could c-c-cure me. Said he did it b-before. He told Mommy we will both be grateful when it-it was done and over with. He-he let me read the ABCs and then some n-n-numbers, and every time I stuttered or ha-ha-had a tic, he hit the metal ruler on my knees. He did it until I bled and M-M-Mommy told him she would call the police. I cried even though Mommy asked me no-no-not to."

Feeling like I, myself, was on the verge of an attack of sorts, I forced myself to keep my voice calm. There was no need to scare Tinder any more than he already was, but the violent urge to take him away from this family left me gasping for air.

"Is this the first time your daddy has done this to you?"

I couldn't let go of the memory of Andrew shaking his son when the latter had trouble explaining himself.

"No." Tinder picked off the salt from his pretzel absentmindedly. "One time, after we came back from a party where I embarrassed him, he put my head in a si-si-si-sink full of water, in and out, in a-and out. He-He-He said that he would only stop if I stopped a-acting like a weirdo. Bu-but it worked because I stopped for a whole week."

I couldn't blink.

Swallow.

Breathe.

My world collapsed under the weight of the unspoken truth that landed on my feet, and suddenly, everything became crystal clear.

I stepped onto a mine Cillian was trying to keep me well away from. Unraveling a secret that wasn't for me to find.

"Does your daddy treat your mommy and brother this way, too?"

"No. He loves Tree and tells him he will send him to a fancy school in England. I th-think he loves Mommy, too. Even if sometimes he pushes her around. He never pushes too hard." He paused, contemplating his words with a frown. "Other than the time he pushed her off the railings, and she fell downstairs. But she fell to the couch and was-wasn't hurt. And she laughed about it so maybe it was a joke."

Or maybe she didn't want her sons to know what a piece of work their dad was.

I knew I had three problems to deal with.

One was to keep Tinder safe.

The second was to execute my plan as soon as today while I was still welcome in the Arrowsmith household.

And the third was to confront my husband about what I'd suspected all along.

I checked the time on my phone. It was two o'clock. The Arrowsmiths weren't going to be home until at least six. I had a key, though I was expected to pass the time out of the house with Tinder.

They *did* trust me enough to give me a key in case of an emergency. After all, I was in their camp. *Supposedly.* Living separate lives from my husband and despising him as far as they were aware. The different bank accounts, the strategic complaining about Cillian, and letting them in on our separation had paid off.

Now it was time to kick my plan into third gear.

To save Tinder.

To save Cillian.

And who knew? Maybe even my marriage.

I typed a quick text message to Sam Brennan. The first time I'd ever contacted him. I asked Sailor for his special access code shortly after I'd been hired by the Arrowsmiths, knowing there were some things I simply wasn't equipped to do. Once the message had been sent, read, and replied to, I looked up and smiled at the little boy.

"Hey, Tin-Tin, feel like baking some cookies at home while watching *Peter Pan*?"

"S-Sure do!"

I stuffed him into his booster in my Tesla with burning eyes and headed to the Arrowsmith residency for the very last time.

The cookies were going to be almost as bad as the meal I'd tried to cook Cillian on our first "date."

I knew that when I tore open the ready-made mix without bothering to read the instructions. I dumped the powder into a bowl and grabbed the ingredients on the package hurriedly. Tinder protested when I didn't take the time to do everything together with him—crack the eggs, measure the milk, count each drop of vanilla. I kept glancing at the overhead clock, waiting for the doorbell to ring, feeling like a criminal. I *was* a criminal. What I was about to do was against the law. But it wasn't just about saving my husband's company—it was also about Tinder.

We scooped uneven balls onto a pan, shoving it into the oven before it reached the right temperature. Tinder's irritation morphed into confusion. I'd always been the one person he could count on for patience.

"W-What's happening?" He frowned. "I-I don't like doing everything quickly. Are you going anywhere?"

"Not before I make sure you're okay," I muttered, frantically throwing a bag of popcorn into the microwave. I put *Peter Pan* on Disney Plus and sat Tin-Tin in front of the movie with his popcorn and juice.

"I'm going to be a little busy in the next few minutes, okay? But when I'm done, we'll sit down with cookies and some chocolate milk and we'll have a talk. I need to tell you a few things. Don't worry, you are *not* in trouble."

But his father sure was.

When Sam knocked on the door, I jerked him inside at the speed of light. He was wearing a black dress shirt, jeans, and his usual no-bullshit frown.

"His laptop is probably going to be password protected," I warned, still holding the doorjamb, my heart in my throat.

I never broke the law. Ever. For anything or anyone. Hell, I didn't even jaywalk. My obsession with my husband was turning me inside out.

Sam passed the living room, not sparing the young boy a look, and ascended the stairs. I followed him, pointing at Andrew's study. He slipped a pair of elastic gloves on, produced a foldable door lock opener from his backpack, and opened the locked door effortlessly.

We both entered the room. I was hyperaware of Tinder sitting in front of the TV downstairs, waiting for me. Guilt wrecked me. I was going to turn his life upside down, and even though I knew it was the right thing to do, considering his abusive father, I also knew Tinder might never forgive me.

"So Kill was right," Sam said tonelessly, powering up the laptop as he took a seat in Andrew's chair. His fingers were gliding on the

THE Villain

keyboard. He shoved a USB drive into the device. "You're not completely useless, after all."

"You don't think very highly of women, huh?" I turned outside, to the hallway, craning my neck to look downstairs and make sure Tinder was okay.

"I thought you were a gold-digger," Sam said bluntly, clicking away on the laptop, his eyes glued to the screen. "Shit, there's a lot of stuff in his cloud. Amateur mistake."

"Copy everything. I want to sort through all of it," I instructed him, standing at the door, returning to our initial conversation. "And I'm not a gold-digger."

"No shit." He chuckled. "You're risking your ass here. You know that, right? You can get a lot of jail time for what you're doing."

"Really?" I widened my eyes comically. "I had no idea. Dumb it down for me. What's jail? The one with the bars, right? I think I've seen a movie."

Sam's eyes drifted from the screen to me. He smirked.

"So that's why he kept you all this time. You talk back."

I glanced through the window, hugging my midriff, speculating whether Andrew's house was wired like Cillian's or not.

"The coast was clear." Sam read my thoughts. "The house is wired, but the idiot's cameras have crappy street view due to overgrown trees. Apparently, his conscience wouldn't let him trim the fuckers."

He stood, handing me a disc-on-key.

When I reached for it, he tilted it away from my reach.

"You sure you don't want me to go through it myself? That's a lot of data. You can't mess it up."

"I will do a thorough job."

"Let me make a copy for myself. Just in case."

"If you make yourself a copy, I'm going to make sure you lose your job with the Fitzpatricks." I tilted my chin up warningly. "There may be some private things in there I don't want anyone to see."

"Like a sex tape?"

Men.

"Sure."

Sam Brennan was a handsome man. Then so was Ted Bundy. I didn't find him attractive, especially seeing as his weekly body count surpassed Ted Bundy's entire career. I honestly couldn't see what Aisling's fascination was with him. Then again, the same could probably be said about Kill and me.

"You do understand the concept of an arranged marriage, correct? Nothing about what you have with your husband is real."

"Samuel," I used his given name, my tone haughty, as I did when one of my students was misbehaving, "give me the flash drive, please."

He tucked it into my dress pocket, laughing softly.

"I didn't get it at first." He dipped his head down, scanning my face. "I thought he wanted Emmabelle. Every time the three of you were in the same room, his eyes were on her. But then I realized," he dropped his voice, "the timing was peculiar. See, Kill always looked at Emmabelle exactly at the same time you looked at *him*. He wanted to throw you off. To make you jealous. The first and last human thing I'd ever seen him do."

Sam took a step back, looking around the room.

"I'll relock the study. Andrew will never know we've been in here. Proceed as normal when they get here."

He turned around, tapping the doorframe.

The oven dinged downstairs, and I heard Tin-Tin yelping in delight.

We were running out of time.

I thought Sam was going to say some parting words.

About my bold move.

About the risk I'd taken for my husband.

But that would imply Sam Brennan was impressed.

And if there was something I knew with every bone in my body, it was that, unfortunately for Aisling, my friend, woman-hater Sam Brennan would never be impressed by the other sex.

THE *Villain*

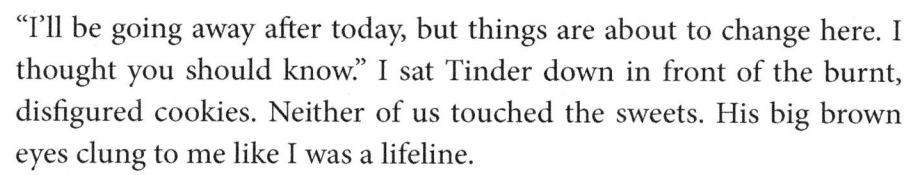

"I'll be going away after today, but things are about to change here. I thought you should know." I sat Tinder down in front of the burnt, disfigured cookies. Neither of us touched the sweets. His big brown eyes clung to me like I was a lifeline.

"C-Change how?"

"Your father is not treating you well. He shouldn't do the things he is doing, and I cannot—*will* not—be able to be here all the time to protect you. There will come a day when you grow up and make your mind up about what I'm about to do. You will either hate me or appreciate me." I shook my head, feeling the tears welling up in my eyes, but held myself back. Tinder deserved more. He deserved my composure and reassurance. He deserved the world. "However you choose to feel about me, I will accept and respect it. I think I'm going to put your daddy in a lot of trouble soon, but you will still have your mommy and your brother, and they're the important part, you hear me? They're the part I want you to focus on."

He nodded slowly, taking it all in. It was a lot. Even I wasn't sure if I fully grasped what I was about to do. I dropped my forehead to Tinder's, breathing him in. If I inhaled really deeply, I could still detect it faintly. That elusive baby smell that made my bones melt.

"Have I ever told you about The Wish Cloud, Tin-Tin?"

He shook his head.

"I'm about to gift you one wish. Something to remember me by. But you'll have to choose your wish carefully. You only get one. And you can only cash in on the wish when you see a lone cloud in an otherwise clear sky."

"I know what I'll ch-ch-choose, Auntie Persy," he said, smiling. "I'll choose what I always choose. I'll choose you."

Two hours later, the rest of the family returned from the charity event. I stood from the couch and walked over to the entrance. As soon as Andrew walked through the door, I pointed at him with my finger, my expression very possibly manic.

Joelle backed away, stumbling with a gasp. Tree looked back and forth between his father and me.

"What's going on?" The young boy sniffed.

"I know what you did to Tinder," I whispered to Andrew. "I need to talk to you two. *Alone.*"

Andrew's eyes zoned in on mine, his nostrils flaring.

"Tree, take your brother and go up to your room," he instructed. The boys bolted up the stairs. Andrew opened his mouth, but I held my hand up. We were still standing at the doorway.

"Save it. I know about the ruler. About the beatings. How you pushed Joelle from the railings."

Joelle shrieked behind her husband, covering her face in her hands and sobbing. Her carefully staged world was collapsing.

"I know about Cillian," I finished softly. I was mostly bluffing but knowing with certainty that burned inside me that he did to my husband something that made him the way he was. That changed him beyond recognition.

Andrew's face paled, his jaw slacking. "He told you?"

I couldn't bring myself to lie, so I smiled in what I hoped resembled confidence, shrugging.

"Your secret is becoming not so secretive. Doesn't bode well for your role as the chairman of Green Living. At any rate, I'm here to tell you that was the last time you hit your son. I am taking this to Child Protective Services. Since it's not my first rodeo with CPS, let me tell you how it's going to play out. I will file a complaint, they'll visit your house within twenty-four hours to check for the wellness of your children, and once they find signs of neglect or abuse—which they will, because Tinder is physically injured—they'll remove the children to a foster home and press charges against you."

Joelle nearly choked.

"Since I've worked with numerous schools during my short career and know quite a few CPS agents, I can probably help Joelle get full custody since she wasn't complicit in the abuse. Now, as for you—" I turned to Joelle, who buckled with her back against the wall, crying on the floor. Her face was wet with sweat, tears, and snot.

"You should put your children above all else. Always."

"I did." Joelle grabbed ahold of my dress, tugging at it desperately. "I do! Do you think I liked what he did? Do you think it's my fault? I had no idea it was going to be this way. I would have never married him, Persy. *Ever.*"

I didn't think it was her fault. She wasn't the abusive party. If anything, she was a victim, too. But I knew her children might not see it that way. They might grow up to resent the woman who clung on their father's arm with a big smile on her face, knowing what he did behind closed doors.

"Doesn't matter what you thought. It's time you take responsibility and step away from this toxic relationship. Put you and the twins first. Consider this my official resignation. Oh, and Andrew? Drop the lawsuit against my husband. You'll either have to resign or get fired within the next few days, and you have bigger legal fish to fry."

I grabbed my keys and bag, glancing behind my shoulder. What I saw broke my heart. Tinder and Tree were huddled together on the last step of the stairway, gaping at me with tears in their eyes.

I broke down, falling to my knees, letting all the tears I kept at bay loose. Starting this job, I knew I'd get attached, but I never thought I was going to love them so fiercely.

"Come here, boys." I opened my arms.

They ran to me, yelping. As always, I fell back from the momentum, from the storm of their embrace, allowing them to bury their heads in my shoulders, crying along with them.

Later that night, I sifted through the material on the disc-on-key Sam gave me.

It took me three hours and two glasses of wine to find the file I'd been looking for. It was simply named. CFF.

Cillian Frances Fitzpatrick.

I double-clicked it, downed the wine, and said a prayer.

I didn't know what I was in for.

I just knew I wasn't ready for this.

Twenty-One

Cillian

The Past.

THE FIRST TIME I STEPPED INTO A JUVENILE TREATMENT CLINIC was at age fourteen.

Earlier that week, I beat myself up so bad, I was still pissing blood and spitting teeth. My face was so swollen, it took three of my peers to recognize who I was when they found me on the library floor.

My mother accompanied me into the Swiss clinic. Reluctantly. I was covered in a coat, hat, and sunglasses to hide my battered figure, like a D-list celebrity zipping through an airport, trying to remain unidentified. Mother remained silent most of the plane journey from England to Zurich, save for a brief conversation, whispered after the stewardesses were out of earshot.

"Your father can't know."

That was the first thing she said.

Not how you are doing.

How'd it happen.

Your father can't know.

I stayed quiet. There was, after all, nothing to say. She was right. *Athair* couldn't know. And at any rate, there was no way to explain what had happened. One second I was sitting in front of my textbooks in the library, studying my ass off to finish first in class as always, the familiar weird pressure—an intangible tension I couldn't explain—skulking up my spine like a spider, and the other, I was on the floor, beaten to a pulp, not sure who did it.

Now I knew who that person was.

It was *me*.

I beat myself up to a point of unconsciousness.

"Cillian Frances, did you hear me?" Mother linked her fingers together over her lap, face rigid, posture perfect.

"Loud and clear." I looked out the window at the passing clouds.

"Good." She frowned at an invisible spot on the cockpit door. "He will blame it on me, somehow. He always does, you know? I can never catch a break with this man."

My mother wasn't a bad person. But she was weak. *Convenient*. Now more than ever, having given birth to my sibling, Hunter, less than three years ago.

The new baby had put a strain on my parents' marriage. When I came for a visit during the summer, they'd barely spoken a word to each other. When my mother asked if I wanted to hold my brother, my initial reaction had been *hell no*, but then she gave me that sheepish, poor-me look, and added, "Your father never holds him."

So I'd held him. Looked down at the tiny, old-looking bald person who stared back at me with big blue eyes that looked nothing like mine and told him, "Buckle up, little bro. You were definitely born into one heck of a family."

"*Anyway*," Mother chimed again on the plane, rearranging her pearl necklace, "I hope this has nothing to do with Andrew Arrowsmith. You won't be seeing much of him anymore outside of Evon."

"I haven't heard or seen him since *Athair* fired his dad," I admitted in a vain attempt to try to get some info.

"His father wouldn't have been fired if he wasn't a crook," Mother huffed.

THE Villain

"I don't care about his father."

"We'll see if he finishes his studies at Evon," she continued, ignoring my words. I'd often wondered why I bothered answering her at all. "Your father is suing him for everything he stole."

"They used to go golfing together. Take annual vacations. Visit casinos in Europe. Go fishing," I said, leaving out the escorts, strip clubs, and underground joints they'd promised to take Andrew and me to when we were older.

She rolled her eyes. "Don't be naïve, Cillian. People will do anything to get close to us Fitzpatricks. We can't have real friendships."

Mother dropped me off at the clinic as soon as we landed, signed the paperwork, and told me she'd come to pick me up in a few hours.

"I would stay," she sighed, "but you know how jittery I get in clinics. They're not my scene. Besides, I have some shopping to do. You understand, don't you, Kill?" She pinched my cheeks. I stepped away, turned around, and left without a word.

A nurse led me to a white small room with a desk and a chair. She locked the door behind me. I sat down, looking up at a security camera that was trained on me. I was obviously being watched.

They kept me like this for twenty minutes or so before a male voice sounded behind a two-way mirror.

"Hi there, Cillian."

"Hello."

I wasn't afraid. I was extremely adaptable. Came with the territory of growing up in the hands of au pairs and attending private schools away from home from age six.

"How're you feeling?"

"Been better. Been worse." I crossed my legs, making myself comfortable.

"That's interesting," the doctor said. It wasn't, really, but I appreciated his sympathy, whether it was genuine or not. It was more than I'd received from my own mother, oftentimes.

"Do you know why you're here?" the pleasant voice asked.

"I'm guessing it's because I have a thing called the Tourette's syndrome." I slouched back in the chair, taking in all the whiteness. The calmness of it pleased me. A long silence stretched from the other side of the window. "How long have you known?"

"About a week."

I heard pages flipping on a clipboard from the other side. I smiled grimly. Normally, it was the patient who was in the dark.

"How can it be? It says here your tic attack took place two days ago," another voice said. A middle-aged female was my guess. Both doctors had accents. One was probably Italian, and the other Swiss from the French border.

"Yes," I said slowly, giving them time to fill in their charts. "But I've been feeling the tension of the attack in the days before building up, so I did some research."

"So you knew you were going to get it?" the woman Swiss doctor asked incredulously. "The attack."

I nodded curtly. She gasped. She actually *gasped*.

"Poor thing," she said. Very un-doctor-like.

"Never been accused of being that before," I muttered, checking my watch for the time.

"Where are your parents?" the female doctor asked, her voice growing closer. Were they going to open the door between our rooms? I hoped not. Eye contact wasn't my favorite.

"My father is in Boston, handling the family business, and my mother is shopping. Zurich is one of her favorite retail spots."

Knowing Mother, she was going to pick me up with bags full of new shoes, cuff links, and summer clothes for me. Her version of being maternal.

"Why didn't you tell anyone?" the male doctor asked. "About the Tourette's syndrome."

"What was the point?" I brushed my dress pants from lint. "Knowing my family, we will be keeping my condition under wraps. So either you prescribe me with shit, try new treatment on me, or let me go. I'll figure out a way to hide it."

"It's a neurological disorder," the female doctor explained, her voice

THE Villain

turning even softer. "Caused by an array of very complex things, mostly because of abnormalities in certain brain regions. The tics will come and go, and even though we can offer some treatments to relieve and ease the disorder, it is mostly here to stay. You can't control it. The very definition of Tourette's is that your tics are involuntarily. You cannot train your nerves. They are everywhere in your body. To numb them, you will have to stop feeling completely."

Perfect.

"Then it *is* voluntary." I stood, heading for the door.

"No," the doctor hesitated. "For you to stop the tics, you'll have to stop feeling. I don't think you understand—"

"I understand everything." I curled my fist, knocking on the door three times, signaling the nurse I wanted to get out.

"Mr. Fitzpatrick—"

I didn't answer.

I got what I came here for.

A solution.

Now all I needed was practice.

Operation Cancel Feelings did not get off to a smooth start when I came back to England.

To begin with, I wasn't big on feelings. That was not to say I hadn't felt any. I was capable of being sad, happy, hungry, amused, and jealous. I hated a lot of people—certainly more than a boy my age should—and even loved a little.

Mainly my baby brother, who had the advantage of not being able to talk back, hence not being able to piss me off. But I also loved other things. Polo and Christmas and sticking my tongue out when it rained. The alluring taste of winter.

I also liked my friendship with Andrew Arrowsmith. A lot.

Not in the same way I liked girls. The way they moved and smelled and existed, which I found both magical and confusing. I knew I was one hundred percent straight. I liked Andy because he got me. Because we were the two kids with the Boston accents who did everything together. We studied and hung out and watched movies and shows and played the same sports. We pulled dangerous pranks together. We farted and blamed it on his dogs during dinnertime. We watched our first porno together, and fought over football, and ran away from the cops that one time when we accidentally set a trash can in the country club on fire...

We were being kids and shared whatever childhood our parents allowed us to have together.

He was the closest thing to family I'd had. Which was why I was furious with Andrew Senior for stealing money from Royal Pipelines, and with my own father for finding out, and also with *Athair* for acting on the betrayal.

Yes, Andy's dad stole from our company, but Andy was my lifeline. Couldn't *Athair* let this shit go?

After weeks of not hearing or seeing Andy at Evon, I finally ran into him at the main chapel. My relief was mixed with dread.

I waved at him from across the chapel. There was a swarm of students between us, and all of us were wearing the same uniform. Andrew noticed me and looked away.

The tinge of pain in my chest alarmed me. I couldn't afford to feel. Feelings would inspire more nerve attacks, and nerve attacks would make *Athair* disown me. While I truly liked baby Hunter, I didn't want to see him snagging the eldest son's title as the heir to Royal Pipelines.

Not to mention, *Athair*, Mother, and Hunter were the only family I had left, now that Andy probably hated my guts.

I strode across the lawn after Sunday Mass, hands clasped behind my back, frowning at the lush grass. I didn't even care much that I had Tourette's. It was inconvenient, for sure, but after gulping down a few medical journals and a couple of books about the syndrome, I'd decided I would overcome it before graduating and moving on to college.

And when I decided something, I never failed, no matter the means it took to achieve it.

The back of my neck seared with sudden pain. I stopped, bringing my hand to rub at it. It felt warm and sleek. I withdrew my palm, glancing at it. It was full of blood. I turned around. Andrew strode toward me with some of his friends, tossing a rock in his hand.

He grinned.

"What the fuck, Arrowsmith?"

"The fuck is your father is a jealous asshole, and my mates here told me that you're a freak. I heard about the library *accident*."

I figured he would. I straightened my posture, reminding myself that there was no need to waste any feelings over this nonsense. He wasn't the first person to leave. He wasn't going to be the last, either.

"Yeah? Well, I h-h-heard your da-da-dad stole money to pay your way through Evon. Short on money, Arrowsmith?" I punched my own face out of nowhere.

What the fuck?

Andrew's eyes gleamed as he advanced toward me, picking up speed. His friends followed suit.

"Oh, man, you're stuttering now!"

"I'm not stuttering." I let out a low growl, slapping my own face again.

No. No. No.

I wasn't in an empty library this time. I had an audience, and they were watching, laughing, getting a glimpse of the freak show. I had to stop.

Stop feeling.
Stop wanting.
Stop hurting right now.

"The good thing"—Andrew stopped only when he was next to me—"is that I'm not a Fitzpatrick. An Arrowsmith always comes to his friend's rescue. And you need to be rescued, don't you, Kill?"

His friends laughed, hands tucked inside their pockets, glaring at me, waiting for the word *go*.

I looked behind me, slapping my own face again. I could probably run, but there was no point. The tics were going to slow me down, and anyway, I'd always been faster on a horse than with my feet.

I looked back at them. Now was as good a time as any to check the pain box on my list and make sure I couldn't feel it.

Andrew cracked his knuckles loudly.

I did the same thing.

Note to self: cracking one's knuckles is very soothing.

"I'm about to fuck your ugly face up even worse than you did, Fitzy."

I smiled, feeling blissfully numb. "Give it your best shot, Oliver Twist."

Andrew ended up filming some of his abuse, probably to stash it and remind himself it happened.

But he wasn't an idiot and was careful to never show his face.

It was one of the very things we'd been taught. Never film anything incriminating. The infamous Bullingdon Club had cost Oxford University enough embarrassment, and nobody at fine British institutions wanted their reputation to be stained by a bunch of teenage dirtbags.

The abuse wasn't one-sided.

In fact, during our first fight, I'd noticed when Andrew beat me up, I stopped feeling. The tics had stopped. And so, I sought Andrew out. Went to his room on a weekly basis. Goaded him into fighting, abusing, and messing with me.

Andrew took over. We crossed the lines many times.

Broken bones. Permanent scars. Cigarette burns.

I grew stronger and more indifferent each time.

And he? He cried when he did those things to me. Cried like a baby.

Going through the trials and tribulations of being bullied—burned, waterboarded, slapped across the face each time I stuttered or hit myself, each time I *twitched*—proved to be highly effective.

By fifteen, the year when I'd found out Andrew Arrowsmith wasn't going to complete his education at Evon, I was free of symptoms.

Outwardly, anyway.

I still popped my knuckles.

Still breathed deep and slow to lower my heart rate.

Still resisted any type of feelings, smashing them whenever they tried to rise above the surface.

The more I controlled the tics, the worse they had become. Fortunately, I always unleashed them when I was in the privacy of my room.

I kicked, screamed, hit myself, broke walls, tore furniture, and devastated everything around me. But I did it on my terms, and only when I felt I was ready. That was how successfully I managed to suppress my emotions.

Until one day, the tics stopped completely.

Feelings were so far away from my realm of existence that I didn't have to worry anymore.

But the tapes were still out there, and Andrew had them.

Like the one of me lying in a puddle of my own vomit.

Or the one where I sat at the bottom of the pool for a minute at a time until I was blue. Every time I miscalculated the time and rose to the surface too quickly, he'd strike me.

One thing was for sure: Andrew wanted revenge, I wanted complete control, and we both got what we wanted.

By the time we parted ways, his job was done, and so was mine.

I thought we were even.

I thought we both got what we deserved.

I thought I was immune to feelings ever again.

Turned out, every single one of those assumptions was wrong.

Persephone

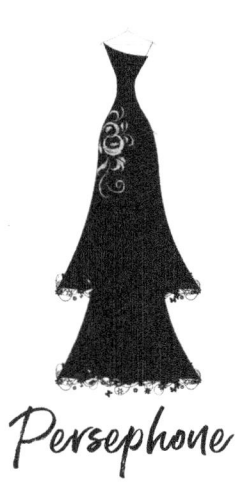

The third time I ran to the bathroom to throw up, I threw in the towel and shut my laptop, stashing it under my bed, like the videos could haunt me. I had enough of seeing my husband—then a teenager—abused.

Beaten.

Smashed.

Broken.

Stuttering.

Crying.

Laughing.

Losing it.

Finding it.

I wanted to kill Andrew Arrowsmith with my own hands.

And knew with a confidence that frightened me that I was capable of doing that, too, given the opportunity.

Andrew's face wasn't on the tapes. But his voice was there. So were his motives to do what he did.

At six thirty in the morning, I rose to my feet and walked over to the shower. My eyes were puffy from crying all night.

There were two things I knew without a shadow of a doubt:

THE Villain

One—I was going to make sure Arrowsmith was ruined, even if it was the last thing I did in my life.

Two—Cillian was truly incapable of feeling anything after everything he'd been through. But even the unloving deserved to be loved. Even he deserved peace, belonging, and a home.

From now on, I was going to let him have me on his terms.

Even if it slayed my bleeding heart.

Twenty-Two

Cillian

"Sir, you have a visitor."

I didn't look up from the screen, still typing out a message to my legal team regarding Green Living.

"Do you have eyes, Serena?"

"Sophia," she corrected mildly as though the mistake was her fault. "I do, sir."

"Then I suggest you make use of them and look at my planner. It is wide open for a reason. I do not accept visitors at this time."

She was still standing on my threshold, wondering how to approach her new boss. At times, I was certain the definition of hell was new personal assistants going through orientation. Sophia needed to be spoon-fed everything, and her only saving grace was that, unlike Ms. Brandt, she wasn't a world-class bitch who looked like a half-melted Barbie

"It's your wife." She physically cringed, bracing herself for a verbal whipping.

I resisted the urge to look up from my laptop and steal a glance at Flower Girl through the glass wall.

To tell Sophia to let her in.

Nothing good was going to come out of this.

She was probably here to give me the third degree about

THE Villain

threatening her ex-husband at gunpoint. Or maybe she finally realized how much of a fuckup I am and decided to help Andrew with his lawsuit. To testify.

My wife knew my secret.

Sam had told me about her little stint at Andrew Arrowsmith's place as soon as he walked out my enemy's door. I knew Persephone had seen the videos.

She had no right.

No right to butt into my business. No right to uncover what I wanted to keep a secret. No right to peel off the layers I'd refused to shed when she tried the nice way.

"Turn her away," I ordered, my eyes still on my monitor.

"I'm afraid she can't and won't do that. Also, don't take that tone with her. She is your assistant, not your servant." I heard a throaty, sweet voice from the doorway. This time, I did look up.

Flower Girl stood at the doorway. She wore a sunny dress and a stern look. I wanted to take both of them off her.

"You've fired Ms. Brandt." She closed the door on Sophia, stepping into my office. "Why?"

"That's not any of your business." I closed the laptop.

"Try again." She crossed her arms over her chest.

"Because you hated her," I spat out, disgusted with myself.

She smiled.

I died a little inside.

Oh, how the mighty have fallen.

I stood, gathering the paperwork on my desk to keep my traitorous eyes from wandering her way. Watching my wife was akin to watching the sun. The euphoric, blinding notion you were both immortal and pathetically human grabbing you by the throat.

"I suppose you're here because your ex-husband has dumped you again. Am I the consolation prize?" I stuffed my paperwork into my briefcase, itching to go somewhere—*anywhere*—that was far away from this woman.

The pressure signaling an impending attack pressed against my sternum. Every time she walked into the room, I had to regain my control.

"You knew he was in town?" Her peacock blue eyes followed me intently.

"Your security cameras," I pointed out, in case she planned on accusing me of slapping her with more private investigators.

She stalked in my direction.

"I threw him out the night he showed up. You'd have known that if you'd bothered to answer any of my calls or actually go through the pain of giving me the time of the day when I tried to visit you at your house."

Your house.

Of course it was my house.

Why would it be ours? I'd plucked her out of the clinical apartment I'd put her in, stuck her in one of the guest rooms, and expected her to…what? Form any sort of attachment to the place?

"Would you like a prize for remaining faithful?" I arched an eyebrow. She stopped right in front of me. Her scent was everywhere in the room, drowning my senses, and I wanted to grab her by the shoulders and shake her. Kick her out, kiss her, fuck her, yell at her. All these possibilities exhibited both emotion and complete lack of control.

"Sam told you, didn't he?" She tilted her head, examining me. She meant Andrew Arrowsmith's laptop. The tapes she must have watched.

"He *is* on my payroll."

"So is the rest of the city."

"You included, so do yourself a favor and stop sniffing around my business before I cut you off."

"We both know I'm not here for the money. Now, I want to talk about what I've learned."

She treaded carefully into the conversation.

"No," I said flatly. "You had no right."

"Had no right?" She laughed sadly. "I'm your wife, Kill. Whether

THE *Villain*

you accept it or not. I wanted to help you. That's why I decided to work for Andrew in the first place. To extract information. To get a glimpse into his most intimate place. I knew there was too much riding on this operation, and that you'd try to stop me because you're too righteous to accept you needed my help."

"Your job is not to save me."

"Why?" She parked a hand on her waist. "Why isn't it my job to save you? I've lost count of the times *you've* saved *me*. You saved me from Byrne and Kaminski, from a horse, from a poisonous flower, from my ex-husband. The list goes on and on. Why is it okay for you to give up your entire existence for the world, to put your father's needs before yours, to walk through fire for the people you care about, but I can't do you this one solid?"

"Because you didn't accomplish anything!" I boomed in her face, baring my teeth. "You pretty little idiot, the videos you found won't hold up in court. They are not legal evidence. They're stolen, and probably fuzzy, and don't capture his face. You've worked for *nothing*."

The frustration of knowing she'd seen me at my worst, and for no good reason at all, maddened me. I grabbed my wife's arms. "Your little stunt did nothing more than put another ten-foot dent in our marriage, which, by the way, was the worst mistake of my life."

The words flew out before I could stop them. I'd heard of people saying things they didn't mean while angry but had never experienced it because, well, I was never angry. This was an unwelcome, humanizing first. My wife's blue eyes glittered with rage. I wanted to apologize but knew that the entire floor was watching through my glass office walls, and that an apology would achieve nothing.

We were done.

I was faulty. Broken beyond repair, and she wasn't going to stick around long enough to try to fix me.

"You don't know what I found out," she said quietly.

"I don't fucking care!"

In my periphery, I could see Hunter marching from his office to mine. He waved away the curious audience forming outside my door, shooting me a *pull it together* look.

I'd officially hit rock bottom. Nothing said you were a world-class loser more than Hunter goddamn Fitzpatrick telling you to chill.

I turned my attention back to Persephone, lowering my voice but still feeling that undeniable shake. "Nothing you found on Andrew's laptop can help me win this case. The only thing you did was give him more ammo on me. Now he is probably telling people I sent my wife to sniff around his work and made her perform two jobs to try to dig up some dirt about him. Not only did you not help me, but you also put yourself at risk, and I…"

That's where I stopped. And *what?*

Persephone slanted one eyebrow up, studying me with eyes so hungry, if I had a heart, it would break for her. She clearly wanted me to care.

"And you what, hubs?" she asked softly. "What would have happened had Andrew done something to me?"

A violent shudder ran through me.

The waterboarding.

The burns.

The beatings.

Getting locked in the confession booth for hours at a time in a dark church with only my demons to keep me company.

Coming back to him, asking him for more. To atone for my father's sins. To grieve our friendship. To numb my feelings.

And just like that, I remembered who I was.

Who Andrew Arrowsmith had made me.

Who my father—my whole family—expected me to be.

A grim smirk slashed my face like a wound. I leaned down, my lips brushing my wife's ear, my hot breath fanning her pale hair.

"And I wish he'd finished the job, Flower Girl, so I could finally go ahead and marry someone in my own league. You were a mistake. A foolish, horny mistake. Divorce couldn't come fast enough."

THE Villain

I felt, rather than saw her take a step back. That was when I realized I'd closed my eyes like a pathetic moron, inhaling her.

With her head tilted up and her spine stiff, she pulled a stack of papers from her bag and slammed it against my chest.

"In that case, congratulations. You've worked really hard to show me Andrew turned you into a heartless monster. Consider yourself free from this marriage. Here's your parting gift from me. A Child Protective Service report deeming Andrew a dangerous, unfit father. Thought it might be of interest to you, since he's lost custody of his children, and will be losing his job next."

She took a ragged breath that shook her entire tiny body.

"I love you, Cillian Fitzpatrick. I've always loved you. From the moment we first met at the charity ball when I spotted you across the room. You were a god among mortals. Vital yet dead. And when you looked at me—when you looked *past* me—I saw my whole future in your eyes. I knew you were rich, and handsome, and powerful. Yet the only thing I truly ever wanted from you, Kill, was *you*. To peel off the layers, shed them with my fingernails, and have you, and love you, and *save* you. I thought I could change you. And I tried. I really did. But I cannot change someone who doesn't want to change. I love you, but I love me, too. And I deserve more than you've given me. More than you are willing to part ways with. So I'm saving you this one time, for all the times you saved me, and saying goodbye."

She rose to her tiptoes and pressed a cold, impersonal kiss on my lips, her eyelashes brushing against my nose.

"We've always been so bad at respecting each other's boundaries. We broke our contract again and again and again. If you have a shred of sympathy for me in that cold heart of yours, don't contact me anymore. No matter what happens, no matter how much you want to tell me something, leave me alone. I need time to digest, to lick my wounds, to move on. Don't show up at my sister's house, or at my workplace, or anywhere I might be. Let me get over you. My heart can't take another blow."

She turned around and walked away.

Leaving me to stand with my get-out-of-jail monopoly card, the perfect evidence against Andrew Arrowsmith, and my heart in my throat.

It beat, loud and fast.

Alive.

Angry.

And full of emotions.

Rather than extinguishing the five hundred fires wreaking havoc in my life, I opted to take the car, drive to the closest liquor store, stock up on the cheapest, most punishing brand of vodka—the type certain to give me a hangover from hell—and drive to the ranch.

I got drunk with my horses (I did all the drinking; they were there to watch me through the half doors of their stalls), with my phone turned off. Flower Girl was finally done with me. Mission accomplished. Now when I had Andrew's downfall in my back pocket, when I knew he'd drop the lawsuit thanks to her, all I wanted to do was go down in flames right along with him.

I took a swig from the vodka, slouching against the wall in the barn, surrounded by horse shit.

I closed my eyes. A snippet of a few weeks ago played behind my eyelids.

Of Persephone pulling me to the laundry room—I had no idea where that room was, exactly, before that moment—hopping on a working washing machine, spreading her thighs for me, and moaning my name as I fucked her hard.

I opened my eyes, rubbing at them. It was dark outside. I must've passed out a few hours ago and blacked out.

THE Villain

Excellent. A few more months of this, and I should be good to go back into my previous state of numbness.

Yellow headlights shimmered from outside the open door of the barn. Tires crunched hay outside. Someone was coming.

I let go of the empty vodka bottle, watching as it rolled all the way to Hamilton's stall. The asshole almost cost me a wife. *Fucker*.

The intruder killed the engine, flung the driver's door open, and stepped out, the crisp sound of leaves under their boots grating on my nerves.

"Kill? Are you there?" Hunter's baritone demanded. Since when did my brother turn into an authoritative, respectable figure?

"No," I growled, knowing he was going to come in anyway.

He did just that, halting at the door to the barn with his hands on his hips.

"Sailor had the baby. I have a daughter."

I expected to feel the relief of him not having a son, a true heir, someone to take over Royal Pipelines, but all I felt was emptiness. I knew normal people would be happy for their brother. I wasn't normal.

"Congratulations," I said monotonously. "Are the mother and daughter healthy?"

"Very."

"Good. I opened a trust fund in your child's honor. Three grand a month until college."

"Thanks, but that's not why I'm here." He took a step inside, closing the door behind him. "Sam found out Andrew put Paxton Veitch on the plane back to Boston. That's how he got here. Arrowsmith was obviously trying to stir shit."

Paxton was no longer a threat.

He was probably never a threat.

The only person standing in my way to having Persephone Penrose was me, and I did a hell of a job at keeping us apart.

I unscrewed another bottle of vodka. My bladder was screaming at me to stop drinking, but my brain urged me to keep going until the blissful numbness was restored.

"I know," I drawled. "I got it out of Paxton myself. Apparently, I'm the only son of a bitch around qualified to get shit done."

"Doubt it." Hunter sighed.

"Why?"

"Because you're currently trying to loosen the bottom of a liquor bottle."

My brother grabbed the vodka from my hand, turning it upside down. I took the opportunity to wobble to my feet. I turned around and took a piss. Strictly speaking, pissing in my horse stable was vandalizing my own property. Then again, punishing myself seemed like a good idea.

I turned back around. *Ceann beag* handed me the bottle silently. I glared at him. At all six versions of him.

"I took care of the Arrowsmith problem," I said blandly. "Well, my wife did."

"That's not why I'm here, either."

"Why *are* you here?" I squinted. "Go be with your family."

Hunter had a family of his own. A *real* family, shaped and molded by him and his wife. His wasn't rotten from the inside, built on the ruins of social standing, old money, and greed.

"I *am* with my family." He grabbed the bottle in my hand, throwing it aside with a frown. "With the family who needs me right now. And I'd very much like to go back to the one I've just created, so would you tell me what the fuck is going on with you?"

I zigzagged to the door, flung it open, and stepped out of the barn. Hunter grunted, following me. It wasn't lost on me that the tables had turned. I was the shitshow brother now, and he was the responsible family man.

"She saved my ass," I said as my brother tracked me down the dirt path back to the main cabin. "Tutoring that asshole's kids. Digging up dirt on him. She did it for me. All this time, I thought she was just getting back at me for being cruel to her."

"You cursed," he noted.

No fucking shit, Sherlock.

And it felt too good to fucking stop, dammit.

Since Tourette's syndrome was known as "that cursing disorder," I'd made it a point to never utter a swear word. There was no better way to distance myself from the stigma. But profanity was never my problem. I'd never cursed during my attacks.

At that moment, though, I had an acute case of not giving a fuck.

Not giving a fuck if people found out.

Not giving a fuck if cursing wasn't proper or well-mannered.

Not noble enough for the heir of Royal Pipelines.

"Persy's in love with you," he grumbled, still following me.

"She's in love with the *idea* of me." Many women were. "What it comes down to is this, *ceann beag*. She is, and always will be, a woman I'd bought like a sack of potatoes. She came with a price tag, like all the women before her. And if you can buy it, you can replace it. I'll find someone else. And Persephone? She'll marry again, too."

Hunter stopped. I soldiered on, past the cabin, toward my car. I needed to get over this little self-pity party, drive back to the office, and start putting things in motion.

Suddenly, I felt something heavy and damp plastered to my back. I turned around. My brother had thrown manure on me.

"What the f—"

"You asswipe!" He crouched down, grabbing another ball of manure in the dark. I'd never fought with my younger brother. And we'd definitely never been physical. There was nothing brotherly about us, other than the title.

He knew it.

I knew it.

Hunter aimed—and caught—my shoulder.

"Stop it," I growled, narrowing my eyes at him.

He ignored me, kneeling to grab more manure. A childish zing of vengeance sparked inside me. I lowered myself to grab as much manure as I could find.

"She was never in love with your persona, assface." Hunter swung his arm backward, like a baseball player, and caught me in the chest. I aimed my ball of shit to his face, striking a good portion of his neck and chin.

Now we were both in deep shit. *Literally.*

"Stalin had a more loveable character, you moron. She was always stupidly—and may I add *unreasonably*—in love with your ass!"

He threw another ball at me.

I threw one back at him.

"She owed a lot of money," I yelled back. "I paid her debt. That's why she married me."

"I know!" Hunter laughed hysterically, deserting the manure and pouncing on me. He shoved me to the ground, twisting the lapels of my blazer as he pinned me down. "I know, because after the night Persy came to accept your offer in the blizzard, I knocked on her door. I knew I had to make it right. Not for her, or for you, but for my wife. I didn't want anything to upset Sailor so early in the pregnancy. Persy told me about her debt. I offered to pay it in full and wrote a check right in front of her."

I blinked at him, confused and disappointed with myself for wanting to hear the rest, blood thundering through my head.

"You wrote a check?" I growled. "Doesn't your generation Venmo?"

He lowered his head to mine, his eyes burning with rage. "She tore the bitch up in front of my face and told me she was marrying your sorry ass. She *wanted* to marry you! Stipulations and assholery included. Now my question is this—how did you manage to lose her? How did you let the only girl you've ever loved just…go?"

"I don't—"

"Of course you do!" He smashed my head against the dirt. I twisted, grabbing him by the shirt and rolling him over, switching our positions so I was on top of him now.

THE Villain

"You fool, anyone with a pair of working eyes could see you're crazy about her. You couldn't look Persephone in the eye like a six-year-old for as long as you've known her. You couldn't bring yourself to attend her goddamn wedding. You've had it bad for her from the moment you saw her. You let her go because of your stupid insecurities. Because you are so convinced you're Hades, doomed, dark, and unredeemable, you haven't even bothered to read the myth all the way."

He reached to wrap his fingers around my throat, pressing, draining the oxygen out of me.

"*Persephone!*" He clasped harder.

"*Loved!*" He shook me by the neck.

"*Hades!*"

"I don't l-l-l-love her." I heaved, plummeting into his face with my fists. Stuttering. Losing it.

Hunter smiled through the pain.

"Say it louder," he whispered.

"I don't lo-lo-lo dammit! Love her!" I punched him again. This time his jawline.

"Louder."

"Are you an idiot?" I didn't know why I asked this question. I was already well aware my brother possessed the intelligence of a turkey. A cum-stuffed one, for that matter. "I don't love my wife."

He punched me back, laughing. We rolled on the ground, hitting each other, yanking hair, poking eyes, cursing, and grunting like two cavemen.

Like two *brothers*.

I kept saying I didn't love her, and Hunter kept cackling as if that was the funniest thing he'd ever heard.

I didn't know how much time had passed, but when we were done, we both looked and smelled like horse shit.

Panting and sweating, we were covered in mud and manure head-to-toe.

Hunter was the first to stand and stomp back to his car.

"Apologize," I demanded to his retreating back. He waved me off.

"Siblings don't apologize. They just start acting nice to each other. Now, you ain't driving anywhere after polishing off a bottle of vodka. Get your ass in my car. I'm throwing you in the shower and taking you to see your niece."

I opened my mouth to say something. Even though he couldn't see me, he still raised his palm in warning.

"Save it, bro. I don't care. And if you're worried about seeing your estranged wife at the hospital, don't. By the time we get there, she'll be at work. You didn't even ask what my daughter's name was." He threw the driver's door to his Audi open.

"What is it?"

Please don't let it be Grinder or Nature Valley.

The smile that broke on his face threatened to crack it in two.

"Rooney."

Twenty-Three

Cillian

I drove to Andrew Arrowsmith's house as soon as I kissed my new niece, Rooney, hello.

She was a pink ball with a head full of red hair just like her mother and blue eyes like her father. The lungs, she probably got from Michael Phelps. The kid could blow off the roof with her screams.

All in all, Rooney was one of the cutest babies I'd laid eyes on and a welcome addition to the family.

I'd appreciated how Sailor refrained from pointing out that I was a complete and utter piece of human garbage for what I did to her best friend. She accepted my congratulations with a lukewarm smile even though it was obvious I was responsible for the fact her husband had arrived back in her hospital room beaten up to a pulp and sporting two shiners.

A few hours later, I caught Andrew wobbling from his front door to a U-Haul truck with a cardboard box tucked under his arm. The dirty sweatpants and disheveled hair were a far cry from his usual pretty boy attire.

Parking behind the U-Haul and blocking his way, I slid out of my Aston Martin, my sunglasses and fresh suit hiding my less than pristine condition.

"Moving so fast, Arrowsmith? We haven't even had a chance to have brunch."

He dumped the cardboard box at his feet, groaning.

"I'm handing in my resignation tomorrow. I took some time off to move out, as you can see." He motioned for the truck, implying that I was delaying his progress.

"Doesn't work for me, I'm afraid," I *tsked*, scanning the half-full truck. "You'll hand in your resignation by the end of the workday and drop the lawsuit by three o'clock. If not, I will sue you for every single penny I've spent in legal fees since this bullshit started."

His jaw dropped.

Yes, I cursed.

No, I wasn't afraid for the truth coming out anymore.

I'd already lost the most valuable thing I had—my wife—and anyone else's opinion of me didn't matter. Least of all his.

"Why?" he asked, rearing his head back to squint at me. "Why would I do things your way? All your nasty wife has on me is a bad report from a social worker."

The speed in which I pinned him to the truck by the throat made him gasp.

"Your mouth is not worthy of referring to my wife, let alone calling her nasty."

Choking, he curled his fingers around my wrist, which was the width of his neck. Pissing me off was not his best idea this year. Unfortunately for him, he realized it a moment too late.

Andrew turned pink, then purple before I eased the pressure on his windpipe.

"As for your question—it is more than a report, and we both know it. You are abusing a child with a disorder. Your *own* child. And let's not forget the battery charge for what you did to your wife. That's not very *charitable*, now, is it, Andy?"

I'd read the report against Arrowsmith all night, over and over again, resisting the urge to pick up the phone and beg Persephone for forgiveness. She did a thorough job handing me my enemy on a silver platter.

Andrew sagged, taking a ragged breath.

"I wasn't...I didn't..." He shook his head, turning his back to me, plastering his forehead to the truck and closing his eyes. "I love Tinder. I just didn't know why me. Why did it happen to my child? How was it fair that I had to raise a child as screwed up as the man I hated the most—"

Me.

"My only sin was being the son of the man who hurt your family."

He turned back to me.

"Well, hating *him* was futile, wasn't it? He had a good reason to do what he did to my dad. Plus, it wasn't like I had any access to him. You represented the Fitzpatricks. You were the person I'd seen day in and day out. I felt betrayed and played. Our paths, that had always been parallel, were now forking in different directions. I felt deprived. Robbed of opportunity and prospects and a future I deserved."

He took a sharp breath, tilting his head skywards.

"I used to toss and turn in bed hoping the Fitzpatricks would adopt me." There was a pause. "My wish—my fantasy—was to be you. And when I found out you were less than golden, less than *mo òrga*, I used it to my advantage."

I looked away, cracking my knuckles. I was experiencing an array of negative emotions toward Arrowsmith, from resentment to pity.

I was feeling again, whether I wanted to or not.

"You and I, we were in the business of pain. But with Tinder..." Andrew scrubbed his face. "I never realized I was hurting him. I thought I was helping him. Your wife said she will make this go away if I attend therapy three times a week and live in a different house. I gave Joelle full custody yesterday morning. I can only see my own children while supervised now."

My wife was fucking fantastic. It was hard to believe I'd mistaken her for a nervous, innocent girl who couldn't stand up for herself.

Persephone was both the goddess of spring and the queen of the underworld.

"You have until the end of the day," I repeated, taking a step back. The need to leave made the soles of my feet itch. I had better places to be. Better things to do. All of them connected to what mattered. To the person who mattered. "Drop the lawsuit and resign, then write an extensive press release kissing my ass and admitting your wrongdoings."

I turned around to leave, knowing he was going to play into my hands.

"Cillian," Andrew called out. I stopped, not turning around.

"How'd you do it?" he asked. "Teach yourself to feel again."

I had a hunch I knew why he was asking me this question.

That, in fact, I wasn't the only person who learned how to stop feeling in the process we'd gone through together that year in England.

Andrew was scarred and battered, too.

I shook my head as I slid back into my car.

"I didn't," I muttered. "She taught me."

***

Driving back to my house, I realized that I'd taken two full days off work—more than I had since I'd finished college. I went up to my study and retrieved the contract. The one in which I'd handed over my soul to Persephone.

I was going to leave it for her in the mail. Emmabelle's mail. Persephone had moved back to her sister's house yesterday, after visiting my office.

I'd tried to implement rules, terms, and conditions for my wife to have my soul. Never taking into consideration the fact that the goddamn L-word did not ask for permission to be felt.

It didn't matter what I wanted to give Persephone.

Because my love for her was a given.

And it was time she knew it.

Twenty-Four

Persephone

"This came in the mail for you." Belle tossed a thick envelope onto the kitchenette table as she made her way to the shower, stretching her arms.

It was seven in the morning. I was freshly showered, dressed, and ready for work. I hadn't been able to sleep last night, or the night before it.

Ever since I'd left Cillian, I could barely function, but I knew I had to let him go.

For him.

For me.

"Don't forget, we promised to visit Sailor at five. Let me know if you want me to pick you up from work." Belle proceeded into the bathroom after a long night of work. Goes without saying, I left the Telsa back at the apartment Kill had given me.

Grabbing the envelope, I frowned.

I flipped it back and forth before tearing the thing open.

My soul-purchasing contract was there, duly signed, notarized, and apostilled.

My heart hammered against my rib cage. I unfolded the contract with shaky fingers. When a note slipped out of it, I recognized my husband's long, bold strokes.

My soul is yours.
No terms attached.
Let me know if you have any conditions for keeping it.
I will meet them all.
Cillian

Tears welled up in my eyes.

Kill didn't believe in souls. He was giving me something that was of no value to him. As much as I wanted to believe it, I knew I shouldn't. Every time I chose optimism over realism in our relationship, I got burned.

Supply and demand.

It wasn't that *I* didn't believe he had a soul. I didn't question the existence of what he'd offered me. But as I ripped the contract to shreds, disposing it in the garbage can, I began to follow the footprints of Cillian's mind.

He knew Sailor had given birth to Rooney.

Figured the sword was close to his neck, that it was only a matter of time until Hunter produced male heirs.

Wanted me back in his house.

Back, *period*.

To use.

To get his rocks off.

To impregnate and discard.

I wasn't falling into his cobweb. He saved me. I saved him. As far as I was concerned, we'd settled the score.

It was time we both moved on.

I turned around, grabbed my bag, and hurried out the door to the bike I'd parked outside the building.

Nothing of his was mine anymore.

THE Villain

The next day, I received a text message from my husband first thing in the morning.

I had to rub my eyes twice to make sure I wasn't hallucinating. He never texted me. At least, he never initiated the texts. I proceeded with caution, wondering what he'd sent me.

It was a picture of a cloud floating in a clear sky.

Cillian: Your aunt paid me a visit. She told me I was a cunt. I did not disagree.

Cillian: Have dinner with me.

I snorted out a laugh.

He was bad, but he was trying, and the fact he did made my heart thaw, no matter how badly I knew I needed to quit him.

Belle stretched beside me in bed, letting out a soft snore.

"Is it Kill?"

"Yeah." I pressed the phone to my chest, feeling protective of him even after everything that happened.

"Don't answer." She shook her head. "He needs to sweat a little. See that you have a backbone."

I deleted the message before the urge to answer it won and went about my day.

Six weeks had passed.

Six weeks, thirteen pictures from Cillian of Auntie Tilda in the sky, and a request to meet.

Now with the lawsuit out of the picture, Kill had time to put his heir plan into high gear.

I never answered any of his messages.

It wasn't about punishing my husband; it was about making sure

I had my own back. I refused to be owned, even if, initially, I had been bought.

Six weeks after Rooney Fitzpatrick came into this world, I filled out my divorce papers.

I sat at the family lawyer's office that smelled and bled of the eighties, feeling her eyes on me the entire time as I signed all the paperwork.

"You sure you wanna do this?" she asked for the thousandth time, letting out a smoker's cough. She reminded me of Joey from *Friends* agent, Estelle. "I mean, you won't hear any complaints from me. I'm getting my fee, but the Fitzpatricks aren't a bad family to marry into, child."

"I'm sure." I signed the last page, pushing it across the desk in her direction. "Can you send it to him, please?"

She shook her head.

"Sorry. Your spouse must be served in person. And it has to be by a sheriff, who will then give you proof via return of service."

A sheriff.

The list of people I knew who would pay good money to watch Cillian being served divorce papers by law enforcement was longer than *War and Peace*. But I didn't want to cause Kill any more trouble or humiliation.

"Is it really necessary?"

Just this morning, Cillian left me another message with a cloud.

Cillian: Spoke to your aunt (if you tell anyone I conversed with a cloud, I will flat out deny it). She said I should take you on a honeymoon. I bought tickets.

He seemed undeterred. At the same time, I appreciated him giving me my space. He never once showed up on my doorstep or bulldozed into my life like he used to.

"Yes," said the lawyer, bobbing her head like a dashboard dog. "Maybe you should talk to him if you're so unsure. If you're going to divorce a man, at least give him the courtesy of expecting it."

I stood, collecting the papers.

THE *Villain*

"I'll let him know."

I had to.

I wasn't going to stay in a loveless marriage.

Even if it was to the love of my life.

"Can I turn on the local news?" Ms. Gwen swooped the remote control from one of the round tables in the teachers' lounge, pointing it at the television and switching the channel from sports. A couple of the male teachers groaned in protest.

I poked at my microwaved pasta, sitting in the back of the room, trying not to think about how Belle had promised to deliver the divorce papers to Cillian as soon as she woke up today, which should be at about two in the afternoon.

I couldn't go forward with the sheriff thing. I just couldn't imagine putting him through this. The humiliation. The embarrassment. The publicity of all this.

Still, the limbo had to stop. I had to move on.

"What are we watching?" Ms. Hazel plopped next to Ms. Gwen and me, popping a salt and vinegar chip into her mouth. "Wait, is that a press conference?"

"*Breaking* news." Ms. Michelle sounded startled. I kept my head down as they cranked up the volume. I heard the muttering of press people ahead of a conference, and then the intense hushed voices and loud clicks of the cameras when the person who was speaking got onstage. I refused to lift my eyes from the dish I wasn't even eating. I had this thing again where I knew if I made one move—even trail my gaze up an inch—the tears would start falling.

"Hey, Pers, what's your hot guy doing on the news?" Ms. Michelle chirped.

"Breaking her poor colleagues' hearts, that's what he's doing." Ms. Gwen chuckled. "Emphasis on the word *poor*. What're you still doing here, Persy? Did you not get the memo you're loaded?"

"Why, hello there, honey," whistled Ms. Regina to the TV screen in a manner I knew Cillian would hate. "You can ruin my natural resources *any* day of the week."

"Ladies and gentlemen, thank you so much for coming here today. As I mentioned, this statement will be brief, and, like my temper, short."

My eyes snapped up from my frozen meal. My throat clogged.

Cillian was standing there. My husband—at least for now—in one of his gloriously dark gray suits, dashing silk dark hair, and the hooded expression of a predator on the prowl. Seeing his face again reminded me why I'd insisted he would never seek me out. It disarmed me completely.

His voice. His presence. His smoky amber eyes.

The cameras clicked enthusiastically. It was bizarre to see the man I'd spent countless nights with on a television screen, delivering a message to the city of Boston.

Was he announcing our divorce?

Did Belle serve him yet?

"Despite proving to be a great financial resource and revealing strong potential in getting our hands on more oil, Royal Pipelines has decided to stop the Arctic exploration drillings immediately and indefinitely. All the scheduled rigs will be shut down, future plans are shelved, and the current running trials will cease to operate as of"—he raised his arm, checking his designer watch with a frown—"exactly fifteen minutes from now."

Murmurs and gasps exploded across Royal Pipelines' media room. Journalists and reporters shouted questions about Green Living, Andrew Arrowsmith, and the potential clash with Greenpeace, who were rumored to pick up the lawsuit where Arrowsmith left off.

My heart beat so fast I thought I was going to faint.

THE *Villain*

Kill raised his hand nonchalantly, stopping the stream of questions.

"As I said, the statement will be brief, and I will not be taking any questions. In addition to stopping all oil-rig actions, as of this afternoon, I am also the proud owner of the surrounding Arctic areas which have shown potential and promise to discover oil, meaning Royal Pipelines currently holds all the reserves and options for anyone to drill in the Arctic. Ever.

"I will explore cleaner options in my bid to grow Royal Pipelines' capital and am still committed to employ tens of thousands of Americans. In fact, I would like to inform our investors that I already got my hands on something far more lucrative than the Arctic and not nearly as destructive."

The winning, villainous smile he shot the camera was of someone who was having a checkmate moment, not someone who had just given up his flagship operation. But that was Cillian. Always three steps ahead of the game.

"The reason for my executive decision has nothing to do with Green Living. As you're aware, Green Living had decided to drop the case against Royal Pipelines. As of today, no one had managed to pick it up and carry it through. The reason for my decision is entirely personal.

"As some of you know, I married less than a year ago. One of the things my wife taught me was to listen. This is me listening to what she had to say. She's been outspoken against drilling in the Arctic throughout our short marriage." He paused, twisting his mouth grimly. "She drives a Tesla, you see."

The journalists and photographers erupted in laughter. A few colleagues shot me curious glances. My peers always asked me what I was doing here. As if waking up for work was some sort of punishment. Like they wouldn't miss our students if they quit work. I mostly ignored it, but the truth was, I liked keeping my job because I didn't know if Cillian was going to keep *me*.

I tried to blink back the tears, averting my gaze from the TV.

I told him not to contact me, and he kept on finding new and creative ways to reach out to me.

It took me months to turn my back on us, but I never took into consideration there may be a game changer.

That Cillian might wake up and fight for us.

Cillian

"Anyone interested in hearing a joke about that time Kill drilled the Arctic but stopped because someone thawed his icy heart?"

Hunter snorted when I got off the stage, pacing behind me. Devon followed.

"No," Devon and I barked in unison.

Hunter nodded. "'Kay. Good talk."

We slipped through the back door, taking the elevator back to the management floor. I kept checking my watch, wondering when an appropriate time would be to try calling my wife. I finally got it. How badly it sucked to be ignored. I'd ignored Persephone for months when I had her in my bed, sweet and willing.

Her texts, her words, her quirky observations. They were all mine for the taking.

Now I had to do the chasing, and I had to admit—they weren't kidding when they called Karma a bitch.

The elevator dinged. I strode out to my office, waving at Hunter to get as far as humanly possible away from me. I was a surly son of a bitch these days. I cursed. I shouted at employees. I did a lot of mortal

THE Villain

things people weren't used to from me. The other day, I said *fuck* while golfing with my father. He almost had a stroke.

Speaking of *Athair*, I spotted the old sod pacing the boardroom from the corner of my eye and made a quick, sharp turn toward it. An overhead TV replaying my press conference danced on the wall behind him. Upon a closer look, I saw Mother was there, too, perched on one of the seats by the kidney-shaped desk, fixing her makeup.

I opened the door, closed it, and waited for the storm. I didn't have to wait long.

"You little piece of—"

"I would not finish that sentence if I were you." I raised my open palm, wearing an easy smile on my face. "You're talking to the CEO of Royal Pipelines. Disrespect me, and you'll find yourself escorted out of my building."

"*Your* building?" he sputtered. "That's a good one. No. You would never," my father spat out. I didn't have to grace that with an answer. He already knew I was capable of pretty much anything.

He fell into one of the seats, grabbing his head in his hands, shaking it. "I don't understand."

"I am under no obligation to make sense to you," I informed him.

"Green Living dropped the lawsuit. This could've been the most lucrative oil-rig operation in the world. I mean, *you* were the one who pushed for it. You were the head of research. You spent three goddamn months living on an iceberg, managing this project closely. This was your baby, Cillian."

"Yes," I said. "And now I'm interested in another baby. A human one. Which is why I'd like my wife to be as content as she can be."

"This is what it's about?" Mother jumped to her feet, finally justifying her oxygen consumption in the room. "Sweetie, we appreciate you marrying this...this sweet, *common* girl, but there are others out there. Just as pretty, and they won't interfere with your business. *I* didn't interfere with your father's business."

"No," I agreed. "You also had jack-shit to say about anything, from our upbringing to our education. At the risk of sounding disrespectful—which, by the way, I am happy to take—I don't want your kind of marriage. It looks awful, inside and out. I don't want *manageable*. I don't want my wife to be a ghost of a mother. A yes woman. A prop. And I like my common wife just fine, Mother."

More than like her.

Persephone sacrificed more for me in our short marriage than Mother did since I was born.

"This beats the entire purpose of you getting married!" my father thundered, jumping to his feet. "Losing this 1.4-billion-dollar opportunity for a…for a…"

"Say it." I smirked. "For pussy, right? No other organ in a woman's body counts for you. Least of all a heart."

It didn't for me, either. Not until recently.

"Yes!" my father boomed, throwing his arms in the air, his face red, a drop of saliva staining his lower lip. "If I knew that was the case, I'd have never pushed you to get married."

"I'm glad you did." I opened the glass door. "This marriage has taught me an important lesson. A lesson Evon, Yale, and Harvard combined couldn't. Now, allow me to apply some of the conclusions I've come to in recent months and throw you the hell out of my office—yes, *my* office, if I put in the sixty hour work week, I'm the one calling the shots—with this tip: never, *ever* tell me what to do with my job, my life, and my marriage."

I jerked my chin out the door. Both my parents stared at me, wide-eyed.

"Go on. You know how to use your legs, don't you?"

Walked away from me enough times in your lives, I was tempted to add.

Mother's eyes glittered while she tried to pull herself together while *Athair* kept a solemn, dignified expression. The line had been drawn. They began to make their way out of the office. Mother stopped by the door and cupped my cheeks, gazing up at me.

"I'm sorry," she whispered, her voice so soft only I could hear her. "I'm sorry for everything. You are right. You deserve better than what we made of our lives, Cillian."

I kissed her cheek. "All forgiven."

"Really?"

I gave her a curt nod. "Now get out."

Next, it was my father's turn to stop by the door. His eyes crinkled with a mixture of annoyance and delight.

"*Mo òrga*." He inclined his head. "You keep surprising me with your strength. Your brother has always been a wild card but simple to crack. That's why I unleashed the Brennan girl on him. Your sister… well, she is a saint I don't have to worry about, but you." He inhaled, closing his eyes. "You were my damaged child, which made you so much more dangerous because we both knew you could survive anything. You think I don't know," he whispered in my ear, getting close, too close—the closest he'd ever been to me physically—"but I do. I know about your demons, Cillian. The same ones live in the basement of my heart. Only difference is, you seemed to have slayed yours. Good for you, son."

Disoriented and in need of a stiff drink, I strode to my office.

"Mr. Fitzpatrick!" Sophia jumped from her station, sprinting in my direction as soon as I walked out of the boardroom. "You have a visitor."

"Who?"

"Ms. Penrose."

"Call her that one more time and you are permanently blacklisted from working at any respectable Boston company."

Forcing myself to keep my steps even, I made my way to my office, finding Emmabelle Penrose sitting in my executive chair, her long legs draped over my chrome desk. She wore a pair of Louboutins I was pretty sure belonged to my wife, a pencil skirt, and a blouse that didn't leave much to the imagination.

And the day just keeps better and better.

"Never mind. Wrong sister." I waved Sophia off, pushing open the glass door and closing it after me. I leaned a shoulder against the glass wall, tucking my hands into my front pockets.

"Cillian! How's life treating you?" Emmabelle purred, looking up from her phone.

"Like I fucked its underage daughter, and now it's out for revenge," I answered blandly, pushing off the wall and taking a seat in front of her. I was—and always would be—unruffled by her entire Dita Von Teese on steroids act. Her cry for attention fell on deaf ears in my case.

"Feet off the table," I instructed. "Unless you want them broken."

"Oh, dear, someone's in a mood." She removed her legs from my desk, dumping her ugly secondhand Prada bag on top of my laptop. I resisted the urge to hurl her out of my window. I doubted it would win me any points with my wife. "I'm afraid things are about to go from bad to worse."

"I sincerely doubt there's room for deterioration," I lunged back.

"Then I'm here to prove you the sky is the limit, baby." She plucked something from her bag—a stack of papers—and slid it across my desk with her pointy scarlet fingernail. "You've been served."

I didn't touch the papers. I glanced down and saw my wife's handwriting. Curvy. Romantic. Small. Like her.

For a second, the temptation not to feel was overwhelming.

To laugh it off.

To kick Emmabelle out.

To show her that I didn't care.

Then I remembered it was exactly why I had to fight to get my wife back.

"The answer is no," I said mildly, cracking my knuckles under the table. "I told Persephone divorce wasn't an option. It is tacky, brings bad press, and besides, she's yet to fulfill her part of the bargain."

"You realize you're not God, right?" Emmabelle cocked her head sideways. "You can't just snap your fingers and make people fall in line."

THE Villain

I stared at her. "Prove it."

"She doesn't want you anymore."

"I can change her mind."

"What makes you think that?" Belle grinned, her eyes glittering.

"She wanted me before I even tried. Now that I intend to make an effort, she won't be able to resist me. Either way, we both know you're walking out of here with the divorce petition if I have to fucking feed it to you. This has no legal ground. You're not the sheriff, and I'm not a guy you can push around. If it comes to court, I'll ask the judge for couple's therapy—and will receive it—seeing as we've been married for a short period and no adultery or abuse has occurred."

"That's what I thought." Emmabelle chuckled, withdrawing the papers from my desk and tucking them back into her bag. "Look, I'm not your biggest fan for numerous reasons. At the top of them is the fact you planned to lock my baby sister in a suburban McMansion and have her produce heirs for you while you stayed here and lived the big life. But I've come to accept that, despite your sociopathic shortcomings, you've truly grown to love her. Am I right?"

There were many offensive things on the tip of my tongue, but Emmabelle had the advantage today. I had to let her have her day in the sun, even if I wanted to burn her down.

"Yes," I agreed sullenly. "I love your sister very much."

So much it goddamn fucking hurts.

"Well, maybe it's time to tell her how you feel." Belle stood, scooping her bag and hurling it over her shoulder. "You've been apologizing for the wrong thing the entire time. Persephone didn't leave you because you're an asshole. Heck, I'm sure it's half of your charm. She left you because she thinks you're incapable of feeling. Prove her wrong."

"How the hell can I do that, seeing as I'm not supposed to see her?"

"Says who?" She blinked in surprise.

"Says *her*," I growled. "She told me not to come after her."

365

"Since when do you listen to what my sister says? One of the very things she loves about you is that you do whatever the hell you want. Always."

Of course, the one time I decided to obey, it was to the wrong fucking instruction.

My sister-in-law tapped my shoulder as she exited my office.

"Go get her. She's waiting, and I'm growing tired of taking my flings back to their apartments because she's in my bed."

It was time to break one more promise.

Twenty-Five

Persephone

"**There's a cloud in our backyard!**" Dahlia, one of my students, gasped, pointing her chubby finger out the window behind me.

"*Whoa!*" Reid's tar eyes rounded, his pupils dilating like two splashes of ink. "That is one giant, *humongous* cloud."

"Now, friends," I said from over the rim of the book I was reading. They sat around me on the colorful alphabet carpet. The fog outside distracted them. "Crisscross applesauce. Everybody sit down and pay attention to the story. We need to finish reading about Paddington attending the Busy Bee Adventure Trail before we can play outside."

"Collecting B-words is b-o-r-r-i-n-g!" Noah spelled the word wrong, tossing his limbs about the carpet in frustration. "Mommy says teachers are not very smart, or they wouldn't be teachers. I want to play with the giant cloud!"

Well, Noah, Mommy is a B for bitc…

"Please!" Dahlia cried.

"Oh, Ms. Persy!" Reid whined.

The kids swarmed me, crawling onto my lap while pressing their palms together pleadingly. "Please, please, please can we play with the cloud? The nice man wants us to join him so badly. Look at him playing all by himself."

The nice man?
Playing with himself?

Thinking now was a great time to call the police and make use of my pepper spray, I whipped my head, my jaw slacking.

My husband—who according to Belle refused the divorce papers yesterday and kicked her out of his office—was standing in Little Genius' backyard, sleeves rolled, hair tousled, one knee on the ground as he created a huge, white, solitary cloud that floated above his head. It was the size of a hot air balloon. Big and fluffy and white. My eyes darted to the ground. How did he make it?

I spotted a metal tray, a stirrer, a match, and a Mason jar scattered underneath him.

We stared at each other wordlessly through the glass wall.

The book slipped from my fingers. I felt the herd of kids as they ran past me, dashing to the window, pressing their sticky fingers and noses to the glass as they squealed excitedly.

Avoiding my husband was no longer an option.

He brought me a cloud.

He brought me *Auntie Tilda*.

My legs carried me to the glass wall. He walked over, meeting me behind the thin barrier.

I put my hand on the glass. Cillian mirrored the action, our fingertips touching through the wall.

"I told you not to come here." I swallowed hard.

"I told you a lot of things I regret," he answered. "I hope maybe what you said was one of yours."

"I've already used my Cloud Wish, Kill. I can't have another one." My voice broke.

"The wish is not for you to make, Persephone." He smiled. "It's for me."

THE *Villain*

The children poured into the backyard like hot lava, spreading fast, crackling with delight.

Their small arms reached for the cloud, trying to grasp the ungraspable, stretching their fingers in an attempt to capture its magic.

I was the last to get out to the yard, stopping a few good feet away from my husband. Seeing him after weeks felt like dropping a heavy camping bag at the doorstep of your home. I wanted to bury my nose in his neck and breathe him in.

I didn't ask him what he was doing here. I was afraid to believe. To hope.

Descending from Olympus didn't make my husband any less regal and beautiful, and the Greek gods had a history of making mortals play into their own hands.

"This one is Dahlia." He pointed at one of the kids, who was punching the smoke, trying to bring it to submission. "You call her The Little Mouse. Sassy, sweet, stubborn. This is Teo," he continued, jerking his chin to Teo, "shy and reserved but observant. And that's Joe," he continued, looking at Joel, one of my favorite pupils. A dreamer with a shock of bright red hair.

"How did you know?" I whispered.

"I've been listening during our dinners," he admitted. "To every word you said. Even if I pretended otherwise."

My heart soared.

"You're claiming your Cloud Wish?" I wrung my fingers together in my lap, turning into the same girl he'd met years ago in the bridal suite. Innocent. Unsure.

"Yes."

"Who said you have one?" A smile fluttered on my lips.

"Your aunt." There was no hint of mockery in his voice, which I appreciated, considering he was fluent in sarcasm. "She said I have to be careful. That you only get one wish in a lifetime."

Wait a minute...

It was the same thing Auntie Tilda told me. And I didn't

remember ever telling Kill about this particular part. It couldn't be. It made no sense at all.

"What's your wish?" I whispered.

The children were teeming around us, and I thought it was symbolic, that the reason we were brought together—heirs—engulfed us even though I hadn't conceived.

"I want an hour with you. Sixty minutes of your time. That's all I ask. When are you getting off work?"

"Four," I answered. "Same as always."

"I'll wait."

At least he hadn't told me to ditch work this time.

"How did you make a cloud?" I pointed behind him.

"NASA has a manual. It's nothing."

"It's amazing."

"Third graders can do it."

"I don't care." I shook my head. "Will you wait for me?" I motioned around us, to the school.

He smiled. "Persephone, my dear, I've been waiting for eight years. Four more hours won't kill me."

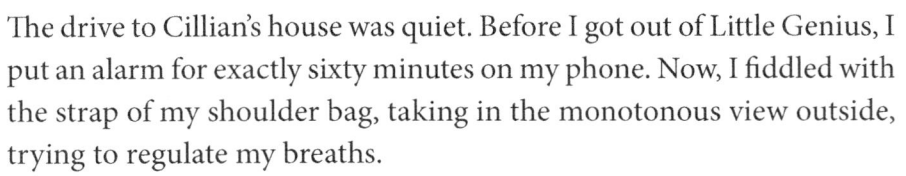

The drive to Cillian's house was quiet. Before I got out of Little Genius, I put an alarm for exactly sixty minutes on my phone. Now, I fiddled with the strap of my shoulder bag, taking in the monotonous view outside, trying to regulate my breaths.

It was make or break time. A part of me always knew Cillian wasn't going to simply accept the divorce. Maybe that was why I went ahead with the paperwork. Subconsciously, I knew it would be a call for him to come closer.

To seek me out.

To defy me.

"You stopped the drilling in the Arctic." I cleared my throat, still looking out the window. It was twenty past. Damn Boston traffic. We had forty more minutes. Technically, anyway.

"Yes."

"That was…nice."

"Giving you flowers is nice. Losing approximately 1.4 billion dollars a year in revenue is, at the very least, a romantic gesture of Shakespearean proportions."

He said it so incredulously—so seriously—I couldn't help but snort out a laugh.

"I'm not even sure how many zeroes that entails."

"Nine." His fingers tapped his knee, and I knew he was itching for a cigar but trying to be on his best behavior. "Ten, including me, if my plan today doesn't work and I find out I did this for nothing."

When we got to his house, I noticed Petar was out. So was the rest of the staff. I'd never seen the place so empty. I had a feeling it was planned.

"Should we go to your study?" I asked politely. A part of me still considered him a complete stranger.

He shook his head. "I want to show you something."

Motioning for me to follow him to the backyard, he opened the double doors in his living room, and we proceeded outside. I'd visited his garden religiously. Not only was it gorgeous but I was still on the lookout for the elusive demon fountain. For the mysterious part of Cillian's property I'd yet to discover.

I followed him, holding my breath when he stopped by the ivy-laced door with the high walls. I'd tried opening it twice, but it was firmly locked. Kill produced a key and unlocked it, pushing it open.

We both stepped in, and there was the demon fountain. With water pouring out of the bat-like monster with pointy teeth.

It was a small space—maybe as big as Belle's apartment—and I wondered what made him close this section and isolate it from the rest of the garden.

Kill crouched down, hands-on-thighs, squinting. There was something about his body language that jarred me. A certain stiffness that was gone. His composure was an inch less than perfect. I liked it.

"What are we looking at?" I came to stand beside him, leaning forward. He caught me by the waist, tugging softly at my dress to keep me from getting too close to the flowers.

To the sea of flowers.

I just realized this section of the house was jam-packed with wildflowers. And not just *any* flowers. The pink and white flowers were shaped as little sad hearts. I swallowed, taking a step back.

"How long have you had those?"

"Almost four years." He turned to me with a slight frown. "About a month after Hunter and Sailor's wedding, my landscaper called me outside, insisting I had to see this. He said it was peculiar. That he didn't plant the bleeding heart, so he had no idea how the flower had gotten here. His best guess was seeds from a nearby garden blew in the wind and settled here. But I remembered that after I took the flowers from your hair, I put them in a napkin. Later that night, when I arrived home, I went out to the garden to smoke a cigar, found the napkin, and tossed it. It was just the one flower, and my landscaper asked if I wanted to keep it. I immediately thought about your curse—*wish*," he amended, "and said no. He yanked the bleeding heart out from its root the same day. A month later, another bleeding heart grew in the same spot. I had him wrench it out again. This time he went as far as poisoning the soil. On the fourth time, I gave up. A part of me wanted to see how damn stubborn you were. And look at it now. My garden's full of them."

I pressed my lips together, fighting a smile.

He barricaded a part of his garden because it reminded him of me. Caged it where no one could see it.

"So I lived with your bleeding heart. A poisonous reminder of how much I wanted you. Not much later, I found out you were getting married."

THE *Villain*

"You never answered my wedding invitation." I felt color rising on my skin.

"Everyone has their limits. I draw mine at celebrating my idiocy of pushing you into another man's arms. Time went by. I'd forgotten about you, mostly. The wheels of life kept on spinning, and no matter how fast or slow they went, I barely even remembered I was on board. Then Paxton left, I'd been appointed CEO of Royal Pipelines, and you showed up at my office, looking for a favor. My initial reaction was to put as much space between us as possible."

"You didn't want to feel," I said softly. He shook his head.

"At this point, I wasn't even concerned about the possibility of feeling. I was mainly still annoyed about the damn flowers that kept showing up out of nowhere in my backyard. Like you snuck in at night and planted them there. But then the need for a bride arose…"

"Yes, and you had multiple candidates to choose from. You canceled the engagement to Minka Gomes. Why?"

He frowned at the bed of flowers.

"She wasn't you."

"She could've been pregnant by now."

"It was never about having an heir," he quipped. A gorgeous, irresistible king who was misjudged and misunderstood. "Deep down, I wasn't altruistic enough to give a fuck about the lineage."

I glanced at my phone. We had half an hour at most before his wish was over.

"Tell me about the Tourette's," I pleaded. "Everything, right from the beginning. I've only seen a few videos, but they were enough to show me what you've been through."

"It started with simple tics, right after my father fired Andrew Senior, and moved to full-blown attacks by the time I'd gotten back to England after summer break. The lonelier I felt, the worse they became. I'd been in and out of clinics, and on top of Tourette's, I also received comorbid diagnosis of having OCD and ASD. To me, it felt like the end of the world. People think of Tourette's as crazy people who shout out obscenities against their own will in rags on the street, OCD as compulsively obsessive maniacs who wash their hands fifteen times an hour, and ASD means I'm on the autism spectrum. Which basically makes people think I'm some sort of Rain Man. Good with numbers, dumb at everything else.

"Quickly, I'd realized I needed to rein in this condition if I wanted to become all the things I was born to be. I learned that while I couldn't control the tics, I could control what made them happen. And what made them happen was my being overwhelmed with emotion. *Any* type of emotion. Whether it was sadness, distress, anger, fear, or even joy. If I was excited—if my heart raced—the pressure of an attack usually followed. As long as I didn't allow myself to feel, I kept the tics at bay. It was very simple and worked for everyone involved."

This explained so much.

Why Cillian was so fond of his leather gloves—he didn't like touching strange things, due to his OCD.

Why he managed to disconnect from his feelings so efficiently when they became a complication.

Why he always cracked his knuckles—to regulate his breaths, to self-soothe. It was a tic. A reminder of what he had to live with. He couldn't switch off who he was. Not fully. No matter how hard he tried.

Why he always kept his guard up.

Why he ignored me for years instead of caving in to temptation.

"Everyone but you. You're the one who couldn't feel anything."

"I survived fine."

"Surviving is not enough."

"I know that now." His sultry eyes twinkled at me. "Thanks to you."

The air between us became thick and charged. He took my hand in his. Such a simple gesture, yet it felt as though he plucked the stars from the sky for me. He pressed my hand against his heart. It raced beneath my palm, thudding violently, desperate to smash the barrier between us and jump into my fist.

THE Villain

The strongest hearts have the most scars.

"Keep it here until I'm done," he instructed, drawing a deep breath.

"I want you." He lifted one finger. "I've always wanted you with a hunger that made my chest ache and my mouth dry. That's one emotion. I am jealous and possessive of you. In case you haven't noticed." He erected two more fingers in the air. "I worry and fear for you. When I discovered why you'd decided to work for Andrew, I wanted to skin you alive for putting yourself at risk for me. That's two more." He splayed his entire hand over an invisible screen between us, stretching all five fingers.

"Five emotions down, five more to go. You've made me the happiest I've ever been. Also the saddest." He now lifted two fingers of his other hand. "And caused me an infinite amount of pain and pleasure."

There was only one finger left curled now.

One emotion he still hadn't unveiled.

The watch on his wrist said it was five to five. Only five more minutes before Auntie Tilda's wish evaporated and we ran out of time to say all the things we wanted to say.

My breath hitched.

"I love you, Persephone," he growled. "I love you so fucking hard. Somewhere along the way, I softened. I may have saved you from a bleeding heart, but your bleeding heart saved *me*. Ten emotions are not twenty-seven. There's still more to go, but I want to take this journey with you.

"We are not Hades and Persephone, Flower Girl. Never were. I didn't drag you down a dark path. You pulled me into the light. Helpless, I followed. Blindly, I got burned. I am Icarus." The clock hit five. Our sixty minutes were up. The alarm on my phone beeped to tell me so, but I smacked the side button to silence it. "I love you as he loved the sun. Too close. Too hard. Too fast."

He dipped his head, his mouth closing in on mine. I went limp in his arms. He gathered me to his chest, strong and resilient, steadfast.

A cold king in his poisonous garden, finally letting the sunrays touch his skin.

We sank down to the ground on our knees, and I no longer feared the earth would open its jaw and swallow me into the underworld.

Kill's mouth moved over mine. He pried my lips apart, rolling his tongue with mine teasingly, tasting me. I moaned, bracketing his cheekbones, deepening our kiss as I climbed onto his lap, the only place that had ever felt like home.

We kissed for hours. By the time our lips broke, my mouth was dry, my lips cracked, and a velvet blue shadow colored the sky.

My husband slid his nose down the bridge of mine.

"The contract still stands. My soul is yours."

"I never wanted your soul." I smiled into his lips, my eyes meeting his. "I tore it to shreds the minute I got it in the mail. I've only ever wanted your heart. Now that I have it, I have a secret to tell you."

He arched an eyebrow.

I put my lips to his ears.

"I didn't believe in souls, either, before."

"Before?"

"Before I met you."

Epilogue

Persephone

A year later.

"You look like you're about to burst."

I wanted to strangle my sister, even if her words were delivered with genuine concern.

Objectively speaking, I *did* look like an orange. I was forty-one weeks pregnant with our first child. It was clear that my son, like his father, was not to be rushed. Rather, he'd decided to opt for a grand entrance while fashionably late, something my body did *not* appreciate.

My breasts were the size of watermelons and constantly sore, my lower back felt like nothing but pointy needles supported it, and my hormones were all over the place.

This past week, I couldn't even bring myself to get out of bed. I had to rely on Cillian for food and entertainment. Oh, and reaching those pesky parts I could no longer scrub while taking a shower.

I leaned over my headboard with a pout, wiggling my toes even though they were nothing but a distant memory I couldn't see anymore.

"When are the mood swings going to be over?" I pondered aloud. Sailor and Aisling were in the room, too, fawning over me.

"I'm tired of bursting into tears every time I see a Super Bowl commercial and whenever a Katy Perry song comes on the radio."

"You cry because she sucks, right?" Belle slumped on the foot of my bed, massaging my feet. "Just want to confirm your hormones are only messing with your feelings and not your taste in music."

I snorted, giving her a playful kick. "I'm serious."

"My mood swings never passed," Sailor said, draped on a recliner in the corner of our master bedroom. "I remember pushing Rooney's stroller along a jogging trail, looking at a squirrel running about, thinking how its tail would be perfect for cleaning baby bottles. In my defense, it *was* really fluffy."

"No offense, bitch, but you're not such a great example." Belle placed my right ankle over her thigh, digging her thumbs deep into the arch of my foot. "You got knocked up again before Rooney graduated from seeing shades to recognizing voices. Does your husband know he can put it away every now and again?"

"No," we all said in unison, laughing. Aisling scrunched her nose. She was standing at the window, watching my lush garden. The day I'd moved back into the mansion was also the day the bleeding heart had begun to wilt and eventually die. It was like it served its purpose and then retired. I always thought of it as Auntie Tilda finally taking a breath after she granted my wish.

"Gross. It's my brother we're talking about." Ash shuddered. "Come to think of it, other than you, Belle, all my friends are also my sisters-in-law, and all of them got knocked up by my brothers. It's alarming."

"What's alarming is this baby is still inside me." I pointed at my huge belly.

"Lucky kid." My husband strolled into our room, cool and collected in his designer suit. His posture alone made me drool a little. Cillian had been most accommodating when we found out my pregnancy came with an increased sexual appetite. However, in the past couple of months, having sex became such a chore, these days we were relying on oral favors and Netflix to keep us busy at night.

"Satan," Belle saluted. My sister and my husband got along fine these days. He'd even helped her buy out her two business partners, so now she was the sole owner of Madame Mayhem.

"Lucifer," Sailor greeted.

She, too, had no beef with her brother-in-law anymore.

"Kill." Ash nodded.

He ignored the women in the room, sauntering in my direction to lean down and press a long, close-mouthed kiss to my forehead.

"How're you doing, Flower Girl?"

"Tired. Sleepy." I stretched lazily, smiling up at him.

He rubbed my stomach through the stretchy orange fabric of my pajamas.

"And the little guy?"

"Great. I think he's going to be a soccer player. He's been kicking up a storm all morning."

Cillian raised his eyebrows. "Whatever floats his boat during adolescence. But once he's out of university, he's going to have to take his place at Royal Pipelines."

Groaning, I grabbed the tip of my husband's tie and tugged him to me, shutting him up with a kiss. "We've been through this, hubs. He is going to be whatever he wants to be. He is not you."

We'd had a lot of discussions about what it meant for Cillian to be Cillian. The heir to Royal Pipelines. How maybe, if it weren't for the burden of his lineage, he wouldn't have had to find creative and destructive ways to deal with his disorder. A disorder that still—apart from myself, Andrew, and Joelle Arrowsmith—no one knew anything about.

Not even his mother, who—Kill told me once—probably blocked the memory of that Swiss lab in order to protect herself.

"Of course," he said flatly. "He can be whatever he wants. A soccer player, a musician, a pool boy."

I shot him a look.

"But he'll want to be a CEO," Kill finished, grinning.

"All righty." Belle tapped my ankles. "I think we're going to leave you to it before you rip off each other's clothes and have *very* pregnant sex in front of us. It's been real. Pers, Mom says she is coming this week, and that she's staying. She has a feeling you will pop over the weekend." She stood, motioning for my friends to follow.

"I'll have Petar get one of the guest rooms ready," Kill said.

"But I haven't rubbed Persy's tummy yet today!" Ash protested.

"God, Ash, you need your own baby." Sailor laughed, pushing her out.

"I've a feeling she'll get one soon," Belle murmured, closing the door behind them.

Kill flashed the door an irritated look, then turned his gaze back to me.

I raised my palms up. "I can't help what leaves my sister's mouth."

"If you could, you'd have a full-time job managing it. Have you heard from Joelle this week? She asked when she could stop by."

Shortly after Cillian and I got back together, I resumed my communication with Joelle Arrowsmith. She was going through a divorce from Andrew, who was still in therapy, working in the private sector as a legal consultant and trying to become a better father for Tree and Tinder. Joelle was relieved when I started visiting her again, often with Cillian, who kept an eye on Tinder and often provided Joelle advice and guidance.

I'd even taken the kids and my husband to see Mrs. Veitch for a Christmas celebration at her nursing home. She died a few weeks after in her sleep.

"I need to call her back, but I'm hoping the next time I see her, I'll have a baby in my hands. Can you help me up? I need a shower." I wobbled about the bed.

"I've got you." He scooped me up in his arms and carried me into our en suite. There, I stood under the streaming showerheads, steam clouding the glass doors while Kill leaned against the marble countertops, keeping me company.

THE *Villain*

"Sailor is starting to show," I observed, lathering my arms with soap.

"Hmm," Kill answered noncommittally. I could see him stroking his chin from the mirror in front of us. "Does Ash really want a baby?"

I shrugged. "Wouldn't surprise me. I'm twenty-seven. That makes her…what? Twenty-six? Not too farfetched even though she still has her residency to complete." Ash was a doctor now. "We've always been the romantics out of the bunch. We've always wanted big families."

"With the slight distinction that you were never obsessed with the king of the underworld," Kill noted.

Sam Brennan was his friend, but he was also a man he didn't want for his sister.

"No," I agreed. "I simply fell in love with the media's favorite villain." I smiled, turning off the water stream and patting the tiles for my bathrobe. "Don't worry, we've got your sister. We'll keep her safe and won't let her do anything too wild."

"Just like they kept you from marrying me," Kill said, unconvinced. "You are sweet but stubborn, and my sister's much the same. I'm old enough to remember that when she was five, she almost dragged a fucking live opossum into the house because my parents had refused to grant her the pet she wanted so much."

My husband cursed. Not often, and only in front of me and a small cluster of friends and family, but he did.

I flicked my hand to turn off the water.

Wait, haven't I done this already?

"…will break every bone in his body and reassemble him to look like a Picasso painting if he as much as touches a hair on her head…"

"Kill," I breathed.

"What?" He stopped talking, turning to face the shower.

"I turned off the water…" I murmured, looking down. "But the water's still running."

His eyes darted between my legs.

"Sweetheart, your water broke."

We both looked at each other.

"Ready, Daddy Kill?"

"Let's get it, Flower Girl."

Cillian

Astor Damian Archibald Fitzpatrick was born on the warmest day in Boston's history. Warmer than the unfortunate day on our belated honeymoon in Namibia, when my wife fulfilled her dream to lie on a velvety yellow dune and look up at the sun defiantly. At one hundred and ten degrees, I sweated my balls off nearby, waiting for her patiently with a cold bottle of water.

It was so scorching hot, the power went down, generators had to be used to keep the electricity running at the hospital, and my wife looked like a liquid version of her former self.

Then he came into the world and everything ceased to matter.

"And my fourth-grade teacher said nothing would come out of me." Persephone pumped the air when the doctor scooped the baby, laughing and crying at the same time, which, I'd learned during my time being with her, was apparently a completely valid thing to do for a human being.

"What's her name?" I demanded. "I'll make sure—"

"God, Kill, who cares about Ms. Merrill! Give me my baby!" There was definitely more laughing than crying now.

Astor did not come out kicking and screaming, as babies do, rejecting the very idea of leaving the comfort and warm safety of the womb in which they were created.

THE *Villain*

He came out quiet and stern. Too quiet, in fact. So much so, that the doctor swooped him away to a nearby table before we could see him properly and began patting him with a towel and suctioning fluid out of his mouth.

"I'm just trying to stimulate his first cry," Dr. Braxman said calmly. "His pulse and color are fine, so I'm sure it is nothing. Probably just a tough, resilient baby."

Persephone wrapped my hand in hers, squeezing me with the remainder of her energy, dripping sweat. After a twelve-hour labor, I was surprised she was still awake.

"Kill," she moaned, cupping her mouth. I pulled her into a hug, craning my neck at the same time to see what Dr. Braxton was doing.

"It's fine. Everything is fine. I'll go take a look."

She nodded.

As I made my way to the doctor, who was still patting and touching my baby, surrounded by two nurses, trying to make him cry, the escalating force of an impending Tourette's attack crawled up my spine. My heart raced. My knuckles popped. My desire to protect my child burned so fiercely in me, I was pretty sure I could destroy the entire building with my two hands if something happened to him.

Just as I took the last step toward Dr. Braxman, Astor opened his tiny red mouth and let out a wail that nearly shattered the windows, curling his tiny fists and thrusting them in the air like Rocky.

"Ah. There we are." Dr. Braxman wrapped my son like a burrito, then handed him to me, supporting his head. "Ten fingers, ten toes, a set of healthy lungs, and a lot of personality."

The doctor moved quickly, settling back between my wife's thighs, which had been covered with a cloth, and began stitching her up.

I frowned down at my son.

The so-called goal. The endgame. My mission after successfully ticking all the boxes on my way to taking over the reins of the Fitzpatrick family.

And out of all the feelings I had felt—joy, pleasure, awe, happiness, wild anticipation, and violent protectiveness, even a little fear tossed in—I couldn't, for the life of me, see myself passing him the burden of going through what I had to go through to make my parents proud.

It wasn't fair to him. To me. To Hunter's and Aisling's children, and all the future offspring we were going to have.

Studying his face, I admired his perfection. Nature had cherry-picked our best features for him. He had huge blue eyes like his mother, my dark hair, and a prominent nose like mine. But his ears were small, like my wife's, and he had that look—the look that could make empires fall—that only Persephone Penrose had ever managed to hone.

A look that disarmed me.

A look that told me I might not be the bad cop in the household, after all.

"Excuse me," Persephone sing-songed from her place on the bed, waving at me. "My apologies for interrupting, but is there any way I could see my own son, too?"

I laughed, walking over to her. Astor was still screaming and throwing his little fists at me. He had surprisingly long fingernails for a newborn, but they looked thin and brittle. I lowered him to her chest, which was only partly covered by her hospital gown.

The mother and the baby stared at each other, and the world around them stopped on its axis. Astor got very quiet and very serious. Persephone sucked in a breath, and I stopped breathing, the pressure of the attack easing down.

"Hello, little angel." She smiled down at him.

He stared at her, mesmerized.

I know the feeling, son.

I stood back and watched them.

My own little family.

A perfect thing in this imperfect world.

Knowing I might've passed Astor the very thing that life had cursed me with because it was hereditary.

Knowing that, in all probability, my father had it, too.

And vowing to make sure Astor would never get locked in a church confession booth with his demons.

That he, too, would one day be able to bask in the light.

The End.

Acknowledgements

This book was definitely a ride to write. It took a lot from me mentally and physically. I don't think I would have been able to write it without my support group. So here goes:

To my beta readers: Tijuana Turner (who is also my momager and my fairy godmother), Vanessa Villegas, Lana Kart, Amy Halter, and Chelsea Humphrey. Thank you for your valuable input and your dedication to this story. You definitely made working on it so much fun.

To my editing team, Cate Hogan, Mara White, Paige Maroney Smith and Jenny Sim. Your attention to detail and dedication to the written word and the quality of the story in front of you never ceases to amaze me. I am forever grateful to have you by my side.

To my wiz cover designer, Letitia Hasser, who has yet to divorce me—thanks for that. I appreciate your patience, your hard work and your overwhelming talent so, so much. You're stuck with me forever! And also to Stacey Blake of Champagne Formatting, another personal favorite who is always there for me and always delivers!

To my agent, Kimberly Brower, at Brower Literary, for being one of my most amazing supporters, and to my KICK-ASS street team, who are much more than a street team: Avivit, Vanessa, Lulu, Ratula, Sheena, Sarah Plocker, Sarah Grim Sentz, Chele, Jacquie, Ariadna, Yamina, Nadine, Nina, Leeann, Samantha, Stacey, Summer, Isa, Sher, Lisa, Tanaka, Marta, Keri, Rebecca, Betty and Lin. If you see reoccurring names each release, it's because they're my ride or die.

And to my best friends in the whole entire world, Charleigh Rose, Ava Harrison, Parker S. Huntington, Tijuana Turner, and Vanessa Villegas. Thank you for being my support system. Always.

Stay connected

Join my Newsletter
http://eepurl.com/b8pSuP

Follow me on Instagram
www.instagram.com/authorljshen

Add me on Facebook
www.facebook.com/authorljshen

Also by L.J. SHEN

Sinners of Saint:
Defy (#0.5)
Vicious (#1)
Ruckus (#2)
Scandalous (#3)
Bane (#4)

All Saints High:
Pretty Reckless (#1)
Broken Knight (#2)
Angry God (#3)

Boston Belles:
The Hunter (#1)
The Villain (#2)
The Monster (#3, TBA 2021)
The Take (#4, TBA 2021)

Standalones:
Tyed
Sparrow
Blood to Dust
Midnight Blue
Dirty Headlines
In the Unlikely Event
The Kiss Thief
Playing with Fire

Excerpt from *The Kiss Thief*

Before you go, here's a small excerpt of *The Kiss Thief*. If you enjoyed Cillian Fitzpatrick, you are going to love Wolfe Keaton…

PROLOGUE

What sucked the most was that I, Francesca Rossi, had my entire future locked inside an unremarkable old wooden box.

Since the day I'd been made aware of it—at six years old—I knew that whatever waited for me inside was going to either kill or save me. So it was no wonder that yesterday at dawn, when the sun kissed the sky, I decided to rush fate and open it.

I wasn't supposed to know where my mother kept the key.

I wasn't supposed to know where my father kept the box.

But the thing about sitting at home all day and grooming yourself to death so you could meet your parents' next-to-impossible standards? You have time—in spades.

"Hold still, Francesca, or I'll prick you with the needle," Veronica whined underneath me.

My eyes ran across the yellow note for the hundredth time as my mother's stylist helped me get into my dress as if I was an invalid. I inked the words to memory, locking them in a drawer in my brain no one else had access to.

Excitement blasted through my veins like a jazzy tune, my eyes zinging with determination in the mirror in front of me. I folded the piece of paper with shaky fingers and shoved it into the cleavage under my unlaced corset.

I started pacing in the room again, too animated to stand still, making Mama's hairdresser and stylist bark at me as they chased me around the dressing room comically.

I am Groucho Marx in Duck Soup. *Catch me if you can.*

Veronica tugged at the end of my corset, pulling me back to the mirror as if I were on a leash.

"Hey, ouch." I winced.

"Stand still, I said!"

It was not uncommon for my parents' employees to treat me like a glorified, well-bred poodle. Not that it mattered. I was going to kiss Angelo Bandini tonight. More specifically—I was going to let *him* kiss *me*.

I'd be lying if I said I hadn't thought about kissing Angelo every night since I returned a year ago from the Swiss boarding school my parents threw me in. At nineteen, Arthur and Sofia Rossi had officially decided to introduce me to the Chicagoan society and let me have my pick of a future husband from the hundreds of eligible Italian-American men who were affiliated with The Outfit. Tonight was going to kick-start a chain of events and social calls, but I already knew whom I wanted to marry.

Papa and Mama had informed me that college wasn't in the cards for me. I needed to attend to the task of finding the perfect husband, seeing as I was an only child and the sole heir to the Rossi businesses. Being the first woman in my family to ever earn a degree had been a dream of mine, but I was nowhere near dumb enough to defy them. Our maid, Clara, often said, "You don't need to meet a husband, Frankie. You need to meet your parents' expectations."

She wasn't wrong. I was born into a gilded cage. It was spacious, but locked, nonetheless. Trying to escape it was risking death. I didn't like being a prisoner, but I imagined I'd like it much less than being six feet under. And so I'd never even dared to peek through the bars of my prison and see what was on the other side.

My father, Arthur Rossi, was the head of The Outfit.

The title sounded painfully merciless for a man who'd braided my hair, taught me how to play the piano, and even shed a fierce tear at my London recital when I played the piano in front of an audience of thousands.

Angelo—you guessed it—was the perfect husband in the eyes of my parents. Attractive, well-heeled, and thoroughly moneyed. His family owned every second building on University Village, and most of the properties were used by my father for his many illicit projects.

I'd known Angelo since birth. We watched each other grow the way flowers blossom. Slowly, yet fast at the same time. During luxurious summer vacations and under the strict supervision of our relatives, Made Men—men who had been formally inducted as full members of the mafia—and bodyguards.

Angelo had four siblings, two dogs, and a smile that would melt the Italian ice cream in your palm. His father ran the accounting firm that worked with my family, and we both took the same annual Sicilian vacations in Syracuse.

Over the years, I'd watched as Angelo's soft blond curls darkened and were tamed with a trim. How his glittering, ocean-blue eyes became less playful and broodier, hardened by the things his father no doubt had shown and taught him. How his voice had deepened, his Italian accent sharpened, and he began to fill his slender boy-frame with muscles and height and confidence. He became more mysterious and less impulsive, spoke less often, but when he did, his words liquefied my insides.

Falling in love was so tragic. No wonder it made people so sad.

And while I looked at Angelo as if he could melt ice cream, I wasn't the only girl who melted from his constant frown whenever he looked at me.

It made me sick to think that when I went back to my all-girls' Catholic school, he'd gone back to Chicago to hang out and talk and *kiss* other girls. But he'd always made me feel like I was The Girl. He sneaked flowers into my hair, let me sip some of his wine when no one was looking, and laughed with his eyes whenever I spoke. When his younger brothers taunted me, he flicked their ears and warned them off. And every summer, he found a way to steal a moment with me and kiss the tip of my nose.

"Francesca Rossi, you're even prettier than you were last summer."

"You always say that."

"And I always mean it. I'm not in the habit of wasting words."

"Tell me something important, then."

"You, my goddess, will one day be my wife."

I tended to every memory from each summer like it was a sacred garden, guarded it with fenced affection, and watered it until it grew to a fairy-tale-like recollection.

More than anything, I remembered how, each summer, I'd hold my breath until he snuck into my room, or the shop I'd visit, or the tree I'd read a book under. How he began to prolong our "moments" as the years ticked by and we entered adolescence, watching me with open amusement as I tried—and failed—to act like one of the boys when I was so painfully and brutally a girl.

I tucked the note deeper into my bra just as Veronica dug her meaty fingers into my ivory flesh, gathering the corset behind me from both ends and tightening it around my waist.

"To be nineteen and gorgeous again," she bellowed rather dramatically. The silky cream strings strained against one another, and I gasped. Only the royal crust of the Italian Outfit still used stylists and maids to get ready for an event. But as far as my parents were concerned—we were the Windsors. "Remember the days, Alma?"

The hairdresser snorted, pinning my bangs sideways as she completed my wavy chignon updo. "Honey, get off your high horse. You were pretty like a Hallmark card when you were nineteen. Francesca, here, is *The Creation of Adam*. Not the same league. Not even the same ball game."

I felt my skin flare with embarrassment. I had a sense that people enjoyed what they saw when they looked at me, but I was mortified by the idea of beauty. It was powerful yet slippery. A beautifully wrapped gift I was bound to lose one day. I didn't want to open it or ravish in its perks. It would only make parting ways with it more difficult.

The only person I wanted to notice my appearance tonight at the Art Institute of Chicago masquerade was Angelo. The theme of the gala was Gods and Goddesses through the Greek and Roman mythologies. I knew most women would show up as Aphrodite or Venus. Maybe Hera or Rhea, if originality struck them. Not me. I was Nemesis, the goddess of retribution. Angelo had always called me a deity, and tonight, I was going to justify my pet name by showing up as the most powerful goddess of them all.

It may have been silly in the 21st century to want to get married at nineteen in an arranged marriage, but in The Outfit, we all bowed to tradition. Ours happened to belong firmly in the 1800s.

"What was in the note?" Veronica clipped a set of velvety black wings to my back after sliding my dress over my body. It was a strapless gown the color of the clear summer sky with magnificent organza blue scallops. The tulle trailed two feet behind me, pooling like an ocean at my maids' feet. "You know, the one you stuck in your corset for safekeeping." She snickered, sliding golden feather-wing earrings into my ears.

"That"—I smiled dramatically, meeting her gaze in the mirror in front of us, my hand fluttering over my chest where the note rested—"is the beginning of the rest of my life."

CHAPTER ONE

Francesca

"I DIDN'T KNOW VENUS HAD WINGS."

Angelo kissed the back of my hand at the doors to the Art Institute of Chicago. My heart sank before I pushed the silly disappointment aside. He was only baiting me. Besides, he looked so dazzlingly handsome in his tux tonight, I could forgive any mistake he made, short of coldhearted murder.

The men, unlike the women at the gala, wore a uniform of tuxedos and demi-masks. Angelo complemented his suit with a golden-leafed Venetian masquerade mask that took over most of his face. Our parents exchanged pleasantries while we stood in front of each other, drinking in every freckle and inch of flesh on one another. I didn't explain my Nemesis costume to him. We'd have time—an entire lifetime—to discuss mythology. I just needed to make sure that tonight we'd have another fleeting summer moment. Only this time, when he kissed my nose, I'd look up and lock our lips, and fate, together.

I am Cupid, shooting an arrow of love straight into Angelo's heart.

"You look more beautiful than the last time I saw you." Angelo clutched the fabric of his suit over where his heart beat, feigning surrender. Everyone around us had gone quiet, and I noticed our fathers staring at one another conspiratorially.

Two powerful, wealthy Italian-American families with strong mutual ties.

Don Vito Corleone would be proud.

"You saw me a week ago at Gianna's wedding." I fought the urge to lick my lips as Angelo stared me straight in the eyes.

"Weddings suit you, but having you all to myself suits you more," he said simply, throwing my heart into fifth gear, before twisting toward my father. "Mr. Rossi, may I escort your daughter to the table?"

My father clasped my shoulder from behind. I was only vaguely aware of his presence as a thick fog of euphoria engulfed me. "Keep your hands where I can see them."

"Always, sir."

Angelo and I entwined our arms together as one of the dozens of waiters showed us to our seats at the table clothed in gold and graced with fine black china. Angelo leaned and whispered in my ear, "Or at least until you're officially mine."

The Rossis and Bandinis had been placed a few seats away from each other—much to my disappointment, but not to my surprise. My father was always at the heart of every party and paid a pretty penny to have the best seats everywhere he went. Across from me, the governor of Illinois, Preston Bishop, and his wife fretted over the wine list. Next to them was a man I didn't know. He wore a simple all-black demi-mask and a tux that must've cost a fortune by its rich fabric and impeccable cut. He was seated next to a boisterous blonde in a white French tulle camisole gown. One of dozens of Venuses who arrived in the same number.

The man looked bored to death, swirling the whiskey in his glass as he ignored the beautiful woman by his side. When she tried to lean in and speak to him, he turned the other way and checked his phone, before completely losing interest in all things combined and staring at the wall behind me.

A pang of sorrow sliced through me. She deserved better than what he was offering. Better than a cold, foreboding man who sent chills down your spine without even looking at you.

I bet he could keep ice cream chilled for days on end.

"You and Angelo seem to be taken with one another," Papa remarked conversationally, glancing at my elbows, which were propped on the table. I withdrew them immediately, smiling politely.

"He's nice." I'd say 'super nice', but my father absolutely detested modern slang.

"He fits the puzzle," Papa snipped. "He asked if he could take you out next week, and I said yes. With Mario's supervision, of course."

Of course. Mario was one of Dad's dozens of musclemen. He had the shape and IQ of a brick. I had a feeling Papa wasn't going to let me sneak anywhere he couldn't see me tonight, precisely because he knew Angelo and I got along a little too well. Papa was overall supportive, but he wanted things to be done a certain way. A way most people my age would find backward or maybe even borderline barbaric. I wasn't stupid. I knew I was digging myself a hole by not fighting for my right for education and gainful employment. I knew that *I* should be the one to decide whom I wanted to marry.

But I also knew that it was his way or the highway. Breaking free came with the price of leaving my family behind—and my family was my entire world.

Other than tradition, The Chicagoan Outfit was vastly different from the version they portrayed in the movies. No gritty alleyways, slimy drug addicts, and bloody combats with the law. Nowadays, it was all about money laundering, acquisition, and recycling. My father openly courted the police, mingled with top-tier politicians, and even helped the FBI nail high-profile suspects.

In fact, that was precisely why we were here tonight. Papa had agreed to donate a staggering amount of money to a new charity foundation designed to help at-risk youth acquire a higher education.

Oh, irony, my loyal friend.

I sipped champagne and stared across the table at Angelo, making conversation with a girl named Emily whose father owned the biggest baseball stadium in Illinois. Angelo told her he was about to enroll into a master's program at Northwestern, while simultaneously joining his father's accounting firm. The truth was, he was going to launder money for my father and serve The Outfit until the rest of his days. I was getting lost in their conversation when Governor Bishop turned his attention to me.

"And what about you, Little Rossi? Are you attending college?"

Everyone around us was conversing and laughing, other than the man in front of me. He still ignored his date in favor of downing his drink and disregarding his phone, which flashed with a hundred messages a minute. Now that he looked at me, he also looked *through* me. I vaguely wondered how old he was. He looked older than me, but not quite Papa's age.

"Me?" I smiled courteously, my spine stiffening. I smoothed my napkin over my lap. My manners were flawless, and I was well versed in mindless conversations. I'd learned Latin, etiquette, and general knowledge at school. I could entertain anyone, from world leaders to a piece of chewed gum. "Oh, I just graduated a year ago. I'm now working toward expanding my social repertoire and forming connections here in Chicago."

"In other words, you neither work nor study," the man in front of me commented flatly, knocking his drink back and shooting my father a vicious grin. I felt my ears pinking as I blinked at my father for help. He mustn't have heard because he seemed to let the remark brush him by.

"Jesus Christ," the blond woman next to the rude man growled, reddening. He waved her off.

"We're among friends. No one would leak this."

Leak this? Who the hell was he?

I perked up, taking a sip of my drink. "There are other things I do, of course."

"Do share," he taunted in mock fascination. Our side of the table fell silent. It was a grim kind of silence. The type that hinted a cringeworthy moment was upon us.

"I love charities…"

"That's not an actual activity. What do you *do?*"

Verbs, Francesca. Think verbs.

"I ride horses and enjoy gardening. I play the piano. I…ah, shop for all the things I need." I was making it worse, and I knew it. But he wouldn't let me divert the conversation elsewhere, and no one else stepped in to my rescue.

"Those are hobbies and luxuries. What's your contribution to society, Miss Rossi, other than supporting the US economy by buying enough clothes to cover North America?"

Utensils cluttered on fine china. A woman gasped. The leftovers of chatter stopped completely.

"That's enough," my father hissed, his voice frosty, his eyes dead. I flinched, but the man in the mask remained composed, straight-spined and, if anything, gaily amused at the turn the conversation had taken.

"I tend to agree, Arthur. I think I've learned everything there is to know about your daughter. And in a minute, no less."

"Have you forgotten your political and public duties at home, along with your manners?" my father remarked, forever well mannered.

The man grinned wolfishly. "On the contrary, Mr. Rossi. I think I remember them quite clearly, much to your future disappointment."

Preston Bishop and his wife extinguished the social disaster by asking me more questions about my upbringing in Europe, my recitals, and what I wanted to study (botany, though I wasn't stupid enough to point out that college was not in my cards). My parents smiled at my flawless conduct, and even the woman next to the rude stranger tentatively joined the conversation, talking about her European trip during her gap year. She was a journalist and had traveled all over the world.

But no matter how nice everyone was, I couldn't shake the terrible humiliation I'd suffered under the sharp tongue of her date, who—by the way—got back to staring at the bottom of his freshly poured tumbler with an expression that oozed boredom.

I contemplated telling him he didn't need another drink but professional help could work wonders.

After dinner came the dancing. Each woman in attendance had a dance card filled with names of those who made an undisclosed bid. All the profits went to charity.

I went to check my card on the long table containing the names of the women who'd attended. My heart beat faster as I scanned it, spotting Angelo's name. My exhilaration was quickly replaced with dread when I realized my card was full to the brim with Italian-sounding names, much longer than the others scattered around it, and I would likely spend the rest of the night dancing until my feet were numb. Sneaking a kiss with Angelo was going to be tricky.

My first dance was with a federal judge. Then a raging Italian-American playboy from New York, who told me he'd come here just to see if the rumors about my looks were true. He kissed the hem of my skirt like a medieval duke before his friends dragged his drunken butt back to their table. *Please don't ask my father for a date*, I groaned inwardly. He seemed like the kind of rich tool who'd make my life some variation of *The Godfather*. The third was Governor Bishop, and the fourth was Angelo. It was a relatively short waltz, but I tried not to let it dampen my mood.

"There she is." Angelo's face lit up when he approached me and the governor for our dance.

Chandeliers seeped from the ceiling, and the marble floor sang with the clinking heels of the dancers. Angelo dipped his head to mine, taking my hand in his, and placing his other hand on my waist.

"You look beautiful. Even more so than two hours ago," he breathed, sending warm air to my face. Tiny, velvety butterfly wings tickled at my heart.

"Good to know, because I can't breathe in this thing." I laughed, my eyes wildly searching his. I knew he couldn't kiss me now, and a dash of panic washed over the butterflies, drowning them in dread. What if we couldn't catch each other at all? Then the note would be useless.

This wooden box will save me or kill me.

"I'd love to give you mouth-to-mouth whenever you're out of breath." He skimmed my face, his throat bobbing with a swallow. "But I would start with a simple date next week, if you are interested."

"I'm interested," I said much too quickly. He laughed, his forehead falling to mine.

"Would you like to know when?"

"When we're going out?" I asked dumbly.

"That, too. Friday, by the way. But I meant when was the point in which I knew you were going to be my wife?" he asked without missing a beat. I could barely bring myself to nod. I wanted to cry. I felt his hand tightening around my waist and realized I was losing my balance.

"It was the summer you turned sixteen. I was twenty. Cradle snatcher." He laughed. "We arrived at our Sicilian cabin late. I was rolling my suitcase by the river next to our adjoined cabins when I spotted you threading flowers into a crown on the dock. You were smiling at the flowers, so pretty and elusive, and I didn't want to break the spell by talking to you. Then the wind swiped the flowers everywhere. You didn't even hesitate. You jumped headfirst into the river and retrieved every single flower that had drifted from the crown, even though you knew it wouldn't survive. Why did you do that?"

"It was my mother's birthday," I admitted. "Failure was not an option. The birthday crown turned out pretty, by the way."

My eyes drifted to the useless space between our chests.

"Failure is not an option," Angelo repeated thoughtfully.

"You kissed my nose in the restroom of that restaurant that day," I pointed out.

"I remember."

"Are you going to steal a nose-kiss tonight?" I asked.

"I would never steal from you, Frankie. I'd buy my kiss from you at full price, down to the penny," he sparred good-naturedly, winking at me, "but I'm afraid that between your shockingly full card and my obligations to mingle with every Made Man who was lucky enough to snatch an invitation to this thing, a raincheck may be required. Don't worry, I've already told Mario I'd tip him generously for taking his time fetching our car from the valet on Friday."

The trickle of panic was now a full-blown downpour of terror. If he wasn't going to kiss me tonight, the note's prediction would go to waste.

"Please?" I tried to smile brighter, masking my terror with eagerness. "My legs could use the break."

He bit his fist and laughed. "So many sexual innuendos, Francesca."

I didn't know if I wanted to cry with despair or scream with frustration. Probably both. The song hadn't ended yet, and we were still swaying in each other's arms, lulled inside a dark spell, when I felt a firm, strong hand plastered on the bare part of my upper back.

"I believe it's my turn." I heard the low voice booming behind me. I turned around with a scowl to find the rude man in the black demi-mask staring back at me.

He was tall—six-foot-three or four—with tousled ink-black hair smoothed back to tantalizing perfection. His sinewy, hard physique was slim yet broad. His eyes were pebble gray, slanted, and menacing, and his too-square jaw framed his bowed lips perfectly, giving his otherwise too-handsome appearance a gritty edge. A scornful, impersonal smirk graced his lips and I wanted to slap it off his face. He was obviously still amused with what he thought was a bunch of nonsense I spat out at the dinner table. And we clearly had an audience as I noticed half the room was now glaring at us with open interest. The women looked at him like hungry sharks in a fishbowl. The men had half-curved grins of hilarity.

"Mind your hands," Angelo snarled when the song changed, and he could no longer keep me in his arms.

"Mind your business," the man deadpanned.

"Are you sure you're on my card?" I turned to the man with a polite yet distant smile. I was still disoriented from the exchange with Angelo when the stranger pulled me against his hard body and pressed a possessive hand lower than socially acceptable on my back, a second from groping my butt.

"Answer me," I hissed.

"My bid on your card was the highest," he replied dryly.

"The bids are anonymous. You don't know how much other people have paid," I kept my lips pursed to keep myself from yelling.

"I know it's nowhere near the realm of what this dance is worth."

Un-freaking-believable.

We began to waltz around the room as other couples were not only spinning and mingling but also stealing envious glances at us. Naked, raw ogles that told me that whomever the blonde he'd come to the masquerade with was, she wasn't his wife. And that I might have been all the rage in The Outfit, but the rude man was in high demand, too.

I was stiff and cold in his arms, but he didn't seem to notice—or mind. He knew how to waltz better than most men, but he was technical, and lacked warmth and Angelo's playfulness.

"Nemesis." He took me by surprise, his rapacious gaze stripping me bare. "Distributing glee and dealing misery. Seems at odds with the submissive girl who entertained Bishop and his horsey wife at the table."

I choked on my own saliva. Did he just call the governor's wife horsey? And *me* submissive? I looked away, ignoring the addictive scent of his cologne, and the way his marble body felt against mine.

"Nemesis is my spirit animal. She was the one to lure Narcissus to a pool where he saw his own reflection and died of vanity. Pride is a terrible illness." I flashed him a taunting smirk.

"Some of us could use catching it." He bared his straight white teeth.

"Arrogance is a disease. Compassion is the cure. Most gods didn't like Nemesis, but that's because she had a backbone."

"Do you?" He arched a dark eyebrow.

"Do I…?" I blinked, the courteous grin on my face crumpling. He was even ruder when we were alone.

"Have a backbone," he provided. He stared at me so boldly and intimately, it felt like he breathed fire into my soul. I wanted to step out of his touch and jump into a pool full of ice.

"Of course, I do," I responded, my spine stiffening. "What's with the manners? Were you raised by wild coyotes?"

"Give me an example," he said, ignoring my quip. I was beginning to draw away from him, but he jerked me back into his arms. The glitzy ballroom distorted into a backdrop, and even though I was starting to notice that the man behind the demi-mask was unusually beautiful, the ugliness of his behavior was the only thing that stood out.

I am a warrior and a lady…and a sane person who can deal with this horrid man.

"I really like Angelo Bandini." I dropped my voice, slicing my gaze from his eyes and toward the table where Angelo's family had been seated. My father was sitting a few seats away, staring at us coldly, surrounded by Made Men who chatted away.

"And see, in my family, we have a tradition dating back ten generations. Prior to her wedding, a Rossi bride is to open a wooden chest—carved and made by a witch who lived in my ancestors' Italian village—and read three notes written to her by the last Rossi girl to marry. It's kind of a good luck charm mixed with a talisman and a bit of fortunetelling. I stole the chest tonight and opened one of the notes, all so I could rush fate. It said that tonight I was going to be kissed by the love of my life, and well…" I drew my lower lip into my mouth and sucked it, peering under my eyelashes at Angelo's empty seat. The man stared at me stoically, as though I was a foreign film he couldn't understand. "I'm going to kiss him tonight."

"That's your backbone?"

"When I have an ambition, I go for it."

A conceited frown crinkled his mask, as if to say I was a complete and utter moron. I looked him straight in the eye. My father taught me that the best way to deal with men like him was to confront, not run. Because, this man? He'd chase.

Yes, I believe in that tradition.

No, I don't care what you think.

Then it occurred to me that over the course of the evening, I'd offered him my entire life story and didn't even ask for his name. I didn't want to know, but etiquette demanded that I at least pretend.

"I forgot to ask who you are."

"That's because you didn't care," he quipped.

He regarded me with the same taciturnity. It was an oxymoron of fierce boredom. I said nothing because it was true.

"Senator Wolfe Keaton." The words rolled off his tongue sharply.

"Aren't you a little young to be a senator?" I complimented him on principal to see if I could defrost the thick layer of asshole he'd built around himself. Some people just needed a tight hug. Around the neck. Wait, I was actually thinking about choking him. Not the same thing.

"Thirty. Celebrated in September. Got elected this November."

"Congratulations." *I couldn't care less.* "You must be thrilled."

"Over the goddamn moon." He drew me even closer, pulling my body flush against his.

"Can I ask you a personal question?" I cleared my throat.

"Only if I can do the same," he shot.

I considered it.

"You can."

He dipped his chin down, giving me permission to continue.

"Why did you ask to dance with me, not to mention paid good

money for the dubious pleasure, if you obviously think everything I stand for is shallow and distasteful?"

For the first time tonight, something that resembled a smile crossed his face. It looked unnatural, almost illusory. I decided he was not in the habit of laughing often. Or at all.

"I wanted to see for myself if the rumors about your beauty were true."

That again. I resisted the urge to stomp on his foot. Men were such simple creatures. But, I reminded myself, Angelo thought I was pretty even *before*. When I still had braces, a blanket of freckles covering my nose and cheeks, and unruly, mousy-brown hair I had yet to learn how to tame.

"My turn," he said, without voicing his verdict on my looks. "Have you picked out names for your children with your Bangini yet?"

It was an odd question, one that was no doubt designed to make fun of me. I wanted to turn around and walk away from him right there and then. But the music was fading, and it was stupid to throw in the towel on an encounter that would end shortly. Besides, everything that came out of my mouth seemed to bother him. Why ruin a perfect strike?

"*Bandini.* And yes, I have, as a matter of fact. Christian, Joshua, and Emmaline."

Okay, I might've picked the sexes, too. That was what happened when you had too much time on your hands.

Now the stranger in the demi-mask was grinning fully, and if my anger didn't make it feel as though pure venom ran through my veins, I could appreciate his commercial-worthy dental hygiene. Instead of bowing his head and kissing my hand, as the brochure for the masquerade had indicated was compulsory, he took a step back and saluted me in mockery. "Thank you, Francesca Rossi."

"For the dance?"

"For the insight."

The night became progressively worse after the cursed dance with

Senator Keaton. Angelo was sitting at a table with a group of men, locked in a heated argument, as I was tossed from one pair of arms to the other, mingling and smiling and losing my hope and sanity, one song at a time. I couldn't believe the absurdity of my situation. I stole my mother's wooden box—the one and only thing I'd ever stolen—to read my note and get the courage to show Angelo how I felt. If he wasn't going to kiss me tonight—if *no one* was going to kiss me tonight—did that mean I was doomed to live a loveless life?

Three hours into the masquerade, I managed to slip out the entrance of the museum and stood on the wide concrete steps, breathing in the crisp spring night. My last dance had to leave early. Thankfully, his wife had gone into labor.

I hugged my own arms, braving the Chicago wind and laughing sadly at nothing in particular. One yellow cab zipped by the tall buildings, and a couple huddled together were zigzagging giddily to their destination.

Click.

It sounded like someone shut down the universe. The lampposts along the street turned off unexpectedly, and all the light faded from view.

It was morbidly beautiful; the only light visible was the shimmering lonely crescent above my head. I felt an arm wrap around my waist from behind. The touch was confident and strong, curving around my body like the man it belonged to had studied it for a while.

For years.

I turned around. Angelo's gold and black masquerade mask stared back at me. All the air left my lungs, my body turning into goo, slacking in his arms with relief.

"You came," I whispered.

His thumb brushed my cheeks. A soft, wordless nod.

Yes.

He leaned down and pressed his lips to mine. My heart squealed inside my chest.

Shut the front door. This is happening.

I grabbed the edges of his suit, pulling him closer. I'd imagined our kiss countless times before, but I'd never expected it to feel like this. Like home. Like oxygen. Like forever. His full lips fluttered over mine, sending hot air into my mouth, and he explored, and nipped, and bit my lower lip before claiming my mouth with his, slanting his head sideways and dipping down for a ferocious caress. He opened his mouth, his tongue peeking out and swiping mine. I returned the favor. He drew me close, devouring me slowly and passionately, pressing his hand to the small of my back and groaning into my mouth like I was water in the desert. I moaned into his lips and licked every corner of his mouth with zero expertise, feeling embarrassed, aroused, and more importantly, free.

Free. In his arms. Was there anything more liberating than feeling loved?

I swayed in the security of his arms, kissing him for a good three minutes before my senses crawled back into my foggy brain. He tasted of whiskey and not the wine Angelo had been drinking all night. He was significantly taller than me—taller than Angelo—even if not by much. Then his aftershave drifted into my nose, and I remembered the icy pebble eyes, raw power, and dark sensuality that licked flames of anger inside my guts. I took a slow breath and felt the burn inside me.

No.

I tore my lips from his and stumbled back, tripping over a stair. He grabbed my wrist and yanked me back to prevent my fall but made no effort to resume our kiss.

"You!" I cried out, my voice shaking. With perfect timing, the streetlamps came back to life, illuminating the sharp curves of his face.

Angelo had soft curves over a defined jaw. This man was all harsh streaks and cut edges. He looked nothing like my crush, even with a demi-mask on.

How did he do that? *Why* did he do that? Tears pooled in my eyes, but I held them back. I didn't want to give this complete stranger the satisfaction of seeing me crumple.

"How dare you," I said quietly, biting my cheeks until the taste of warm blood filled my mouth to keep from screaming.

He took a step back, sliding Angelo's mask off—God knows how he got his hands on it—and tossing it on the stairs like it was contaminated. His unmasked face was unveiled like a piece of art. Brutal and intimidating, it demanded my attention. I took a step sideways, putting more space between us.

"How? Easily." He was so dismissive; he was flirting with open disdain. "A smart girl, however, would have asked for the *why*."

"The why?" I scoffed, refusing to let the last five minutes register. I'd been kissed by someone else. Angelo—according to my family tradition—was not going to be the love of my life. This jerk, however…

Now it was his turn to take a step sideways. His broad back had been blocking the entrance to the museum, so I failed to see who was standing there, his shoulders slack, his mouth agape, his face gloriously unmasked, drinking in the scene.

Angelo took one look at my swollen lips, turned around, and stalked back in with Emily running after him.

The Wolfe was no longer in sheep's clothing as he made his way up the stairs, giving me his back. When he reached the doors, his date poured out as if on cue. Wolfe took her arm in his and led her downstairs, not sparing me a look as I wilted on the cement stairs. I could hear his date murmuring something, his dry response to her, and her laughter ringing in the air like a wind chime.

When the door to their limo slammed shut, my lips stung so bad I had to touch them to make sure he didn't set them on fire. The power outage wasn't coincidental. He did it.

He took the power. *My* power.

I yanked the note out of my corset and threw it against the stair, stomping over it like a tantrum-prone kid.

Wolfe Keaton was a kiss thief.

Printed in Great Britain
by Amazon